THE TURN OF THE SCREW
AND OTHER TALES

broadview editions
series editor: L.W. Conolly

Henry James, 1912, John Singer Sargent (1856-1925).

THE TURN OF THE SCREW
AND OTHER TALES

Henry James

edited by Kimberly C. Reed

broadview editions

Library and Archives Canada Cataloguing in Publication

James, Henry, 1843-1916
    The turn of the screw and other tales / Henry James ; edited by Kimberly C. Reed.

(Broadview editions)
Includes bibliographical references.
ISBN 978-1-55111-911-3

    I. Reed, Kimberly Capps   II. Title.   III. Series: Broadview editions

PS2116.T8 2010   813'.4   C2010-901358-1

Broadview Editions
The Broadview Editions series represents the ever-changing canon of literature in English by bringing together texts long regarded as classics with valuable lesser-known works.

Advisory editor for this volume: Juliet Sutcliffe

Broadview Press is an independent, international publishing house, incorporated in 1985. Broadview believes in shared ownership, both with its employees and with the general public; since the year 2000 Broadview shares have traded publicly on the Toronto Venture Exchange under the symbol BDP.

We welcome comments and suggestions regarding any aspect of our publications— please feel free to contact us at the addresses below or at broadview@broadviewpress.com.

North America
Post Office Box 1243, Peterborough, Ontario, Canada K9J 7H5
2215 Kenmore Avenue, Buffalo, NY, USA 14207
Tel: (705) 743-8990; Fax: (705) 743-8353
email: customerservice@broadviewpress.com

UK, Europe, Central Asia, Middle East, Africa, India, and Southeast Asia
Eurospan Group, 3 Henrietta St., London WC2E 8LU, United Kingdom
Tel: 44 (0) 1767 604972; Fax: 44 (0) 1767 601640
email: eurospan@turpin-distribution.com

Australia and New Zealand
NewSouth Books
c/o TL Distribution, 15-23 Helles Ave., Moorebank, NSW, Australia 2170
Tel: (02) 8778 9999; Fax: (02) 8778 9944
email: orders@tldistribution.com.au

www.broadviewpress.com

This book is printed on paper containing 100% post-consumer fibre.

Typesetting and assembly: True to Type Inc., Claremont, Canada.

PRINTED IN CANADA

Contents

Acknowledgements

I am grateful to have received support from several organizations and individuals. The National Endowment for the Humanities gave me a summer stipend to do research on Henry James's ghost stories; any views, findings, conclusions, or recommendations expressed in this publication do not necessarily reflect those of NEH. Eunice Wells at Beaman Library, Lipscomb University, very kindly helped me with research; Professor N. John Hall of CUNY and Mark Samuels Lasner of the University of Delaware Library graciously helped me track down Max Beerbohm's caricatures of Henry James. The provost at Lipscomb University, Craig Bledsoe, and the English department chair, Matt Hearn, have generously encouraged my work by giving me release time to do research. My editors at Broadview, Marjorie Mather and Leonard Conolly, have always been gracious, helpful, and accommodating. As always, I could not accomplish anything without the love and understanding of my family, Jerry and Olivia.

The frontispiece to the edition is reproduced by permission of The Royal Collection, Copyright © 2010 Her Majesty Queen Elizabeth II. Materials in Appendices A8 and C4 are included with permission of Oxford University Press; in B1 with permission of Harvard University Press, Copyright © 1986 by the President and Fellows of Harvard College; in D1 with permission of Simon and Schuster and the Watkins Loomis Agency, New York; in D3 with the permission of The Society of Authors as the Literary Representative of the Estate of Virginia Woolf; in D4 with permission of the Philadelphia Museum of Art; and in D5 with permission of the National Gallery of Victoria, Australia.

Introduction

A long career in writing fiction allows an author many opportunities to change style and subjects; in a career of more than 50 years, Henry James remained ever alert for new combinations of characters, settings, and plots that would allow him to expand the possibilities of narrative fiction. From his early short stories and novels that often focused on encounters between Americans and Europeans to his complex explorations of consciousness and perspective, James consistently examined issues of great moral heft in his works.

This volume includes four of Henry James's best-known shorter fictional texts; they are often grouped with James's other "ghostly" tales that he wrote over the course of his career. Yet not one of these four actually features a ghost in any kind of unambiguous way. The narrative of the most famous of them all, *The Turn of the Screw*, never makes clear whether the ghosts who seem to terrorize the narrator even exist. In "The Altar of the Dead" and "The Beast in the Jungle," the haunted protagonists are obsessed with the unseen: in the former, the main character devotes his life to remembering the dead, while in the latter, the protagonist spends his entire life awaiting the catastrophe that he is convinced has been reserved exclusively for him. Only "The Jolly Corner" offers an otherworldly being that appears for the reader's scrutiny. In all four stories, however, the ghostly—whether literal or allusive—allowed James a way of figuring abstract questions: how can a writer represent lives unlived, or unspeakable evil? How can an author manipulate narrative techniques, such as point of view, or gesture towards the instability of socio-linguistic conventions?

The Literary Ghost Story

> ... the strange, dizzy lift or swim (I try for terms!) into a stillness, a pause of all life ... Then it was that the others, the outsiders, were there.
>
> —*The Turn of the Screw*

The fact remains, nevertheless, that most ghost stories feature ghosts. Why, then, do we think of these tales by James as ghostly? To answer that question, we must consider what we mean by "ghost" and the ghostly in literature. The word "ghost" has synonyms and near-synonyms in a variety of European languages: "spirit," "sprite," "specter," "*geist*," "*revenant*," "poltergeist," "visitant," "phantom," "phantasm," "spook," "shade," "apparition," and "*doppelgänger*." Each term emphasizes a particular aspect of supernatural phenomena: the French term *revenant*, for example, literally means "re-coming" or returning; a visitant appears deliberately; a poltergeist intends to disrupt; "spirit" is derived from the word for "breath" and evokes the visual insubstantiality of air, and so on.[1] If the concept of the ghostly is conveyed via a multitude of terms, so the ghost story itself appeared in a variety of forms for centuries throughout the Western world by the time Henry James began writing in the 1860s. The ancient Roman historian Pliny the Younger wrote about ghosts who return because their survivors have not laid them to rest properly, while the early Christian church carefully regulated theological beliefs about the departed. Christian rituals for burial developed in part to keep very clear the demarcation between the living and the dead, so that otherworldly visitants could not exert undue (or unorthodox) influence on church members. Nevertheless, tales of ghostly apparitions multiplied throughout the Middle Ages, perhaps as a popular cultural response, as Colin Davis suggests, to the church's monitoring.[2] Ghosts in pre-Reformation Europe come back in order to confess sins, to warn about punishment, to uncover evil-doing, or to proclaim the existence of heaven for the holy.[3] The Reformation, with its rejection of the Catholic concept of purgatory, effectively removed theological options for explaining ghostly returns; Enlightenment philosophers and scientists— worthy heirs of the early modern reformers—attempted to lay to rest once and for all the recurrent popular belief that the dead could return. Denis Diderot, one of the authors of the *Encyclopédie*, wrote dismissively of the subject: "We have applied the term 'phantom' to all the false ideas that impress upon us fear, respect, etc., which torment us and cause unhappiness in our life:

---

1 Ralph Noyes, "The Other Side of Plato's Wall" in *Ghosts: Deconstruction, Psychoanalysis, History*, eds. Peter Buse and Andrew Scott (London: Macmillan, 1999) 245, 247.

2 Colin Davis, *Haunted Subjects: Deconstruction, Psychoanalysis and the Return of the Dead* (Basingstoke, Hampshire: Palgrave Macmillan, 2007) 5.

3 Keith Thomas, *Religion and the Decline of Magic: Studies in Popular Beliefs in Sixteenth- and Seventeenth-Century England* (London: Weidenfeld and Nicolson, 1971) 597.

it is bad education that produces these 'phantoms,' it is experience and philosophy that dissipate them."[1]

As numerous theorists of the Gothic have demonstrated, this restrictive, rationalist dismissal of ghosts and other supernatural manifestations forced writers underground (so to speak) to find expression in narratives that violated the Enlightenment strictures of reason and order. Indeed, the invention of the uncanny, as one scholar has termed this innovation, came about as a direct result of the pressure of Enlightenment ideology.[2] Diderot suggested that ghosts were only a sort of false idea that rationalism could obliterate; rather than disappear, however, the non-rational began to be internalized and given room for free play in the mind and imagination. Small wonder, then, that late eighteenth- and early nineteenth-century fiction featuring imaginative use of the supernatural—what came to be called Gothic literature—tended to take place in the past, often the Middle Ages (generally perceived as a time when ignorance and superstition held sway), confined in isolated settings such as a large house or castle, featuring spectacular, ostensibly supernatural events and characters with dark secrets. The Gothic novel reached an apex in Mary Shelley's *Frankenstein* (1818), although, unlike many Gothic novels of that time, this story takes place in the recent past— indeed, Dr. Frankenstein exemplifies the eighteenth-century scientist, passionate about expanding his knowledge of the secrets of science and medicine until he achieves the ability to create life in a laboratory. His hubristic attitude dooms his experiment, however, setting in motion of series of tragedies that demonstrate the foolishness of such over-reaching. Frankenstein's creature terrorizes and murders those whom Frankenstein loves, exemplifying, as Goya's etching from the late 1790s is titled, the notion that "the sleep of reason produces monsters."

After *Frankenstein*, the trend of interiorizing the irrational continued throughout the nineteenth century, while the burgeoning number of weekly or monthly popular magazines helped create demand for short fiction, including ghost stories. Unlike much Gothic fiction, Victorian supernatural fiction tended to feature contemporary domestic settings; Charlotte Brontë, Charles Dickens, George Eliot, and other nineteenth-century writers pro-

---

1   Denis Diderot, *Encyclopédie, ou dictionnaire raisonné des sciences, des arts et des métiers* (1751–72) <http://portail.atilf.fr/encyclopedie> (my translation).

2   Terry Castle, *The Female Thermometer: Eighteenth-Century Culture and the Invention of the Uncanny* (New York: Oxford UP, 1995) 8.

duced works that featured relatively realistic characters, settings, and events while at the same time interposing supernatural elements, often as a way of representing uncontrollable or unacceptable elements hidden deep within their characters' backgrounds or personalities. In the case of Brontë's *Jane Eyre*, for example, the interiorization of the irrational is quite literal: the novel turns on the mystery of the madwoman in the attic, immured in the family home, doubling Jane both overtly and covertly.

This intimate linkage of the rational and the irrational received theoretical elucidation in a seminal essay by Sigmund Freud, "The Uncanny," published in 1919. In this work, Freud observes that while aesthetic theories of reactions elicited by the beautiful and the attractive abound, few theorists have adequately considered the opposite situation: reactions aroused by that which is distressing or repulsive. Freud chooses the term "uncanny," or *das Unheimliche*, to signify what he calls the "realm of the frightening, of what evokes fear and dread."[1] The crucial point for him resides in the German word itself: if *das Heimliche* can be translated as "homely" in the sense of "belonging to the house, not strange, familiar, tame, dear and intimate, homely, etc.,"[2] then *das Unheimliche* would at first glance appear to mean that which is foreign, strange, alienated. But Freud, after exhaustively analyzing the use of the two words in a survey of German dictionaries and German literature, connects the terms in a paradoxical fashion: time and again, he observes, *das Heimliche* is also used to indicate that which is "removed from the eyes of strangers, hidden, secret."[3] Only a short step leads from that notion to a closely connected one: the *Heimliche* slips into the *Unheimliche*, so that what was "intended to remain secret, hidden away" is now out in the open:[4]

> ... [A]mong those things that are felt to be frightening there must be one group in which it can be shown that the frightening element is something that has been repressed and now returns. This species of the frightening would then constitute the uncanny, and it would be immaterial whether it was itself originally frightening or arose from another affect.... [W]e can

---

1   Sigmund Freud, "The Uncanny," trans. David McClintock, *The Uncanny*, ed. Adam Phillips (New York: Penguin, 2003) 123.
2   Freud 126.
3   Freud 133.
4   Freud 132.

understand why German usage allows the familiar (*das Heim-liche*, the "homely") to switch to its opposite, the uncanny (*das Unheimliche*, the "unhomely"), for this uncanny element is actually nothing new or strange, but something that was long familiar to the psyche and was estranged from it only through being repressed.[1]

Freud's theory of the uncanny drew on his notion of the repressed; in a paper he had written on the subject a few years earlier, he observed that the desire that is repressed necessarily returns, but transformed: "The vanished affect comes back in its transformed shape as social anxiety, moral anxiety, and unlimited self-reproaches."[2] The combination of these Freudian notions—the repressed, the *Heimliche*, the *Unheimliche*—forged new tools for theorizing the use of the ghostly in literature and exerted tremendous influence on subsequent criticism of such fiction. As we will shortly see, Freud's theories of repression and neurosis fueled the spark that ignited the storm of controversy over interpreting *The Turn of the Screw*.

Henry James's Use of the Ghostly in Four Tales

Freud's notion of the uncanny helps us understand James's appropriation of the ghostly in the tales in this volume, for in all these stories, the familiar becomes strange, the comfortable distresses, the repressed returns. In "The Altar of the Dead," George Stransom's new companion, who joins him in mourning at the altar he has erected in memory of his dead, reveals that she has been silently mourning Stransom's bitterest enemy, Acton Hague—the one person whom Stransom had expressly, and vehemently, refused to memorialize at his altar. From the moment of her revelation, everything in Stransom's life is inverted: their friendship grows distant, his enemy's presence looms ever larger despite his death, the candles lose their luster. Stransom's obsession with this dead enemy rivals only his original obsession with his dead loved ones; although Hague himself does not appear as a ghost in the traditional sense of that word, his presence haunts every facet of Stransom's life. Worn down by his friend's refusal to continue mourning with him and thereby

---

1 Freud 148.
2 Sigmund Freud, "Repression" in *On Metapsychology: The Theory of Psy-choanalysis*, vol. 11, trans. James Strachey, ed. Angela Richards (Harmondsworth: Penguin, 1984) 157.

nurture their fledgling relationship, weakened by illness, an idea takes hold in his mind: he could add "just one more" to the collection of candles. "Just one more; just one more" he repeats to himself as he makes his way to the church despite his sharp physical decline that suggests an imminent death. At the end of the story, the motivation for his desire to erect one final candle remains ambiguous: for whom is this candle? for Acton Hague, or for himself? The two characters seem to merge uncannily.

As in "The Altar of the Dead," no ghostly apparition appears in "The Beast in the Jungle," even though, much like George Stransom, John Marcher is consumed by an *idée fixe*, an obsession that rules his life. His conviction that something cataclysmic awaits him takes on the appearance, in his mind, of a crouching beast in a jungle, biding its time before springing on him. Like Stransom, Marcher shares his obsession with a female friend, May Bartram, who divines the identity of the beast long before he does. In a curiously vampiric way, his obsession feeds on May and her companionable support: once she discerns the nature of the beast, she develops a blood disorder that costs her much suffering and finally her life. On her deathbed, she tells him that the beast has sprung despite the fact that he was unaware of it at the time: "your not being aware of it is the strangeness *in* the strangeness. It's the wonder *of* the wonder" ("Beast" 112). May intuitively understands the uncanniness of the beast: within Marcher himself lives a beast fed by an egotism so monstrous that Marcher imagines something incommensurable happening to him and to him alone, an event so exclusive that the tragedy of May's death lies only in her taking the secret identity of the beast to her grave. Critical tradition has tended to read this as one of James's tales of the tragedy of the unlived life, in which Marcher wastes years waiting for nothingness. Eve Kosofsky Sedgwick, however, in an influential essay on the story, finds highly problematic the common reading that "John Marcher *should have desired* May Bartram."[1] Instead, May Bartram, from the time John Marcher tells her his secret, recognizes the closet in which he lives; according to Sedgwick, May hopes that Marcher will move from ignorance about his closeted homosexuality to self-knowledge—a move that allow him to enjoy an authentic sexuality.[2]

---

1 Eve Kosofsky Sedgwick, *Epistemology of the Closet* (Berkeley: U of California P, 1990) 198.
2 Sedgwick 207.

From the haunting by an enemy in "The Altar of the Dead," to the threat of a spring of a beast in "The Beast in the Jungle," we move to perhaps the most literally uncanny of these three shorter tales, "The Jolly Corner." In this story, Spencer Brydon is haunted by none other than himself, by a sort of *doppelgänger*— the man he might have been had he chosen to stay in New York rather than spend much of his adult life in Europe. Exactly what *sort* of man he would have been becomes his "morbid obsession" ("Jolly" 130). He muses on his suspicion that his now-empty boyhood home, the "jolly corner" of the title, in fact shelters his ghostly alter ego; he begins to indulge himself by wandering through the house every evening after socializing with friends who have no idea about his strange belief. As he "let[s] himself go" in his nocturnal visits, Brydon takes pleasure in turning the tables on his ghostly twin by becoming the one who terrifies, rather than the one terrified ("Jolly" 139). However, he begins to experience a "duplication of consciousness" that James renders in a prodigious example of narrative accomplishment:

> ... Brydon at this instant tasted probably of a sensation more complex than had ever before found itself consistent with sanity. It was as if it would have shamed him that a character so associated with his own should triumphantly succeed in just skulking, should to the end not risk the open; so that the drop of this danger was, on the spot, a great lift of the whole situation. Yet with another rare shift of the same subtlety he was already trying to measure by how much more he himself might now be in peril of fear; so rejoicing that he could, in another form, actively inspire that fear, and simultaneously quaking for the form in which he might passively know it. ("Jolly" 139)

The climax of the story, a brilliantly vivid account of Brydon's pursuit of and flight from his Other, ends with the explosion that takes place when the two finally meet: Brydon collapses "under the hot breath and the roused passion of a life larger than his own, a rage of personality" ("Jolly" 148). He both recognizes and refuses to recognize his *doppelgänger* as himself:

> ... the bared identity was too hideous as *his*, and his glare was the passion of his protest. The face, *that* face, Spencer Brydon's?—he searched it still, but looking away from it in dismay and denial, falling straight from his height of sublimity. It was unknown, inconceivable, awful, disconnected from

any possibility—! ... Such an identity fitted his at *no* point, made its alternative monstrous. A thousand times yes, as it came upon him nearer now—the face was the face of a stranger. ("Jolly," 148)

Only his old friend Alice Staverton, who shares his belief that his double haunts his boyhood home, can reassure him that his double's hideous appearance confirms the vast difference between the Brydon who left the United States as a young man and the Brydon who stayed to flourish in business. Yet his very existence in Europe has been upheld by the rents from his New York properties; Alice herself points out to him that if only he had stayed, he might have invented the skyscraper, or conceived of a new architectural plan for New York. The distinction between the two Brydons, then, is blurred; they are inseparably, uncannily linked.

For decades, much critical energy has been expended on the question of who Brydon's double is and whether the ending should be seen as redemptive. For example, given the disdain that Brydon seems to hold for American capitalism, is the double symbolic of that mercenary system? As for the ending, is this story a happy reversal of the endings of "The Altar of the Dead" and "The Beast in the Jungle"? Many critics have seen Alice Staverton's acceptance of both Brydon and his double as a optimistic gesture that allows Brydon to incorporate the ghostly other into his own construction of identity, to live out more fully the possibilities that life offers him. More recently, however, critics have questioned such readings; for example, instead of celebrating the triumph of middle-class heterosexual domesticity, the double represents the closeted homosexual self that early twentieth-century bourgeois culture, in the figure of Alice Staverton, seeks to reclaim.[1]

In all three of these stories, we see the power of obsession, of the *idée fixe* that clamps onto the protagonists' minds and will not let go. As Richard Hocks observes, so potent is this obsession that it can summon the occult.[2] In fact, Hocks argues that much of the fiction of James's so-called major phase, beginning with the publication of *The Ambassadors* in 1903, concerns itself with the

---

1 See Eric Savoy, "The Queer Subject of 'The Jolly Corner,'" *The Henry James Review* 20 (1999): 1–21; Deborah Esch, "A Jamesian About-face: Notes on 'The Jolly Corner,'" *ELH* 50 (1983): 587–605.

2 Richard Hocks, *Henry James: A Study of the Short Fiction* (Boston: Twayne, 1990) 77.

"quasi-supernatural realm." Hocks's definition of the Jamesian quasi-supernatural explains how James used this mode of representation in many of his later works:

[The quasi-supernatural realm] is a felt relationship with the supernatural in which human consciousness, by the sheer extent of its own cultivated activity, its own exploration of its expanding realms or receding limits, thereby comes right up to the edge of the supernatural realm *per se* and stops just short of entering it; but then of admitting (or, if we prefer, not being able *not* to admit, given the proximity) effects and activities that come from just "over the line" making their presence felt *here*, on this side.[1]

James's lifelong interest in sounding the depths of human consciousness inevitably led him to this realm, which he came to realize is brought about by intensity of consciousness, an intensity that takes on the form of an obsession in his characters.

Nowhere is this kind of haunting fixation more apparent than in the fourth tale in this collection, *The Turn of the Screw*. Written in late 1897 for *Collier's Weekly*, the novella grew from an anecdote that Edward White Benson, the Archbishop of Canterbury, recounted to James in 1895. Two days after listening to the story, James made notes to himself so he would remember the idea, the "mere vague, undetailed, faint sketch of it—being all he [the Archbishop] had been told (very badly and imperfectly), by a lady who had no art of relation, and no clearness.... The servants *die* (the story vague about the way of it).... It is all obscure and imperfect, the picture, the story ..."[2] (see Appendix C4). As he wrote years later in his preface to the story, James heard in this anecdote the "vividest little note for sinister romance"; he welcomed the challenge as he envisioned it: a highly controlled "excursion into chaos" that would allow him "to knead the subject of my young friend's, the supposititious narrator's, mystification thick, and yet strain the expression of it so clear and fine that beauty would result."[3] Rather than follow the usual formula

1 Hocks, *Henry James and Pragmatistic Thought* (Chapel Hill: U of North Carolina P, 1974) 198–99.

2 Leon Edel and Lyall H. Powers, eds., *The Complete Notebooks of Henry James* (New York: Oxford UP, 1987) 109.

3 "Preface to *The Aspern Papers, The Turn of the Screw,* 'The Liar,' 'The Two Faces'" in *Henry James: Literary Criticism,* vol. 2 (New York: Library of America, 1984) 1183–85.

for ghost stories or rely on reports of alleged ghostly encounters, he would have his ghosts, his "hovering prowling blighting presences ... reek with the air of Evil" so that as the author, he would be "released from weak specifications" about the nature of that evil while encouraging his readers to imagine the specific horrors.[1] As critics would later observe, James elicits the same response from his readers that the events at Bly trigger in the governess—an intense focus on ghostly traces, echoes, fragments mixed with an irresistible desire, even need, to interpret what they mean. In fact, if the extraordinary interpretive debate this text has generated is one measure of James's accomplishment, then he succeeded beyond his greatest expectations, for very few other English texts have provoked such sustained controversy in the twentieth and twenty-first centuries. James himself anticipated this phenomenon when he wrote in his 1908 preface to the New York edition of his works, "Indeed, if the artistic value of such an experiment be measured by the intellectual echoes it may again, long after, set in motion, the case would make in favour of this little firm fantasy ..."[2] (see Appendix C3).

The very act of interpreting *The Turn of the Screw* reveals an uncanniness inherent in the text in ways both more and less obvious than in James's other ghostly tales. Much of the critical debate stems from how to understand the main narrator's description and interpretation of the events at Bly. It is worth noting that this character—the unnamed governess—is one of three actual narrators in this text. This fact alone has attracted substantial critical attention; rarely does a short story or novella have such an embedded narrative. Of course, there is the simple historical origin of the story, as we have seen, with James listening to his friend the Archbishop recount the fragments of this story, such as he had gleaned from *his* hearing of the story from someone else. Like all good writers, however, James took the basic facts and worked them into a complex fiction that defies easy analysis or summary. We do not ever learn the initial narrator's name (or sex); we know little about Douglas, the second narrator who tells the story that he heard many years ago from the governess. We do learn, however, some crucial information from Douglas about the governess: he met her while he was a college student at Trinity and she was serving as his younger sister's governess; she told him the story then, and left him a

---

1 James, Preface 1186–88.
2 James, Preface 1185.

manuscript detailing the events at Bly. Douglas also provides his little group of listeners with other important information, including an account of the governess's one meeting with her employer, the uncle of the children for whom she was to care. By the time we arrive at the governess's actual words, our impressions of the story have been filtered through a succession of consciousnesses, so that the narrative convention of the mediation of knowledge and interpretation, which forces readers to consider fundamental questions—Who is telling us this story? What is happening? What does it mean?—becomes part and parcel of the story itself.

And so begins one of James's greatest stories of obsession. As an initial reading often has it, *The Turn of the* Screw is the gripping tale of a young, innocent governess who bravely battles wicked ghosts who return to lure her two young charges to their doom. If she occasionally seems overwrought or even hysterical, her behavior merely reflects the monstrosity that she must face almost entirely alone, with only the help of the housekeeper, Mrs. Grose. Some sort of horrific evil has been perpetrated, she comes to believe, on the children by two previous servants, the master's valet, Peter Quint, and the governess, Miss Jessel. Therefore, only Miss Jessel's dismissal, apparently for immoral behavior (possibly a pregnancy by Quint), her subsequent death, and Quint's death in a drunken fall saved the children from a life of unspeakable debauchery. Indeed, the disturbing fact of Miles's expulsion from his school because he said things that were inappropriate confirms Quint's evil influence over the boy. Despite the servants' deaths, however, the governess is confronted with their ghosts, with, as Freud would say, the return of the repressed—the illicit sexual desires and practices that the foursome seemed to have enjoyed. The governess may strike the reader as obsessive in her desire to rid Bly of the presence of the dead servants, but the angelic nature of young Miles and Flora against the unmanageable evil of Quint and Jessel does seem to merit such devotion. With the bewildering injunction from her employer against ever contacting him, she rises to the challenge of her lonely position and finally purges the ghosts' presence from Bly. The fact that Miles dies in the climactic throes of this exorcism is certainly a great tragedy, but her later employment with Douglas's family attests to the esteem in which she was held.

Often, however, a second reading shows gaps or contradictions in the text that cause the reader to question this relatively straightforward understanding of the novella. Rather than admiring the governess for her fortitude and courage in exorcizing the malign influence of the ghosts, a reader who questions the governess's account might instead see her as the instigator of evil, rather than the savior of the children. Why, for example, does the governess habitually finish Mrs. Grose's sentences instead of waiting for her to say what she wants to say? Why does she assume that the children know of the ghosts' presence? Why does she describe Miss Jessel as silent when she sees her in the schoolroom, and yet later tells Mrs. Grose that they had a conversation? Why does she assume that the children's silence about the dead servants is proof of evil? Equally intriguing are the governess's innumerable statements of apparent fact when the reader, or Mrs. Grose, or the children, may arrive at a far different conclusion; for example, when the governess sees Miss Jessel for the second time at the small lake at Bly, she writes, "She was there, so I was justified; she was there, so I was neither cruel nor mad. She was there for poor scared Mrs. Grose, but she was there most for Flora ..." ("Turn" 231)—*despite* the fact that both Mrs. Grose and Flora immediately deny seeing the ghost. She tells Mrs. Grose, as they watch the children together in their "interlocked sweetness," that Miles and Flora are talking "of *them*—they're talking horrors!" She continues that although she may seem "crazy," she is now more "lucid," for she can discern the evil that lurks beneath the children's ostensible beauty and innocence: "Their more than earthly beauty, their absolutely unnatural goodness. It's a game ... it's a policy and a fraud!" ("Turn" 206-07). She either cannot or refuses to consider that Mrs. Grose's constant questioning of her assertions may imply distrust and disbelief rather than desire to learn more "facts." In a text replete with ambiguity, one of the most crucially ambiguous sentences is the last one that Miles utters in their final exchange:

"It's not Miss Jessel! But it's at the window—straight before us. It's *there*—the coward horror, there for the last time!"

At this, after a second in which his head made the movement of a baffled dog's on a scene and then gave a frantic little shake for air and light, he was at me in a white rage, bewildered, glaring vainly over the place and missing wholly, though it now, to my sense, filled the room like the taste of poison, the wide, overwhelming presence. "It's *he*?"

I was so determined to have all my proof that I flashed into ice to challenge him. "Whom do you mean by 'he'?"

"Peter Quint—you devil!" ("Turn" 249)

To the governess, Miles's words are "his supreme surrender of the name and his tribute to my devotion" and exorcise Quint's presence from their lives. She cannot see the irony in her failure to ask Miles whom he means by "you." The thought that *she* might be a devil to Miles is not admissible, despite the fact that his utterance is also his death knell:

> With the stroke of the loss [Quint's disappearance] I was so proud of he uttered the cry of a creature hurled over an abyss, and the grasp with which I recovered him might have been that of catching him in his fall. I caught him, yes, I held him— it may be imagined with what a passion; but at the end of a minute I began to feel what it truly was that I held. We were alone with the quiet day, and his little heart, dispossessed, had stopped. ("Turn" 250)

With such an abrupt, horrifying end to the story, the ambiguities remain and definitive explications of them elude the reader. The text contains both the story of ghosts who terrorize innocent children as well as the story of an obsessive woman bent on eradicating evil, whether real or imaginary. This "both/and" reading exemplifies Freud's notion of the co-originatory status of the *Heimliche* and the *Unheimliche*.

Critical Background of *The Turn of the Screw*

Only relatively recently has *The Turn of the Screw* been seen as a text that allows for both interpretations: the so-called apparitionist, in which the governess is seen as defending the children from very real ghosts, versus the "non-apparitionist," in which the governess is seen as mad, imagining the ghosts and therefore wreaking havoc—not to mention, of course, other approaches that do not focus on the ontological status of the ghosts at all. Henry James himself, in his preface to the New York Edition of *The Turn of the Screw*, called Quint and Jessel "goblins, elves, imps, demons as loosely constructed as those of the old trials for witchcraft."[1] James's contemporaries tended to read the story as a more or less straightforward ghost story, albeit with the usual Jamesian propensity towards indirection and ambiguity.

Two critics in the 1920s wrote essays arguing that the ghosts

---

1 James, Preface 1187.

were not real. Harold C. Goddard's "A Pre-Freudian Reading of *The Turn of the Screw*" established a coherent rationale for suspecting the governess's view of events. To Goddard, the governess's infatuation with the children's uncle, her hints of problems in her family, the mystery of Miles's dismissal from school, and Mrs. Grose's dislike of the previous servants all combine to create a "witch's broth" that boils over into the hysterical denunciations and actions of the governess.[1] However, Goddard's essay was not published until 1957; therefore, it was Edna Kenton's article, published in 1924, that was one of the earliest published with the thesis that the governess imagines the ghosts. Kenton drew on James's comments in his preface to the story to buttress her argument that the ghosts exist only in the governess's mind. To be sure, other writers in the early part of the century perceived the complexity of the text; for example, Oliver Elton observed as early as 1907 that the question of whether the ghosts are real is never answered.[2] Virginia Woolf wrote in 1921 that while "[i]t is Quint who hangs about us in the dark; who is there in that corner and again there in that," we fear not so much Quint as "something, perhaps, in ourselves."[3] Kenton's interpretation received more support with Edmund Wilson's essay of 1934, "The Ambiguity of Henry James." Given Wilson's status as an eminent critic, his argument, based on a Freudian reading, received much more attention than Kenton's and ignited the flames of the controversy that were to burn for much of the century. Wilson pronounced the governess to be a "neurotic case of sex repression" who hallucinates the ghosts; she serves as a variation on a Jamesian theme—the "thwarted Anglo-Saxon spinster."[4] Wilson revised his essay twice, with the third version published in 1948. In that final version, he acknowledges problems with his original essay: for example, he had tried too hard to explain away Mrs. Grose's identification of Peter Quint from the governess's description of the man she saw. Wilson also acknowledges that information found in James's recently published notebooks had influenced his reading; not only did James apparently intend to write a ghost

---

1   Harold C. Goddard, "A Pre-Freudian Reading of *The Turn of the Screw*," *Nineteenth-Century Fiction* 12 (1957): 7.

2   Oliver Elton, "The Novels of Mr. Henry James," *Modern Studies* (London: Edward Arnold, 1907) 255–56.

3   Virginia Woolf, "Henry James's Ghost Stories" in *Granite and Rainbow: Essays by Virginia Woolf* (London: Hogarth Press, 1981) 72.

4   Edmund Wilson, "The Ambiguity of Henry James" in *The Triple Thinkers* (New York: Oxford UP, 1948) 88, 95.

story, Wilson observes, but other events in James's life had perhaps caused him to question his grasp of reality: "the doubts that some readers feel as to the soundness of the governess' story are, I believe the reflection of James's doubts, communicated unconsciously by James himself."[1] Wilson expands his Freudian reading of the text to psychoanalysis of James's life, arguing that James suffered from sexual neuroses that manifested themselves in many of his works.

Wilson's essays provoked a number of arguments in favor of reading the story as involving real ghosts who, as the governess asserts, come back to harm the children. In 1947 and 1948, Robert N. Heilman published two articles on the novella. In the first, "A Freudian Reading of *The Turn of the Screw*," Heilman attacks Wilson on several points: Wilson's belief that what James meant by "authority" (an attribute that James gave the governess in his preface) should actually be understood as "tyranny"; Wilson's argument that the governess confuses the appearance of Quint with that of the master, and so on.[2] In "*The Turn of the Screw* as Poem," Heilman argues that the story is laden with religious symbolism: Miles and Flora evoke Adam and Eve, with Quint as Satan and the governess serving a priestly function in her attempts to rescue the children from the malignancy of the dead servants. According to Heilman, James's use of rich Biblical and allegorical motifs is especially appropriate, since the story treats the "oldest of themes—the struggle of evil to possess the human soul."[3] Other critics agreed with Heilman's allegorical reading of the story but also showed a debt to Wilson's Freudian interpretation. For example, Joseph J. Firebaugh sees the uncle as an absent God who set up Eden at Bly, with a governess who believes that knowledge is evil and therefore cannot cope with the fall that has happened due to the children's relationship with Quint and Jessel.[4] Firebaugh's article, published in 1957, is one of several that postulated a kind of synthesis of the two opposed camps: many critics believed that the ghosts do haunt Bly—but that the governess is deeply flawed and therefore botches her attempt to manage the horrific situation.

---

1   Wilson 124.

2   Robert B. Heilman, "The Freudian Reading of *The Turn of the Screw*," *Modern Language Notes* 62 (Nov 1947): 433–45.

3   Heilman, "*The Turn of the* Screw as Poem" rpt. in Gerald Willen, ed., *A Casebook on Henry James's "The Turn of the Screw,"* 2nd ed. (New York: Thomas Y. Crowell, 1969) 175.

4   Joseph J. Firebaugh, "Inadequacy in Eden: Knowledge and *The Turn of the Screw*," *Modern Fiction Studies* 3 (1957): 59.

By the 1960s, book-length studies of the novella began to appear. Gerald Willen's *A Casebook on Henry James's "The Turn of the Screw"* (1960) collected essays that focused on the Freudian/anti-Freudian readings from the previous decades, while Thomas M. Cranfill's and Robert L. Clark's *An Anatomy of "The Turn of the Screw"* psychoanalyzed the governess, finding her obsessive love for the children's uncle terrifying, given the resultant events. At the same time, other critics were exploring the implications of the ambiguities of the text; Dorothea Krook argues that the text "in fact—not possibly or probably but actually—yields two meanings, both equally self-consistent and self-complete."[1] Several critics brilliantly amplified her argument in the 1970s. Tzvetan Todorov, in *The Fantastic: A Structural Approach to a Literary Genre*, placed the fantastic in a continuum of modes, in which the text's events require a reader (or character) to determine whether an apparently supernatural event has a natural explanation. Those texts whose events cannot be so interpreted, whose characters or readers must exist in a constant state of epistemological hesitation, are operating in the mode of the fantastic. According to Todorov, *The Turn of the Screw* is an unusual example of a text that refuses to resolve and thus is a remarkable instance of the fantastic.[2] In 1976 and 1977, Christine Brooke-Rose published a three-part essay in which she attacked previous critics for their "non-methodology" wherein they mirror the governess by speaking with certainty about textual elements that are ambiguous, using their own opinions and personal impressions.[3] She then carefully analyzes the text using the theories of psychoanalyst Jacques Lacan and of Russian formalists in an attempt to show that the story is perfectly and permanently ambiguous. Similarly and at the same time, Shlomith Rimmon wrote *The Concept of Ambiguity—the Example of James*, in which she, like Brooke-Rose, methodically examines the ways in which the text undermines any certainty of interpretation. Both Brooke-Rose and Rimmon provide a refreshing corrective to the either/or impasse at which so many critics had arrived.

The *tour de force*, however, was Shoshana Felman's "Turning the Screw of Interpretation" from 1977, a work that is now

---

1   Dorothea Krook, *The Ordeal of Consciousness in Henry James* (Cambridge: Harvard UP, 1962) 388.

2   Tzvetan Todorov, *The Fantastic: A Structural Approach to a Literary Genre* (Ithaca, NY: Cornell UP, 1975) 43.

3   Christine Brooke-Rose, *A Rhetoric of the Unreal* (New York: Cambridge UP, 1981) 132.

regarded as one of the seminal theoretical writings in the twentieth century. In this work, Felman focuses on how the text implicates the reader in the interpretative process. She examines the critical controversy that the text had generated, paying close attention to Edmund Wilson's arguments. Rather than taking sides, Felman demonstrates how the critical debate echoes the struggles in the story itself: Edmund Wilson's identification of the governess as mad, for example, mirrors the governess's identification of the children as possessed, so that the very act of interpretation forces us to repeat the actions of the text. Felman observes that a contemporary review denounced the tale for causing its readers to assist "in an outrage upon the holiest and sweetest fountain of human innocence, and helping to debauch— at least by helplessly standing by—the pure and trusting nature of children." The reader is thus "forced to participate in the scandal," Felman argues, and take on the role of the governess, who is the interpreter of the events:

> To demystify the governess is only possible on one condition: the condition of *repeating* the governess's very gesture. The text thus constitutes a reading of its two possible readings, both of which, in the course of that reading, it deconstructs. James's trap is then the simplest and the most sophisticated in the world: the trap is but a text, that is, an invitation to the reader, a simple invitation to undertake its reading. But in the case of *The Turn of the Screw*, the invitation to undertake a reading of the text is perforce an invitation to *repeat* the text, to enter into its labyrinth of mirrors, from which it is henceforth impossible to escape.[1]

With these more postmodern readings of the text, criticism of *The Turn of the Screw* in the last quarter of the twentieth century moved away from the debates over the existence of the ghosts and the sanity of the governess. More recent critics have used the insights of deconstruction and psychoanalysis to examine how social constructs such as gender relations, socioeconomic status, and sexual orientation are called into question by the text.[2]

---

1 Shoshana Felman, *Literature and Psychoanalysis: The Question of Reading: Otherwise* (Baltimore: Johns Hopkins UP, 1982) 97, 190.

2 See, for example, John Carlos Rowe, "Psychoanalytical Significances: The Use and Abuse of Uncertainty in *The Turn of the Screw*" in *The Theoretical Dimensions of Henry James* (Madison: U of Wisconsin P,   (continued)

Biographical Background

> Humanity is immense, and reality has a myriad forms...
> —Henry James, "The Art of Fiction."[1]

Henry James Jr. was born on 15 April 1843, to Henry and Mary Walsh James in New York City. His father was independently wealthy, living on an inheritance from his father, William James of Albany, New York, an Irish immigrant who made a fortune after he arrived in the United States in 1789. Thanks to his inheritance, Henry James Sr. was able to pursue a life of the mind, lecturing and writing on a variety of subjects. Equally as important in the family's life was the ability to travel at will and live abroad as the elder Henry liked. In fact, Henry Jr. spent several years in Europe during his boyhood on three different occasions and was indelibly shaped by the exposure to European art, history, and foreign languages that his family's sojourns abroad afforded him, just as he soaked up the cultural offerings that New York and New England offered as well. For the rest of his life, the relationship between the American and the European would serve him well in his attempts to render the moral lives of his characters. One of his earliest works of fiction, *Daisy Miller*, which explored the collision of the two cultures in the person of a young American woman who goes to Europe, became a best seller in 1878 and helped establish James as an important young author. Although he continued to manipulate this theme in such works as *The Portrait of a Lady*, *The Ambassadors*, *The Wings of the Dove*, and *The Golden Bowl*, he moved beyond the relative straightforward tragicomedy of *Daisy Miller* to more sophisticated experiments in depicting consciousness and perception. Thanks largely to his family inheritance, he was able to devote himself full time to his writing, which included twenty novels, over 100 stories and novellas, and a large body of non-fiction work, including literary reviews and travel essays. James, who never married, lived most of his adult life in Europe (primarily England) and enjoyed

---

1984) 120–46; Graham McMaster, "Henry James and India: A Historical Reading of *The Turn of the Screw*," *Clio* 18 (1988): 23–40; T.J. Lustig, *Henry James and the Ghostly* (Cambridge: Cambridge UP, 1994); Kevin Ohi, "'Blameless and Foredoomed': Innocence and Haste in *The Turn of the Screw*" in *Innocence and Rapture: The Erotic Child in Pater, Wilde, James, and Nabokov* (New York: Palgrave Macmillan, 2005) 123–53.

1   Henry James, *Literary Criticism, Volume 1: Essays on Literature, American Writers & English Writers* (New York: Library of America, 1984) 52.

friendships with a large number of the artistic and intellectual lights of his time. He became a British citizen not long before his death in 1916.

We have seen that James used the ghostly as a way of grappling with moral and aesthetic issues. As befits an author whose writing thematizes ambivalence, however, his attitude towards ghost stories—especially *his* ghost stories—never coalesced into a critical or theoretical stance. Indeed, James's own relationship to the ghostly was a complicated one, shaped in part by the attitudes and experiences of those closest to him. Connecting an author's biography to his or her writings can devolve into a sort of reductive treasure hunt, in which every character, event, or setting must have its analogue in the life and times of the author, thereby eliding the importance of the creative impulse. Nevertheless, even a cursory glance at some events in James's life allows us to see reflections of the struggles in his fiction between social engagement and artistic devotion, between past happiness and present pain, between expansive possibilities and stultifying realities. These struggles require his characters to make choices that often come back to haunt them, just as some of James's own encounters and experiences came back—whether invited or unwanted—to haunt him.

When Henry Jr. was only a toddler, his father unexpectedly experienced an overwhelming epiphany about the presence of evil. Not many years before he died, the elder James wrote about the moment, in which he felt the presence of a "damnèd shape," which was "raying out from his fetid personality influences fatal to life"[1] (see Appendix A2). This "vastation," as Henry Sr. later called his experience, was a turning point for him; he realized that all his previous work—indeed his entire life—had grown out of his own egotistical sense of his capabilities. In an effort to comprehend the significance of the event, he turned to the writings of Emmanuel Swedenborg, the eighteenth-century Swedish mystic whose ideas were widely discussed in mid-nineteenth-century America and Europe. Swedenborg's visions of heaven and hell, of conversations with angels and spirits, intrigued his readers, particularly given that he had begun his career as a scientist in an era when reason was of paramount importance. With the benefit of years of studying Swedenborg's extensive writings, Henry Sr. could later look back on his experience with a measure of under-

---

1   R.W.B. Lewis, *The Jameses: A Family Narrative* (New York: Farrar, Straus and Giroux, 1991) 51.

standing; he had undergone a terrifying emptying of self—the first step, he believed, in recognizing "the radical menace of individual selfhood."[1] He would spend his life pursuing this view of the self in relation to the universe, advocating what Martin Marty calls a "republicanization of religious impulses," with each individual equally close to God.[2]

Like father, like son: all of his life William James, the eldest child of Henry James Sr. found himself intrigued by the implications of the supernatural, beginning with his father's experience and expanding into his research into the psychology of belief in the supernatural. Indeed, William experienced his own sort of vastation, dramatically depicted many years later in *The Varieties of Religious Experience*. The fact that William felt the need to attribute the story to someone else suggests an intensity of experience that he could not acknowledge. He claims to quote another person's narrative that has been translated from the French, but it is in fact his own revelation that he describes. Having suffered an emotional and physical collapse in 1870, he says, the writer had a vision of himself in another form, that of an "idiotic" patient in an asylum who sat like "a sort of sculptured Egyptian cat or Peruvian mummy, moving nothing but his black eyes and looking absolutely non-human."[3]

Far from experiencing evil as a merely intellectual problem, William argues, those who experience such visions undergo a "grisly blood-freezing heart-palsying sensation of it close upon one, and no other conception or sensation able to live for a moment in its presence"[4] (see Appendix A3). As had been the case with his father, the vastation focuses on a nightmarish figure, but unlike his father, William immediately recognized—and acknowledged, however privately—the very real possibility that the figure was himself.

Trained to be a doctor, appointed professor of philosophy, inclined towards psychology, William spent his life mingling the scientific with the philosophic, the verifiable with the intangible, as evidenced by his participation in the Society for Psychical Research (SPR), founded in England in 1882 with the American branch founded by William in 1885. The organization was com-

---

1 Lewis 54.
2 Martin Marty, "Introduction" in William James, *The Varieties of Religious Experience* (New York: Penguin, 1982) xi.
3 William James, *The Varieties of Religious Experience* (New York: Penguin, 1982) 160.
4 William James 162.

posed of highly respected and respectable academics, philosophers, scientists, writers, and others who wanted to study the possibility of supernatural phenomena with some degree of scientific objectivity and thereby rehabilitate reports of paranormal events. The SPR acquired a much-needed mantle of respectability when philosopher and Cambridge don Henry Sidgwick agreed to serve as its first president. Sidgwick had been part of a society formed in the 1850s at Cambridge's Trinity College to study reports of supernatural phenomena in order to determine their veracity.[1] For William, membership in this society held both professional and familial attractions; from a professional perspective, as Martha Banta writes, he hoped that psychical research would lead to a "psychology deemed truly scientific because it included all human nature—the chaotic as well as the calm, the dark as well as the light."[2] Personally, he saw his work with psychical research as a way of linking his father's mysticism with the positivism of the latter part of the nineteenth century. William spent well over a year collecting Henry Sr.'s writings and annotating them with his own commentaries before publishing them as *The Literary Remains of the Late Henry James* in 1884. Unfortunately, the book was almost completely ignored by critics; the one major journal that did review it did so only to dismiss Henry Sr.'s writings as unimportant to anyone except philosophers.

Such harshness, especially coming at the same time as the failure of the serialization of *The Bostonians*, caused Henry Jr. to despair, as he wrote to William:

> But how can one murmur at one's success not being what one would like when one thinks of the pathetic, tragic ineffectualness of poor Father's lifelong effort, & the silence & oblivion that seems to have swallowed it up? ... It is terribly touching &—when I think of the evolution of his production and ideas, fills me with tears.[3]

---

1 Peter G. Beidler has noted the fact that in *The Turn of the Screw*, Douglas, the narrator who has the late governess's manuscript, was a student at Trinity College while the governess worked for his family. See Peter G. Beidler, ed., *The Turn of the Screw Henry James* (Boston: Bedford, 2004) 24.

2 Martha Banta, *Henry James and the Occult: The Great Extension* (Bloomington: Indiana UP, 1972) 25.

3 Philip Horne, *Henry James: A Life in Letters* (New York: Viking, 1999) 181.

James's perception of his father's failure reverberated throughout the rest of his career, lurking as a warning about the possibility of his own failure, echoing time and again in his fictional characters' lives. He would attempt to stave off such silence and oblivion for his own work many years later through his creation of his New York Edition, which he intended to be a magisterial compendium demonstrating once and for all his mastery of the art of fiction. Yet, as Alfred Habegger notes, "[b]eneath the monumental New York Edition lies a corpse that haunted James, the *Remains of Henry James, Sr.*... This was a saint's corpse, one of the cherished dead for whom James burned a votive candle."[1] When the New York Edition failed to earn any significant amount of money or critical attention, Henry James's fear became a reality: his life's work threatened to vanish into nothingness, a threat that led him into a serious depression and eventual breakdown—both physical and emotional—in 1909 and 1910.

Only a few months after William founded the American SPR, his youngest child, 18-month-old Herman, succumbed to whooping cough. Seeking consolation for their grief, William and his wife Alice invited a medium, Mrs. Leonora Piper, to conduct seances in their home in Cambridge, Massachusetts, during which (as William wrote in an account for the American SPR in 1886) Mrs. Piper showed a knowledge of family stories to which she had had no previous access. In 1890, William submitted another report on Mrs. Piper's contact with the dead to the British SPR, who invited Henry to read it at their fall meeting (see Appendix B1). To express their gratitude for Henry's efforts, the society presented him with Volume VI of the society's *Proceedings*, covering the years 1889–90. Numerous details from the narratives included in that volume make their way, albeit imaginatively transformed, into James's ghostly tales of the 1890s. In fact, E.A. Sheppard argues convincingly that organizations such as the SPR created a new sort of reader, well versed in the various narratives that were being published and interested in ghost stories as intellectual conundrums rather than as terrifying tales.[2] Such readerly attitudes were congenial to James, of course, given his own preference for irony and ambiguity. With this new

---

1 David McWhirter, *Henry James's New York Edition: The Construction of Authorship* (Stanford: Stanford UP, 1995) 195.

2 E.A. Sheppard, *Henry James and "The Turn of the Screw"* (Auckland: Auckland UP, 1974) 126–27. Sheppard has an extended discussion of the relationship between the SPA's collected narratives and James's ghost stories of the 1890s.

respectability surrounding the ghostly narrative, his artistic aspirations no longer precluded his satisfying his financial needs by publishing such "potboilers," as he called such tales.[1] He would adapt the conventions of the ghostly to suit his own purposes.

Because Henry described belief in spiritualism to be "alien" to him, his response to his sister-in-law Alice's report of yet another seance with Mrs. Piper, this one in 1905, is remarkable in its passionate intensity. According to Alice, Henry's deceased mother had a cryptic message for her son: "He must be anxious no more for the end shall be as he desires." Despite William's prediction that Henry would doubt the message and find it distressing, Henry in fact welcomed it with great joy. He had been consumed with anxiety, he confided to Alice by letter, over "a matter known to no one in the world but myself," and had been yearning for "some mystic or revealed guarantee that 'anxiety' is superfluous." He could not communicate the effect that this revelation had on him: "I have been hugely affected and emotionné by what you tell me," while considering his beloved mother's "unextinguished consciousness breaking through the interposing vastness of the universe and pouncing upon the first occasion helpfully to get at me." In their reply to his enthusiastic letter, both Alice and William agreed that the dead somehow communicate with the living. "[W]hat it all means, I don't know," William wrote, "but it means at any rate that the world our 'normal' consciousness makes use of is only a fraction of the whole world in which we have our being."[2] Both Henry's and William's responses exemplify Martha Banta's distinction between the facts of scientific studies of the supernatural and the fictions that James spun from them: "To James, the scientist as spectator of the consciousness renounced involvement with drama and style in order to register facts of life," while the "artist as spectator of the consciousness renounced whatever denied drama and style in order to create fables of life."[3]

James had experienced just such a drama when he was young, one that he would later use to create fables of life. As a boy, he had developed a fascination for his first cousin Mary (Minny) Temple, the orphaned daughter of his father's sister. Minny's *joie de vivre*, her outspokenness, her cheerful resistance to prescriptive social expectations enthralled her quieter cousin. They shared an

---

1 Horne 314.

2 Lewis 497–99.

3 Banta 49.

intense desire to experience life, to explore beyond the narrow provinciality that they both detested. With a financially comfortable peripatetic father, the young Henry had already been to Europe three times for extended stays, while Minny yearned to see Europe and to visit Henry there when he departed in February 1869. But in late 1868, she became ill with tuberculosis. Without parents, surrounded by sisters who were successfully finding husbands, living with a strict, unimaginative brother-in-law, Minny saw her chances at escape and exploration quickly receding. One of those who enjoyed and encouraged her freedom of thought—Henry—was far away, exactly where she dreamed of going. Her letters to him during his sojourn demonstrate the depths of her need to flee while also suggesting a flirtatiousness that perhaps disguised a more serious attraction. "If you were not my cousin," she wrote him in June 1869, "I would write and ask you to marry me and take me with you, but as it is, it wouldn't do. I will console myself, however, with the thought, that in that case you might not accept my offer, which would be much worse than it is now." When he avoided answering her inquiries about joining him in Europe, she recognized that he was ambivalent about her presence there, yet she delicately, plaintively continued to press the issue: "If I were, by hook or by crook, to spend next winter, with friends, in Rome, should I see you, at all?"[1] Indeed, Minny's bantering tone belies a desperate desire to escape the stifling circumstances in which she was forced to exist. When another Temple sister became engaged to the brother of her sister's husband—in both cases, with a generation-wide age gap between the husbands and wives—Minny wrote to Henry, "I must flee this spot, unless I wish to become the prey of a bald-headed Emmet [the family name of the brothers-in-law]—There seems to be a fatality about it, which I would fain escape." But she also makes clear to him the threat of a real fatality, a threat that she believes the warm climate of Italy could avert: "I am afraid that another winter might go far toward finishing me up & I would give anything to have a winter in Italy."[2] James apparently never directly answered her hints or outright questions; perhaps he did not recognize the urgency and desperation that lay behind them. Or then again, perhaps he did—but was too involved in his own need for distance and independence in order

---

1 Leon Edel, *Henry James: The Untried Years: 1843–1870* (New York: Avon, 1953) 314–15.

2 Lyndall Gordon, *A Private Life of Henry James: Two Women and His Art* (New York: W.W. Norton, 1999) 102.

to pursue the career he envisioned. To chaperone Minny would infringe on that precious freedom to develop his art; it would also bring him uncomfortably close to a young woman whose intellect and insight attracted him. In any event, Minny never saw Europe. Her premonitions of fatality, of being finished, were tragically exactly right. In March 1870, the tuberculosis that she had fought with such vigor proved fatal.

While alive, Minny was an amusement and a challenge to him; dead, she emanated a golden glow. Writing to William a few days after receiving word of her death, Henry spoke as if directly to her: "In exchange for you, dearest Minny, we'll keep your future...."[1] His rambling letter to his mother, replying to her letter with the news, is striking in his numerous references to the future: "Twenty years hence what a pure eloquent vision she will be.... What a pregnant reference in future years—what a secret from those who never knew her!... But how much—how long— we have got to live without her!"[2] Minny would live, as Lyndall Gordon notes, as a "continuation of a living voice,"[3] one who would speak again in some of his greatest characters. He would summon her ghost while creating Daisy Miller, born to *épater la bourgeoisie* with her mixture of candor and flirtation, or Isabel Archer in *The Portrait of a Lady*, struggling to exercise her independence in a society suffocated by strictures for women, or Milly Theale in *The Wings of the Dove*, fighting death with all the desperation of a young woman just entering adult life.

He would end his memoir of youth by hailing Minny in the valediction to his *Notes of a Son and Brother*. James's recollections of her and the letters that he chose to include combine to resurrect an irrepressible intelligence that almost leaps off the page; the fascination that she had exerted on him clearly had never waned. In one letter that he quotes, Minny writes tartly about her disappointment after hearing a well-known minister preach about Christianity: "The mystery of this world grows and grows, and sticks out of every apparently trivial thing, instead of lessening."[4] True companionship was difficult for Minny to find with a family who could not understand her: "If by chance I say anything or ask a question that lies at all near my heart my sisters all tell me I am 'queer' and that they 'wouldn't be me for anything,'—which

1 Gordon 124–25.
2 Horne 37–38.
3 Gordon 125.
4 Henry James, *Notes of a Son and Brother* (n.p.: Kessinger Publishing, 2005) 451.

is, no doubt, sensible on their part, but which puts an end to anything but conversation of the most superficial kind on mine."[1] A person who understood that the mystery of the world existed in every trivial thing was a person on whom, as James would later say of great artists, nothing was lost; surely this was Minny's greatest attraction for him. At the end of his own life, looking back through the years at this long-lost cousin and friend, he acknowledged her centrality to his life's work:

> ... death, at the last, was dreadful to her; she would have given anything to live—and the image of this, which was long to remain with me, appeared so of the essence of tragedy that I was in the far-off aftertime to seek to lay the ghost by wrapping it, a particular occasion aiding, in the beauty and dignity of art. The figure that was to hover as the ghost has at any rate been of an extreme pertinence, I feel, to my doubtless too loose and confused general picture, vitiated perhaps by the effort to comprehend more than it contains.[2]

Her death marked "the end of our youth," he wrote in his final words of the memoir (see Appendix A4).

Just as James had predicted in his youthful letter to his mother, Minny did in fact continue to live for him; whether resurrected through his writings or lingering as a ghost, she figured the finely tuned consciousness that he always sought to depict. In James's short story "The Altar of the Dead" (1895), George Stransom becomes obsessed with honoring his dead loved ones. He remembers a dear friend whose husband remarried too soon after her untimely death:

> ... his eyes, in the swarming void of things, seemed to have caught Kate Creston's, and it was into their sad silences he looked. It was to him her sentient spirit had turned, knowing that it was of her he would think. He thought, for a long time, of how the closed eyes of dead women could still live—how they could open again, in a quiet lamplit room, long after they had looked their last. They had looks that remained, as great poets had quoted lines. ("Altar" 55)

"It is from the dead that James's truest, richest inspiration comes," wrote Leslie A. Fiedler in *Love and Death in the American*

---

1 James 460.
2 James 479.

Novel, "from a fascination with and a love for the dead, for death itself; and it is no accident that his Muse and his America are both figured forth by the image of a girl who died at twenty-four."[1] If Minny haunted James, then, she did so at his own summoning, a ghostly Muse who sparked some of his greatest works.

William and Henry had three younger siblings; their two brothers, Robertson and Wilkerson, apparently did not share in the creative drive that their father and older brothers enjoyed. The only daughter in the family, Alice James, displayed many of the same gifts from which her brothers benefited. Unfortunately, ill health plagued her for much of her life and turned her into a permanent invalid, but she managed nonetheless to write lengthy letters, keep a diary, hold salons, teach correspondence courses, and read voraciously. "The moral and philosophical questions that Henry wrote up as fiction and William as science," Alice James's biographer observes, "Alice simply lived."[2] She suffered from debilitating pain, fainting spells, headaches, stomach problems, intermittently paralyzed legs, depression, and nervous collapses; her father described her at one point as "on the verge of insanity and suicide."[3] Despite her afflictions, she managed to retain her wit, her vigorous curiosity, and her desire to sound the moral depths of her life—all qualities that endeared her to her family, especially to William and Henry.

The James children lost both their parents in 1882, which left Alice living alone in Boston. Sometime later, she recorded in her diary her desolation in words that both evoke the descriptions of "vastations" recorded by Henry Sr. and William and presage the haunted Jolly Corner that Henry would later create:

> In those ghastly days, when I was by myself in the little house in Mt. Vernon St., how I longed to flee in to the firemen next door & escape from the "Alone! Alone!" that echoed thro' the house, rustled down the stairs, whispered from the walls & confronted me, like a material presence, as I sat waiting, counting the moments as they turned themselves from today into tomorrow....[4]

---

1 Leslie A. Fiedler, *Love and Death in the American Novel* (Normal, IL: Dalkey Archive P, 1997) 303.

2 Jean Strouse, *Alice James: A Biography* (Boston: Houghton Mifflin, 1980) xiv.

3 Ruth Bernard Yeazell, *The Death and Letters of Alice James* (Berkeley: U of California P, 1981) 15.

4 Qtd. In Yeazell 24.

In 1884, she moved to London along with her close friend and companion, Katharine Peabody Loring, where she spent the remaining eight years of her life. After Alice's death, Katharine had her diary privately printed and gave copies to William and Henry. Although Henry agonized at the thought of the family's privacy being invaded, he immediately recognized Alice's literary gifts, as he wrote to William:

> ... I have been immensely impressed with the thing as a reve-
> lation of a moral and personal picture. It is heroic in its indi-
> viduality, its independence—its face-to-face with the universe
> for and by herself—and the beauty and eloquence with which
> she often expresses this, let alone the rich irony and humour,
> constitute (I wholly agree with you) a new claim for the family
> renown. This last element—her style, her power to write—are
> indeed to me a delight—for I never had many letters from
> her.[1]

Alice's death was one of a number of traumas in the 1890s, a period that James's biographer Leon Edel calls "the treacherous years." He made a concerted effort to succeed as a playwright, but never managed to thrive in that arena; indeed, he suffered a great humiliation on the opening night of his play *Guy Domville* in 1895, when he was called on the stage after the performance ended, only to be greeted with a combination of cheers, hisses, and catcalls. *Guy Domville* was soon replaced by a new work written by the very popular Oscar Wilde. *The Importance of Being Earnest* brought yet more success to its author, but James was horrified and shaken by the scandal that erupted over Wilde's homosexuality not long after the play premiered. While scholars disagree over how to describe James's own sexuality, most would agree that James was attracted to men; whether or not he engaged in actual homosexual relations, the Wilde tragedy certainly served as a harsh reminder of Anglo-American attitudes towards any sexual expression outside heterosexual marriage.

In the mid-1890s, James lost several close friends. In 1894, he received distressing word from Samoa that his beloved friend Robert Louis Stevenson had died after years of ill health. Earlier that year another friend had died in a manner that upset James tremendously. James had met the American writer Constance

---

1 Qtd. in Strouse 321–22.

Fenimore Woolson in 1880 and the two quickly became friends, for James recognized a kindred spirit in this fiercely intelligent, independent woman who, like him, sought artistic and intellectual stimulation in Europe. On the whole, James appreciated her fiction and encouraged her literary aspirations. So mutually beneficial was their relationship that for a few weeks in December 1886, they actually shared a villa overlooking Florence, a fact that James took some pains to disguise from his family and friends—as he also hid the fact that his month-long stay in Geneva in 1888 included Woolson's companionship.

The nature of their relationship will always remain unclear; several of James's biographers believe that Woolson cared a great deal for James, but, since she believed that he would never marry, she settled for an intense platonic friendship. At some point in their relationship, they made a pact that they would destroy each other's letters, thereby allowing themselves the luxury of honesty in their communications. Woolson felt free to criticize as well as praise James's writings, as when she disputed some of Isabel Archer's reactions in *The Portrait of a Lady* while lauding James's understanding of intelligent women like Isabel. In fact, in Woolson James found a rarity: someone as interested as he in the knotty aesthetic problems inherent in trying to create the interior lives of characters.

When James received a telegram in January 1894 announcing Woolson's death in Venice, he was shocked—but even more so when the news arrived that she likely had committed suicide by jumping out of her hotel room window. At that point, he later remembered, he collapsed from the horror, torturing himself with questions about his own role in Woolson's death—whether there was something he could have done to prevent it, whether he had abandoned her to loneliness and depression. In April he traveled to Venice to help Woolson's sister sort through her effects, at which point he may well have burned the letters he had written her. Soon thereafter he visited her grave in the Protestant cemetery in Rome—the very cemetery where, many years before, he had placed the grave of Daisy Miller. That fall, he took lodgings in the same building in Oxford where Woolson had lived for over a year in the early 1890s; in those rooms, he conceived "The Altar of the Dead" and shortly thereafter made his first extensive notes for what would become *The Wings of the Dove*.

Henry James's works reverberate with echoes from his own experience: the anxieties about his life's work, the punitive Victorian attitudes towards any sort of non-conformity (especially

sexual), the deaths of family and friends, the hallucinatory creatures who visited his father and his brother, his strange mixture
of sorrow and exaltation over Minny's death, the thwarted bril-
liance of his sister Alice's life, his anguish at the tragedy of Constance Woolson's life and death—all find their way into these four
ghostly tales. In these stories, James sought, as he said, to lay his
ghosts through the exercising—and perhaps exorcising—of his
art. In his fiction, though, the ghosts remain, perpetually bidden
to open their eyes, to speak, to walk, to live, to haunt—all a
worthy measure of James's extraordinary achievement.

Works Cited

Banta, Martha. *Henry James and the Occult: The Great Extension.*
Bloomington: Indiana UP, 1972.

Beidler, Peter G., ed. Henry James, *The Turn of the Screw/Henry
James.* Boston: Bedford, 2004.

Brooke-Rose, Christine. *A Rhetoric of the Unreal.* New York: Cambridge UP, 1981.

Castle, Terry. *The Female Thermometer: Eighteenth-Century Culture and
the Invention of the Uncanny.* New York: Oxford UP, 1995.

Cranfill, Thomas M. and Robert L. Clark. *An Anatomy of "The Turn
of the Screw."* Austin: U of Texas P, 1965.

Davis, Colin. *Haunted Subjects: Deconstruction, Psychoanalysis and the
Return of the Dead.* Basingstoke, Hampshire: Palgrave Macmillan,
2007.

Diderot, Denis. *Encyclopédie, ou dictionnaire raisonné des sciences, des
arts et des métiers* (1751-52). <http://portail.atilf.fr/encyclopedie>.

Edel, Leon and Lyall H. Powers, eds. *The Complete Notebooks of
Henry James.* New York: Oxford UP, 1987.

Edel, Leon. *Henry James: The Untried Years: 1843–1870.* New York:
Avon, 1953.

Elton, Oliver. *Modern Studies.* London: Edward Arnold, 1907.

Esch, Deborah. "A Jamesian About-face: Notes on 'The Jolly
Corner.'" *ELH* 50 (1983): 587–605.

Felman, Shoshana. *Literature and Psychoanalysis: The Question of
Reading: Otherwise.* Baltimore: Johns Hopkins UP, 1982.

Fiedler, Leslie A. *Love and Death in the American Novel.* Normal, IL:
Dalkey Archive P, 1997.

Firebaugh, Joseph J. "Inadequacy in Eden: Knowledge and *The Turn
of the Screw.*" *Modern Fiction Studies* 3 (1957): 57–63.

Freud, Sigmund. "Repression." *On Metapsychology: The Theory of Psychoanalysis,* Vol. 22. Trans. James Strachey. Ed. Angela Richards.
Harmondsworth: Penguin, 1984.

——. *The Uncanny.* Trans. David McClintock. Ed. Adam Phillips.
New York: Penguin, 2003 (1957). 123–62.

Goddard, Harold. "A Pre-Freudian Reading of *The Turn of the Screw.*" *Nineteenth-Century Fiction* 12 (1957): 1–36.

Gordon, Lyndall. *A Private Life of Henry James: Two Women and His Art.* New York: W.W. Norton, 1999.

Heilman, Robert B. "The Freudian Reading of *The Turn of the Screw.*" *Modern Language Notes* 62 (1947): 433–45.

———. "*The Turn of the Screw* as Poem." Rpt. in Gerald Willen, ed., *A Casebook on Henry James's "The Turn of the Screw."* 2nd ed. New York: Thomas Y. Crowell, 1969. 174–88.

Hocks, Richard. *Henry James: A Study of the Short Fiction.* Boston: Twayne, 1990.

———. *Henry James and Pragmatistic Thought.* Chapel Hill: U of North Carolina P, 1974.

Horne, Philip. *Henry James: A Life in Letters.* New York: Viking, 1999.

James, Henry. "The Art of Fiction." *Henry James: Literary Criticism: Essays on Literature, American Writers & English Writers.* Vol. 1. New York: Library of America, 1984. 44–65.

———. *Notes of a Son and Brother.* Kessinger Publishing, 2005.

———. "Preface to *The Aspern Papers, The Turn of the Screw*, 'The Liar,' 'The Two Faces.'" *Henry James: Literary Criticism: French Writers, Other European Writers, The Prefaces to the New York Edition.* Vol. 2. New York: Library of America, 1984. 1173–91.

Kenton, Edna. "Henry James to the Ruminant Reader: *The Turn of the Screw.*" *The Arts* Nov. 1924: 245-55.

Krook, Dorothea. *The Ordeal of Consciousness in Henry James.* Cambridge: Harvard UP, 1962.

Lewis, R.W.B. *The Jameses: A Family Narrative.* New York: Farrar, Straus and Giroux, 1991.

Lustig, T.J. *Henry James and the Ghostly.* Cambridge: Cambridge UP, 1994.

Marty, Martin. Introduction. *The Varieties of Religious Experience.* By William James. New York: Penguin, 1982. vii–xxvii.

McMaster, Graham. "Henry James and India: A Historical Reading of *The Turn of the Screw.*" *Clio* 18 (1988): 23–40.

McWhirter, David. *Henry James's New York Edition: The Construction of Authorship.* Stanford: Stanford UP, 1995.

Noyes, Ralph. "The Other Side of Plato's Wall." *Ghosts: Deconstruction, Psychoanalysis, History.* Eds. Peter Buse and Andrew Scott. London: Macmillan, 1999. 244–62.

Ohi, Kevin. "'Blameless and Foredoomed': Innocence and Haste in *The Turn of the Screw.*" *Innocence and Rapture: The Erotic Child in Pater, Wilde, James, and Nabokov.* New York: Palgrave Macmillan, 2005. 123–53.

Rimmon, Shlomith. *The Concept of Ambiguity—The Case of Henry James.* Chicago: The U of Chicago P, 1977.

Rowe, John Carlos. "Psychoanalytical Significances: The Use and Abuse of Uncertainty in *The Turn of the Screw.*" *The Theoretical*

Dimensions of Henry James. Madison: U of Wisconsin P, 1984. 120–46.

Savoy, Eric. "The Queer Subject of 'The Jolly Corner.'" *The Henry James Review* 20 (1999): 1–21.

Sedgwick, Eve Kosofsky. *Epistemology of the Closet*. Berkeley: U of California P, 1990.

Sheppard, E.A. *Henry James and "The Turn of the Screw."* Auckland: Auckland UP, 1974.

Strouse, Jean. *Alice James: A Biography*. Boston: Houghton Mifflin, 1980.

Thomas, Keith. *Religion and the Decline of Magic: Studies in Popular Beliefs in Sixteenth- and Seventeenth-Century England*. London: Weidenfeld and Nicolson, 1971.

Todorov, Tzvetan. *The Fantastic: A Structural Approach to a Literary Genre*. Ithaca, NY: Cornell UP, 1975.

Willen, Gerald, ed. *A Casebook on Henry James's "The Turn of the Screw."* New York: Crowell, 1960.

Wilson, Edmund. "The Ambiguity of Henry James." *The Triple Thinkers*. New York: Oxford UP, 1948. 48–132.

Woolf, Virginia. "Henry James's Ghost Stories." *Granite and Rainbow: Essays by Virginia Woolf*. London: Hogarth Press, 1981.

Yeazell, Ruth Bernard. *The Death and Letters of Alice James*. Berkeley: U of California P, 1981.

Henry James: A Brief Chronology

1843 Henry James is born April 15 in New York City to Henry James Sr. and Mary Walsh James, joining older brother William (born January 11, 1842).

1843 In October, Henry James, Sr., takes family to live in Europe, moving back and forth between England and France over a period of almost two years.

1845 James family returns to New York, with extended stays with James family in Albany. Garth Wilkinson (Wilky) James is born July 21.

1846 Robertson (Bob) James is born August 29.

1848 Alice James is born August 7.

1855 James family leaves New York for Europe, traveling and living in England, France, Switzerland; Henry learns to speak French fluently.

1858 Family returns to US, settling in Newport, Rhode Island.

1859 Henry James Sr. decides to take family back to Switzerland because of his preference for the educational system in Geneva.

1860 Family returns to Newport so that William can study art with William Morris Hunt.

1861 Henry Sr.'s Temple nieces move to Newport; Henry Jr. and his cousin Mary (Minny) Temple become close; Henry suffers "obscure hurt" while helping extinguish fire in Newport.

1862 Wilkinson James enlists in the Massachusetts 44th Regiment, later moving to the black 54th Regiment led by Colonel Robert Gould Shaw; Henry enrolls in Harvard Law School but later withdraws in order to pursue literary career.

1863 Wilkinson James is critically injured in regiment's attack on Fort Wagner in Charleston, South Carolina.

1864 Henry James's first short story is published ("A Tragedy of Error") in *Continental Monthly* and his first review is published for *North American Review*; the James family moves to Boston.

1865 James's first signed short story ("The Story of a Year") appears in *Atlantic Monthly*; he also writes reviews for *Nation* and *North American Review*.

1866   The Jameses move to Cambridge, Massachusetts; Henry
       continues publishing reviews and fictional works.

1869   Henry departs for Europe, where he first stays in
       London and encounters Leslie Stephen, William Morris,
       George Eliot, Charles Eliot Norton, John Ruskin, Dante
       Gabriel Rossetti, Charles Darwin, and Edward Burne-
       Jones; goes to Paris and Geneva, and travels through
       Italy.

1870   James leaves Italy to travel in France, then goes on to
       England; learns of Minny Temple's death in March;
       departs for the United States in April.

1872   James returns to Europe along with his Aunt Kate and
       sister Alice in May; Aunt Kate and Alice return home in
       October, while James travels in France, Italy, Switzer-
       land, and Germany; William James joins him and the two
       stay in Florence and Rome.

1874   William returns home; Henry stays in Florence for
       several months, then leaves Italy to travel through
       Switzerland, Germany, Holland, and Belgium on his way
       back to England and then home.

1875   After publishing fiction, reviews, and travel essays, James
       leaves in October for Europe, where he settles in Paris
       and will meet in the next year Ivan Turgenev, Gustave
       Flaubert, Edmond de Goncourt, Emile Zola, Alphonse
       Daudet, and Guy de Maupassant.

1876   *The American* begins serialization (published as a book in
       1877); James leaves Paris for London.

1878   *Daisy Miller* appears in *Cornhill Magazine* in June and
       July (published as a book in November) and becomes
       James's best selling work so far; he will later report being
       asked to dinner in London 107 times during the winter
       of 1878–79.

1880   *Washington Square* is serialized and then published in
       December; *The Portrait of a Lady* begins serialization
       (published in November 1881).

1881   James returns to the United States, where he visits his
       family in Cambridge.

1882   James travels to Washington where he meets President
       Chester A. Arthur and Oscar Wilde (on a speaking tour);
       recalled to Cambridge due to his mother's illness but
       arrives too late to see her before she dies in late January;
       returns to England in May via Ireland; visits France and
       writes travel essays that become *A Little Tour in France*;

recalled in December to American due to his father's illness, but arrives after his father's death on December 18; goes to his parents' graves in Cambridge and reads aloud a farewell letter to their father from William, who is in London.

1883 James visits his brothers Wilkinson and Robertson in Milwaukee, Wisconsin, and returns to Boston to serve as executor of his father's will; spends his 40th birthday on April 15 in New York City; returns to London at the end of the summer; play version of *Daisy Miller* published; *Collected Edition* of James's novels and tales (14 volumes) published by Macmillan; Wilkinson James dies in November.

1884 Alice James arrives in England with her friend, Katherine Loring; James develops friendships with the American painter John Singer Sargent and the British writer Robert Louis Stevenson.

1885 *The Bostonians* and *The Princess Casamassima* begin serialization (both published in 1886).

1886 James leaves England for extended stay in Italy, spending time with his friend and fellow novelist, Constance Fenimore Woolson.

1888 Publication of several works, including *The Reverberator* and *The Aspern Papers*

1889 *The Tragic Muse* begins serialization (published in 1890); James is asked to dramatize *The American* for an English theatre company.

1890 While traveling in Italy, James receives word that his sister Alice has had a complete collapse in England and returns to be with her.

1891 James's dramatic version of his novel *The American* opens in London to mixed reviews; Alice is diagnosed with breast cancer.

1892 Alice James dies in London in March; James writes short stories and plays.

1894 Constance Fenimore Woolson dies in Venice, apparently by suicide, in January; in the spring, James goes to Venice to help Woolson's family settle her affairs; death of Robert Louis Stevenson in December.

1895 Premiere of James's play, *Guy Domville*; James is both cheered and booed when escorted to the stage after the performance; *The Better Sort*, a collection of short stories including "The Altar of the Dead," is published.

1896   *The Spoils of Poynton* begins serialization under the title *The Old Things* and is published in 1897; *The Other House* is serialized and published.

1897   *What Maisie Knew* is serialized and published; James buys typewriter and hires stenographer to take dictation to avoid further damage to his wrist; decides to move to the town of Rye, Sussex, and live in an eighteenth-century house called Lamb House.

1898   *The Turn of the Screw* is serialized in spring and published later in the year in *The Two Magics*, which also includes another novella, *Covering End*; *The Awkward Age* is serialized (published in 1899).

1900   Death of Stephen Crane, the American writer who lived near Rye and with whom James was friends.

1901   *The Sacred Fount* is published.

1902   *The Wings of the Dove* is published.

1903   *The Ambassadors* is serialized and published; *The Better Sort*, a collection of short stories including "The Beast in the Jungle," is published.

1904   *The Golden Bowl* is published; James travels to America for first visit in over 20 years; visits many people including Edith Wharton at her Berkshire home The Mount; his brothers William and Robertson and their families; travels to Washington where he dines at the White House with President Theodore Roosevelt; stays with the Vanderbilts at their home, the Biltmore, in North Carolina; travels to South Carolina and Florida; to St. Louis, Chicago, Los Angeles, San Diego, San Francisco, Portland, Seattle, Albany, New York City, Baltimore, and Cambridge (among other cities).

1905   James begins publishing essays about his travels, which are later collected (with some changes) and published as *The American Scene* (1907).

1906   James works on prefaces for the New York Edition and begins process of revising works for inclusion; 24 volumes will be published between 1907 and 1909.

1907   James goes to Paris to stay with Edith Wharton and take a motor car tour through the countryside before traveling on his own to Italy.

1908   Continues work for the New York Edition; "The Jolly Corner" published in December.

1910   Suffers from stomach problems and depression; William's son Henry and then William and his wife Alice come to be with him; William, Alice, and Henry go to Bad Nauheim in Germany due to William's increasing heart problems; Robertson James dies in July; William, Alice, and Henry sail to America in August; William dies soon after their arrival at his home in New Hampshire.

1911 James receives honorary degree from Harvard University; leaves the United States for the last time in August.

1912 James leases flat in Chelsea (London); works on his autobiography, *A Small Boy and Others* (published in 1913); receives honorary Doctor of Letters from Oxford.

1913 On April 15, James celebrates 70th birthday by receiving gifts organized by a large number of friends; these gifts include an antique bowl and the opportunity to sit for a portrait by his friend John Singer Sargent; London newspapers feature articles and editorials praising James, and he receives card and telegrams from friends all over Europe and America.

1914 James publishes second volume of his autobiography, *Notes of a Son and Brother*; World War I begins; James becomes honorary president of the American Volunteer Motor Ambulance Corps.

1915 James becomes British citizen in July; suffers series of strokes in December; Alice James (widow of William) arrives to oversee his care.

1916 On New Year's Day, James receives the Order of Merit from the king, George V; condition continues to decline and James dies on February 28; a funeral service is held in Chelsea Old Church; Alice brings his ashes to Cambridge, Massachusetts, where they are buried in the family cemetery plot.

A Note on the Texts

Many of Henry James's short stories were published in at least three versions: in a periodical, then later with other stories in a book, and finally in the collection of James's *oeuvre*, the New York Edition. Before publishing his stories the second or third time, James would often make changes to the text, sometimes minor, sometimes more significant. Determining which version to use for new editions, therefore, requires careful consideration. Complicating this process is the fact that the English and American texts sometimes varied from each other.

Two of the four tales collected here are exceptions to the general rule of first appearing in a periodical. "The Altar of the Dead" originally appeared as part of a short-story collection, *Terminations*, published in London by William Heinemann in May 1895 and in New York by Harper and Brothers in June 1895. "The Beast in the Jungle" likewise first was published in *The Better Sort*, published in London by Methuen and in New York by Charles Scribner's Sons in February 1903. "The Turn of the Screw" was the only one of the four to be serialized; it appeared in the periodical *Collier's Weekly* from 27 January until 16 April 1898, and was published as a complete novella, *The Turn of the Screw*, in a collection titled *The Two Magics* in October 1898 by William Heinemann in London and by the Macmillan Company in New York. "The Jolly Corner" was published in one volume of *The English Review* in December 1908.

All four of these stories also appeared in *The Novels and Tales of Henry James*, The New York Edition, the 1907–09 edition of his works published by Charles Scribner's Sons. Having been inspired by the 1875 appearance of Honoré de Balzac's collected works, which had motivated James's first essay on that great novelist, James envisioned the New York Edition as his version of Balzac's *Comédie humaine*. Revising his life's work was a monumental task, one that took up much of his time between 1904 and 1909; James pored over the texts he had chosen for inclusion, often making extensive alterations, with the result that the New York Edition contains the final versions that James himself authorized. The edition is notable for another facet of James's contributions to literature: he wrote a set of prefaces to his works in which he articulated his theory of fiction, reminisced about the origins of many of his stories, and reflected on the relationship between life and art. Because of the significance of this undertaking and the fact that it contains James's last, definitive revisions, I have chosen to use the texts of the stories from the New York Edition as the copytexts for this volume.

It is worth noting that James's changes for the New York Edition of *The Turn of the Screw* were more substantial than those made to the other three texts in this volume: as Deborah Esch and Jonathan Warren note, James moved the focus away from actions and towards reactions, especially those experienced by the governess.[1] I have kept the spelling and punctuation as they appeared in that edition with one exception: I have changed James's spelling of two-syllable contractions such as "did n't" to the now standard form.

---

1 Deborah Esch and Jonathan Warren, eds., *The Turn of the Screw*, 2nd ed. (New York: W.W. Norton, 1999) 89.

THE TALES

The Altar of the Dead

I

He had a mortal dislike, poor Stransom, to lean anniversaries, and loved them still less when they made a pretence of a figure. Celebrations and suppressions were equally painful to him, and but one of the former found a place in his life. He had kept each year in his own fashion the date of Mary Antrim's death. It would be more to the point perhaps to say that this occasion kept *him*: it kept him at least effectually from doing anything else. It took hold of him again and again with a hand of which time had softened but never loosened the touch. He waked to his feast of memory as consciously as he would have waked to his marriage-morn. Marriage had had of old but too little to say to the matter: for the girl who was to have been his bride there had been no bridal embrace. She had died of a malignant fever after the wedding-day had been fixed, and he had lost before fairly tasting it an affection that promised to fill his life to the brim.

Of that benediction, however, it would have been false to say this life could really be emptied: it was still ruled by a pale ghost, still ordered by a sovereign presence. He had not been a man of numerous passions, and even in all these years no sense had grown stronger with him than the sense of being bereft. He had needed no priest and no altar to make him for ever widowed. He had done many things in the world—he had done almost all but one: he had never, never forgotten. He had tried to put into his existence whatever else might take up room in it, but had failed to make it more than a house of which the mistress was eternally absent. She was most absent of all on the recurrent December day that his tenacity set apart. He had no arranged observance of it, but his nerves made it all their own. They drove him forth without mercy, and the goal of his pilgrimage was far. She had been buried in a London suburb, a part then of Nature's breast, but which he had seen lose one after another every feature of freshness. It was in truth during the moments he stood there that his eyes beheld the place least. They looked at another image, they opened to another light. Was it a credible future? Was it an incredible past? Whatever the answer it was an immense escape from the actual.

It's true that if there weren't other dates than this there were other memories; and by the time George Stransom was fifty-five such memories had greatly multiplied. There were other ghosts in his life than the ghost of Mary Antrim. He had perhaps not had more losses than most men, but he had counted his losses more; he hadn't seen death more closely, but had in a manner felt it more deeply. He had formed little by little the habit of numbering his Dead: it had come to him early in life that there was something one had to do for them. They were there in their simplified intensified essence, their conscious absence and expressive patience, as personally there as if they had only been stricken dumb. When all sense of them failed, all sound of them ceased, it was as if their purgatory were really still on earth: they asked so little that they got, poor things, even less, and died again, died every day, of the hard usage of life. They had no organised service, no reserved place, no honour, no shelter, no safety. Even ungenerous people provided for the living, but even those who were called most generous did nothing for the others. So on George Stransom's part had grown up with the years a resolve that he at least would do something, do it, that is, for his own— would perform the great charity without reproach. Every man *had* his own, and every man had, to meet this charity, the ample resources of the soul.

It was doubtless the voice of Mary Antrim that spoke for them best; as the years at any rate went by he found himself in regular communion with these postponed pensioners, those whom indeed he always called in his thoughts the Others. He spared them the moments, he organised the charity. Quite how it had risen he probably never could have told you, but what came to pass was that an altar, such as was after all within everybody's compass, lighted with perpetual candles and dedicated to these secret rites, reared itself in his spiritual spaces. He had wondered of old, in some embarrassment, whether he had a religion; being very sure, and not a little content, that he hadn't at all events the religion some of the people he had known wanted him to have. Gradually this question was straightened out for him: it became clear to him that the religion instilled by his earliest consciousness had been simply the religion of the Dead. It suited his inclination, it satisfied his spirit, it gave employment to his piety. It answered his love of great offices, of a solemn and splendid ritual; for no shrine could be more bedecked and no ceremonial more stately than those to which his worship was attached. He had no imagination about these things but that they were accessible to any who should feel the need of them. The poorest could build such temples of the spirit—could make them blaze with candles and smoke with incense, make them flush with pictures and flowers. The cost, in the common phrase, of keeping them up fell wholly on the generous heart.

II

He had this year, on the eve of his anniversary, as happened, an emotion not unconnected with that range of feeling. Walking home at the close of a busy day he was arrested in the London street by the particular effect of a shop-front that lighted the dull brown air with its mercenary grin and before which several persons were gathered. It was the window of a jeweller whose diamonds and sapphires seemed to laugh, in flashes like high notes of sound, with the mere joy of knowing how much more they were "worth" than most of the dingy pedestrians staring at them from the other side of the pane. Stransom lingered long enough to suspend, in a vision, a string of pearls about the white neck of Mary Antrim, and then was kept an instant longer by the sound of a voice he knew. Next him was a mumbling old woman, and beyond the old woman a gentleman with a lady on his arm. It was from him, from Paul Creston, the voice had proceeded: he was talking with the lady of some precious object in the window. Stransom had no sooner recognised him than the old woman turned away; but just with this growth of opportunity came a felt strangeness that stayed him in the very act of laying his hand on his friend's arm. It lasted but the instant, only that space sufficed for the flash of a wild question. Was *not* Mrs. Creston dead?—the ambiguity met him there in the short drop of her husband's voice, the drop conjugal, if it ever was, and in the way the two figures leaned to each other. Creston, making a step to look at something else, came nearer, glanced at him, started and exclaimed—behaviour the effect of which was at first only to leave Stransom staring, staring back across the months at the different face, the wholly other face, the poor man had shown him last, the blurred ravaged mask bent over the open grave by which they had stood together. That son of affliction wasn't in mourning now; he detached his arm from his companion's to grasp the hand of the older friend. He coloured as well as smiled in the strong light of the shop when Stransom raised a tentative hat to the lady. Stransom had just time to see she was pretty before he found himself gaping at a fact more portentous. "My dear fellow, let me make you acquainted with my wife."

Creston had blushed and stammered over it, but in half a minute, at the rate we live in polite society, it had practically become, for our friend, the mere memory of a shock. They stood there and laughed and talked; Stransom had instantly whisked the shock out of the way, to keep it for private consumption. He felt himself grimace, he heard himself exaggerate the proper, but was conscious of turning not a little faint. That new woman, that hired performer Mrs. Creston? Mrs. Creston had been more living for him than any woman but one. This lady had a face that shone as publicly as the jeweller's window, and in the happy candour with which she wore her monstrous character was an effect of gross immodesty. The character of Paul Creston's wife thus attributed to her was monstrous for reasons Stransom could judge his friend to know perfectly that he knew. The happy pair had just arrived from America, and Stransom hadn't needed to be told this to guess the nationality of the lady. Somehow it deepened the foolish air that her husband's confused cordiality was unable to conceal. Stransom recalled that he had heard of poor Creston's having, while his bereavement was still fresh, crossed the sea for what people in such predicaments call a little change. He had found the little change indeed, he had brought the little change back; it was the little change that stood there and that, do what he would, he couldn't, while he showed those high front teeth of his, look other than a conscious ass about. They were going into the shop, Mrs. Creston said, and she begged Mr. Stransom to come with them and help to decide. He thanked her, opening his watch and pleading an engagement for which he was already late, and they parted while she shrieked into the fog, "Mind now you come to see me right away!" Creston had had the delicacy not to suggest that, and Stransom hoped it hurt him somewhere to hear her scream it to all the echoes.

He felt quite determined, as he walked away, never in his life to go near her. She was perhaps a human being, but Creston oughtn't to have shown her without precautions, oughtn't indeed to have shown her at all. His precautions should have been those of a forger or a murderer, and the people at home would never have mentioned extradition. This was a wife for foreign service or purely external use; a decent consideration would have spared her the injury of comparisons. Such was the first flush of George Stransom's reaction; but as he sat alone that night—there were particular hours he always passed alone—the harshness dropped from it and left only the pity. *He* could spend an evening with Kate Creston, if the man to whom she had given everything couldn't. He had known her twenty years, and she was the only woman for whom he might perhaps have been unfaithful. She was all cleverness and sympathy and charm; her house had been the very easiest in all the world and her friendship the very firmest. Without accidents he had loved her, without accidents every one had loved her: she had made the passions about her as regular as the moon makes the tides. She had been also of course far too good for her husband, but he never suspected it, and in nothing had she been more admirable than in the exquisite art with which she tried to keep every one else (keeping Creston was no trouble) from finding it out. Here was a man to whom she had devoted her life and for whom she had given it up—dying to bring into the world a child of his bed; and she had had only to submit to her fate to have, ere the grass was green on her grave, no more existence for him than a domestic servant he had replaced. The frivolity, the indecency of it made Stransom's eyes fill; and he had that evening a sturdy sense that he alone, in a world without delicacy, had a right to hold up his head. While he smoked, after dinner, he had a book in his lap, but he had no eyes for his page: his eyes, in the swarming void of things, seemed to have caught Kate Creston's, and it was into their sad silences he looked. It was to him her sentient spirit had turned, knowing it to be of her he would think. He thought for a long time of how the closed eyes of dead women could still live—how they could open again, in a quiet lamplit room, long after they had looked their last. They had looks that survived—had them as great poets had quoted lines.

The newspaper lay by his chair—the thing that came in the afternoon and the servants thought one wanted; without sense for what was in it he had mechanically unfolded and then dropped it. Before he went to bed he took it up, and this time, at the top of a paragraph, he was caught by five words that made him start. He stood staring, before the fire, at the "Death of Sir Acton Hague, K.C.B.,"[1] the man who ten years earlier had been the nearest of his friends and whose deposition from this eminence had practically left it without an occupant. He had seen him after their rupture, but hadn't now seen him for years. Standing there before the fire he turned cold as he read what had befallen him. Promoted a short time previous to the governorship of the Westward Islands, Acton Hague had died, in the bleak honour of this exile, of an illness consequent on the bite of a poi-

---

1 Knight Commander of the Bath, one of the classes of the Order of the Bath, a chivalric order founded in 1725 by George I, awarded at the time of the story to high-ranking military or civil servants.

sonous snake. His career was compressed by the newspaper into a dozen lines, the perusal of which excited on George Stransom's part no warmer feeling than one of relief at the absence of any mention of their quarrel, an incident accidentally tainted at the time, thanks to their joint immersion in large affairs, with a horrible publicity. Public indeed was the wrong Stransom had, to his own sense, suffered, the insult he had blankly taken from the only man with whom he had ever been intimate; the friend, almost adored, of his University years, the subject, later, of his passionate loyalty: so public that he had never spoken of it to a human creature, so public that he had completely overlooked it. It had made the difference for him that friendship too was all over, but it had only made just that one. The shock of interests had been private, intensely so; but the action taken by Hague had been in the face of men. To-day it all seemed to have occurred merely to the end that George Stransom should think of him as "Hague" and measure exactly how much he himself could resemble a stone. He went cold, suddenly and horribly cold, to bed.

III

The next day, in the afternoon, in the great grey suburb, he knew his long walk had tired him. In the dreadful cemetery alone he had been on his feet an hour. Instinctively, coming back, they had taken him a devious course, and it was a desert in which no circling cabman hovered over possible prey. He paused on a corner and measured the dreariness; then he made out through the gathered dusk that he was in one of those tracts of London which are less gloomy by night than by day, because, in the former case, of the civil gift of light. By day there was nothing, but by night there were lamps, and George Stransom was in a mood that made lamps good in themselves. It wasn't that they could show him anything, it was only that they could burn clear. To his surprise, however, after a while, they did show him something: the arch of a high doorway approached by a low terrace of steps, in the depth of which—it formed a dim vestibule—the raising of a curtain at the moment he passed gave him a glimpse of an avenue of gloom with a glow of tapers at the end. He stopped and looked up, recognising the place as a church. The thought quickly came to him that since he was tired he might rest there; so that after a moment he had in turn pushed up the leathern curtain and gone in. It was a temple of the old persuasion, and there had evidently been a function—perhaps a service for the dead; the high altar was still a blaze of candles. This was an exhibition he always liked, and he dropped into a seat with relief. More than it had ever yet come home to him it struck him as good there should be churches.

This one was almost empty and the other altars were dim; a verger shuffled about, an old woman coughed, but it seemed to Stransom there was hospitality in the thick sweet air. Was it only the savour of the incense or was it something of larger intention? He had at any rate quitted the great grey suburb and come nearer to the warm centre. He presently ceased to feel intrusive, gaining at last even a sense of community with the only worshipper in his neighbourhood, the sombre presence of a woman, in mourning unrelieved, whose back was all he could see of her and who had sunk deep into prayer at no great distance from him. He wished he could sink, like her, to the very bottom, be as motionless, as rapt in prostration. After a few moments he shifted his seat; it was almost indelicate to be so aware of her. But Stransom subsequently quite lost himself, floating away on the sea of light. If occasions like this had been more frequent in his life he would have had more present the great original type, set up in a myriad temples, of the unapproachable shrine he had erected in his mind. That shrine had begun in vague likeness to church pomps, but the echo had ended by growing more distinct than the sound. The sound now rang out, the type blazed at him with all its fires and with a mystery of radiance in which endless meanings could glow. The thing became as he sat there his appropriate altar and each starry candle an appropriate vow. He numbered them, named them, grouped them—it was the silent roll-call of his Dead. They made together a brightness vast and intense, a brightness in which the mere chapel of his thoughts grew so dim that as it faded away he asked himself if he shouldn't find his real comfort in some material act, some outward worship.

This idea took possession of him while, at a distance, the black-robed lady continued prostrate; he was quietly thrilled with his conception, which at last brought him to his feet in the sudden excitement of a plan. He wandered softly through the aisles, pausing in the different chapels, all save one applied to a special devotion. It was in this clear recess, lampless and unapplied, that he stood longest—the length of time it took him fully to grasp the conception of gilding it with his bounty. He should snatch it from no other rites and associate it with nothing profane; he would simply take it as it should be given up to him and make it a masterpiece of splendour and a mountain of fire.

Tended sacredly all the year, with the sanctifying church round it, it would always be ready for his offices. There would be difficulties, but from the first they presented themselves only as difficulties surmounted. Even for a person so little affiliated the thing would be a matter of arrangement. He saw it all in advance, and how bright in especial the place would become to him in the intermissions of toil and the dusk of afternoons; how rich in assurance at all times, but especially in the indifferent world. Before withdrawing he drew nearer again to the spot where he had first sat down, and in the movement he met the lady whom he had seen praying and who was now on her way to the door. She passed him quickly, and he had only a glimpse of her pale face and her unconscious, almost sightless eyes. For that instant she looked faded and handsome.

This was the origin of the rites more public, yet certainly esoteric, that he at last found himself able to establish. It took a long time, it took a year, and both the process and the result would have been—for any who knew—a vivid picture of his good faith. No one did know, in fact—no one but the bland ecclesiastics whose acquaintance he had promptly sought, whose objections he had softly overridden, whose curiosity and sympathy he had artfully charmed, whose assent to his eccentric munificence he had eventually won, and who had asked for concessions in exchange for indulgences. Stransom had of course at an early stage of his enquiry been referred to the Bishop, and the Bishop had been delightfully human, the Bishop had been almost amused. Success was within sight, at any rate, from the moment the attitude of those whom it concerned became liberal in response to liberality. The altar and the sacred shell that half-encircled it, consecrated to an ostensible and customary worship, were to be splendidly maintained; all that Stransom reserved to himself was the number of his lights and the free enjoyment of his intention. When the intention had taken complete effect the enjoyment became even greater than he had ventured to hope. He liked to think of this effect when far from it, liked to convince himself of it yet again when near. He was not often indeed so near as that a visit to it hadn't perforce something of the patience of a pilgrimage; but the time he gave to his devotion came to seem to him more a contribution to his other interests than a betrayal of them. Even a loaded life might be easier when one had added a new necessity to it.

How much easier was probably never guessed by those who simply knew there were hours when he disappeared and for many of whom there was a vulgar reading of what they used to call his plunges. These plunges were into depths quieter than the deep sea-caves, and the habit had at the end of a year or two become the one it would have cost him most to relinquish. Now they had really, his Dead, something that was indefeasibly theirs; and he liked to think that they might in cases be the Dead of others, as well as that the Dead of others might be invoked there under the protection of what he had done. Whoever bent a knee on the carpet he had laid down appeared to him to act in the spirit of his intention. Each of his lights had a name for him, and from time to time a new light was kindled. This was what he had fundamentally agreed for, that there should always be room for them all. What those who passed or lingered saw was simply the most resplendent of the altars called suddenly into vivid usefulness, with a quiet elderly man, for whom it evidently had a fascination, often seated there in a maze or a doze; but half the satisfaction of the spot for this mysterious and fitful worshipper was that he found the years of his life there, and the ties, the affections, the struggles, the submissions, the conquests, if there had been such, a record of that adventurous journey in which the beginnings and the endings of human relations are the lettered mile-stones. He had in general little taste for the past as a part of his own history; at other times and in other places it mostly seemed to him pitiful to consider and impossible to repair; but on these occasions he accepted it with something of that positive gladness with which one adjusts one's self to an ache that begins to succumb to treatment. To the treatment of time the malady of life begins at a given moment to succumb; and these were doubtless the hours at which that truth most came home to him. The day was written for him there on which he had first become acquainted with death, and the successive phases of the acquaintance were marked each with a flame.

The flames were gathering thick at present, for Stransom had entered that dark defile of our earthly descent in which some one dies every day. It was only yesterday that Kate Creston had flashed out her white fire; yet already there were younger stars ablaze on the tips of the tapers. Various persons in whom his interest had not been intense drew closer to him by entering this company. He went over it, head by head, till he felt like the shepherd of a huddled flock, with all a shepherd's vision of differences imperceptible. He knew his candles apart, up to the colour of the flame, and would still have known them had their positions all been changed. To other imaginations they might stand for other things—that they should stand for something to be hushed before was all he desired; but he was intensely conscious of the personal note of each and of the distinguishable way it contributed to the concert. There were hours at which he almost caught himself wishing that certain of his friends would now die, that he might establish with them in this manner a connexion more charming than, as it happened, it was possible to enjoy with them in life. In regard to those from whom one was separated by the long curves of the globe such a connexion could only be an improvement: it brought them instantly within reach. Of course there were gaps in the constellation, for Stransom knew he could only pretend to act for his own, and it wasn't every figure passing before his eyes into the great obscure that was entitled to a memorial. There was a strange sanctification in death, but some characters were more sanctified by being forgotten than by being remembered. The greatest blank in the shining page was the memory of Acton Hague, of which he inveterately tried to rid himself. For Acton Hague no flame could ever rise on any altar of his.

IV

Every year, the day he walked back from the great graveyard, he went to church as he had done the day his idea was born. It was on this occasion, as it happened, after a year had passed, that he began to observe his altar to be haunted by a worshipper at least as frequent as himself. Others of the faithful, and in the rest of the church, came and went, appealing sometimes, when they disappeared, to a vague or to a particular recognition; but this unfailing presence was always to be observed when he arrived and still in possession when he departed. He was surprised, the first time, at the promptitude with which it assumed an identity for him—the identity of the lady whom two years before, on his anniversary, he had seen so intensely bowed, and of whose tragic face he had had so flitting a vision. Given the time that had passed, his recollection of her was fresh enough to make him wonder. Of himself she had of course no impression, or rather had had none at first: the time came when her manner of transacting her business suggested her having gradually guessed his call to be of the same order. She used his altar for her own purpose—he could only hope that, sad and solitary as she always struck him, she used it for her own Dead. There were interruptions, infidelities, all on his part, calls to other associations and duties; but as the months went on he found her whenever he returned, and he ended by taking pleasure in the thought that he had given her almost the contentment he had given himself. They worshipped side by side so often that there were moments when he wished he might be sure, so straight did their prospect stretch away of growing old together in their rites. She was younger than he, but she looked as if her Dead were at least as numerous as his candles. She had no colour, no sound, no fault, and another of the things about which he had made up his mind was that she had no fortune. Always black-robed, she must have had a succession of sorrows. People weren't poor, after all, whom so many losses could overtake; they were positively rich when they had had so much to give up. But the air of this devoted and indifferent woman, who always made, in any attitude, a beautiful accidental line, conveyed somehow to Stransom that she had known more kinds of trouble than one.

He had a great love of music and little time for the joy of it; but occasionally, when workaday noises were muffled by Saturday afternoons, it used to come back to him that there were glories. There were moreover friends who reminded him of this and side by side with whom he found himself sitting out concerts. On one of these winter evenings, in Saint James's Hall, he became aware after he had seated himself that the lady he had so often seen at church was in the place next him and was evidently alone, as he also this time happened to be. She was at first too absorbed in the consideration of the programme to heed him, but when she at last glanced at him he took advantage of the movement to speak to her, greeting her with the remark that he felt as if he already knew her. She smiled as she said "Oh yes, I recognise you"; yet in spite of this admission of long acquaintance it was the first he had seen of her smile. The effect of it was suddenly to contribute more to that acquaintance than all the previous meetings had done. He hadn't "taken in," he said to himself, that she was so pretty. Later, that evening—it was while he rolled along in a hansom on his way to dine out—he added that he hadn't taken in that she was so interesting. The next morning in the midst of his work he quite suddenly and irrelevantly reflected that his impression of her, beginning so far back, was like a winding river that had at last reached the sea.

His work in fact was blurred a little all that day by the sense of what had now passed between them. It wasn't much, but it had just made the difference. They had listened together to Beethoven and Schumann;[1] they had talked in the pauses, and at the end, when at the door, to which they moved together, he had asked her if he could help her in the matter of getting away. She had thanked him and put up her umbrella, slipping into the crowd without an allusion to their meeting yet again and leaving him to remember at leisure that not a word had been exchanged about the usual scene of that coincidence. This omission struck him now as natural and then again as perverse. She mightn't in the least have allowed his warrant for speaking to her, and yet if she hadn't he would have judged her an underbred woman. It was odd that when nothing had really ever brought them together he should have been able successfully to assume they were in a manner old friends—that this negative quantity was somehow more than they could express. His success, it was true, had been qualified by her quick escape, so that there grew up in him an absurd desire to put it to some better test. Save in so far as some other poor chance might help him, such a test could be only to meet her afresh at church. Left to himself he would have gone to church the very next afternoon, just for the curiosity of seeing if he should find her there. But he wasn't left to himself, a fact he discovered quite at the last, after he had virtually made up his mind to go. The influence that kept him away really revealed to him how little to himself his Dead *ever* left him. He went only for *them*—for nothing else in the world.

The force of this revulsion kept him away ten days: he hated to connect the place with anything but his offices or to give a glimpse of the curiosity that had been on the point of moving him. It was absurd to weave a tangle about a matter so simple as a custom of devotion that might with ease have been daily or hourly; yet the tangle got itself woven. He was sorry, he was disappointed: it was as if a long happy spell had been broken and he had lost a familiar security. At the last, however, he asked himself if he was to stay away for ever from the fear of this muddle about motives. After an interval neither longer nor shorter than usual he re-entered the church with a clear conviction that he should scarcely heed the presence or the absence of the lady of the concert. This indifference didn't prevent his at once noting that for the only time since he had first seen her she wasn't on the spot. He had now no scruple about giving her time to arrive, but she didn't arrive, and when he went away still missing her he was

---

1 Ludwig van Beethoven (1770–1827) and Robert Schumann (1810–56), German composers.

profanely and consentingly sorry. If her absence made the tangle more intricate, that was all her own doing. By the end of another year it was very intricate indeed; but by that time he didn't in the least care, and it was only his cultivated consciousness that had given him scruples. Three times in three months he had gone to church without finding her, and he felt he hadn't needed these occasions to show him his suspense had dropped. Yet it was, incongruously, not indifference, but a refinement of delicacy that had kept him from asking the sacristan, who would of course immediately have recognised his description of her, whether she had been seen at other hours. His delicacy had kept him from asking any question about her at any time, and it was exactly the same virtue that had left him so free to be decently civil to her at the concert.

This happy advantage now served him anew, enabling him when she finally met his eyes—it was after a fourth trial—to pre-determine quite fixedly his awaiting her retreat. He joined her in the street as soon as she had moved, asking her if he might accompany her a certain distance. With her placid permission he went as far as a house in the neighbourhood at which she had business: she let him know it was not where she lived. She lived, as she said, in a mere slum, with an old aunt, a person in con-nexion with whom she spoke of the engrossment of humdrum duties and regular occupations. She wasn't, the mourning niece, in her first youth, and her vanished freshness had left something behind that, for Stransom, represented the proof it had been trag-ically sacrificed. Whatever she gave him the assurance of she gave without references. She might have been a divorced duchess—she might have been an old maid who taught the harp.

V

They fell at last into the way of walking together almost every time they met, though for a long time still they never met but at church. He couldn't ask her to come and see him, and as if she hadn't a proper place to receive him she never invited her friend. As much as himself she knew the world of London, but from an undiscussed instinct of privacy they haunted the region not mapped on the social chart. On the return she always made him leave her at the same corner. She looked with him, as a pretext for a pause, at the depressed things in suburban shop-fronts; and there was never a word he had said to her that she hadn't beauti-fully understood. For long ages he never knew her name, any more than she had ever pronounced his own; but it was not their names that mattered, it was only their perfect practice and their common need.

These things made their whole relation so impersonal that they hadn't the rules or reasons people found in ordinary friendships. They didn't care for the things it was supposed necessary to care for in the intercourse of the world. They ended one day—they never knew which of them expressed it first—by throwing out the idea that they didn't care for each other. Over this idea they grew quite intimate; they rallied to it in a way that marked a fresh start in their confidence. If to feel deeply together about certain things wholly distinct from themselves didn't constitute a safety, where was safety to be looked for? Not lightly nor often, not without occasion nor without emotion, any more than in any other reference by serious people to a mystery of their faith; but when something had happened to warm, as it were, the air for it, they came as near as they could come to calling their Dead by name. They felt it was coming very near to utter their thought at all. The word "they" expressed enough; it limited the mention, it had a dignity of its own, and if, in their talk, you had heard our friends use it, you might have taken them for a pair of pagans of old alluding decently to the domesticated gods. They never knew—at least Stransom never knew—how they had learned to be sure about each other. If it had been with each a question of what the other was there for, the certitude had come in some fine way of its own. Any faith, after all, has the instinct of propagation, and it was as natural as it was beautiful that they should have taken pleasure on the spot in the imagination of a following. If the following was for each but a following of one it had proved in the event sufficient. Her debt, however, of course, was much greater than his, because while she had only given him a worshipper he had given her a splendid temple. Once she said she pitied him for the length of his list—she had counted his candles almost as often as himself—and this made him wonder what could have been the length of hers. He had wondered before at the coincidence of their losses, especially as from time to time a new candle was set up. On some occasion some accident led him to express this curiosity, and she answered as if in surprise that he hadn't already understood. "Oh for me, you know, the more there are the better—there could never be too many. I should like hundreds and hundreds—I should like thousands; I should like a great mountain of light."

Then of course in a flash he understood. "Your Dead are only One?"

She hung back at this as never yet. "Only One," she answered, colouring as if now he knew her guarded secret. It really made him feel he knew less than before, so difficult was it for him to reconstitute a life in which a single experience had so belittled all others. His own life, round its central hollow, had been packed close enough. After this she appeared to have regretted her confession, though at the moment she spoke there had been pride in her very embarrassment. She declared to him that his own was the larger, the dearer possession—the portion one would have chosen if one had been able to choose; she assured him she could perfectly imagine some of the echoes with which his silences were peopled. He knew she couldn't: one's relation to what one had loved and hated had been a relation too distinct from the relations of others. But this didn't affect the fact that they were growing old together in their piety. She was a feature of that piety, but even at the ripe stage of acquaintance in which they occasionally arranged to meet at a concert or to go together to an exhibition she was not a feature of anything else. The most that happened was that his worship became paramount. Friend by friend dropped away till at last there were more emblems on his altar than houses left him to enter. She was more than any other the friend who remained, but she was unknown to all the rest. Once when she had discovered, as they called it, a new star, she used the expression that the chapel at last was full.

"Oh no," Stransom replied, "there's a great thing wanting for that! The chapel will never be full till a candle is set up before which all the others will pale. It will be the tallest candle of all."

Her mild wonder rested on him. "What candle do you mean?"

"I mean, dear lady, my own."

He had learned after a long time that she earned money by her pen, writing under a pseudonym she never disclosed in magazines he never saw. She knew too well what he couldn't read and what she couldn't write, and she taught him to cultivate indifference with a success that did much for their good relations. Her invisible industry was a convenience to him; it helped his contented thought of her, the thought that rested in the dignity of her proud obscure life, her little remunerated art and her little impenetrable home. Lost, with her decayed relative, in her dim suburban world, she came to the surface for him in distant places. She was really the priestess of his altar, and whenever he quitted England he committed it to her keeping. She proved to him afresh that women have more of the spirit of religion than men; he felt his fidelity pale and faint in comparison with hers. He often said to her that since he had so little time to live he rejoiced in her having so much; so glad was he to think she would guard the temple when he should have been called. He had a great plan for that, which of course he told her too, a bequest of money to keep it up in undiminished state. Of the administration of this fund he would appoint her superintendent, and if the spirit should move her she might kindle a taper even for him.

"And who will kindle one even for me?" she then seriously asked.

VI

She was always in mourning, yet the day he came back from the longest absence he had yet made her appearance immediately told him she had lately had a bereavement. They met on this occasion as she was leaving the church, so that postponing his own entrance he instantly offered to turn round and walk away with her. She considered, then she said: "Go in now, but come and see me in an hour." He knew the small vista of her street, closed at the end and as dreary as an empty pocket, where the pairs of shabby little houses, semi-detached but indissolubly united, were like married couples on bad terms. Often, however, as he had gone to the beginning he had never gone beyond. Her aunt was dead—that he immediately guessed, as well as that it made a difference; but when she had for the first time mentioned her number he found himself, on her leaving him, not a little agitated by this sudden liberality. She wasn't a person with whom, after all, one got on so very fast: it had taken him months and months to learn her name, years and years to learn her address. If she had looked, on this reunion, so much older to him, how in the world did he look to her? She had reached the period of life he had long since reached, when, after separations, the marked clock-face of the friend we meet announces the hour we have tried to forget. He couldn't have said what he expected as, at the end of his waiting, he turned the corner where for years he had always paused; simply not to pause was a sufficient cause for emotion. It was an event, somehow; and in all their long acquaintance there had never been an event. This one grew larger when, five minutes later, in the faint elegance of her little drawing-room, she quavered out a greeting that showed the measure she took of it. He had a strange sense of having come for something in particular; strange because literally there was nothing particular between them, nothing save that they were at one on their great point, which had long ago become a magnificent matter of course. It was true that after she had said "You can always come now, you know," the thing he was there for seemed already to have happened. He asked her if it was the death of her aunt that made the difference; to which she replied: "She never knew I knew you. I wished her not to." The beautiful clearness of her candour—her faded beauty was like a summer twilight—disconnected the words from any image of deceit. They might have struck him as the record of a deep dissimulation, but she had always given him a sense of noble reasons. The vanished aunt was present, as he looked about him, in the small complacencies of the room, the beaded velvet and the fluted moreen;[1] and though, as we know, he had the worship of the Dead, he found himself not definitely regretting this lady. If she wasn't in his long list, however, she was in her niece's short one, and Stransom presently observed to the latter that now at least, in the place they haunted together, she would have another object of devotion.

"Yes, I shall have another. She was very kind to me. It's that that's the difference."

He judged, wondering a good deal before he made any motion to leave her, that the difference would somehow be very great and would consist of still other things than her having let him come in. It rather chilled him, for they had been happy together as they were. He extracted from her at any rate an intimation that she should now have means less limited, that her aunt's tiny fortune had come to her, so that there was henceforth only one to consume what had formerly been made to suffice for two. This was a joy to Stransom, because it had hitherto been equally impossible for him either to offer her presents or contentedly to stay his hand. It was too ugly to be at her side that way, abounding himself and yet not able to overflow—a demonstration that would have been signally a false note. Even her better situation too seemed only to draw out in a sense the loneliness of her future. It would merely help her to live more and more for their small ceremonial, and this at a time when he himself had begun wearily to feel that, having set it in motion, he might depart. When they had sat a while in the pale parlour she got up—"This isn't *my* room: let us go into mine." They had only to cross the narrow hall, as he found, to pass quite into another air. When she had closed the door of the second room, as she called it, he felt at last in real possession of her. The place had the flush of life—

---

1 Heavy fabric, often used for upholstery.

it was expressive; its dark red walls were articulate with memories and relics. These were simple things—photographs and water-colours, scraps of writing framed and ghosts of flowers embalmed; but a moment sufficed to show him they had a common meaning. It was here she had lived and worked, and she had already told him she would make no change of scene. He read the reference in the objects about her—the general one to places and times; but after a minute he distinguished among them a small portrait of a gentleman. At a distance and without their glasses his eyes were only so caught by it as to feel a vague curiosity. Presently this impulse carried him nearer, and in another moment he was staring at the picture in stupefaction and with the sense that some sound had broken from him. He was further conscious that he showed his companion a white face when he turned round on her gasping: "Acton Hague!"

She matched his great wonder. "Did you know him?"

"He was the friend of all my youth—of my early manhood. And *you* knew him?"

She coloured at this and for a moment her answer failed; her eyes embraced everything in the place, and a strange irony reached her lips as she echoed: "Knew him?"

Then Stransom understood, while the room heaved like the cabin of a ship, that its whole contents cried out with him, that it was a museum in his honour, that all her later years had been addressed to him and that the shrine he himself had reared had been passionately converted to this use. It was all for Acton Hague that she had knelt every day at his altar. What need had there been for a consecrated candle when he was present in the whole array? The revelation so smote our friend in the face that he dropped into a seat and sat silent. He had quickly felt her shaken by the force of his shock, but as she sank on the sofa beside him and laid her hand on his arm he knew almost as soon that she mightn't resent it as much as she'd have liked.

VII

He learned in that instant two things: one being that even in so long a time she had gathered no knowledge of his great intimacy and his great quarrel; the other that in spite of this ignorance, strangely enough, she supplied on the spot a reason for his stupor. "How extraordinary," he presently exclaimed, "that we should never have known!"

She gave a wan smile which seemed to Stransom stranger even than the fact itself. "I never, never spoke of him."

He looked again about the room. "Why then, if your life had been so full of him?"

"Mayn't I put you that question as well? Hadn't your life also been full of him?"

"Any one's, every one's life who had the wonderful experience of knowing him. *I* never spoke of him," Stransom added in a moment, "because he did me—years ago—an unforgettable wrong." She was silent, and with the full effect of his presence all about them it almost startled her guest to hear no protest escape her. She accepted his words; he turned his eyes to her again to see in what manner she accepted them. It was with rising tears and a rare sweetness in the movement of putting out her hand to take his own. Nothing more wonderful had ever appeared to him than, in that little chamber of remembrance and homage, to see her convey with such exquisite mildness that as from Acton Hague any injury was credible. The clock ticked in the stillness—Hague had probably given it to her—and while he let her hold his hand with a tenderness that was almost an assumption of responsibility for his old pain as well as his new, Stransom after a minute broke out: "Good God, how he must have used *you!*"

She dropped his hand at this, got up and, moving across the room, made straight a small picture to which, on examining it, he had given a slight push. Then turning round on him with her pale gaiety recovered, "I've forgiven him!" she declared.

"I know what you've done," said Stransom; "I know what you've done for years." For a moment they looked at each other through it all with their long community of service in their eyes. This short passage made, to his sense, for the woman before him, an immense, an absolutely naked confession; which was presently, suddenly blushing red and changing her place again, what she appeared to learn he perceived in it. He got up and "How you must have loved him!" he cried.

"Women aren't like men. They can love even where they've suffered."

"Women are wonderful," said Stransom. "But I assure you I've forgiven him too."

"If I had known of anything so strange I wouldn't have brought you here."

"So that we might have gone on in our ignorance to the last?"

"What do you call the last?" she asked, smiling still.

At this he could smile back at her. "You'll see—when it comes."

She thought of that. "This is better perhaps; but as we were—it was good."

He put her the question. "Did it never happen that he spoke of me?"

Considering more intently she made no answer, and he then knew he should have been adequately answered by her asking how often he himself had spoken of their terrible friend. Suddenly a brighter light broke in her face and an excited idea sprang to her lips in the appeal: "You *have* forgiven him?"

"How, if I hadn't, could I linger here?"

She visibly winced at the deep but unintended irony of this; but even while she did so she panted quickly: "Then in the lights on your altar—?"

"There's never a light for Acton Hague!"

She stared with a dreadful fall. "But if he's one of your Dead?"

"He's one of the world's, if you like—he's one of yours. But he's not one of mine. Mine are only the Dead who died possessed of me. They're mine in death because they were mine in life."

"*He* was yours in life then, even if for a while he ceased to be. If you forgave him you went back to him. Those whom we've once loved—"

"Are those who can hurt us most," Stransom broke in.

"Ah it's not true—you've *not* forgiven him!" she wailed with a passion that startled him.

He looked at her as never yet. "What was it he did to you?"

"Everything!" Then abruptly she put out her hand in farewell. "Good-bye."

He turned as cold as he had turned that night he read the man's death. "You mean that we meet no more?"

"Not as we've met—not *there!*"

He stood aghast at this snap of their great bond, at the renouncement that rang out in the word she so expressively sounded. "But what's changed—for you?"

She waited in all the sharpness of a trouble that for the first time since he had known her made her splendidly stern. "How can you understand now when you didn't understand before?"

"I didn't understand before only because I didn't know. Now that I know, I see what I've been living with for years," Stransom went on very gently.

She looked at him with a larger allowance, doing this gentleness justice. "How can I then, on this new knowledge of my own, ask you to continue to live with it?"

"I set up my altar, with its multiplied meanings," Stransom began; but she quickly interrupted him.

"You set up your altar, and when I wanted one most I found it magnificently ready. I used it with the gratitude I've always shown you, for I knew it from of old to be dedicated to Death. I told you long ago that my Dead weren't many. Yours were, but all you had done for them was none too much for *my* worship! You had placed a great light for Each—I gathered them together for One!"

"We had simply different intentions," he returned. "That, as you say, I perfectly knew, and I don't see why your intention shouldn't still sustain you."

"That's because you're generous—you can imagine and think. But the spell's broken."

It seemed to poor Stransom, in spite of his resistance, that it really was, and the prospect stretched grey and void before him. All he could say, however, was: "I hope you'll try before you give up."

"If I had known you had ever known him I should have taken for granted he had his candle," she presently answered. "What's changed, as you say, is that on making the discovery I find he never has had it. That makes *my* attitude"—she paused as thinking how to express it, then said simply—"all wrong."

"Come once again," he pleaded.

"Will you give him his candle?" she asked.

He waited, but only because it would sound ungracious; not because of a doubt of his feeling. "I can't do that!" he declared at last.

"Then good-bye." And she gave him her hand again.

He had got his dismissal; besides which, in the agitation of everything that had opened out to him, he felt the need to recover himself as he could only do in solitude. Yet he lingered—lingered to see if she had no compromise to express, no attenuation to propose. But he only met her great lamenting eyes, in which indeed he read that she was as sorry for him as for any one else. This made him say: "At least, in any case, I may see you here."

"Oh yes, come if you like. But I don't think it will do."

He looked round the room once more, knowing how little he was sure it would do. He felt also stricken and more and more cold, and his chill was like an ague in which he had to make an effort not to shake. Then he made doleful reply: "I must try on my side—if you can't try on yours." She came out with him to the hall and into the doorway, and here he put her the question he held he could least answer from his own wit. "Why have you never let me come before?"

"Because my aunt would have seen you, and I should have had to tell her how I came to know you."

"And what would have been the objection to that?"

"It would have entailed other explanations; there would at any rate have been that danger."

"Surely she knew you went every day to church," Stransom objected.

"She didn't know what I went for."

"Of me then she never even heard?"

"You'll think I was deceitful. But I didn't need to be!"

He was now on the lower door-step, and his hostess held the door half-closed behind him. Through what remained of the opening he saw her framed face. He made a supreme appeal. "What *did* he do to you?"

"It would have come out—*she* would have told you. That fear at my heart—that was my reason!" And she closed the door, shutting him out.

VIII

He had ruthlessly abandoned her—that of course was what he had done. Stransom made it all out in solitude, at leisure, fitting the unmatched pieces gradually together and dealing one by one with a hundred obscure points. She had known Hague only after her present friend's relations with him had wholly terminated; obviously indeed a good while after; and it was natural enough that of his previous life she should have ascertained only what he had judged good to communicate. There were passages it was quite conceivable that even in moments of the tenderest expansion he should have withheld. Of many facts in the career of a man so in the eye of the world there was of course a common knowledge; but this lady lived apart from public affairs, and the only time perfectly clear to her would have been the time following the dawn of her own drama. A man in her place would have "looked up" the past—would even have consulted old newspapers. It remained remarkable indeed that in her long contact with the partner of her retrospect no accident had lighted a train; but there was no arguing about that; the accident had in fact come: it had simply been that security had prevailed. She had taken what

Hague had given her, and her blankness in respect of his other connexions was only a touch in the picture of that plasticity Stransom had supreme reason to know so great a master could have been trusted to produce.

This picture was for a while all our friend saw: he caught his breath again and again as it came over him that the woman with whom he had had for years so fine a point of contact was a woman whom Acton Hague, of all men in the world, had more or less fashioned. Such as she sat there to-day she was ineffaceably stamped with him. Beneficent, blameless as Stransom held her, he couldn't rid himself of the sense that he had been, as who should say, swindled. She had imposed upon him hugely, though she had known it as little as he. All this later past came back to him as a time grotesquely misspent. Such at least were his first reflexions; after a while he found himself more divided and only, as the end of it, more troubled. He imagined, recalled, reconstituted, figured out for himself the truth she had refused to give him; the effect of which was to make her seem to him only more saturated with her fate. He felt her spirit, through the whole strangeness, finer than his own to the very degree in which she might have been, in which she certainly had been, more wronged. A women, when wronged, was always more wronged than a man, and there were conditions when the least she could have got off with was more than the most he could have to bear. He was sure this rare creature wouldn't have got off with the least. He was awestruck at the thought of such a surrender—such a prostration. Moulded indeed she had been by powerful hands, to have converted her injury into an exaltation so sublime. The fellow had only had to die for everything that was ugly in him to be washed out in a torrent. It was vain to try to guess what had taken place, but nothing could be clearer than that she had ended by accusing herself. She absolved him at every point, she adored her very wounds. The passion by which he had profited had rushed back after its ebb, and now the tide of tenderness, arrested for ever at flood, was too deep even to fathom. Stransom sincerely considered that he had forgiven him; but how little he had achieved the miracle that she had achieved! His forgiveness was silence, but hers was mere unuttered sound. The light she had demanded for his altar would have broken his silence with a blare; whereas all the lights in the church were for her too great a hush.

She had been right about the difference—she had spoken the truth about the change: Stransom was soon to know himself as perversely but sharply jealous. *His* tide had ebbed, not flowed; if he had "forgiven" Acton Hague, that forgiveness was a motive with a broken spring. The very fact of her appeal for a material sign, a sign that should make her dead lover equal there with the others, presented the concession to her friend as too handsome for the case. He had never thought of himself as hard, but an exorbitant article might easily render him so. He moved round and round this one, but only in widening circles—the more he looked at it the less acceptable it seemed. At the same time he had no illusion about the effect of his refusal; he perfectly saw how it would make for a rupture. He left her alone a week, but when at last he again called this conviction was cruelly confirmed. In the interval he had kept away from the church, and he needed no fresh assurance from her to know she hadn't entered it. The change was complete enough: it had broken up her life. Indeed it had broken up his, for all the fires of his shrine seemed to him suddenly to have been quenched. A great indifference fell upon him, the weight of which was in itself a pain; and he never knew what his devotion had been for him till in that shock it ceased like a dropped watch. Neither did he know with how large a confidence he had counted on the final service that had now failed: the mortal deception was that in this abandonment the whole future gave way.

These days of her absence proved to him of what she was capable; all the more that he never dreamed she was vindictive or even resentful. It was not in anger she had forsaken him; it was in simple submission to hard reality, to the stern logic of life. This came home to him when he sat with her again in the room in which her late aunt's conversation lingered like the tone of a cracked piano. She tried to make him forget how much they were estranged, but in the very presence of what they had given up it was impossible not to be sorry for her. He had taken from her so much more than she had taken from him. He argued with her again, told her she could now have the altar to herself; but she only shook her head with pleading sadness, begging him not to waste his breath on the impossible, the extinct. Couldn't he see that in relation to her private need the rites he had established were practically an elaborate exclusion? She regretted nothing that had happened; it had all been right so long as she didn't know, and it was only that now she knew too much and that from the moment their eyes were open they would simply have to conform. It had doubtless been happiness enough for them to go on together so long. She was gentle, grateful, resigned; but this was only the form of a deep immoveability. He saw he should never more cross the threshold of the second room, and he felt how much this alone would make a stranger of him and give a conscious stiffness to his visits. He would have hated to plunge again into that well of reminders, but he enjoyed quite as little the vacant alternative.

After he had been with her three or four times it struck him that to have come at last into her house had had the horrid effect of diminishing their intimacy. He had known her better, had liked her in greater freedom, when they merely walked together or kneeled together. Now they only pretended; before they had been nobly sincere. They began to try their walks again, but it proved a lame imitation, for these things, from the first, beginning or ending, had been connected with their visits to the church. They had either strolled away as they came out or gone in to rest on the return. Stransom, besides, now faltered; he couldn't walk as of old. The omission made everything false; it was a dire mutilation of their lives. Our friend was frank and monotonous, making no mystery of his remonstrance and no secret of his predicament. Her response, whatever it was, always came to the same thing— an implied invitation to him to judge, if he spoke of predicaments, of how much comfort she had in hers. For him indeed was no comfort even in complaint, since every allusion to what had befallen them but made the author of their trouble more present. Acton Hague was between them—that was the essence of the matter, and never so much between them as when they were face to face. Then Stransom, while still wanting to banish him, had the strangest sense of striving for an ease that would involve having accepted him. Deeply disconcerted by what he knew, he was still worse tormented by really not knowing. Perfectly aware that it would have been horribly vulgar to abuse his old friend or to tell his companion the story of their quarrel, it yet vexed him that her depth of reserve should give him no opening and should have the effect of a magnanimity greater even than his own.

He challenged himself, denounced himself, asked himself if he were in love with her that he should care so much what adventures she had had. He had never for a moment allowed he was in love with her; therefore nothing could have surprised him more than to discover he was jealous. What but jealousy could give a man that sore contentious wish for the detail of what would make him suffer? Well enough he knew indeed that he should never have it from the only person who to-day could give it to him. She let him press her with his sombre eyes, only smiling at him with an exquisite mercy and breathing equally little the word that would expose her secret and the word that would appear to deny his literal right to bitterness. She told nothing, she judged nothing; she accepted everything but the possibility of her return to the old symbols. Stransom divined that for her too they had been vividly individual, had stood for particular hours or particular attributes—particular links in her chain. He made it clear to himself, as he believed, that his difficulty lay in the fact that the very nature of the plea for his faithless friend constituted a prohibition; that it happened to have come from *her* was precisely the vice that attached to it. To the voice of impersonal generosity he felt sure he would have listened; he would have deferred to an advocate who, speaking from abstract justice, knowing of his denial without having known Hague, should have had the imagination to say: "Ah remember only the best of him; pity him; provide for him." To provide for him on the very ground of having discovered another of his turpitudes was not to pity but to glorify him. The more Stransom thought the more he made out that whatever this relation of Hague's it could only have been a deception more or less finely practised. Where had it come into the life that all men saw? Why had one never heard of it if it had had the frankness of honourable things? Stransom knew enough of his other ties, of his obligations and appearances, not to say enough of his general character, to be sure there had been some infamy. In one way or another this creature had been coldly sacrificed. That was why at the last as well as the first he must still leave him out and out.

IX

And yet this was no solution, especially after he had talked again to his friend of all it had been his plan she should finally do for him. He had talked in the other days, and she had responded with a frankness qualified only by a courteous reluctance, a reluctance that touched him, to linger on the question of his death. She had then practically accepted the charge, suffered him to feel he could depend upon her to be the eventual guardian of his shrine; and it was in the name of what had so passed between them that he appealed to her not to forsake him in his age. She listened at present with shining coldness and all her habitual forbearance to insist on her terms; her deprecation was even still tenderer, for it expressed the compassion of her own sense that he was abandoned. Her terms, however, remained the same, and scarcely the less audible for not being uttered; though he was sure that secretly even more than he she felt bereft of the satisfaction his solemn trust was to have provided her. They both missed the rich future, but she missed it most, because after all it was to have been entirely hers; and it was her acceptance of the loss that gave him the full measure of her preference for the thought of Acton Hague over any other thought whatever. He had humour enough to laugh rather grimly when he said to himself: "Why the deuce does she like him so much more than she likes me?"—the reasons being really so conceivable. But even his faculty of analysis left the irritation standing, and this irritation proved perhaps the greatest misfortune that had ever overtaken him. There had been nothing yet that made him so much want to give up. He had of course by this time well reached the age of renouncement; but it had not hitherto been vivid to him that it was time to give up everything.

Practically, at the end of six months, he had renounced the friendship once so charming and comforting. His privation had two faces, and the face it had turned to him on the occasion of his last attempt to cultivate that friendship was the one he could look at least. This was the privation he inflicted; the other was the privation he bore. The conditions she never phrased he used to murmur to himself in solitude: "One more, one more—only just one." Certainly he was going down; he often felt it when he caught himself, over his work, staring at vacancy and giving voice to that inanity. There was proof enough besides in his being so weak and so ill. His irritation took the form of melancholy, and his melancholy that of the conviction that his health had quite failed. His altar moreover had ceased to exist; his chapel, in his dreams, was a great dark cavern. All the lights had gone out—all his Dead had died again. He couldn't exactly see at first how it had been in the power of his late companion to extinguish them, since it was neither for her nor by her that they had been called into being. Then he understood that it was essentially in his own soul the revival had taken place, and that in the air of this soul they were now unable to breathe. The candles might mechanically burn, but each of them had lost its lustre. The church had become a void; it was his presence, her presence, their common presence, that had made the indispensable medium. If anything was wrong everything was—her silence spoiled the tune.

Then when three months were gone he felt so lonely that he went back; reflecting that as they had been his best society for years his Dead perhaps wouldn't let him forsake them without doing something more for him. They stood there, as he had left them, in their tall radiance, the bright cluster that had already made him, on occasions when he was willing to compare small things with great, liken them to a group of sea-lights on the edge of the ocean of life. It was a relief to him, after a while, as he sat there, to feel they had still a virtue. He was more and more easily tired, and he always drove now; the action of his heart was weak and gave him none of the reassurance conferred by the action of his fancy. None the less he returned yet again, returned several times, and finally, during six months, haunted the place with a renewal of frequency and a strain of impatience. In winter the church was unwarmed and exposure to cold forbidden him, but the glow of his shrine was an influence in which he could almost bask. He sat and wondered to what he had reduced his absent associate and what she now did with the hours of her absence. There were other churches, there were other altars, there were other candles; in one way or another her piety would still operate; he couldn't absolutely have deprived her of her rites. So he argued, but without contentment; for he well enough knew there was no other such rare semblance of the mountain of light she had once mentioned to him as the satisfaction of her need. As this semblance again gradually grew great to him and his pious practice more regular, he found a sharper and sharper pang in the imagination of her darkness; for never so much as in these weeks had his rites been real, never had his gathered company seemed so to respond and even to invite. He lost himself in the large lustre, which was more and more what he had from the first wished it to be—as dazzling as the vision of heaven in the mind of a child. He wandered in the fields of light; he passed, among the tall tapers, from tier to tier, from fire to fire, from name to name, from the white intensity of one clear emblem, of one saved soul, to another. It was in the quiet sense of having saved his souls that his deep strange instinct rejoiced. This was no dim theological rescue, no boon of a contingent world; they were saved better than faith or works could save them, saved for the warm world they had shrunk from dying to, for actuality, for continuity, for the certainty of human remembrance.

By this time he had survived all his friends; the last straight flame was three years old, there was no one to add to the list. Over and over he called his roll, and it appeared to him compact and complete. Where should he put in another, where, if there were no other objection, would it stand in its place in the rank? He reflected, with a want of sincerity of which he was quite conscious, that it would be difficult to determine that place. More and more, besides, face to face with his little legion, reading over endless histories, handling the empty shells and playing with the silence—more and more he could see that he had never introduced an alien. He had had his great compassions, his indulgences—there were cases in which they had been immense; but what had his devotion after all been if it hadn't been at bottom a respect? He was, however, himself surprised at his stiffness; by the end of the winter the responsibility of it was what was uppermost in his thoughts. The refrain had grown old to them, that plea for just one more. There came a day when, for simple exhaustion, if symmetry should demand just one he was ready so far to meet symmetry. Symmetry was harmony, and the idea of harmony began to haunt him; he said to himself that harmony was of course everything. He took, in fancy, his composition to pieces, redistributing it into other lines, making other juxtapositions and contrasts. He shifted this and that candle, he made the spaces different, he effaced the disfigurement of a possible gap. There were subtle and complex relations, a scheme of cross-reference, and moments in which he seemed to catch a glimpse of the void so sensible to the woman who wandered in exile or sat where he had seen her with the portrait of Acton Hague. Finally, in this way, he arrived at a conception of the total, the ideal, which left a clear opportunity for just another figure. "Just one more—to round it off; just one more, just one," continued to hum in his head. There was a strange confusion in the thought, for he felt the day to be near when he too should be one of the Others. What in this event would the Others matter to him, since they only mattered to the living? Even as one of the Dead what would his altar matter to him, since his particular dream of keeping it up had melted away? What had harmony to do with the case if his lights were all to be quenched? What he had hoped for was an instituted thing. He might perpetuate it on some other pretext, but his special meaning would have dropped. This meaning was to have lasted with the life of the one other person who understood it.

In March he had an illness during which he spent a fortnight in bed, and when he revived a little he was told of two things that had happened. One was that a lady whose name was not known to the servants (she left none) had been three times to ask about him; the other was that in his sleep and on an occasion when his mind evidently wandered he was heard to murmur again and again: "Just one more—just one." As soon as he found himself able to go out, and before the doctor in attendance had pronounced him so, he drove to see the lady who had come to ask about him. She was not at home; but this gave him the opportunity, before his strength should fail again, to take his way to the church. He entered it alone; he had declined, in a happy manner he possessed of being able to decline effectively, the company of his servant or of a nurse. He knew now perfectly what these good people thought; they had discovered his clandestine connexion, the magnet that had drawn him for so many years, and doubtless attached a significance of their own to the odd words they had repeated to him. The nameless lady was the clandestine connexion—a fact nothing could have made clearer than his indecent haste to rejoin her. He sank on his knees before his altar while his head fell over on his hands. His weakness, his life's weariness overtook him. It seemed to him he had come for the great surrender. At first he asked himself how he should get away; then, with the failing belief in the power, the very desire to move gradually left him. He had come, as he always came, to lose himself; the fields of light were still there to stray in; only this time, in straying, he would never come back. He had given himself to his Dead, and it was good: this time his Dead would keep him. He couldn't rise from his knees; he believed he should never rise again; all he could do was to lift his face and fix his eyes on his lights. They looked unusually, strangely splendid, but the one that always drew him most had an unprecedented lustre. It was the central voice of the choir, the glowing heart of the brightness, and on this occasion it seemed to expand, to spread great wings of flame. The whole altar flared—dazzling and blinding; but the source of the vast radiance burned clearer than the rest, gathering itself into form, and the form was human beauty and human charity, was the far-off face of Mary Antrim. She smiled at him from the glory of heaven—she brought the glory down with her to take him. He bowed his head in submission and at the same moment another wave rolled over him. Was it the quickening of joy to pain? In the midst of his joy at any rate he felt his buried face grow hot as with some communicated knowledge that had the force of a reproach. It suddenly made him contrast that very rapture with the bliss he had refused to another. This breath of the passion immortal was all that other had asked; the descent of Mary Antrim opened his spirit with a great compunctious throb for the descent of Acton Hague. It was as if Stransom had read what her eyes said to him.

After a moment he looked round in a despair that made him feel as if the source of life were ebbing. The church had been empty—he was alone; but he wanted to have something done, to make a last appeal. This idea gave him strength for an effort; he rose to his feet with a movement that made him turn, supporting himself by the back of a bench. Behind him was a prostrate figure, a figure he had seen before; a woman in deep mourning, bowed in grief or in prayer. He had seen her in other days—the first time of his entrance there, and he now slightly wavered, looking at her again till she seemed aware he had noticed her. She raised her head and met his eyes: the partner of his long worship had come back. She looked across at him an instant with a face wondering and scared; he saw he had made her afraid. Then quickly rising she came straight to him with both hands out.

"Then you *could* come? God sent you!" he murmured with a happy smile.

"You're very ill—you shouldn't be here," she urged in anxious reply.

"God sent me too, I think. I was ill when I came, but the sight of you does wonders." He held her hands, which steadied and quickened him. "I've something to tell you."

"Don't tell me!" she tenderly pleaded; "let me tell you. This afternoon, by a miracle, the sweetest of miracles, the sense of our difference left me. I was out—I was near, thinking, wandering alone, when, on the spot, something changed in my heart. It's my confession—there it is. To come back, to come back on the instant—the idea gave me wings. It was as if I suddenly saw something—as if it all became possible. I could come for what you yourself came for: that was enough. So here I am. It's not for my own—that's over. But I'm here for *them*." And breathless, infinitely relieved by her low precipitate explanation, she looked with eyes that reflected all its splendour at the magnificence of their altar.

"They're here for you," Stransom said, "they're present to-night as they've never been. They speak for you—don't you see?—in a passion of light; they sing out like a choir of angels. Don't you hear what they say?—they offer the very thing you asked of me."

"Don't talk of it—don't think of it; forget it!" She spoke in hushed supplication, and while the alarm deepened in her eyes she disengaged one of her hands and passed an arm round him to support him better, to help him to sink into a seat.

He let himself go, resting on her; he dropped upon the bench and she fell on her knees beside him, his own arm round her shoulder. So he remained an instant, staring up at his shrine.

"They say there's a gap in the array—they say it's not full, complete. Just one more," he went on, softly—"isn't that what you wanted? Yes, one more, one more."

"Ah no more—no more!" she wailed, as with a quick new horror of it, under her breath.

"Yes, one more," he repeated, simply; "just one!" And with this his head dropped on her shoulder; she felt that in his weakness he had fainted. But alone with him in the dusky church a great dread was on her of what might still happen, for his face had the whiteness of death.

I

What determined the speech that startled him in the course of
their encounter scarcely matters, being probably but some words
spoken by himself quite without intention—spoken as they lingered and slowly moved together after their renewal of acquaintance. He had been conveyed by friends an hour or two before to
the house at which she was staying; the party of visitors at the
other house, of whom he was one, and thanks to whom it was his
theory, as always, that he was lost in the crowd, had been invited
over to luncheon. There had been after luncheon much dispersal,
all in the interest of the original motive, a view of Weatherend
itself and the fine things, intrinsic features, pictures, heirlooms,
treasures of all the arts, that made the place almost famous; and
the great rooms were so numerous that guests could wander at
their will, hang back from the principal group and in cases where
they took such matters with the last seriousness give themselves
up to mysterious appreciations and measurements. There were
persons to be observed, singly or in couples, bending toward
objects in out-of-the-way corners with their hands on their knees
and their heads nodding quite as with the emphasis of an excited
sense of smell. When they were two they either mingled their
sounds of ecstasy or melted into silences of even deeper import,
so that there were aspects of the occasion that gave it for Marcher
much the air of the "look round," previous to a sale highly adver-
tised, that excites or quenches, as may be, the dream of acquisition. The dream of acquisition at Weatherend would have had to
be wild indeed, and John Marcher found himself, among such
suggestions, disconcerted almost equally by the presence of those
who knew too much and by that of those who knew nothing. The
great rooms caused so much poetry and history to press upon
him that he needed some straying apart to feel in a proper relation with them, though this impulse was not, as happened, like
the gloating of some of his companions, to be compared to the
movements of a dog sniffing a cupboard. It had an issue promptly
enough in a direction that was not to have been calculated.

It led, briefly, in the course of the October afternoon, to his
closer meeting with May Bartram, whose face, a reminder, yet
not quite a remembrance, as they sat much separated at a very
long table, had begun merely by troubling him rather pleasantly.
It affected him as the sequel of something of which he had lost

the beginning. He knew it, and for the time quite welcomed it, as a continuation, but didn't know what it continued, which was an interest or an amusement the greater as he was also somehow aware—yet without a direct sign from her—that the young woman herself hadn't lost the thread. She hadn't lost it, but she wouldn't give it back to him, he saw, without some putting forth of his hand for it; and he not only saw that, but saw several things more, things odd enough in the light of the fact that at the moment some accident of grouping brought them face to face he was still merely fumbling with the idea that any contact between them in the past would have had no importance. If it had had no importance he scarcely knew why his actual impression of her should so seem to have so much; the answer to which, however, was that in such a life as they all appeared to be leading for the moment one could but take things as they came. He was satisfied, without in the least being able to say why, that this young lady might roughly have ranked in the house as a poor relation; satisfied also that she was not there on a brief visit, but was more or less a part of the establishment—almost a working, a remunerated part. Didn't she enjoy at periods a protection that she paid for by helping, among other services, to show the place and explain it, deal with the tiresome people, answer questions about the dates of the building, the styles of the furniture, the authorship of the pictures, the favourite haunts of the ghost? It wasn't that she looked as if you could have given her shillings[1]—it was impossible to look less so. Yet when she finally drifted toward him, distinctly handsome, though ever so much older—older than when he had seen her before—it might have been as an effect of her guessing that he had, within the couple of hours, devoted more imagination to her than to all the others put together, and had thereby penetrated to a kind of truth that the others were too stupid for. She *was* there on harder terms than any one; she was there as a consequence of things suffered, one way and another, in the interval of years; and she remembered him very much as she was remembered—only a good deal better.

By the time they at last thus came to speech they were alone in one of the rooms—remarkable for a fine portrait over the chimney-place—out of which their friends had passed, and the charm of it was that even before they had spoken they had practically arranged with each other to stay behind for talk. The

---

1 Coin used until the British monetary system was decimalized in 1971; a shilling was 1/20 of a pound.

charm, happily, was in other things too—partly in there being scarce a spot at Weatherend without something to stay behind for. It was in the way the autumn day looked into the high windows as it waned; the way the red light, breaking at the close from under a low sombre sky, reached out in a long shaft and played over old wainscots, old tapestry, old gold, old colour. It was most of all perhaps in the way she came to him as if, since she had been turned on to deal with the simpler sort, he might, should he choose to keep the whole thing down, just take her mild attention for a part of her general business. As soon as he heard her voice, however, the gap was filled up and the missing link supplied; the slight irony he divined in her attitude lost its advantage. He almost jumped at it to get there before her. "I met you years and years ago in Rome. I remember all about it." She confessed to disappointment—she had been so sure he didn't; and to prove how well he did he began to pour forth the particular recollections that popped up as he called for them. Her face and her voice, all at his service now, worked the miracle—the impression operating like the torch of a lamplighter who touches into flame, one by one, a long row of gas-jets. Marcher flattered himself the illumination was brilliant, yet he was really still more pleased on her showing him, with amusement, that in his haste to make everything right he had got most things rather wrong. It hadn't been at Rome—it had been at Naples; and it hadn't been eight years before—it had been more nearly ten. She hadn't been, either, with her uncle and aunt, but with her mother and brother; in addition to which it was not with the Pembles *he* had been, but with the Boyers, coming down in their company from Rome—a point on which she insisted, a little to his confusion, and as to which she had her evidence in hand. The Boyers she had known, but didn't know the Pembles, though she had heard of them, and it was the people he was with who had made them acquainted. The incident of the thunderstorm that had raged round them with such violence as to drive them for refuge into an excavation—this incident had not occurred at the Palace of the Caesars,[1] but at Pompeii,[2] on an occasion when they had been present there at an important find.

---

1 Home for Roman emperors located on the Palatine Hills in Rome, beginning with Augustus (63 BCE–19 BCE) and enlarged by his successors.
2 Small city in southern Italy that was destroyed by the volcano, Mt. Vesuvius, in 79 CE.

· He accepted her amendments, he enjoyed her corrections, though the moral of them was, she pointed out, that he *really* didn't remember the least thing about her; and he only felt it as a drawback that when all was made strictly historic there didn't appear much of anything left. They lingered together still, she neglecting her office—for from the moment he was so clever she had no proper right to him—and both neglecting the house, just waiting as to see if a memory or two more wouldn't again breathe on them. It hadn't taken them many minutes, after all, to put down on the table, like the cards of a pack, those that constituted their respective hands; only what came out was that the pack was unfortunately not perfect—that the past, invoked, invited, encouraged, could give them, naturally, no more than it had. It had made them anciently meet—her at twenty, him at twenty-five; but nothing was so strange, they seemed to say to each other, as that, while so occupied, it hadn't done a little more for them. They looked at each other as with the feeling of an occasion missed; the present would have been so much better if the other, in the far distance, in the foreign land, hadn't been so stupidly meagre. There weren't, apparently, all counted, more than a dozen little old things that had succeeded in coming to pass between them; trivialities of youth, simplicities of freshness, stupidities of ignorance, small possible germs, but too deeply buried—too deeply (didn't it seem?) to sprout after so many years. Marcher could only feel he ought to have rendered her some service—saved her from a capsized boat in the Bay or at least recovered her dressing-bag, filched from her cab in the streets of Naples by a lazzarone[1] with a stiletto. Or it would have been nice if he could have been taken with fever all alone at his hotel, and she could have come to look after him, to write to his people, to drive him out in convalescence. *Then* they would be in possession of the something or other that their actual show seemed to lack. It yet somehow presented itself, this show, as too good to be spoiled; so that they were reduced for a few minutes more to wondering a little helplessly why—since they seemed to know a certain number of the same people—their reunion had been so long averted. They didn't use that name for it, but their delay from minute to minute to join the others was a kind of confession that they didn't quite want it to be a failure. Their attempted supposition of reasons for their not having met but showed how little they knew of each other. There came in fact a

---

1 Beggar (Italian).

moment when Marcher felt a positive pang. It was vain to pretend she was an old friend, for all the communities were wanting, in spite of which it was as an old friend that he saw she would have suited him. He had new ones enough—was surrounded with them for instance on the stage of the other house; as a new one he probably wouldn't have so much as noticed her. He would have liked to invent something, get her to make-believe with him that some passage of a romantic or critical kind *had* originally occurred. He was really almost reaching out in imagination—as against time—for something that would do, and saying to himself that if it didn't come this sketch of a fresh start would show for quite awkwardly bungled. They would separate, and now for no second or no third chance. They would have tried and not succeeded. Then it was, just at the turn, as he afterwards made it out to himself, that, everything else failing, she herself decided to take up the case and, as it were, save the situation. He felt as soon as she spoke that she had been consciously keeping back what she said and hoping to get on without it; a scruple in her that immensely touched him when, by the end of three or four minutes more, he was able to measure it. What she brought out, at any rate, quite cleared the air and supplied the link—the link it was so odd he should frivolously have managed to lose.

"You know you told me something I've never forgotten and that again and again has made me think of you since; it was that tremendously hot day when we went to Sorrento, across the bay, for the breeze. What I allude to was what you said to me, on the way back, as we sat under the awning of the boat enjoying the cool. Have you forgotten?"

He had forgotten, and was even more surprised than ashamed. But the great thing was that he saw in this no vulgar reminder of any "sweet" speech. The vanity of women had long memories, but she was making no claim on him of a compliment or a mistake. With another woman, a totally different one, he might have feared the recall possibly even some imbecile "offer." So, in having to say that he had indeed forgotten, he was conscious rather of a loss than of a gain; he already saw an interest in the matter of her mention. "I try to think—but I give it up. Yet I remember the Sorrento day."

"I'm not very sure you do," May Bartram after a moment said; "and I'm not very sure I ought to want you to. It's dreadful to bring a person back at any time to what he was ten years before. If you've lived away from it," she smiled, "so much the better."

"Ah if *you* haven't why should I?" he asked.

"Lived away, you mean, from what I myself was?"

"From what *I* was. I was of course an ass," Marcher went on; "but I would rather know from you just the sort of ass I was than—from the moment you have something in your mind—not know anything."

Still, however, she hesitated. "But if you've completely ceased to be that sort—?"

"Why I can then all the more bear to know. Besides, perhaps I haven't."

"Perhaps. Yet if you haven't," she added, "I should suppose you'd remember. Not indeed that *I* in the least connect with my impression the invidious name you use. If I had only thought you foolish," she explained, "the thing I speak of wouldn't so have remained with me. It was about yourself." She waited as if it might come to him; but as, only meeting her eyes in wonder, he gave no sign, she burnt her ships. "Has it ever happened?"

Then it was that, while he continued to stare, a light broke for him and the blood slowly came to his face, which began to burn with recognition. "Do you mean I told you—?" But he faltered, lest what came to him shouldn't be right, lest he should only give himself away.

"It was something about yourself that it was natural one shouldn't forget—that is if one remembered you at all. That's why I ask you," she smiled, "if the thing you then spoke of has ever come to pass?"

Oh then he saw, but he was lost in wonder and found himself embarrassed. This, he also saw, made her sorry for him, as if her allusion had been a mistake. It took him but a moment, however, to feel it hadn't been, much as it had been a surprise. After the first little shock of it her knowledge on the contrary began, even if rather strangely, to taste sweet to him. She was the only other person in the world then who would have it, and she had had it all these years, while the fact of his having so breathed his secret had unaccountably faded from him. No wonder they couldn't have met as if nothing had happened. "I judge," he finally said, "that I know what you mean. Only I had strangely enough lost any sense of having taken you so far into my confidence."

"Is it because you've taken so many others as well?"

"I've taken nobody. Not a creature since then."

"So that I'm the only person who knows?"

"The only person in the world."

"Well," she quickly replied, "I myself have never spoken. I've never, never repeated of you what you told me." She looked at him so that he perfectly believed her. Their eyes met over it in such a way that he was without a doubt. "And I never will."

She spoke with an earnestness that, as if almost excessive, put him at ease about her possible derision. Somehow the whole question was a new luxury to him—that is from the moment she was in possession. If she didn't take the sarcastic view she clearly took the sympathetic, and that was what he had had, in all the long time, from no one whomsoever. What he felt was that he couldn't at present have begun to tell her, and yet could profit perhaps exquisitely by the accident of having done so of old. "Please don't then. We're just right as it is."

"Oh I am," she laughed, "if you are!" To which she added: "Then you do still feel in the same way?"

It was impossible he shouldn't take to himself that she was really interested, though it all kept coming as a perfect surprise. He had thought of himself so long as abominably alone, and lo he wasn't alone a bit. He hadn't been, it appeared, for an hour— since those moments on the Sorrento boat. It was *she* who had been, he seemed to see as he looked at her—she who had been made so by the graceless fact of his lapse of fidelity. To tell her what he had told her—what had it been but to ask something of her? something that she had given, in her charity, without his having, by a remembrance, by a return of the spirit, failing another encounter, so much as thanked her. What he had asked of her had been simply at first not to laugh at him. She had beautifully not done so for ten years, and she was not doing so now. So he had endless gratitude to make up. Only for that he must see just how he had figured to her. "What, exactly, was the account I gave—?"

"Of the way you did feel? Well, it was very simple. You said you had had from your earliest time, as the deepest thing within you, the sense of being kept for something rare and strange, possibly prodigious and terrible, that was sooner or later to happen to you, that you had in your bones the foreboding and the conviction of, and that would perhaps overwhelm you."

"Do you call that very simple?" John Marcher asked.

She thought a moment. "It was perhaps because I seemed, as you spoke, to understand it."

"You do understand it?" he eagerly asked.

Again she kept her kind eyes on him. "You still have the belief?"

"Oh!" he exclaimed helplessly. There was too much to say.

"Whatever it's to be," she clearly made out, "it hasn't yet come."

He shook his head in complete surrender now. "It hasn't yet come. Only, you know, it isn't anything I'm to *do*, to achieve in the world, to be distinguished or admired for. I'm not such an ass as *that*. It would be much better, no doubt, if I were."

"It's to be something you're merely to suffer?"

"Well, say to wait for—to have to meet, to face, to see suddenly break out in my life; possibly destroying all further consciousness, possibly annihilating me; possibly, on the other hand, only altering everything, striking at the root of all my world and leaving me to the consequences, however they shape themselves."

She took this in, but the light in her eyes continued for him not to be that of mockery. "Isn't what you describe perhaps but the expectation—or at any rate the sense of danger, familiar to so many people—of falling in love?"

John Marcher wondered. "Did you ask me that before?"

"No—I wasn't so free-and-easy then. But it's what strikes me now."

"Of course," he said after a moment, "it strikes you. Of course it strikes *me*. Of course what's in store for me may be no more than that. The only thing is," he went on, "that I think if it had been that I should by this time know."

"Do you mean because you've *been* in love?" And then as he but looked at her in silence: "You've been in love, and it hasn't meant such a cataclysm, hasn't proved the great affair?"

"Here I am, you see. It hasn't been overwhelming."

"Then it hasn't been love," said May Bartram.

"Well, I at least thought it was. I took it for that—I've taken it till now. It was agreeable, it was delightful, it was miserable," he explained. "But it wasn't strange. It wasn't what *my* affair's to be."

"You want something all to yourself—something that nobody else knows or *has* known?"

"It isn't a question of what I 'want'—God knows I don't want anything. It's only a question of the apprehension that haunts me—that I live with day by day."

He said this so lucidly and consistently that he could see it further impose itself. If she hadn't been interested before she'd have been interested now. "Is it a sense of coming violence?"

Evidently now too again he liked to talk of it. "I don't think of it as—when it does come—necessarily violent. I only think of it as natural and as of course above all unmistakeable. I think of it simply as *the* thing. *The* thing will of itself appear natural."

"Then how will it appear strange?"

Marcher bethought himself. "It won't—to *me*."

"To whom then?"

"Well," he replied, smiling at last, "say to you."

"Oh then I'm to be present?"

"Why you *are* present—since you know."

"I see." She turned it over. "But I mean at the catastrophe."

At this, for a minute, their lightness gave way to their gravity; it was as if the long look they exchanged held them together. "It will only depend on yourself—if you'll watch with me."

"Are you afraid?" she asked.

"Don't leave me *now*," he went on.

"Are you afraid?" she repeated.

"Do you think me simply out of my mind?" he pursued instead of answering." Do I merely strike you as a harmless lunatic?"

"No," said May Bartram. "I understand you. I believe you."

"You mean you feel how my obsession—poor old thing!—may correspond to some possible reality?"

"To some possible reality."

"Then you *will* watch with me?"

She hesitated, then for the third time put her question. "Are you afraid?"

"Did I tell you I was—at Naples?"

"No, you said nothing about it."

"Then I don't know. And I should *like* to know," said John Marcher. "You'll tell me yourself whether you think so. If you'll watch with me you'll see."

"Very good then." They had been moving by this time across the room, and at the door, before passing out, they paused as for the full wind-up of their understanding. "I'll watch with you," said May Bartram.

II

The fact that she "knew"—knew and yet neither chaffed[1] him nor betrayed him—had in a short time begun to constitute between them a goodly bond, which became more marked when, within the year that followed their afternoon at Weatherend, the opportunities for meeting multiplied. The event that thus promoted these occasions was the death of the ancient lady her great-aunt, under whose wing, since losing her mother, she had

---

1 Teased.

to such an extent found shelter, and who, though but the widowed mother of the new successor to the property, had succeeded—thanks to a high tone and a high temper—in not forfeiting the supreme position at the great house. The deposition of this personage arrived but with her death, which, followed by many changes, made in particular a difference for the young woman in whom Marcher's expert attention had recognized from the first a dependent with a pride that might ache though it didn't bristle. Nothing for a long time had made him easier than the thought that the aching must have been much soothed by Miss Bartram's now finding herself able to set up a small home in London. She had acquired property, to an amount that made that luxury just possible, under her aunt's extremely complicated will, and when the whole matter began to be straightened out, which indeed took time, she let him know that the happy issue was at last in view. He had seen her again before that day, both because she had more than once accompanied the ancient lady to town and because he had paid another visit to the friends who so conveniently made of Weatherend one of the charms of their own hospitality. These friends had taken him back there; he had achieved there again with Miss Bartram some quiet detachment; and he had in London succeeded in persuading her to more than one brief absence from her aunt. They went together, on these latter occasions, to the National Gallery[1] and the South Kensington Museum,[2] where, among vivid reminders, they talked of Italy at large—not now attempting to recover, as at first, the taste of their youth and their ignorance. That recovery, the first day at Weatherend, had served its purpose well, had given them quite enough; so that they were, to Marcher's sense, no longer hovering about the head-waters of their stream, but had felt their boat pushed sharply off and down the current.

They were literally afloat together; for our gentleman this was marked, quite as marked as that the fortunate cause of it was just the buried treasure of her knowledge. He had with his own hands dug up this little hoard, brought to light—that is to within reach of the dim day constituted by their discretions and privacies—the object of value the hiding-place of which he had, after putting it into the ground himself, so strangely, so long forgotten. The rare luck of his having again just stumbled on the spot made him

---

1 Art gallery in central London.
2 Museum of decorative arts in London, renamed the Victoria and Albert Museum (the V & A) in 1899.

indifferent to any other question; he would doubtless have devoted more time to the odd accident of his lapse of memory if he hadn't been moved to devote so much to the sweetness, the comfort, as he felt, for the future, that this accident itself had helped to keep fresh. It had never entered into his plan that any one should "know," and mainly for the reason that it wasn't in him to tell any one. That would have been impossible, for nothing but the amusement of a cold world would have waited on it. Since, however, a mysterious fate had opened his mouth betimes, in spite of him, he would count that a compensation and profit by it to the utmost. That the right person *should* know tempered the asperity of his secret more even than his shyness had permitted him to imagine; and May Bartram was clearly right, because—well, because there she was. Her knowledge simply settled it; he would have been sure enough by this time had she been wrong. There was that in his situation, no doubt, that disposed him too much to see her as a mere confidant, taking all her light for him from the fact—the fact only—of her interest in his predicament; from her mercy, sympathy, seriousness, her consent not to regard him as the funniest of the funny. Aware, in fine, that her price for him was just in her giving him this constant sense of his being admirably spared, he was careful to remember that she had also a life of her own, with things that might happen to *her*, things that in friendship one should likewise take account of. Something fairly remarkable came to pass with him, for that matter, in this connexion—something represented by a certain passage of his consciousness, in the suddenest way, from one extreme to the other.

He had thought himself, so long as nobody knew, the most disinterested person in the world, carrying his concentrated burden, his perpetual suspense, ever so quietly, holding his tongue about it, giving others no glimpse of it nor of its effect upon his life, asking of them no allowance and only making on his side all those that were asked. He hadn't disturbed people with the queerness of their having to know a haunted man, though he had had moments of rather special temptation on hearing them say they were forsooth "unsettled." If they were as unsettled as he was—he who had never been settled for an hour in his life—they would know what it meant. Yet it wasn't, all the same, for him to make them, and he listened to them civilly enough. This was why he had such good—though possibly such rather colourless—manners; this was why, above all, he could regard himself, in a greedy world, as decently—as in fact perhaps even a little sublimely—unselfish. Our point is accordingly that he valued this character quite sufficiently to measure his present danger of letting it lapse, against which he promised himself to be much on his guard. He was quite ready, none the less, to be selfish just a little, since surely no more charming occasion for it had come to him. "Just a little," in a word, was just as much as Miss Bartram, taking one day with another, would let him. He never would be in the least coercive, and would keep well before him the lines on which consideration for her—the very highest—ought to proceed. He would thoroughly establish the heads under which her affairs, her requirements, her peculiarities—he went so far as to give them the latitude of that name—would come into their intercourse. All this naturally was a sign of how much he took the intercourse itself for granted. There was nothing more to be done about *that*. It simply existed; had sprung into being with her first penetrating question to him in the autumn light there at Weatherend. The real form it should have taken on the basis that stood out large was the form of their marrying. But the devil in this was that the very basis itself put marrying out of the question. His conviction, his apprehension, his obsession, in short, wasn't a privilege he could invite a woman to share; and that consequence of it was precisely what was the matter with him. Something or other lay in wait for him, amid the twists and the turns of the months and the years, like a crouching beast in the jungle. It signified little whether the crouching beast were destined to slay him or to be slain. The definite point was the inevitable spring of the creature; and the definite lesson from that was that a man of feeling didn't cause himself to be accompanied by a lady on a tiger-hunt. Such was the image under which he had ended by figuring his life.

They had at first, none the less, in the scattered hours spent together, made no allusion to that view of it; which was a sign he was handsomely alert to give that he didn't expect, that he in fact didn't care, always to be talking about it. Such a feature in one's outlook was really like a hump on one's back. The difference it made every minute of the day existed quite independently of discussion. One discussed of course *like* a hunchback, for there was always, if nothing else, the hunchback face. That remained, and she was watching him; but people watched best, as a general thing, in silence, so that such would be predominantly the manner of their vigil. Yet he didn't want, at the same time, to be tense and solemn; tense and solemn was what he imagined he too much showed for with other people. The thing to be, with the one person who knew, was easy and natural—to make the reference rather than be seeming to avoid it, to avoid it rather than be seeming to make it, and to keep it, in any case, familiar, facetious even, rather than pedantic and portentous. Some such consideration as the latter was doubtless in his mind for instance when he wrote pleasantly to Miss Bartram that perhaps the great thing he had so long felt as in the lap of the gods was no more than this circumstance, which touched him so nearly, of her acquiring a house in London. It was the first allusion they had yet again made, needing any other hitherto so little; but when she replied, after having given him the news, that she was by no means satisfied with such a trifle as the climax to so special a suspense, she almost set him wondering if she hadn't even a larger conception of singularity for him than he had for himself. He was at all events destined to become aware little by little, as time went by, that she was all the while looking at his life, judging it, measuring it, in the light of the thing she knew, which grew to be at last, with the consecration of the years, never mentioned between them save as "the real truth" about him. That had always been his own form of reference to it, but she adopted the form so quietly that, looking back at the end of a period, he knew there was no moment at which it was traceable that she had, as he might say, got inside his idea, or exchanged the attitude of beautifully indulging for that of still more beautifully believing him.

It was always open to him to accuse her of seeing him but as the most harmless of maniacs, and this, in the long run—since it covered so much ground—was his easiest description of their friendship. He had a screw loose for her but she liked him in spite of it and was practically, against the rest of the world, his kind wise keeper, unremunerated but fairly amused and, in the absence of other near ties, not disreputably occupied. The rest of the world of course thought him queer, but she, she only, knew how, and above all why, queer; which was precisely what enabled her to dispose the concealing veil in the right folds. She took his gaiety from him—since it had to pass with them for gaiety—as she took everything else; but she certainly so far justified by her unerring touch his finer sense of the degree to which he had ended by convincing her. *She* at least never spoke of the secret of his life except as "the real truth about you," and she had in fact a wonderful way of making it seem, as such, the secret of her own life too. That was in fine how he so constantly felt her as allowing for him; he couldn't on the whole call it anything else. He allowed for himself, but she, exactly, allowed still more; partly because, better placed for a sight of the matter, she traced his unhappy perversion through reaches of its course into which he could scarce follow it. He knew how he felt, but, besides knowing that, she knew how he *looked* as well; he knew each of the things of importance he was insidiously kept from doing, but she could add up the amount they made, understand how much, with a lighter weight on his spirit, he might have done, and thereby establish how, clever as he was, he fell short. Above all she was in the secret of the difference between the forms he went through—those of his little office under Government, those of caring for his modest patrimony, for his library, for his garden in the country, for the people in London whose invitations he accepted and repaid—and the detachment that reigned beneath them and that made of all behaviour, all that could in the least be called behaviour, a long act of dissimulation. What it had come to was that he wore a mask painted with the social simper, out of the eye-holes of which there looked eyes of an expression not in the least matching the other features. This the stupid world, even after years, had never more than half discovered. It was only May Bartram who had, and she achieved, by an art indescribable, the feat of at once—or perhaps it was only alternately—meeting the eyes from in front and mingling her own vision, as from over his shoulder, with their peep through the apertures.

So while they grew older together she did watch with him, and so she let this association give shape and colour to her own existence. Beneath *her* forms as well detachment had learned to sit, and behaviour had become for her, in the social sense, a false account of herself. There was but one account of her that would have been true all the while and that she could give straight to nobody, least of all to John Marcher. Her whole attitude was a virtual statement, but the perception of that only seemed called to take its place for him as one of the many things necessarily crowded out of his consciousness. If she had moreover, like himself, to make sacrifices to their real truth, it was to be granted that her compensation might have affected her as more prompt and more natural. They had long periods, in this London time, during which, when they were together, a stranger might have listened to them without in the least pricking up his ears; on the other hand the real truth was equally liable at any moment to rise to the surface, and the auditor would then have wondered indeed what they were talking about. They had from an early hour made up their mind that society was, luckily, unintelligent, and the margin allowed them by this had fairly become one of their commonplaces. Yet there were still moments when the situation turned almost fresh—usually under the effect of some expression drawn from herself. Her expressions doubtless repeated themselves, but her intervals were generous. "What saves us, you know, is that we answer so completely to so usual an appearance: that of the man and woman whose friendship has become such a daily habit—or almost—as to be at last indispensable." That for instance was a remark she had frequently enough had occasion to make, though she had given it at different times different developments. What we are especially concerned with is the turn it happened to take from her one afternoon when he had come to see her in honour of her birthday. This anniversary had fallen on a Sunday, at a season of thick fog and general outward gloom; but he had brought her his customary offering, having known her now long enough to have established a hundred small traditions. It was one of his proofs to himself, the present he made her on her birthday, that he hadn't sunk into real selfishness. It was mostly nothing more than a small trinket, but it was always fine of its kind, and he was regularly careful to pay for it more than he thought he could afford. "Our habit saves you, at least, don't you see? because it makes you, after all, for the vulgar, indistinguishable from other men. What's the most inveterate mark of men in general? Why the capacity to spend endless time with dull women—to spend it I won't say without being bored, but without minding that they are, without being driven off at a tangent by it; which comes to the same thing. I'm your dull woman, a part of the daily bread for which you pray at church. That covers your tracks more than anything."

"And what covers yours?" asked Marcher, whom his dull woman could mostly to this extent amuse. "I see of course what you mean by your saving me, in this way and that, so far as other people are concerned—I've seen it all along. Only what is it that saves *you*? I often think, you know, of that."

She looked as if she sometimes thought of that too, but rather in a different way. "Where other people, you mean, are concerned?"

"Well, you're really so in with me, you know—as a sort of result of my being so in with yourself. I mean of my having such an immense regard for you, being so tremendously mindful of all you've done for me. I sometimes ask myself if it's quite fair. Fair I mean to have so involved and—since one may say it—interested you. I almost feel as if you hadn't really had time to do anything else."

"Anything else but be interested?" she asked. "Ah what else does one ever want to be? If I've been 'watching' with you, as we long ago agreed I was to do, watching's always in itself an absorption."

"Oh certainly," John Marcher said, "if you hadn't had your curiosity—! Only doesn't it sometimes come to you as time goes on that your curiosity isn't being particularly repaid?"

May Bartram had a pause. "Do you ask that, by any chance, because you feel at all that yours isn't? I mean because you have to wait so long."

Oh he understood what she meant! "For the thing to happen that never does happen? For the beast to jump out? No, I'm just where I was about it. It isn't a matter as to which I can *choose*, I can decide for a change. It isn't one as to which there *can* be a change. It's in the lap of the gods. One's in the hands of one's law—there one is. As to the form the law will take, the way it will operate, that's its own affair."

"Yes," Miss Bartram replied; "of course one's fate's coming, of course it *has* come in its own form and its own way, all the while. Only, you know, the form and the way in your case were to have been—well, something so exceptional and, as one may say, so particularly *your* own."

Something in this made him look at her with suspicion. "You say 'were to *have* been,' as if in your heart you had begun to doubt."

"Oh!" she vaguely protested.

"As if you believed," he went on, "that nothing will now take place."

She shook her head slowly but rather inscrutably. "You're far from my thought."

He continued to look at her. "What then is the matter with you?"

"Well," she said after another wait, "the matter with me is simply that I'm more sure than ever my curiosity, as you call it, will be but too well repaid."

They were frankly grave now; he had got up from his seat, had turned once more about the little drawing-room to which, year after year, he brought his inevitable topic; in which he had, as he might have said, tasted their intimate community with every sauce, where every object was as familiar to him as the things of his own house and the very carpets were worn with his fitful walk very much as the desks in old counting-houses are worn by the elbows of generations of clerks. The generations of his nervous moods had been at work there, and the place was the written history of his whole middle life. Under the impression of what his friend had just said he knew himself, for some reason, more aware of these things; which made him, after a moment, stop again before her. "Is it possibly that you've grown afraid?"

"Afraid?" He thought, as she repeated the word, that his question had made her, a little, change colour; so that, lest he should have touched on a truth, he explained very kindly: "You remember that that was what you asked *me* long ago—that first day at Weatherend."

"Oh yes, and you told me you didn't know—that I was to see for myself. We've said little about it since, even in so long a time."

"Precisely," Marcher interposed—"quite as if it were too delicate a matter for us to make free with. Quite as if we might find, on pressure, that I *am* afraid. For then," he said, "we shouldn't, should we? quite know what to do."

She had for the time no answer to this question. "There have been days when I thought you were. Only, of course," she added, "there have been days when we have thought almost anything."

"Everything. Oh!" Marcher softly groaned, as with a gasp, half-spent, at the face, more uncovered just then than it had been for a long while, of the imagination always with them. It had always had its incalculable moments of glaring out, quite as with the very eyes of the very Beast, and, used as he was to them, they could still draw from him the tribute of a sigh that rose from the depths of his being. All they had thought, first and last, rolled over him; the past seemed to have been reduced to mere barren speculation. This in fact was what the place had just struck him as so full of—the simplification of everything but the state of suspense. That remained only by seeming to hang in the void surrounding it. Even his original fear, if fear it had been, had lost itself in the desert. "I judge, however," he continued, "that you see I'm not afraid now."

"What I see, as I make it out, is that you've achieved something almost unprecedented in the way of getting used to danger. Living with it so long and so closely you've lost your sense of it; you know it's there, but you're indifferent, and you cease even, as of old, to have to whistle in the dark. Considering what the danger is," May Bartram wound up, "I'm bound to say I don't think your attitude could well be surpassed."

John Marcher faintly smiled. "It's heroic?"

"Certainly—call it that."

It was what he would have liked indeed to call it. "I *am* then a man of courage?"

"That's what you were to show me."

He still, however, wondered. "But doesn't the man of courage know what he's afraid of—or not afraid of? I don't know *that*, you see. I don't focus it. I can't name it. I only know I'm exposed."

"Yes, but exposed—how shall I say?—so directly. So intimately. That's surely enough."

"Enough to make you feel then—as what we may call the end and the upshot of our watch—that I'm not afraid?"

"You're not afraid. But it isn't," she said, "the end of our watch. That is it isn't the end of yours. You've everything still to see."

"Then why haven't *you*?" he asked. He had had, all along, to-day, the sense of her keeping something back, and he still had it. As this was his first impression of that it quite made a date. The case was the more marked as she didn't at first answer; which in turn made him go on. "You know something I don't." Then his voice, for that of a man of courage, trembled a little. "You know what's to happen." Her silence, with the face she showed, was almost a confession—it made him sure. "You know, and you're afraid to tell me. It's so bad that you're afraid I'll find out."

All this might be true, for she did look as if, unexpectedly to her, he had crossed some mystic line that she had secretly drawn round her. Yet she might, after all, not have worried; and the real climax was that he himself, at all events, needn't. "You'll never find out."

III

It was all to have made, none the less, as I have said, a date; which came out in the fact that again and again, even after long intervals, other things that passed between them were in relation to this hour but the character of recalls and results. Its immediate effect had been indeed rather to lighten insistence—almost to provoke a reaction; as if their topic had dropped by its own weight and as if moreover, for that matter, Marcher had been visited by one of his occasional warnings against egotism. He had kept up, he felt, and very decently on the whole, his consciousness of the importance of not being selfish, and it was true that he had never sinned in that direction without promptly enough trying to press the scales the other way. He often repaired his fault, the season permitting, by inviting his friend to accompany him to the opera; and it not infrequently thus happened that, to show he didn't wish her to have but one sort of food for her mind, he was the cause of her appearing there with him a dozen nights in the month. It even happened that, seeing her home at such times, he occasionally went in with her to finish, as he called it, the evening, and, the better to make his point, sat down to the frugal but always careful little supper that awaited his pleasure. His point was made, he thought, by his not eternally insisting with her on himself; made for instance, at such hours, when it befell that, her piano at hand and each of them familiar with it, they went over passages of the opera together. It chanced to be on one of these occasions, however, that he reminded her of her not having answered a certain question he had put to her during the talk that had taken place between them on her last birthday. "What is it that saves *you*?"—saved her, he meant, from that appearance of variation from the usual human type. If he had practically escaped remark, as she pretended, by doing, in the most important particular, what most men do—find the answer to life in patching up an alliance of a sort with a woman no better than himself—how had she escaped it, and how could the alliance, such as it was, since they must suppose it had been more or less noticed, have failed to make her rather positively talked about?

"I never said," May Bartram replied, "that it hadn't made me a good deal talked about."

"Ah well then you're not 'saved.'"

"It hasn't been a question for me. If you've had your woman I've had," she said, "my man."

"And you mean that makes you all right?"

Oh it was always as if there were so much to say! "I don't know why it shouldn't make me—humanly, which is what we're speaking of—as right as it makes you."

"I see," Marcher returned. "'Humanly,' no doubt, as showing that you're living for something. Not, that is, just for me and my secret."

May Bartram smiled. "I don't pretend it exactly shows that I'm not living for you. It's my intimacy with you that's in question."

He laughed as he saw what she meant. "Yes, but since, as you say, I'm only, so far as people make out, ordinary, you're—aren't you? no more than ordinary either. You help me to pass for a man like another. So if I *am*, as I understand you, you're not compromised. Is that it?"

She had another of her waits, but she spoke clearly enough. "That's it. It's all that concerns me—to help you to pass for a man like another."

He was careful to acknowledge the remark handsomely. "How kind, how beautiful, you are to me! How shall I ever repay you?"

She had her last grave pause, as if there might be a choice of ways. But she chose. "By going on as you are."

It was into this going on as he was that they relapsed, and really for so long a time that the day inevitably came for a further sounding of their depths. These depths, constantly bridged over by a structure firm enough in spite of its lightness and of its occasional oscillation in the somewhat vertiginous air, invited on occasion, in the interest of their nerves, a dropping of the plummet and a measurement of the abyss. A difference had been made moreover, once for all, by the fact that she had all the while not appeared to feel the need of rebutting his charge of an idea within her that she didn't dare to express—a charge uttered just before one of the fullest of their later discussions ended. It had come up for him then that she "knew" something and that what she knew was bad—too bad to tell him. When he had spoken of it as visibly so bad that she was afraid he might find it out, her reply had left the matter too equivocal to be let alone and yet, for Marcher's special sensibility, almost too formidable again to touch. He circled about it at a distance that alternately narrowed and widened and that still wasn't much affected by the consciousness in him that there was nothing she could "know," after all, any better than he did. She had no source of knowledge he hadn't equally—except of course that she might have finer nerves. That was what women had where they were interested; they made out things, where people were concerned, that the people often couldn't have made out for themselves. Their nerves, their sensibility, their imagination, were conductors and revealers, and the beauty of May Bartram was in particular that she had given herself so to his case. He felt in these days what, oddly enough, he had never felt before, the growth of a dread of losing her by some catastrophe—some catastrophe that yet wouldn't at all be *the* catastrophe: partly because she had almost of a sudden begun to strike him as more useful to him than ever yet, and partly by reason of an appearance of uncertainty in her health, coincident and equally new. It was characteristic of the inner detachment he had hitherto so successfully cultivated and to which our whole account of him is a reference, it was characteristic that his complications, such as they were, had never yet seemed so as at this crisis to thicken about him, even to the point of making him ask himself if he were, by any chance, of a truth, within sight or sound, within touch or reach, within the immediate jurisdiction, of the thing that waited.

When the day came, as come it had to, that his friend confessed to him her fear of a deep disorder in her blood, he felt somehow the shadow of a change and the chill of a shock. He immediately began to imagine aggravations and disasters, and above all to think of her peril as the direct menace for himself of personal privation. This indeed gave him one of those partial recoveries of equanimity that were agreeable to him—it showed him that what was still first in his mind was the loss she herself might suffer. "What if she should have to die before knowing, before seeing—?" It would have been brutal, in the early stages of her trouble, to put that question to her; but it had immediately sounded for him to his own concern, and the possibility was what most made him sorry for her. If she did "know," moreover, in the sense of her having had some—what should he think?—mystical irresistible light, this would make the matter not better, but worse, inasmuch as her original adoption of his own curiosity had quite become the basis of her life. She had been living to see what would *be* to be seen, and it would quite lacerate her to have to give up before the accomplishment of the vision. These reflexions, as I say, quickened his generosity; yet, make them as he might, he saw himself, with the lapse of the period, more and more disconcerted. It lapsed for him with a strange steady sweep, and the oddest oddity was that it gave him, independently of the threat of much inconvenience, almost the only positive surprise his career, if career it could be called, had yet offered him. She kept the house as she had never done; he had to go to her to see her—she could meet him nowhere now, though there was scarce a corner of their loved old London in which she hadn't in the past, at one time or another, done so; and he found her always seated by her fire in the deep old-fashioned chair she was less and less able to leave. He had been struck one day, after an absence exceeding his usual measure, with her suddenly looking much older to him than he had ever thought of her being; then he recognised that the suddenness was all on his side—he had just simply and suddenly noticed. She looked older because inevitably, after so many years, she *was* old, or almost; which was of course true in still greater measure of her companion. If she was old, or almost, John Marcher assuredly was, and yet it was her showing of the lesson, not his own, that brought the truth home to him. His surprises began here; when once they had begun they multiplied; they came rather with a rush: it was as if, in the oddest way in the world, they had all been kept back, sown in a thick cluster, for the late afternoon of life, the time at which for people in general the unexpected has died out.

One of them was that he should have caught himself—for he *had* so done—*really* wondering if the great accident would take form now as nothing more than his being condemned to see this charming woman, this admirable friend, pass away from him. He had never so unreservedly qualified her as while confronted in thought with such a possibility; in spite of which there was small doubt for him that as an answer to his long riddle the mere effacement of even so fine a feature of his situation would be an abject anticlimax. It would represent, as connected with his past attitude, a drop of dignity under the shadow of which his existence could only become the most grotesques of failures. He had been far from holding it a failure—long as he had waited for the appearance that was to make it a success. He had waited for quite another thing, not for such a thing as that. The breath of his good faith came short, however, as he recognised how long he had waited, or how long at least his companion had. That she, at all events, might be recorded as having waited in vain—this affected him sharply, and all the more because of his at first having done little more than amuse himself with the idea. It grew more grave as the gravity of her condition grew, and the state of mind it produced in him, which he himself ended by watching as if it had been some definite disfigurement of his outer person, may pass for another of his surprises. This conjoined itself still with another, the really stupefying consciousness of a question that he would have allowed to shape itself had he dared. What did everything mean—what, that is, did *she* mean, she and her vain waiting and her probable death and the soundless admonition of it all—unless that, at this time of day, it was simply, it was overwhelmingly too late? He had never at any stage of his queer consciousness admitted the whisper of such a correction; he had never till within these last few months been so false to his conviction as not to hold that what was to come to him had time, whether *he* struck himself as having it or not. That at last, at last, he certainly hadn't it, to speak of, or had it but in the scantiest measure—such, soon enough, as things went with him, became the inference with which his old obsession had to reckon: and this it was not helped to do by the more and more confirmed appearance that the great vagueness casting the long shadow in which he had lived had, to attest itself, almost no margin left. Since it was in Time that he was to have met his fate, so it was in Time that his fate was to have acted; and as he waked up to the sense of no longer being young, which was exactly the sense of being stale, just as that, in turn, was the sense of being weak, he waked up to another matter beside. It all hung together; they were subject, he and the great vagueness, to an equal and indivisible law. When the possibilities themselves had accordingly turned stale, when the secret of the gods had grown faint, had perhaps even quite evaporated, that, and that only, was failure. It wouldn't have been failure to be bankrupt, dishonoured, pilloried, hanged; it was failure not to be anything. And so, in the dark valley into which his path had taken its unlooked-for twist, he wondered not a little as he groped. He didn't care what awful crash might overtake him, with what ignominy or what monstrosity he might yet be associated—since he wasn't after all too utterly old to suffer—if it would only be decently proportionate to the posture he had kept, all his life, in the threatened presence of it. He had but one desire left—that he shouldn't have been "sold."

IV

Then it was that, one afternoon, while the spring of the year was young and new she met all in her own way his frankest betrayal of these alarms. He had gone in late to see her, but evening hadn't settled and she was presented to him in that long fresh light of waning April days which affects us often with a sadness sharper than the greyest hours of autumn. The week had been warm, the spring was supposed to have begun early, and May Bartram sat, for the first time in the year, without a fire; a fact that, to Marcher's sense, gave the scene of which she formed part a smooth and ultimate look, an air of knowing, in its immaculate order and cold meaningless cheer, that it would never see a fire again. Her own aspect—he could scarce have said why—intensified this note. Almost as white as wax, with the marks and signs in her face as numerous and as fine as if they had been etched by a needle, with soft white draperies relieved by a faded green scarf on the delicate tone of which the years had further refined, she was the picture of a serene and exquisite but impenetrable sphinx,[1] whose head, or indeed all whose person, might have been powdered with silver. She was a sphinx, yet with her white petals and green fronds she might have been

---

1   An ancient mythological creature, usually depicted with the head of a
    human and the recumbent body of a lion. The sphinx often guarded the
    entrance to a temple or a city; in the ancient Greek story of Oedipus, a
    sphinx guards the entrance to the city of Thebes and all those who wish
    to enter must answer her riddle or be killed.

a lily too—only an artificial lily, wonderfully imitated and constantly kept, without dust or stain, though not exempt from a
slight droop and a complexity of faint creases, under some clear
glass bell. The perfection of household care, of high polish and
finish, always reigned in her rooms, but they now looked most as
if everything had been wound up, tucked in, put away, so that
she might sit with folded hands and with nothing more to do.
She was "out of it," to Marcher's vision; her work was over; she
communicated with him as across some gulf or from some island
of rest that she had already reached, and it made him feel
strangely abandoned. Was it—or rather wasn't it—that if for so
long she had been watching with him the answer to their question must have swum into her ken and taken on its name, so that
her occupation was verily gone? He had as much as charged her
with this in saying to her, many months before, that she even
then knew something she was keeping from him. It was a point
he had never since ventured to press, vaguely fearing as he did
that it might become a difference, perhaps a disagreement,
between them. He had in this later time turned nervous, which
was what he in all the other years had never been; and the oddity
was that his nervousness should have waited till he had begun to
doubt, should have held off so long as he was sure. There was
something, it seemed to him, that the wrong word would bring
down on his head, something that would so at least ease off his
tension. But he wanted not to speak the wrong word; that would
make everything ugly. He wanted the knowledge he lacked to
drop on him, if drop it could, by its own august weight. If she
was to forsake him it was surely for her to take leave. This was
why he didn't directly ask her again what she knew; but it was
also why, approaching the matter from another side, he said to
her in the course of his visit: "What do you regard as the very
worst that at this time of day *can* happen to me?"

He had asked her that in the past often enough; they had, with
the odd irregular rhythm of their intensities and avoidances,
exchanged ideas about it and then had seen the ideas washed
away by cool intervals, washed like figures traced in sea-sand. It
had ever been the mark of their talk that the oldest allusions in it
required but a little dismissal and reaction to come out again,
sounding for the hour as new. She could thus at present meet his
enquiry quite freshly and patiently. "Oh yes, I've repeatedly
thought, only it always seemed to me of old that I couldn't quite
make up my mind. I thought of dreadful things, between which
it was difficult to choose; and so must you have done."

"Rather! I feel now as if I had scarce done anything else. I appear to myself to have spent my life in thinking of nothing *but* dreadful things. A great many of them I've at different times named to you, but there were others I couldn't name."

"They were too, too dreadful?"

"Too, too dreadful—some of them."

She looked at him a minute, and there came to him as he met it, an inconsequent sense that her eyes, when one got their full clearness, were still as beautiful as they had been in youth, only beautiful with a strange cold light—a light that somehow was a part of the effect, if it wasn't rather a part of the cause, of the pale hard sweetness of the season and the hour. "And yet," she said at last, "there are horrors we've mentioned."

It deepened the strangeness to see her, as such a figure in such a picture, talk of "horrors," but she was to do in a few minutes something stranger yet—though even of this he was to take the full measure but afterwards—and the note of it already trembled. It was, for the matter of that, one of the signs that her eyes were having again the high flicker of their prime. He had to admit, however, what she said. "Oh yes, there were times when we did go far." He caught himself in the act of speaking as if it all were over. Well, he wished it were; and the consummation depended for him clearly more and more on his friend.

But she had now a soft smile. "Oh far—!"

It was oddly ironic. "Do you mean you're prepared to go further?"

She was frail and ancient and charming as she continued to look at him, yet it was rather as if she had lost the thread. "Do you consider that we went far?"

"Why I thought it the point you were just making—that we *had* looked most things in the face."

"Including each other?" She still smiled. "But you're quite right. We've had together great imaginations, often great fears; but some of them have been unspoken."

"Then the worst—we haven't faced that. I *could* face it, I believe, if I knew what you think it. I feel," he explained, "as if I had lost my power to conceive such things." And he wondered if he looked as blank as he sounded. "It's spent."

"Then why do you assume," she asked, "that mine isn't?"

"Because you've given me signs to the contrary. It isn't a question for you of conceiving, imagining, comparing. It isn't a question now of choosing." At last he came out with it. "You know something I don't. You've shown me that before."

These last words had affected her, he made out in a moment, exceedingly, and she spoke with firmness. "I've shown you, my dear, nothing."

He shook his head. "You can't hide it."

"Oh, oh!" May Bartram sounded over what she couldn't hide. It was almost a smothered groan.

"You admitted it months ago, when I spoke of it to you as of something you were afraid I should find out. Your answer was that I couldn't, that I wouldn't, and I don't pretend I have. But you had something therefore in mind, and I see now how it must have been, how it still is, the possibility that, of all possibilities, has settled itself for you as the worst. This," he went on, "is why I appeal to you. I'm only afraid of ignorance to-day—I'm not afraid of knowledge." And then as for a while she said nothing: "What makes me sure is that I see in your face and feel here, in this air and amid these appearances, that you're out of it. You've done. You've had your experience. You leave me to my fate."

Well, she listened, motionless and white in her chair, as on a decision to be made, so that her manner was fairly an avowal, though still, with a small fine inner stiffness, an imperfect surrender. "It *would* be the worst," she finally let herself say. "I mean the thing I've never said."

It hushed him a moment. "More monstrous than all the monstrosities we've named?"

"More monstrous. Isn't that what you sufficiently express," she asked, "in calling it the worst?"

Marcher thought. "Assuredly—if you mean, as I do, something that includes all the loss and all the shame that are thinkable."

"It would if it *should* happen," said May Bartram. "What we're speaking of, remember, is only my idea."

"It's your belief," Marcher returned. "That's enough for me. I feel your beliefs are right. Therefore if, having this one, you give me no more light on it, you abandon me."

"No, no!" she repeated. "I'm with you—don't you see?—still." And as to make it more vivid to him she rose from her chair—a movement she seldom risked in these days—and showed herself, all draped and all soft, in her fairness and slimness. "I haven't forsaken you."

It was really, in its effort against weakness, a generous assurance, and had the success of the impulse not, happily, been great, it would have touched him to pain more than to pleasure. But the cold charm in her eyes had spread, as she hovered before him, to all the rest of her person, so that it was for the minute almost a recovery of youth. He couldn't pity her for that; he could only take her as she showed—as capable even yet of helping him. It was as if, at the same time, her light might at any instant go out; wherefore he must make the most of it. There passed before him with intensity the three or four things he wanted most to know; but the question that came of itself to his lips really covered the others. "Then tell me if I shall consciously suffer."

She promptly shook her head. "Never!"

It confirmed the authority he imputed to her, and it produced on him an extraordinary effect. "Well, what's better than that? Do you call that the worst?"

"You think nothing is better?" she asked.

She seemed to mean something so special that he again sharply wondered, though still with the dawn of a prospect of relief. "Why not, if one doesn't *know*?" After which, as their eyes, over his question, met in a silence, the dawn deepened, and something to his purpose came prodigiously out of her very face. His own, as he took it in, suddenly flushed to the forehead, and he gasped with the force of a perception to which, on the instant, everything fitted. The sound of his gasp filled the air; then he became articulate. "I see—if I don't suffer!"

In her own look, however, was doubt. "You see what?"

"Why what you mean—what you've always meant."

She again shook her head. "What I mean isn't what I've always meant. It's different."

"It's something new?"

She hung back from it a little. "Something new. It's not what you think. I see what you think."

His divination drew breath then; only her correction might be wrong. "It isn't that I *am* a blockhead?" he asked between faintness and grimness. "It isn't that it's all a mistake?"

"A mistake?" she pityingly echoed. *That* possibility, for her, he saw, would be monstrous; and if she guaranteed him the immunity from pain it would accordingly not be what she had in mind. "Oh no," she declared; "it's nothing of that sort. You've been right."

Yet he couldn't help asking himself if she weren't, thus pressed, speaking but to save him. It seemed to him he should be most in a hole if his history should prove all a platitude. "Are you telling me the truth, so that I shan't have been a bigger idiot than I can bear to know? I *haven't* lived with a vain imagination, in the most besotted illusion? I haven't waited but to see the door shut in my face?"

She shook her head again. "However the case stands *that* isn't the truth. Whatever the reality, it *is* a reality. The door isn't shut. The door's open," said May Bartram.

"Then something's to come?"

She waited once again, always with her cold sweet eyes on him. "It's never too late." She had, with her gliding step, diminished the distance between them, and she stood nearer to him, close to him, a minute, as if still charged with the unspoken. Her movement might have been for some finer emphasis of what she was at once hesitating and deciding to say. He had been standing by the chimney-piece, fireless and sparely adorned, a small perfect old French clock and two morsels of rosy Dresden constituting all its furniture; and her hand grasped the shelf while she kept him waiting, grasped it a little as for support and encouragement. She only kept him waiting, however; that is he only waited. It had become suddenly, from her movement and attitude, beautiful and vivid to him that she had something more to give him; her wasted face delicately shone with it—it glittered almost as with the white lustre of silver in her expression. She was right, incontestably, for what he saw in her face was the truth, and strangely, without consequence, while their talk of it as dreadful was still in the air, she appeared to present it as inordinately soft. This, prompting bewilderment, made him but gape the more gratefully for her revelation, so that they continued for some minutes silent, her face shining at him, her contact imponderably pressing, and his stare all kind but all expectant. The end, none the less, was that what he had expected failed to come to him. Something else took place instead, which seemed to consist at first in the mere closing of her eyes. She gave way at the same instant to a slow fine shudder, and though he remained staring—though he stared in fact but the harder—turned off and regained her chair. It was the end of what she had been intending, but it left him thinking only of that.

"Well, you don't say—?"

She had touched in her passage a bell near the chimney and had sunk back strangely pale. "I'm afraid I'm too ill."

"Too ill to tell me?" it sprang up sharp to him, and almost to his lips, the fear she might die without giving him light. He checked himself in time from so expressing his question, but she answered as if she had heard the words.

"Don't you know—now?"

"'Now'—?" She had spoken as if some difference had been made within the moment. But her maid, quickly obedient to her bell, was already with them. "I know nothing." And he was afterwards to say to himself that he must have spoken with odious impatience, such an impatience as to show that, supremely disconcerted, he washed his hands of the whole question.

"Oh!" said May Bartram.

"Are you in pain?" he asked as the woman went to her.

"No," said May Bartram.

Her maid, who had put an arm round her as if to take her to her room, fixed on him eyes that appealingly contradicted her; in spite of which, however, he showed once more his mystification. "What then has happened?"

She was once more, with her companion's help, on her feet, and, feeling withdrawal imposed on him, he had blankly found his hat and gloves and had reached the door. Yet he waited for her answer. "What *was* to," she said.

V

He came back the next day, but she was then unable to see him, and as it was literally the first time this had occurred in the long stretch of their acquaintance he turned away, defeated and sore, almost angry—or feeling at least that such a break in their custom was really the beginning of the end—and wandered alone with his thoughts, especially with the one he was least able to keep down. She was dying and he would lose her; she was dying and his life would end. He stopped in the Park, into which he had passed, and stared before him at his recurrent doubt. Away from her the doubt pressed again; in her presence he had believed her, but as he felt his forlornness he threw himself into the explanation that, nearest at hand, had most of a miserable warmth for him and least of a cold torment. She had deceived him to save him—to put him off with something in which he should be able to rest. What could the thing that was to happen to him be, after all, but just this thing that had begun to happen? Her dying, her death, his consequent solitude—*that* was what he had figured as the Beast in the Jungle, that was what had been in the lap of the gods. He had had her word for it as he left her—what else on earth could she have meant? It wasn't a thing of a monstrous order; not a fate rare and distinguished; not a stroke of fortune that overwhelmed and immortalised; it had only the stamp of the common doom. But poor Marcher at this hour judged the common doom sufficient. It would serve his turn, and even as the consummation of infinite waiting he would bend his pride to accept it. He sat down on a bench in the twilight. He hadn't been a fool. Something had *been*, as she had said, to come. Before he rose indeed it had quite struck him that the final fact really matched with the long avenue through which he had had to reach it. As sharing his suspense and as giving herself all, giving her life, to bring it to an end, she had come with him every step of the way. He had lived by her aid, and to leave her behind would be cruelly, damnably to miss her. What could be more overwhelming than that?

Well, he was to know within the week, for though she kept him a while at bay, left him restless and wretched during a series of days on each of which he asked about her only again to have to turn away, she ended his trial by receiving him where she had always received him. Yet she had been brought out at some hazard into the presence of so many of the things that were, consciously, vainly, half their past, and there was scant service left in the gentleness of her mere desire, all too visible, to check his obsession and wind up his long trouble. That was clearly what she wanted; the one thing more for her own peace while she could still put out her hand. He was so affected by her state that, once seated by her chair, he was moved to let everything go; it was she herself therefore who brought him back, took up again, before she dismissed him, her last word of the other time. She showed how she wished to leave their business in order. "I'm not sure you understood. You've nothing to wait for more. It *has* come."

Oh how he looked at her! "Really?"

"Really."

"The thing that, as you said, *was* to?"

"The thing that we began in our youth to watch for."

Face to face with her once more he believed her; it was a claim to which he had so abjectly little to oppose. "You mean that it has come as a positive definite occurrence, with a name and a date?"

"Positive. Definite. I don't know about the 'name,' but, oh with a date!"

He found himself again too helplessly at sea. "But come in the night—come and passed me by?"

May Bartram had her strange faint smile. "Oh no, it hasn't passed you by!"

"But if I haven't been aware of it and it hasn't touched me—?"

"Ah your not being aware of it"—and she seemed to hesitate an instant to deal with this—"your not being aware of it is the strangeness *in* the strangeness. It's the wonder *of* the wonder." She spoke as with the softness almost of a sick child, yet now at last, at the end of all, with the perfect straightness of a sibyl. She visibly knew that she knew, and the effect on him was of something co-ordinate, in its high character, with the law that had ruled him. It was the true voice of the law; so on her lips would the law itself have sounded. "It *has* touched you," she went on. "It has done its office. It has made you all its own."

"So utterly without my knowing it?"

"So utterly without your knowing it." His hand, as he leaned to her, was on the arm of her chair, and, dimly smiling always now, she placed her own on it. "It's enough if *I* know it."

"Oh!" he confusedly breathed, as she herself of late so often had done.

"What I long ago said is true. You'll never know now, and I think you ought to be content. You've *had* it," said May Bartram.

"But had what?"

"Why what was to have marked you out. The proof of your law. It has acted. I'm too glad," she then bravely added, "to have been able to see what it's *not*."

He continued to attach his eyes to her, and with the sense that it was all beyond him, and that *she* was too, he would still have sharply challenged her hadn't he so felt it an abuse of her weakness to do more than take devoutly what she gave him, take it hushed as to a revelation. If he did speak, it was out of the foreknowledge of his loneliness to come. "If you're glad of what it's 'not' it might then have been worse?"

She turned her eyes away, she looked straight before her; with which after a moment: "Well, you know our fears."

He wondered. "It's something then we never feared?"

On this slowly she turned to him. "Did we ever dream, with all our dreams, that we should sit and talk of it thus?"

He tried for a little to make out that they had; but it was as if their dreams, numberless enough, were in solution in some thick cold mist through which thought lost itself. "It might have been that we couldn't talk?"

"Well"—she did her best for him—"not from this side. This, you see," she said, "is the *other* side."

"I think," poor Marcher returned, "that all sides are the same to me." Then, however, as she gently shook her head in correction: "We mightn't, as it were, have got across—?"

"To where we are—no. We're *here*"—she made her weak emphasis.

"And much good does it do us!" was her friend's frank comment.

"It does us the good it can. It does us the good that *it* isn't here. It's past. It's behind," said May Bartram. "Before—" but her voice dropped.

He had got up, not to tire her, but it was hard to combat his yearning. She after all told him nothing but that his light had failed—which he knew well enough without her. "Before—?" he blankly echoed.

"Before you see, it was always to *come*. That kept it present."

"Oh I don't care what comes now! Besides," Marcher added, "it seems to me I liked it better present, as you say, than I can like it absent with *your* absence."

"Oh mine!"—and her pale hands made light of it.

"With the absence of everything." He had a dreadful sense of standing there before her for—so far as anything but this proved, this bottomless drop was concerned—the last time of their life. It rested on him with a weight he felt he could scarce bear, and this weight it apparently was that still pressed out what remained in him of speakable protest. "I believe you; but I can't begin to pretend I understand. *Nothing*, for me, is past; nothing *will* pass till I pass myself, which I pray my stars may be as soon as possible. Say, however," he added, "that I've eaten my cake, as you contend, to the last crumb—how can the thing I've never felt at all be the thing I was marked out to feel?"

She met him perhaps less directly, but she met him unperturbed. "You take your 'feelings' for granted. You were to suffer your fate. That was not necessarily to know it."

"How in the world—when what is such knowledge but suffering?"

She looked up at him a while in silence. "No—you don't understand."

"I suffer," said John Marcher.

"Don't, don't!"

"How can I help at least *that*?"

"*Don't!*" May Bartram repeated.

She spoke it in a tone so special, in spite of her weakness, that he stared an instant—stared as if some light, hitherto hidden, had shimmered across his vision. Darkness again closed over it, but the gleam had already become for him an idea. "Because I haven't the right—?"

"Don't *know*—when you needn't," she mercifully urged. "You needn't—for we shouldn't."

"Shouldn't?" If he could but know what she meant!

"No—it's too much."

"Too much?" he still asked but with a mystification that was the next moment of a sudden to give way. Her words, if they meant something, affected him in this light—the light also of her wasted face—as meaning *all*, and the sense of what knowledge had been for herself came over him with a rush which broke through into a question. "Is it of that then you're dying?"

She but watched him, gravely at first, as to see, with this, where he was, and she might have seen something or feared something that moved her sympathy. "I would live for you still— if I could." Her eyes closed for a little, as if, withdrawn into herself, she were for a last time trying. "But I can't!" she said as she raised them again to take leave of him.

She couldn't indeed, as but too promptly and sharply appeared, and he had no vision of her after this that was anything but darkness and doom. They had parted for ever in that strange talk; access to her chamber of pain, rigidly guarded, was almost wholly forbidden him; he was feeling now moreover, in the face of doctors, nurses, the two or three relatives attracted doubtless by the presumption of what she had to "leave," how few were the rights, as they were called in such cases, that he had to put forward, and how odd it might even seem that their intimacy shouldn't have given him more of them. The stupidest fourth cousin had more, even though she had been nothing in such a person's life. She had been a feature of features in *his*, for what else was it to have been so indispensable? Strange beyond saying were the ways of existence, baffling for him the anomaly of his lack, as he felt it to be, of producible claim. A woman might have been, as it were, everything to him, and it might yet present him in no connexion that any one seemed held to recognise. If this was the case in these closing weeks it was the case more sharply on the occasion of the last offices rendered, in the great grey London cemetery, to what had been mortal, to what had been precious, in his friend. The concourse at her grave was not numerous, but he saw himself treated as scarce more nearly concerned with it than if there had been a thousand others. He was in short from this moment face to face with the fact that he was to profit extraordinarily little by the interest May Bartram had taken in him. He couldn't quite have said what he expected, but he hadn't surely expected this approach to a double privation. Not only had her interest failed him, but he seemed to feel himself unattended—and for a reason he couldn't seize—by the distinction, the dignity, the propriety, if nothing else, of the man markedly bereaved. It was as if, in the view of society he had not *been* markedly bereaved, as if there still failed some sign or proof of it, and as if none the less his character could never be affirmed nor the deficiency ever made up. There were moments as the weeks went by when he would have liked, by some almost aggressive act, to take his stand on the intimacy of his loss, in order that it *might* be questioned and his retort, to the relief of his spirit, so recorded; but the moments of an irritation more helpless followed fast on these, the moments during which, turning things over with a good conscience but with a bare horizon, he found himself wondering if he oughtn't to have begun, so to speak, further back.

He found himself wondering indeed at many things, and this last speculation had others to keep it company. What could he have done, after all, in her lifetime, without giving them both, as it were, away? He couldn't have made known she was watching him, for that would have published the superstition of the Beast. This was what closed his mouth now—now that the Jungle had been thrashed to vacancy and that the Beast had stolen away. It sounded too foolish and too flat; the difference for him in this particular, the extinction in his life of the element of suspense, was such as in fact to surprise him. He could scarce have said what the effect resembled; the abrupt cessation, the positive prohibition, of music perhaps, more than anything else, in some place all adjusted and all accustomed to sonority and to attention. If he could at any rate have conceived lifting the veil from his image at some moment of the past (what had he done, after all, if not lift it to *her*?) so to do this to-day, to talk to people at large of the Jungle cleared and confide to them that he now felt it as safe, would have been not only to see them listen as to a goodwife's tale, but really to hear himself tell one. What it presently came to in truth was that poor Marcher waded through his beaten grass, where no life stirred, where no breath sounded, where no evil eye seemed to gleam from a possible lair, very much as if vaguely looking for the Beast, and still more as if acutely missing it. He walked about in an existence that had grown strangely more spacious, and, stopping fitfully in places where the undergrowth of life struck him as closer, asked himself yearningly, wondered secretly and sorely, if it would have lurked here or there. It would have at all events *sprung*; what was at least complete was his belief in the truth itself of the assurance given him. The change from his old sense to his new was absolute and final: what was to happen *had* so absolutely and finally happened that he was as little able to know a fear for his future as to know a hope; so absent in short was any question of anything still to come. He was to live entirely with the other question, that of his unidentified past, that of his having to see his fortune impenetrably muffled and masked.

The torment of this vision became then his occupation; he couldn't perhaps have consented to live but for the possibility of guessing. She had told him, his friend, not to guess; she had forbidden him, so far as he might, to know, and she had even in a sort denied the power in him to learn: which were so many things, precisely, to deprive him of rest. It wasn't that he wanted, he argued for fairness, that anything past and done should repeat itself; it was only that he shouldn't, as an anticlimax, have been taken sleeping so sound as not to be able to win back by an effort of thought the lost stuff of consciousness. He declared to himself at moments that he would either win it back or have done with consciousness for ever; he made this idea his one motive in fine, made it so much his passion that none other, to compare with it, seemed ever to have touched him. The lost stuff of consciousness became thus for him as a strayed or stolen child to an unappeasable father; he hunted it up and down very much as if he were knocking at doors and enquiring of the police. This was the spirit in which, inevitably, he set himself to travel; he started on a journey that was to be as long as he could make it; it danced before him that, as the other side of the globe couldn't possibly have less to say to him, it might, by a possibility of suggestion, have more. Before he quitted London, however, he made a pilgrimage to May Bartram's grave, took his way to it through the endless avenues of the grim suburban metropolis, sought it out in the wilderness of tombs, and, though he had come but for the renewal of the act of farewell, found himself, when he had at last stood by it, beguiled into long intensities. He stood for an hour, powerless to turn away and yet powerless to penetrate the darkness of death; fixing with his eyes her inscribed name and date, beating his forehead against the fact of the secret they kept, drawing his breath, while he waited, as if some sense would in pity of him rise from the stones. He kneeled on the stones, however, in vain; they kept what they concealed; and if the face of the tomb did become a face for him it was because her two names became a pair of eyes that didn't know him. He gave them a last long look, but no palest light broke.

VI

He stayed away, after this, for a year; he visited the depths of Asia, spending himself on scenes of romantic interest, of superlative sanctity; but what was present to him everywhere was that for a man who had known what *he* had known the world was vulgar and vain. The state of mind in which he had lived for so many years shone out to him, in reflexion, as a light that coloured and refined, a light beside which the glow of the East was garish cheap and thin. The terrible truth was that he had lost—with everything else—a distinction as well; the things he saw couldn't help being common when he had become common to look at them. He was simply now one of them himself—he was in the dust, without a peg for the sense of difference; and there were hours when, before the temples of gods and the sepulchres of kings, his spirit turned for nobleness of association to the barely discriminated slab in the London suburb. That had become for him, and more intensely with time and distance, his one witness of a past glory. It was all that was left to him for proof or pride, yet the past glories of Pharaohs[1] were nothing to him as he thought of it. Small wonder then that he came back to it on the morrow of his return. He was drawn there this time as irresistibly as the other, yet with a confidence, almost, that was doubtless the effect of the many months that had elapsed. He had lived, in spite of himself, into his change of feeling, and in wandering over the earth had wandered, as might be said, from the circumference to the centre of his desert. He had settled to his safety and accepted perforce his extinction; figuring to himself, with some colour, in the like- ness of certain little old men he remembered to have seen, of whom, all meagre and wizened as they might look, it was related that they had in their time fought twenty duels or been loved by ten princesses. They indeed had been wondrous for others while he was but wondrous for himself; which, however, was exactly the cause of his haste to renew the wonder by getting back, as he might put it, into his own presence. That had quickened his steps and checked his delay. If his visit was prompt it was because he had been separated so long from the part of himself that alone he now valued.

It's accordingly not false to say that he reached his goal with a certain elation and stood there again with a certain assurance. The creature beneath the sod *knew* of his rare experience, so that, strangely now, the place had lost for him its mere blankness of expression. It met him in mildness—not, as before, in mockery; it wore for him the air of conscious greeting that we find, after absence, in things that have closely belonged to us and which seem to confess of themselves to the connexion. The plot of

---

1 Ancient Egyptian rulers.

ground, the graven tablet, the tended flowers affected him so as belonging to him that he resembled for the hour a contented landlord reviewing a piece of property. Whatever had happened— well, had happened. He had not come back this time with the vanity of that question, his former worrying "What, *what*?" now practically so spent. Yet he would none the less never again so cut himself off from the spot; he would come back to it every month, for if he did nothing else by its aid he at least held up his head. It thus grew for him, in the oddest way, a positive resource; he carried out his idea of periodical returns, which took their place at last among the most inveterate of his habits. What it all amounted to, oddly enough, was that in his finally so simplified world this garden of death gave him the few square feet of earth on which he could still most live. It was as if, being nothing anywhere else for any one, nothing even for himself, he were just everything here, and if not for a crowd of witnesses or indeed for any witness but John Marcher, then by clear right of the register that he could scan like an open page. The open page was the tomb of his friend, and *there* were the facts of the past, there the truth of his life, there the backward reaches in which he could lose himself. He did this from time to time with such effect that he seemed to wander through the old years with his hand in the arm of a companion who was, in the most extraordinary manner, his other, his younger self; and to wander, which was more extraordinary yet, round and round a third presence—not wandering she, but stationary, still, whose eyes, turning with his revolution, never ceased to follow him, and whose seat was his point, so to speak, of orientation. Thus in short he settled to live— feeding all on the sense that he once *had* lived, and dependent on it not alone for a support but for an identity.

It sufficed him in its way for months and the year elapsed; it would doubtless even have carried him further but for an accident, superficially slight, which moved him, quite in another direction, with a force beyond any of his impressions of Egypt or of India. It was a thing of the merest chance—the turn, as he afterwards felt, of a hair, though he was indeed to live to believe that if light hadn't come to him in this particular fashion it would still have come in another. He was to live to believe this, I say, though he was not to live, I may not less definitely mention, to do much else. We allow him at any rate the benefit of the conviction, struggling up for him at the end, that, whatever might have happened or not happened, he would have come round of himself to the light. The incident of an autumn day had put the match to the train laid from of old by his misery. With the light before him he knew that even of late his ache had only been smothered. It was strangely drugged, but it throbbed; at the touch it began to bleed. And the touch, in the event, was the face of a fellow mortal. This face, one grey afternoon when the leaves were thick in the alleys, looked into Marcher's own, at the cemetery, with an expression like the cut of a blade. He felt it, that is, so deep down that he winced at the steady thrust. The person who so mutely assaulted him was a figure he had noticed, on reaching his own goal, absorbed by a grave a short distance away, a grave apparently fresh, so that the emotion of the visitor would probably match it for frankness. This fact alone forbade further attention, though during the time he stayed he remained vaguely conscious of his neighbour, a middle-aged man apparently, in mourning, whose bowed back, among the clustered monuments and mortuary yews, was constantly presented. Marcher's theory that these were elements in contact with which he himself revived, had suffered, on this occasion, it may be granted, a marked, an excessive check. The autumn day was dire for him as none had recently been, and he rested with a heaviness he had not yet known on the low stone table that bore May Bartram's name. He rested without power to move, as if some spring in him, some spell vouchsafed, had suddenly been broken for ever. If he could have done that moment as he wanted he would simply have stretched himself on the slab that was ready to take him, treating it as a place prepared to receive his last sleep. What in all the wide world had he now to keep awake for? He stared before him with the question, and it was then that, as one of the cemetery walks passed near him, he caught the shock of the face.

His neighbour at the other grave had withdrawn, as he himself, with force enough in him, would have done by now, and was advancing along the path on his way to one of the gates. This brought him close, and his pace was slow, so that—and all the more as there was a kind of hunger in his look—the two men were for a minute directly confronted. Marcher knew him at once for one of the deeply stricken—a perception so sharp that nothing else in the picture comparatively lived, neither his dress, his age, nor his presumable character and class; nothing lived but the deep ravage of the features that he showed. He *showed* them—that was the point; he was moved, as he passed, by some impulse that was either a signal for sympathy or, more possibly, a challenge to an opposed sorrow. He might already have been aware of our friend, might at some previous hour have noticed in him the smooth habit of the scene, with which the state of his own senses so scantly consorted, and might thereby have been stirred as by an overt discord. What Marcher was at all events conscious of was in the first place that the image of scarred passion presented to him was conscious too— of something that profaned the air; and in the second that, roused, startled, shocked, he was yet the next moment looking after it, as it went, with envy. The most extraordinary thing that had happened to him—though he had given that name to other matters as well— took place, after his immediate vague stare, as a consequence of this impression. The stranger passed, but the raw glare of his grief remained, making our friend wonder in pity what wrong, what wound it expressed, what injury not to be healed. What had the man *had*, to make him by the loss of it so bleed and yet live?

Something—and this reached him with a pang—that *he*, John Marcher, hadn't; the proof of which was precisely John Marcher's arid end. No passion had ever touched him, for this was what passion meant; he had survived and maundered and pined, but where had been *his* deep ravage? The extraordinary thing we speak of was the sudden rush of the result of this question. The sight that had just met his eyes named to him, as in letters of quick flame, something he had utterly, insanely missed, and what he had missed made these things a train of fire, made them mark themselves in an anguish of inward throbs. He had seen *outside* of his life, not learned it within, the way a woman was mourned when she had been loved for herself: such was the force of his conviction of the meaning of the stranger's face, which still flared for him as a smoky torch. It hadn't come to him, the knowledge, on the wings of experience; it had brushed him, jostled him, upset him, with the disrespect of chance, the insolence of accident. Now that the illumination had begun, however, it blazed to the zenith, and what he presently stood there gazing at was the sounded void of his life. He gazed, he drew breath, in pain; he turned in his dismay, and, turning, he had before him in sharper incision than ever the open page of his story. The name on the table smote him as the passage of his neighbour had done, and what it said to him, full in the face, was that *she* was what he had missed. This was the awful thought, the answer to all the past, the vision at the dread clearness of which he turned as cold as the stone beneath him. Everything fell together, confessed, explained, overwhelmed; leaving him most of all stupefied at the blindness he had cherished. The fate he had been marked for he had met with a vengeance—he had emptied the cup to the lees; he had been the man of his time, *the* man, to whom nothing on earth was to have happened. That was the rare stroke—that was his visitation. So he saw it, as we say, in pale horror, while the pieces fitted and fitted. So *she* had seen it while he didn't, and so she served at this hour to drive the truth home. It was the truth, vivid and monstrous, that all the while he had waited the wait was itself his portion. This the companion of his vigil had at a given moment made out, and she had then offered him the chance to baffle his doom. One's doom, however, was never baffled, and on the day she told him his own had come down she had seen him but stupidly stare at the escape she offered him.

The escape would have been to love her; then, *then* he would have lived. *She* had lived—who could say now with what passion?—since she had loved him for himself; whereas he had never thought of her (ah how it hugely glared at him!) but in the chill of his egotism and the light of her use. Her spoken words came back to him—the chain stretched and stretched. The Beast had lurked indeed, and the Beast, at its hour, had sprung; it had sprung in that twilight of the cold April when, pale, ill, wasted, but all beautiful, and perhaps even then recoverable, she had risen from her chair to stand before him and let him imaginably guess. It had sprung as he didn't guess; it had sprung as she hopelessly turned from him, and the mark, by the time he left her, had fallen where it *was* to fall. He had justified his fear and achieved his fate; he had failed, with the last exactitude, of all he was to fail of; and a moan now rose to his lips as he remembered she had prayed he mightn't know. This horror of waking—*this* was knowledge, knowledge under the breath of which the very tears in his eyes seemed to freeze. Through them, none the less, he tried to fix it and hold it; he kept it there before him so that he might feel the pain. That at least, belated and bitter, had something of the taste of life. But the bitterness suddenly sickened him, and it was as if, horribly, he saw, in the truth, in the cruelty of his image, what had been appointed and done. He saw the Jungle of his life and saw the lurking Beast; then, while he looked, perceived it, as by a stir of the air, rise, huge and hideous, for the leap that was to settle him. His eyes darkened—it was close; and, instinctively turning, in his hallucination, to avoid it, he flung himself, face down, on the tomb.

THE JOLLY CORNER

I

"Every one asks me what I 'think' of everything," said Spencer Brydon; "and I make answer as I can—begging or dodging the question, putting them off with any nonsense. It wouldn't matter to any of them really," he went on, "for, even were it possible to meet in that stand-and-deliver way so silly a demand on so big a subject, my 'thoughts' would still be almost altogether about something that concerns only myself." He was talking to Miss Staverton, with whom for a couple of months now he had availed himself of every possible occasion to talk; this disposition and this resource, this comfort and support, as the situation in fact presented itself, having promptly enough taken the first place in the considerable array of rather unattenuated surprises attending his so strangely belated return to America. Everything was somehow a surprise; and that might be natural when one had so long and so consistently neglected everything, taken pains to give surprises so much margin for play. He had given them more than thirty years—thirty-three, to be exact; and they now seemed to him to have organised their performance quite on the scale of that licence. He had been twenty-three on leaving New York—he was fifty-six today: unless indeed he were to reckon as he had sometimes, since his repatriation, found himself feeling; in which case he would have lived longer than is often allotted to man. It would have taken a century, he repeatedly said to himself, and said also to Alice Staverton, it would have taken a longer absence and a more averted mind than those even of which he had been guilty, to pile up the differences, the newnesses, the queernesses, above all the bignesses, for the better or the worse, that at present assaulted his vision wherever he looked.

The great fact all the while however had been the incalculability; since he *had* supposed himself, from decade to decade, to be allowing, and in the most liberal and intelligent manner, for brilliancy of change. He actually saw that he had allowed for nothing; he missed what he would have been sure of finding, he found what he would never have imagined. Proportions and values were upside-down; the ugly things he had expected, the ugly things of his far-away youth, when he had too promptly waked up to a sense of the ugly—these uncanny phenomena placed him rather, as it happened, under the charm; whereas the "swagger" things, the modern, the monstrous, the famous things, those he had more particularly, like thousands of ingenuous enquirers every year, come over to see, were exactly his sources of dismay. They were as so many set traps for displeasure, above all for reaction, of which his restless tread was constantly pressing the spring. It was interesting, doubtless, the whole show, but it would have been too disconcerting hadn't a certain finer truth saved the situation. He had distinctly not, in this steadier light, come over *all* for the monstrosities; he had come, not only in the last analysis but quite on the face of the act, under an impulse with which they had nothing to do. He had come—putting the thing pompously—to look at his "property," which he had thus for a third of a century not been within four thousand miles of; or, expressing it less sordidly, he had yielded to the humour of seeing again his house on the jolly corner, as he usually, and quite fondly, described it—the one in which he had first seen the light, in which various members of his family had lived and had died, in which the holidays of his over-schooled boyhood had been passed and the few social flowers of his chilled adolescence gathered, and which, alienated then for so long a period, had, through the successive deaths of his two brothers and the termination of old arrangements, come wholly into his hands. He was the owner of another, not quite so "good"—the jolly corner having been, from far back, superlatively extended and consecrated; and the value of the pair represented his main capital, with an income consisting, in these later years, of their respective rents which (thanks precisely to their original excellent type) had never been depressingly low. He could live in "Europe," as he had been in the habit of living, on the product of these flourishing New York leases, and all the better since, that of the second structure, the mere number in its long row, having within a twelvemonth fallen in, renovation at a high advance had proved beautifully possible.

These were items of property indeed, but he had found himself since his arrival distinguishing more than ever between them. The house within the street, two bristling blocks westward, was already in course of reconstruction as a tall mass of flats; he had acceded, some time before, to overtures for this conversion— in which, now that it was going forward, it had been not the least of his astonishments to find himself able, on the spot, and though without a previous ounce of such experience, to participate with a certain intelligence, almost with a certain authority. He had lived his life with his back so turned to such concerns and his face addressed to those of so different an order that he scarce knew what to make of this lively stir, in a compartment of his mind never yet penetrated, of a capacity for business and a sense for construction. These virtues, so common all round him now, had been dormant in his own organism—where it might be said of them perhaps that they had slept the sleep of the just. At present, in the splendid autumn weather—the autumn at least was a pure boon in the terrible place—he loafed about his "work" undeterred, secretly agitated; not in the least "minding" that the whole proposition, as they said, was vulgar and sordid, and ready to climb ladders, to walk the plank, to handle materials and look wise about them, to ask questions, in fine, and challenge explanations and really "go into" figures.

It amused, it verily quite charmed him; and, by the same stroke, it amused, and even more, Alice Staverton, though perhaps charming her perceptibly less. She wasn't however going to be better off for it, as *he* was—and so astonishingly much: nothing was now likely, he knew, ever to make her better-off than she found herself, in the afternoon of life, as the delicately frugal possessor and tenant of the small house in Irving Place to which she had subtly managed to cling through her almost unbroken New York career. If he knew the way to it now better than to any other address among the dreadful multiplied numberings which seemed to him to reduce the whole place to some vast ledger-page, overgrown, fantastic, of ruled and criss-crossed lines and figures—if he had formed, for his consolation, that habit, it was really not a little because of the charm of his having encountered and recognised, in the vast wilderness of the wholesale, breaking through the mere gross generalisation of wealth and force and success, a small still scene where items and shades, all delicate things, kept the sharpness of the notes of a high voice perfectly trained, and where economy hung about like the scent of a garden. His old friend lived with one maid and herself dusted her relics and trimmed her lamps and polished her silver; she stood off, in the awful modern crush, when she could, but she sallied forth and did battle when the challenge was really to "spirit," the spirit she after all confessed to, proudly and a little shyly, as to that of the better time, that of *their* common, their quite far-away and antediluvian social period and order. She made use of the street-cars when need be, the terrible things that people scrambled for as the panic-stricken at sea scramble for the boats; she affronted, inscrutably, under stress, all the public concussions and ordeals; and yet, with that slim mystifying grace of her appearance, which defied you to say if she were a fair young woman who looked older through trouble, or a fine smooth older one who looked young through successful indifference; with her precious reference, above all, to memories and histories into which he could enter, she was as exquisite for him as some pale pressed flower (a rarity to begin with), and, failing other sweetnesses, she was a sufficient reward of his effort. They had communities of knowledge, "their" knowledge (this discriminating possessive was always on her lips) of presences of the other age, presences all over laid, in his case, by the experience of a man and the freedom of a wanderer, overlaid by pleasure, by infidelity, by passages of life that were strange and dim to her, just by "Europe" in short, but still unobscured, still exposed and cherished, under that pious visitation of the spirit from which she had never been diverted.

She had come with him one day to see how his "apartment-house" was rising; he had helped her over gaps and explained to her plans, and while they were there had happened to have, before her, a brief but lively discussion with the man in charge, the representative of the building-firm that had undertaken his work. He had found himself quite "standing-up" to this personage over a failure on the latter's part to observe some detail of one of their noted conditions, and had so lucidly urged his case that, besides ever so prettily flushing, at the time, for sympathy in his triumph, she had afterwards said to him (though to a slightly greater effect of irony) that he had clearly for too many years neglected a real gift. If he had but stayed at home he would have anticipated the inventor of the skyscraper. If he had but stayed at home he would have discovered his genius in time really to start some new variety of awful architectural hare and run it till it burrowed in a gold-mine. He was to remember these words, while the weeks elapsed, for the small silver ring they had sounded over the queerest and deepest of his own lately most disguised and most muffled vibrations.

It had begun to be present to him after the first fortnight, it had broken out with the oddest abruptness, this particular wanton wonderment: it met him there—and this was the image under which he himself judged the matter, or at least, not a little, thrilled and flushed with it—very much as he might have been met by some strange figure, some unexpected occupant, at a turn of one of the dim passages of an empty house. The quaint analogy quite hauntingly remained with him, when he didn't indeed rather improve it by a still intenser form: that of his opening a door behind which he would have made sure of finding nothing, a door into a room shuttered and void, and yet so coming, with a great suppressed start, on some quite erect confronting presence, something planted in the middle of the place and facing him through the dusk. After that visit to the house in construction he walked with his companion to see the other and always so much the better one, which in the eastward direction formed one of the corners, the "jolly" one precisely, of the street now so generally dishonoured and disfigured in its westward reaches, and of the comparatively conservative Avenue. The Avenue still had pretensions, as Miss Staverton said, to decency; the old people had mostly gone, the old names were unknown, and here and there an old association seemed to stray, all vaguely, like some very aged person, out too late, whom you might meet and feel the impulse to watch or follow, in kindness, for safe restoration to shelter.

They went in together, our friends; he admitted himself with his key, as he kept no one there, he explained, preferring, for his reasons, to leave the place empty, under a simple arrangement with a good woman living in the neighbourhood and who came for a daily hour to open windows and dust and sweep. Spencer Brydon had his reasons and was growingly aware of them; they seemed to him better each time he was there, though he didn't name them all to his companion, any more than he told her as yet how often, how quite absurdly often, he himself came. He only let her see for the present, while they walked through the great blank rooms, that absolute vacancy reigned and that, from top to bottom, there was nothing but Mrs. Muldoon's broomstick, in a corner, to tempt the burglar. Mrs. Muldoon was then on the premises, and she loquaciously attended the visitors, preceding them from room to room and pushing back shutters and throwing up sashes—all to show them, as she remarked, how little there was to see. There was little indeed to see in the great gaunt shell where the main dispositions and the general apportionment of space, the style of an age of ampler allowances, had nevertheless for its master their honest pleading message, affecting him as some good old servant's, some lifelong retainer's appeal for a character, or even for a retiring-pension; yet it was also a remark of Mrs. Muldoon's that, glad as she was to oblige him by her noonday round, there was a request she greatly hoped he would never make of her. If he should wish her for any reason to come in after dark she would just tell him, if he "plased," that he must ask it of somebody else.

The fact that there was nothing to see didn't militate for the worthy woman against what one *might* see, and she put it frankly to Miss Staverton that no lady could be expected to like, could she? "craping up to thim top storeys in the ayvil hours." The gas and the electric light were off the house, and she fairly evoked a gruesome vision of her march through the great grey rooms—so many of them as there were too!—with her glimmering taper. Miss Staverton met her honest glare with a smile and the profession that she herself certainly would recoil from such an adventure. Spencer Brydon meanwhile held his peace—for the moment; the question of the "evil" hours in his old home had already become too grave for him. He had begun some time since to "crape," and he knew just why a packet of candles addressed to that pursuit had been stowed by his own hand three weeks before, at the back of a drawer of the fine old sideboard that occupied, as a "fixture," the deep recess in the dining-room. Just now he laughed at his companions—quickly however changing the subject; for the reason that, in the first place, his laugh struck him even at that moment as starting the odd echo, the conscious human resonance (he scarce knew how to qualify it) that sounds made while he was there alone sent back to his ear or his fancy; and that, in the second, he imagined Alice Staverton for the instant on the point of asking him, with a divination, if he ever so prowled. There were divinations he was unprepared for, and he had at all events averted enquiry by the time Mrs. Muldoon had left them, passing on to other parts.

There was happily enough to say, on so consecrated a spot, that could be said freely and fairly; so that a whole train of declarations was precipitated by his friend's having herself broken out, after a yearning look round: "But I hope you don't mean they want you to pull *this* to pieces!" His answer came, promptly, with his re-awakened wrath: it was of course exactly what they wanted, and what they were "at" him for, daily, with the iteration of people who couldn't for their life understand a man's liability to decent feelings. He had found the place, just as it stood and beyond what he could express, an interest and a joy. There were values other than the beastly rent-values, and in short, in short—! But it was thus Miss Staverton took him up. "In short you're to make so good a thing of your sky-scraper that, living in luxury on *those* ill-gotten gains, you can afford for a while to be sentimental here!" Her smile had for him, with the words, the particular mild irony with which he found half her talk suffused; an irony without bitterness and that came, exactly, from her having so much imagination—not, like the cheap sarcasms with which one heard most people, about the world of "society," bid for the reputation of cleverness, from nobody's really having any. It was agreeable to him at this very moment to be sure that when he had answered, after a brief demur, "Well yes: so, precisely, you may put it!" her imagination would still do him justice. He explained that even if never a dollar were to come to him from the other house he would nevertheless cherish this one; and he dwelt, further, while they lingered and wandered, on the fact of the stupefaction he was already exciting, the positive mystification he felt himself create.

He spoke of the value of all he read into it, into the mere sight of the walls, mere shapes of the rooms, mere sound of the floors, mere feel, in his hand, of the old silver-plated knobs of the several mahogany doors, which suggested the pressure of the palms of the dead; the seventy years of the past in fine that these things represented, the annals of nearly three generations, counting his grandfather's, the one that had ended there, and the impalpable ashes of his long-extinct youth, afloat in the very air like microscopic motes. She listened to everything; she was a woman who answered intimately but who utterly didn't chatter. She scattered abroad therefore no cloud of words; she could assent, she could agree, above all she could encourage, without doing that. Only at the last she went a little further than he had done himself. "And then how do you know? You may still, after all, want to live here." It rather indeed pulled him up, for it wasn't what he had been thinking, at least in her sense of the words. "You mean I may decide to stay on for the sake of it?"

"Well, *with* such a home—!" But, quite beautifully, she had too much tact to dot so monstrous an *i*, and it was precisely an illustration of the way she didn't rattle. How could any one—of any wit—insist on any one else's "wanting" to live in New York?

"Oh," he said, "I *might* have lived here (since I had my opportunity early in life); I might have put in here all these years. Then everything would have been different enough—and, I dare say, 'funny' enough. But that's another matter. And then the beauty of it—I mean of my perversity, of my refusal to agree to a 'deal'— is just in the total absence of a reason. Don't you see that if I had a reason about the matter at all it would *have* to be the other way, and would then be inevitably a reason of dollars? There are no reasons here *but* of dollars. Let us therefore have none whatever— not the ghost of one."

They were back in the hall then for departure, but from where they stood the vista was large, through an open door, into the great square main saloon, with its almost antique felicity of brave spaces between windows. Her eyes came back from that reach and met his own a moment. "Are you very sure the 'ghost' of one doesn't, much rather, serve—?"

He had a positive sense of turning pale. But it was as near as they were then to come. For he made answer, he believed, between a glare and a grin: "Oh ghosts—of course the place must swarm with them! I should be ashamed of it if it didn't. Poor Mrs. Muldoon's right, and it's why I haven't asked her to do more than look in."

Miss Staverton's gaze again lost itself, and things she didn't utter, it was clear, came and went in her mind. She might even for the minute, off there in the fine room, have imagined some element dimly gathering. Simplified like the death-mask of a handsome face, it perhaps produced for her just then an effect akin to the stir of an expression in the "set" commemorative plaster. Yet whatever her impression may have been she produced instead a vague platitude. "Well, if it were only furnished and lived in—!"

She appeared to imply that in case of its being still furnished he might have been a little less opposed to the idea of a return. But she passed straight into the vestibule, as if to leave her words behind her, and the next moment he had opened the house-door and was standing with her on the steps. He closed the door and, while he re-pocketed his key, looking up and down, they took in the comparatively harsh actuality of the Avenue, which reminded him of the assault of the outer light of the Desert on the traveller emerging from an Egyptian tomb. But he risked before they stepped into the street his gathered answer to her speech. "For me it *is* lived in. For me it *is* furnished." At which it was easy for her to sigh "Ah yes—!" all vaguely and discreetly; since his parents and his favourite sister, to say nothing of other kin, in numbers, had run their course and met their end there. That represented, within the walls, ineffaceable life.

It was a few days after this that, during an hour passed with her again, he had expressed his impatience of the too flattering curiosity—among the people he met—about his appreciation of New York. He had arrived at none at all that was socially producible, and as for that matter of his "thinking" (thinking the better or the worse of anything there) he was wholly taken up with one subject of thought. It was mere vain egoism, and it was moreover, if she liked, a morbid obsession. He found all things come back to the question of what he personally might have been, how he might have led his life and "turned out," if he had not so, at the outset, given it up. And confessing for the first time to the intensity within him of this absurd speculation—which but proved also, no doubt, the habit of too selfishly thinking—he affirmed the impotence there of any other source of interest, any other native appeal. "What would it have made of me, what would it have made of me? I keep for ever wondering, all idiotically; as if I could possibly know! I see what it has made of dozens of others, those I meet, and it positively aches within me, to the point of exasperation, that it would have made something of me as well. Only I can't make out *what*, and the worry of it, the small rage of curiosity never to be satisfied, brings back what I remember to have felt, once or twice, after judging best, for reasons, to burn some important letter unopened. I've been sorry, I've hated it—I've never known what was in the letter. You may of course say it's a trifle—!"

"I don't say it's a trifle," Miss Staverton gravely interrupted.

She was seated by her fire, and before her, on his feet and restless, he turned to and fro between this intensity of his idea and a fitful and unseeing inspection, through his single eye-glass, of the dear little old objects on her chimney-piece. Her interruption made him for an instant look at her harder. "I shouldn't care if you did!" he laughed, however; "and it's only a figure, at any rate, for the way I now feel. *Not* to have followed my perverse young course—and almost in the teeth of my father's curse, as I may say; not to have kept it up, so, 'over there,' from that day to this, without a doubt or a pang; not, above all, to have liked it, to have loved it, so much, loved it, no doubt, with such an abysmal conceit of my own preference: some variation from *that*, I say, must have produced some different effect for my life and for my 'form.' I should have stuck here—if it had been possible; and I was too young, at twenty-three, to judge, *pour deux sous*,[1] whether it *were* possible. If I had waited I might have seen it was, and then I might have been, by staying here, something nearer to one of these types who have been hammered so hard and made so keen by their conditions. It isn't that I admire them so much—the question of any charm in them, or of any charm, beyond that of the rank money-passion, exerted by their conditions *for* them, has nothing to do with the matter: it's only a question of what fantastic, yet perfectly possible, development of my own nature I mayn't have missed. It comes over me that I had then a strange

---

1 For two cents (French).

alter ego[1] deep down somewhere within me, as the full-blown flower is in the small tight bud, and that I just took the course, I just transferred him to the climate, that blighted him for once and for ever."

"And you wonder about the flower," Miss Staverton said. "So do I, if you want to know; and so I've been wondering these several weeks. I believe in the flower," she continued, "I feel it would have been quite splendid, quite huge and monstrous."

"Monstrous above all!" her visitor echoed; "and I imagine, by the same stroke, quite hideous and offensive."

"You don't believe that," she returned; "if you did you wouldn't wonder. You'd know, and that would be enough for you. What you feel—and what I feel *for* you—is that you'd have had power."

"You'd have liked me that way?" he asked.

She barely hung fire. "How should I not have liked you?"

"I see. You'd have liked me, have preferred me, a billionaire!"

"How should I not have liked you?" she simply again asked.

He stood before her still—her question kept him motionless. He took it in, so much there was of it; and indeed his not otherwise meeting it testified to that. "I know at least what I am," he simply went on; "the other side of the medal's clear enough. I've not been edifying—I believe I'm thought in a hundred quarters to have been barely decent. I've followed strange paths and worshipped strange gods; it must have come to you again and again—in fact you've admitted to me as much—that I was leading, at any time these thirty years, a selfish frivolous scandalous life. And you see what it has made of me."

She just waited, smiling at him. "You see what it has made of *me*."

"Oh you're a person whom nothing can have altered. You were born to be what you are, anywhere, anyway: you've the perfection nothing else could have blighted. And don't you see how, without my exile, I shouldn't have been waiting till now—?" But he pulled up for the strange pang.

"The great thing to see," she presently said, "seems to me to be that it has spoiled nothing. It hasn't spoiled your being here at last. It hasn't spoiled this. It hasn't spoiled your speaking—" She also however faltered.

He wondered at everything her controlled emotion might mean. "Do you believe then—too dreadfully!—that I *am* as good as I might ever have been?"

---

1 Other self (Latin).

"Oh no! Far from it!" With which she got up from her chair and was nearer to him. "But I don't care," she smiled.

"You mean I'm good enough?"

She considered a little. "Will you believe it if I say so? I mean will you let that settle your question for you?" And then as if making out in his face that he drew back from this, that he had some idea which, however absurd, he couldn't yet bargain away: "Oh you don't care either—but very differently: you don't care for anything but yourself."

Spencer Brydon recognised it—it was in fact what he had absolutely professed. Yet he importantly qualified. "*He* isn't myself. He's the just so totally other person. But I do want to see him," he added. "And I can. And I shall."

Their eyes met for a minute while he guessed from something in hers that she divined his strange sense. But neither of them otherwise expressed it, and her apparent understanding, with no protesting shock, no easy derision, touched him more deeply than anything yet, constituting for his stifled perversity, on the spot, an element that was like breatheable air. What she said however was unexpected. "Well, *I've* seen him."

"You—?"

"I've seen him in a dream."

"Oh a 'dream'—!" It let him down.

"But twice over," she continued. "I saw him as I see you now."

"You've dreamed the same dream—?"

"Twice over," she repeated. "The very same."

This did somehow a little speak to him, as it also gratified him. "You dream about me at that rate?"

"Ah about *him*!" she smiled.

His eyes again sounded her. "Then you know all about him." And as she said nothing more: "What's the wretch like?"

She hesitated, and it was as if he were pressing her so hard that, resisting for reasons of her own, she had to turn away. "I'll tell you some other time!"

II

It was after this that there was most of a virtue for him, most of a cultivated charm, most of a preposterous secret thrill, in the particular form of surrender to his obsession and of address to what he more and more believed to be his privilege. It was what in these weeks he was living for—since he really felt life to begin but after Mrs. Muldoon had retired from the scene and, visiting the ample house from attic to cellar, making sure he was alone, he knew himself in safe possession and, as he tacitly expressed it, let himself go. He sometimes came twice in the twenty-four hours; the moments he liked best were those of gathering dusk, of the short autumn twilight; this was the time of which, again and again, he found himself hoping most. Then he could, as seemed to him, most intimately wander and wait, linger and listen, feel his fine attention, never in his life before so fine, on the pulse of the great vague place: he preferred the lampless hour and only wished he might have prolonged each day the deep crepuscular spell. Later—rarely much before midnight, but then for a considerable vigil—he watched with his glimmering light; moving slowly, holding it high, playing it far, rejoicing above all, as much as he might, in open vistas, reaches of communication between rooms and by passages; the long straight chance or show, as he would have called it, for the revelation he pretended to invite. It was practice he found he could perfectly "work" without exciting remark; no one was in the least the wiser for it; even Alice Staverton, who was moreover a well of discretion, didn't quite fully imagine.

He let himself in and let himself out with the assurance of calm proprietorship; and accident so far favoured him that, if a fat Avenue "officer" had happened on occasion to see him entering at eleven-thirty, he had never yet, to the best of his belief, been noticed as emerging at two. He walked there on the crisp November nights, arrived regularly at the evening's end; it was as easy to do this after dining out as to take his way to a club or to his hotel. When he left his club, if he hadn't been dining out, it was ostensibly to go to his hotel; and when he left his hotel, if he had spent a part of the evening there, it was ostensibly to go to his club. Everything was easy in fine; everything conspired and promoted: there was truly even in the strain of his experience something that glossed over, something that salved and simplified, all the rest of consciousness. He circulated, talked, renewed, loosely and pleasantly, old relations—met indeed, so far as he could, new expectations and seemed to make out on the whole that in spite of the career, of such different contacts, which he had spoken of to Miss Staverton as ministering so little, for those who might have watched it, to edification, he was positively rather liked than not. He was a dim secondary social success—and all with people who had truly not an idea of him. It was all mere surface sound, this murmur of their welcome, this popping of their corks—just as his gestures of response were the extravagant shadows, emphatic in proportion as they meant little, of some game of *ombres chinoises*.[1] He projected himself all day, in thought, straight over the bristling line of hard unconscious heads and into the other, the real, the waiting life; the life that, as soon as he had heard behind him the click of his great house-door, began for him, on the jolly corner, as beguilingly as the slow opening bars of some rich music follows the tap of the conductor's wand.

He always caught the first effect of the steel point of his stick on the old marble of the hall pavement, large black-and-white squares that he remembered as the admiration of his childhood and that had then made in him, as he now saw, for the growth of an early conception of style. This effect was the dim reverberating tinkle as of some far-off bell hung who should say where?— in the depths of the house, of the past, of that mystical other world that might have flourished for him had he not, for weal or woe, abandoned it. On this impression he did ever the same thing; he put his stick noiselessly away in a corner—feeling the place once more in the likeness of some great glass bowl, all precious concave crystal, set delicately humming by the play of a moist finger round its edge. The concave crystal held, as it were, this mystical other world, and the indescribably fine murmur of its rim was the sigh there, the scarce audible pathetic wail to his strained ear, of all the old baffled forsworn possibilities. What he did therefore by this appeal of his hushed presence was to wake them into such measure of ghostly life as they might still enjoy. They were shy, all but unappeasably shy, but they weren't really sinister; at least they weren't as he had hitherto felt them—before they had taken the Form he so yearned to make them take, the Form he at moments saw himself in the light of fairly hunting on tiptoe, the points of his evening shoes, from room to room and from storey to storey.

That was the essence of his vision—which was all rank folly, if one would, while he was out of the house and otherwise occupied, but which took on the last verisimilitude as soon as he was placed and posted. He knew what he meant and what he wanted; it was as clear as the figure on a cheque presented in demand for cash. His *alter ego* "walked"—that was the note of his image of him, while his image of his motive for his own odd pastime was the desire to waylay him and meet him. He roamed, slowly, warily, but all restlessly, he himself did—Mrs. Muldoon had been

---

1   Literally, Chinese shadows; shadow play (French).

right, absolutely, with her figure of their "craping"; and the presence he watched for would roam restlessly too. But it would be as cautious and as shifty; the conviction of its probable, in fact its already quite sensible, quite audible evasion of pursuit grew for him from night to night, laying on him finally a rigour to which nothing in his life had been comparable. It had been the theory of many superficially-judging persons, he knew, that he was wasting that life in a surrender to sensations, but he had tasted of no pleasure so fine as his actual tension, had been introduced to no sport that demanded at once the patience and the nerve of this stalking of a creature more subtle, yet at bay perhaps more formidable, than any beast of the forest. The terms, the comparisons, the very practices of the chase positively came again into play; there were even moments when passages of his occasional experience as a sportsman, stirred memories, from his younger time, of moor and mountain and desert, revived for him—and to the increase of his keenness—by the tremendous force of analogy. He found himself at moments—once he had placed his single light on some mantel-shelf or in some recess—stepping back into shelter or shade, effacing himself behind a door or in an embrasure, as he had sought of old the vantage of rock and tree; he found himself holding his breath and living in the joy of the instant, the supreme suspense created by big game alone.

He wasn't afraid (though putting himself the question as he believed gentlemen on Bengal tiger-shoots[1] or in close quarters with the great bear of the Rockies had been known to confess to having put it); and this indeed—since here at least he might be frank!—because of the impression, so intimate and so strange, that he himself produced as yet a dread, produced certainly a strain, beyond the liveliest he was likely to feel. They fell for him into categories, they fairly became familiar, the signs, for his own perception, of the alarm his presence and his vigilance created; though leaving him always to remark, portentously, on his probably having formed a relation, his probably enjoying a consciousness, unique in the experience of man. People enough, first and last, had been in terror of apparitions, but who had ever before so turned the tables and become himself, in the apparitional world, an incalculable terror? He might have found this sublime had he quite dared to think of it; but he didn't too much insist, truly, on that side of his privilege. With habit and repetition he gained to an extraordinary degree the power to penetrate the dusk of dis-

---

1 Hunts for a tiger found primarily in India and other parts of south Asia.

tances and the darkness of corners, to resolve back into their innocence the treacheries of uncertain light, the evil-looking forms taken in the gloom by mere shadows, by accidents of the air, by shifting effects of perspective; putting down his dim luminary he could still wander on without it, pass into other rooms and, only knowing it was there behind him in case of need, see his way about, visually project for his purpose a comparative clearness. It made him feel, this acquired faculty, like some monstrous stealthy cat; he wondered if he would have glared at these moments with large shining yellow eyes, and what it mightn't verily be, for the poor hard-pressed *alter ego*, to be confronted with such a type.

He liked however the open shutters; he opened everywhere those Mrs. Muldoon had closed, closing them as carefully afterwards, so that she shouldn't notice: he liked—oh this he did like, and above all in the upper rooms!—the sense of the hard silver of the autumn stars through the window-panes, and scarcely less the flare of the street-lamps below, the white electric lustre which it would have taken curtains to keep out. This was human actual social; this was of the world he had lived in, and he was more at his ease certainly for the countenance, coldly general and impersonal, that all the while and in spite of his detachment it seemed to give him. He had support of course mostly in the rooms at the wide front and the prolonged side; it failed him considerably in the central shades and the parts at the back. But if he sometimes, on his rounds, was glad of his optical reach, so none the less often the rear of the house affected him as the very jungle of his prey. The place was there more subdivided; a large "extension" in particular, where small rooms for servants had been multiplied abounded in nooks and corners, in closets and passages, in the ramifications especially of an ample back staircase over which he leaned, many a time, to look far down—not deterred from his gravity even while aware that he might, for a spectator, have figured some solemn simpleton playing at hide-and-seek. Outside in fact he might himself make that ironic *rapprochement*;[1] but within the walls, and in spite of the clear windows, his consistency was proof against the cynical light of New York.

It had belonged to that idea of the exasperated consciousness of his victim to become a real test for him; since he had quite put it to himself from the first that, oh distinctly! he could "cultivate" his whole perception. He had felt it as above all open to cultiva-

---

1 Comparison or parallel (French).

tion—which indeed was but another name for his manner of spending his time. He was bringing it on, bringing it to perfection, by practice; in consequence of which it had grown so fine that he was now aware of impressions, attestations of his general postulate, that couldn't have broken upon him at once. This was the case more specifically with a phenomenon at last quite frequent for him in the upper rooms, the recognition—absolutely unmistakeable, and by a turn dating from a particular hour, his resumption of his campaign after a diplomatic drop, a calculated absence of three nights—of his being definitely followed, tracked at a distance carefully taken and to the express end that he should the less confidently, less arrogantly, appear to himself merely to pursue. It worried, it finally quite broke him up, for it proved, of all the conceivable impressions, the one least suited to his book. He was kept in sight while remaining himself—as regards the essence of his position—sightless, and his only recourse then was in abrupt turns, rapid recoveries of ground. He wheeled about, retracing his steps, as if he might so catch in his face at least the stirred air of some other quick revolution. It was indeed true that his fully dislocalised thought of these manoeuvres recalled to him Pantaloon, at the Christmas farce, buffeted and tricked from behind by ubiquitous Harlequin;[1] but it left intact the influence of the conditions themselves each time he was re-exposed to them, so that in fact this association, had he suffered it to become constant, would on a certain side have but ministered to his intenser gravity. He had made, as I have said, to create on the premises the baseless sense of a reprieve, his three absences; and the result of the third was to confirm the after-effect of the second.

On his return, that night—the night succeeding his last intermission—he stood in the hall and looked up the staircase with a certainty more intimate than any he had yet known. "He's *there*, at the top, and waiting—not, as in general, falling back for disappearance. He's holding his ground, and it's the first time—which is a proof, isn't it? that something has happened for him." So Brydon argued with his hand on the banister and his foot on the lowest stair; in which position he felt as never before the air chilled by his logic. He himself turned cold in it, for he seemed

---

1 Pantaloon and Harlequin are traditional stock characters in improvisational theater, such as the Italian *commedia dell'arte*; Harlequin is often a mischievous servant, while Pantaloon is frequently an older rich man known for greediness.

of a sudden to know what now was involved. "Harder pressed?—yes, he takes it in, with its thus making clear to him that I've come, as they say, 'to stay.' He finally doesn't like and can't bear it, in the sense, I mean, that his wrath, his menaced interest, now balances with his dread. I've hunted him till he has 'turned': that, up there, is what has happened—he's the fanged or the antlered animal brought at last to bay." There came to him, as I say—but determined by an influence beyond my notation!—the acuteness of this certainty; under which however the next moment he had broken into a sweat that he would as little have consented to attribute to fear as he would have dared immediately to act upon it for enterprise. It marked none the less a prodigious thrill, a thrill that represented sudden dismay, no doubt, but also represented, and with the selfsame throb, the strangest, the most joyous, possibly the next minute almost the proudest, duplication of consciousness.

"He has been dodging, retreating, hiding, but now, worked up to anger, he'll fight!"—this intense impression made a single mouthful, as it were, of terror and applause. But what was wondrous was that the applause, for the felt fact, was so eager, since, if it was his other self he was running to earth, this ineffable identity was thus in the last resort not unworthy of him. It bristled there—somewhere near at hand, however unseen still—as the hunted thing, even as the trodden worm of the adage *must* at last bristle; and Brydon at this instant tasted probably of a sensation more complex than had ever before found itself consistent with sanity. It was as if it would have shamed him that a character so associated with his own should triumphantly succeed in just skulking, should to the end not risk the open, so that the drop of this danger was, on the spot, a great lift of the whole situation. Yet with another rare shift of the same subtlety he was already trying to measure by how much more he himself might now be in peril of fear; so rejoicing that he could, in another form, actively inspire that fear, and simultaneously quaking for the form in which he might passively know it.

The apprehension of knowing it must after a little have grown in him, and the strangest moment of his adventure perhaps, the most memorable or really most interesting, afterwards, of his crisis, was the lapse of certain instants of concentrated conscious *combat*, the sense of a need to hold on to something, even after the manner of a man slipping and slipping on some awful incline; the vivid impulse, above all, to move, to act, to charge, somehow and upon something—to show himself, in a word, that he wasn't afraid. The state of "holding-on" was thus the state to which he was momentarily reduced; if there had been anything, in the great vacancy, to seize, he would presently have been aware of having clutched it as he might under a shock at home have clutched the nearest chair-back. He had been surprised at any rate—of this he was aware—into something unprecedented since his original appropriation of the place; he had closed his eyes, held them tight, for a long minute, as with that instinct of dismay and that terror of vision. When he opened them the room, the other contiguous rooms, extraordinarily, seemed lighter—so light, almost, that at first he took the change for day. He stood firm, however that might be, just where he had paused; his resistance had helped him—it was as if there were something he had tided over. He knew after a little what this was—it had been in the imminent danger of flight. He had stiffened his will against going; without this he would have made for the stairs, and it seemed to him that, still with his eyes closed, he would have descended them, would have known how, straight and swiftly, to the bottom.

Well, as he had held out, here he was—still at the top, among the more intricate upper rooms and with the gauntlet of the others, of all the rest of the house, still to run when it should be his time to go. He would go at his time—only at his time: didn't he go every night very much at the same hour? He took out his watch—there was light for that: it was scarcely a quarter past one, and he had never withdrawn so soon. He reached his lodgings for the most part at two—with his walk of a quarter of an hour. He would wait for the last quarter—he wouldn't stir till then; and he kept his watch there with his eyes on it, reflecting while he held it that this deliberate wait, a wait with an effort, which he recognised, would serve perfectly for the attestation he desired to make. It would prove his courage—unless indeed the latter might most be proved by his budging at last from his place. What he mainly felt now was that, since he hadn't originally scuttled, he had his dignities—which had never in his life seemed so many—all to preserve and to carry aloft. This was before him in truth as a physical image, an image almost worthy of an age of greater romance. That remark indeed glimmered for him only to glow the next instant with a finer light; since what age of romance, after all, could have matched either the state of his mind or, "objectively," as they said, the wonder of his situation? The only difference would have been that, brandishing his dignities over his head as in a parchment scroll, he might then—that is in the heroic time—have proceeded downstairs with a drawn sword in his other grasp.

At present, really, the light he had set down on the mantel of the next room would have to figure his sword; which utensil, in the course of a minute, he had taken the requisite number of steps to possess himself of. The door between the rooms was open, and from the second another door opened to a third. These rooms, as he remembered, gave all three upon a common corridor as well, but there was a fourth, beyond them, without issue save through the preceding. To have moved, to have heard his step again, was appreciably a help; though even in recognising this he lingered once more a little by the chimney-piece on which his light had rested. When he next moved, just hesitating where to turn, he found himself considering a circumstance that, after his first and comparatively vague apprehension of it, produced in him the start that often attends some pang of recollection, the violent shock of having ceased happily to forget. He had come into sight of the door in which the brief chain of communication ended and which he now surveyed from the nearer threshold, the one not directly facing it. Placed at some distance to the left of this point, it would have admitted him to the last room of the four, the room without other approach or egress, had it not, to his intimate conviction, been closed *since* his former visitation, the matter probably of a quarter of an hour before. He stared with all his eyes at the wonder of the fact, arrested again where he stood and again holding his breath while he sounded its sense. Surely it had been *subsequently* closed—that is it had been on his previous passage indubitably open!

He took it full in the face that something had happened between—that he couldn't not have noticed before (by which he meant on his original tour of all the rooms that evening) that such a barrier had exceptionally presented itself. He had indeed since that moment undergone an agitation so extraordinary that it might have muddled for him any earlier view; and he tried to convince himself that he might perhaps then have gone into the room and, inadvertently, automatically, on coming out, have drawn the door after him. The difficulty was that this exactly was what he never did; it was against his whole policy, as he might have said, the essence of which was to keep vistas clear. He had them from the first, as he was well aware, quite on the brain: the strange apparition, at the far end of one of them, of his baffled "prey" (which had become by so sharp an irony so little the term now to apply!) was the form of success his imagination had most cherished, projecting into it always a refinement of beauty. He had known fifty times the start of perception that had afterwards dropped; had fifty times gasped to himself "There!" under some fond brief hallucination. The house, as the case stood, admirably lent itself; he might wonder at the taste, the native architecture of the particular time, which could rejoice so in the multiplication of doors—the opposite extreme to the modern, the actual almost complete proscription of them; but it had fairly contributed to provoke this obsession of the presence encountered telescopically, as he might say, focussed and studied in diminishing perspective and as by a rest for the elbow.

It was with these considerations that his present attention was charged—they perfectly availed to make what he saw portentous. He *couldn't*, by any lapse, have blocked that aperture; and if he hadn't, if it was unthinkable, why what else was clear but that there had been another agent? Another agent?—he had been catching, as he felt, a moment back, the very breath of him; but when had he been so close as in this simple, this logical, this completely personal act? It was so logical, that is, that one might have *taken* it for personal; yet for what did Brydon take it, he asked himself, while, softly panting, he felt his eyes almost leave their sockets. Ah this time at last they *were*, the two, the opposed projections of him, in presence; and this time, as much as one would, the question of danger loomed. With it rose, as not before, the question of courage—for what he knew the blank face of the door to say to him was "Show us how much you have!" It stared, it glared back at him with that challenge; it put to him the two alternatives: should he just push it open or not? Oh to have this consciousness was to *think*—and to think, Brydon knew, as he stood there, was, with the lapsing moments, not to have acted! Not to have acted—that was the misery and the pang—was even still not to act; was in fact *all* to feel the thing in another, in a new and terrible way. How long did he pause and how long did he debate? There was presently nothing to measure it; for his vibration had already changed—as just by the effect of its intensity. Shut up there, at bay, defiant, and with the prodigy of the thing palpably proveably *done*, thus giving notice like some stark signboard— under that accession of accent the situation itself had turned; and Brydon at last remarkably made up his mind on what it had turned to.

It had turned altogether to a different admonition; to a supreme hint, for him, of the value of Discretion! This slowly dawned, no doubt—for it could take its time; so perfectly, on his threshold, had he been stayed, so little as yet had he either advanced or retreated. It was the strangest of all things that now when, by his taking ten steps and applying his hand to a latch, or even his shoulder and his knee, if necessary, to a panel, all the hunger of his prime need might have been met, his high curiosity crowned, his unrest assuaged—it was amazing, but it was also exquisite and rare, that insistence should have, at a touch, quite dropped from him. Discretion—he jumped at that; and yet not, verily, at such a pitch, because it saved his nerves or his skin, but because, much more valuably, it saved the situation. When I say he "jumped" at it I feel the consonance of this term with the fact that—at the end indeed of I know not how long—he did move again, he crossed straight to the door. He wouldn't touch it—it seemed now that he might *if* he would: he would only just wait there a little, to show, to prove, that he wouldn't. He had thus another station, close to the thin partition by which revelation was denied him; but with his eyes bent and his hands held off in a mere intensity of stillness. He listened as if there had been something to hear, but this attitude, while it lasted, was his own communication. "If you won't then—good: I spare you and I give up. You affect me as by the appeal positively for pity: you convince me that for reasons rigid and sublime—what do I know?—we both of us should have suffered. I respect them then, and, though moved and privileged as, I believe, it has never been given to man, I retire, I renounce—never, on my honour, to try again. So rest for ever—and let *me*!"

That, for Brydon was the deep sense of this last demonstration—solemn, measured, directed, as he felt it to be. He brought it to a close, he turned away; and now verily he knew how deeply he had been stirred. He retraced his steps, taking up his candle, burnt, he observed, well-nigh to the socket, and marking again, lighten it as he would, the distinctness of his footfall; after which, in a moment, he knew himself at the other side of the house. He did here what he had not yet done at these hours—he opened half a casement, one of those in the front, and let in the air of the night; a thing he would have taken at any time previous for a sharp rupture of his spell. His spell was broken now, and it didn't matter—broken by his concession and his surrender, which made it idle henceforth that he should ever come back. The empty street—its other life so marked even by the great lamplit vacancy—was within call, within touch; he stayed there as to be in it again, high above it though he was still perched; he watched as for some comforting common fact, some vulgar human note, the passage of a scavenger or a thief, some night-bird however base. He would have blessed that sign of life; he would have welcomed positively the slow approach of his friend the policeman, whom he had hitherto only sought to avoid, and was not sure that if the patrol had come into sight he mightn't have felt the impulse to get into relation with it, to hail it, on some pretext, from his fourth floor.

The pretext that wouldn't have been too silly or too compromising, the explanation that would have saved his dignity and kept his name, in such a case, out of the papers was not definite to him: he was so occupied with the thought of recording his Discretion—as an effect of the vow he had just uttered to his intimate adversary—that the importance of this loomed large and something had overtaken all ironically his sense of proportion. If there had been a ladder applied to the front of the house, even one of the vertiginous perpendiculars employed by painters and roofers and sometimes left standing overnight, he would have managed somehow, astride of the window-sill, to compass by outstretched leg and arm that mode of descent. If there had been some such uncanny thing as he had found in his room at hotels, a workable fire-escape in the form of notched cable or a canvas shoot, he would have availed himself of it as a proof—well, of his present delicacy. He nursed that sentiment, as the question stood, a little in vain, and even—at the end of he scarce knew, once more, how long—found it, as by the action on his mind of the failure of response of the outer world, sinking back to vague anguish. It seemed to him he had waited an age for some stir of the great grim hush; the life of the town was itself under a spell—so unnaturally, up and down the whole prospect of known and rather ugly objects, the blankness and the silence lasted. Had they ever, he asked himself, the hard-faced houses, which had begun to look livid in the dim dawn, had they ever spoken so little to any need of his spirit? Great builded voids, great crowded stillnesses put on, often, in the heart of cities, for the small hours, a sort of sinister mask, and it was of this large collective negation that Brydon presently became conscious—all the more that the break of day was, almost incredibly, now at hand, proving to him what night he had made of it.

He looked again at his watch, saw what had become of his time-values (he had taken hours for minutes—not, as in other tense situations, minutes for hours) and the strange air of the streets was but the weak, the sullen flush of a dawn in which everything was still locked up. His choked appeal from his own open window had been the sole note of life, and he could but break off at last as for a worse despair. Yet while so deeply demoralised he was capable again of an impulse denoting—at least by his present measure—extraordinary resolution; of retracing his steps to the spot where he had turned cold with the extinction of his last pulse of doubt as to there being in the place another presence than his own. This required an effort strong enough to sicken him; but he had his reason, which overmastered for the moment everything else. There was the whole of the rest of the house to traverse, and how should he screw himself to that if the door he had seen closed were at present open? He could hold to the idea that the closing had practically been for him an act of mercy, a chance offered him to descend, depart, get off the ground and never again profane it. This conception held together, it worked; but what it meant for him depended now clearly on the amount of forbearance his recent action, or rather his recent inaction, had engendered. The image of the "presence," whatever it was, waiting there for him to go—this image had not yet been so concrete for his nerves as when he stopped short of the point at which certainty would have come to him. For, with all his resolution, or more exactly with all his dread, he did stop short—he hung back from really seeing. The risk was too great and his fear too definite: it took at this moment an awful specific form.

He knew—yes, as he had never known anything—that, *should* he see the door open, it would all too abjectly be the end of him. It would mean that the agent of his shame—for his shame was the deep abjection—was once more at large and in general possession; and what glared him thus in the face was the act that this would determine for him. It would send him straight about to the window he had left open, and by that window, be long ladder and dangling rope as absent as they would, he saw himself uncontrollably insanely fatally take his way to the street. The hideous chance of this he at least could avert; but he could only avert it by recoiling in time from assurance. He had the whole house to deal with, this fact was still there; only he now knew that uncertainty alone could start him. He stole back from where he had checked himself—merely to do so was suddenly like safety—and, making blindly for the greater staircase, left gaping rooms and sounding passages behind. Here was the top of the stairs, with a fine large dim descent and three spacious landings to mark off. His instinct was all for mildness, but his feet were harsh on the floors, and, strangely, when he had in a couple of minutes become aware of this, it counted somehow for help. He couldn't have spoken, the tone of his voice would have scared him, and the common conceit or resource of "whistling in the dark" (whether literally or figuratively) have appeared basely vulgar; yet he liked none the less to hear himself go, and when he had reached his first landing—taking it all with no rush, but quite steadily—that stage of success drew from him a gasp of relief.

The house, withal, seemed immense, the scale of space again inordinate; the open rooms to no one of which his eyes deflected, gloomed in their shuttered state like mouths of caverns; only the high skylight that formed the crown of the deep well created for him a medium in which he could advance, but which might have been, for queerness of colour, some watery under-world. He tried to think of something noble, as that his property was really grand, a splendid possession; but this nobleness took the form too of the clear delight with which he was finally to sacrifice it. They might come in now, the builders, the destroyers—they might come as soon as they would. At the end of two flights he had dropped to another zone, and from the middle of the third, with only one more left, he recognised the influence of the lower windows, of half-drawn blinds, of the occasional gleam of street-lamps, of the glazed spaces of the vestibule. This was the bottom of the sea, which showed an illumination of its own and which he even saw paved—when at a given moment he drew up to sink a long look over the banisters—with the marble squares of his childhood. By that time indubitably he felt, as he might have said in a commoner cause, better; it had allowed him to stop and draw breath, and the ease increased with the sight of the old black-and-white slabs. But what he most felt was that now surely, with the element of impunity pulling him as by hard firm hands, the case was settled for what he might have seen above had he dared that last look. The closed door, blessedly remote now, was still closed—and he had only in short to reach that of the house.

He came down further, he crossed the passage forming the access to the last flight; and if here again he stopped an instant it was almost for the sharpness of the thrill of assured escape. It made him shut his eyes—which opened again to the straight slope of the remainder of the stairs. Here was impunity still, but impunity almost excessive; inasmuch as the side-lights and the high fan-tracery of the entrance were glimmering straight into the hall; an appearance produced, he the next instant saw, by the fact that the vestibule gaped wide, that the hinged halves of the inner door had been thrown far back. Out of that again the *question* sprang at him, making his eyes, as he felt, half start from his head, as they had done, at the top of the house, before the sign of the other door. If he had left that one open, hadn't he left this one closed, and wasn't he now in *most* immediate presence of some inconceivable occult activity? It was as sharp, the question, as a knife in his side, but the answer hung fire still and seemed to lose itself in the vague darkness to which the thin admitted dawn, glimmering archwise over the whole outer door, made a semicircular margin, a cold silvery nimbus that seemed to play a little as he looked—to shift and expand and contract.

It was as if there had been something within it, protected by indistinctness and corresponding in extent with the opaque surface behind, the painted panels of the last barrier to his escape, of which the key was in his pocket. The indistinctness mocked him even while he stared, affected him as somehow shrouding or challenging certitude, so that after faltering an instant on his step he let himself go with the sense that here *was* at last something to meet, to touch, to take, to know—something all unnatural and dreadful, but to advance upon which was the condition for him either of liberation or of supreme defeat. The penumbra, dense and dark, was the virtual screen of a figure which stood in it as still as some image erect in a niche or as some black-vizored sentinel guarding a treasure. Brydon was to know afterwards, was to recall and make out, the particular thing he had believed during the rest of his descent. He saw, in its great grey glimmering margin, the central vagueness diminish, and he felt it to be taking the very form toward which, for so many days, the passion of his curiosity had yearned. It gloomed, it loomed, it was something, it was somebody, the prodigy of a personal presence.

Rigid and conscious, spectral yet human, a man of his own substance and stature waited there to measure himself with his power to dismay. This only could it be—this only till he recognised, with his advance, that what made the face dim was the pair of raised hands that covered it and in which, so far from being offered in defiance, it was buried as for dark deprecation. So Brydon, before him, took him in; with every fact of him now, in the higher light, hard and acute—his planted stillness, his vivid truth, his grizzled bent head and white masking hands, his queer actuality of evening-dress, of dangling double eye-glass, of gleaming silk lappet[1] and white linen, of pearl button and gold watch-guard and polished shoe. No portrait by a great modern master

---

1   A loose or overlapping part of a garment.

could have presented him with more intensity, thrust him out of his frame with more art, as if there had been "treatment," of the consummate sort, in his every shade and salience. The revulsion, for our friend, had become, before he knew it, immense—this drop, in the act of apprehension, to the sense of his adversary's inscrutable manoeuvre. That meaning at least, while he gaped, it offered him; for he could but gape at his other self in this other anguish, gape as a proof that *he*, standing there for the achieved, the enjoyed, the triumphant life, couldn't be faced in his triumph. Wasn't the proof in the splendid covering hands, strong and completely spread?—so spread and so intentional that, in spite of a special verity that surpassed every other, the fact that one of these hands had lost two fingers, which were reduced to stumps, as if accidentally shot away, the face was effectually guarded and saved.

"Saved," though, *would* it be?—Brydon breathed his wonder till the very impunity of his attitude and the very insistence of his eyes produced, as he felt, a sudden stir which showed the next instant as a deeper portent, while the head raised itself, the betrayal of a braver purpose. The hands, as he looked, began to move, to open; then, as if deciding in a flash, dropped from the face and left it uncovered and presented. Horror, with the sight, had leaped into Brydon's throat, gasping there in a sound he couldn't utter; for the bared identity was too hideous as *his*, and his glare was the passion of his protest. The face, *that* face, Spencer Brydon's?—he searched it still, but looking away from it in dismay and denial, falling straight from his height and sublimity. It was unknown, inconceivable, awful, disconnected from any possibility—! He had been "sold," he inwardly moaned, stalking such game as this: the presence before him was a presence, the horror within him a horror, but the waste of his nights had been only grotesque and the success of his adventure an irony. Such an identity fitted his at *no* point, made its alternative monstrous. A thousand times yes, as it came upon him nearer now—the face was the face of a stranger. It came upon him nearer now, quite as one of those expanding fantastic images projected by the magic lantern of childhood; for the stranger, whoever he might be, evil, odious, blatant, vulgar, had advanced as for aggression, and he knew himself give ground. Then harder pressed still, sick with the force of his shock, and falling back as under the hot breath and the roused passion of a life larger than his own, a rage of personality before which his own collapsed, he felt the whole vision turn to darkness and his very feet give way. His head went round; he was going; he had gone.

III

What had next brought him back, clearly—though after how long?—was Mrs. Muldoon's voice, coming to him from quite near, from so near that he seemed presently to see her as kneeling on the ground before him while he lay looking up at her; himself not wholly on the ground, but half-raised and upheld—conscious, yes, of tenderness of support and, more particularly, of a head pillowed in extraordinary softness and faintly refreshing fragrance. He considered, he wondered, his wit but half at his service; then another face intervened, bending more directly over him, and he finally knew that Alice Staverton had made her lap an ample and perfect cushion to him, and that she had to this end seated herself on the lowest degree of the staircase, the rest of his long person remaining stretched on his old black-and-white slabs. They were cold, these marble squares of his youth; but *he* somehow was not, in this rich return of consciousness—the most wonderful hour, little by little, that he had ever known, leaving him, as it did, so gratefully, so abysmally passive, and yet as with a treasure of intelligence waiting all round him for quiet appropriation; dissolved, he might call it, in the air of the place and producing the golden glow of a late autumn afternoon. He had come back, yes—come back from further away than any man but himself had ever travelled; but it was strange how with this sense what he had come back *to* seemed really the great thing, and as if his prodigious journey had been all for the sake of it. Slowly but surely his consciousness grew, his vision of his state thus completing itself: he had been miraculously *carried* back—lifted and carefully borne as from where he had been picked up, the uttermost end of an interminable grey passage. Even with this he was suffered to rest, and what had now brought him to knowledge was the break in the long mild motion.

It had brought him to knowledge, to knowledge—yes, this was the beauty of his state; which came to resemble more and more that of a man who has gone to sleep on some news of a great inheritance, and then, after dreaming it away, after profaning it with matters strange to it, has waked up again to serenity of certitude and has only to lie and watch it grow. This was the drift of his patience—that he had only to let it shine on him. He must moreover, with intermissions, still have been lifted and borne; since why and how else should he have known himself, later on, with the afternoon glow intenser, no longer at the foot of his stairs—situated as these now seemed at that dark other end of his tunnel—but on a deep window-bench of his high saloon, over which had been spread, couch-fashion, a mantle of soft stuff lined with grey fur that was familiar to his eyes and that one of his hands kept fondly feeling as for its pledge of truth. Mrs. Muldoon's face had gone, but the other, the second he had recognised, hung over him in a way that showed how he was still propped and pillowed. He took it all in, and the more he took it the more it seemed to suffice: he was as much at peace as if he had had food and drink. It was the two women who had found him, on Mrs. Muldoon's having plied, at her usual hour, her latch-key—and on her having above all arrived while Miss Staverton still lingered near the house. She had been turning away, all anxiety, from worrying the vain bell-handle— her calculation having been of the hour of the good woman's visit; but the latter, blessedly, had come up while she was still there, and they had entered together. He had then lain, beyond the vestibule, very much as he was lying now—quite, that is, as he appeared to have fallen, but all so wondrously without bruise or gash; only in a depth of stupor. What he most took in, however, at present, with the steadier clearance, was that Alice Staverton had for a long unspeakable moment not doubted he was dead.

"It must have been that I *was*." He made it out as she held him. "Yes—I can only have died. You brought me literally to life. Only," he wondered, his eyes rising to her, "only, in the name of all the benedictions, how?"

It took her but an instant to bend her face and kiss him, and something in the manner of it, and in the way her hands clasped and locked his head while he felt the cool charity and virtue of her lips, something in all this beatitude somehow answered everything. "And now I keep you," she said.

"Oh keep me, keep me" he pleaded while her face still hung over him: in response to which it dropped again and stayed close, clingingly close. It was the seal of their situation—of which he tasted the impress for a long blissful moment in silence. But he came back. "Yet how did you know—?"

"I was uneasy. You were to have come, you remember—and you had sent no word."

"Yes, I remember—I was to have gone to you at one today." It caught on to their "old" life and relation—which were so near and so far. "I was still out there in my strange darkness—where was it, what was it? I must have stayed there so long." He could but wonder at the death and the duration of his swoon.

"Since last night?" she asked with a shade of fear for her possible indiscretion.

"Since this morning—it must have been: the cold dim dawn of today. Where have I been," he vaguely wailed, "where have I been?" He felt her hold him close, and it was as if this helped him now to make in all security his mild moan. "What a long dark day!"

All in her tenderness she had waited a moment. "In the cold dim dawn?" she quavered.

But he had already gone on piecing together the parts of the whole prodigy. "As I didn't turn up you came straight—?"

She barely cast about. "I went first to your hotel—where they told me of your absence. You had dined out last evening and hadn't been back since. But they appeared to know you had been at your club."

"So you had the idea of *this*—?"

"Of what?" she asked in a moment.

"Well—of what has happened."

"I believed at least you'd have been here. I've known, all along," she said, "that you've been coming."

"'Known' it—?"

"Well, I've believed it. I said nothing to you after that talk we had a month ago—but I felt sure. I knew you *would*," she declared.

"That I'd persist, you mean?"

"That you'd see him."

"Ah but I didn't" cried Brydon with his long wail. "There's somebody—an awful beast; whom I brought, too horribly, to bay. But it's not me."

At this she bent over him again, and her eyes were in his eyes. "No—it's not you." And it was as if, while her face hovered, he might have made out in it, hadn't it been so near, some particular meaning blurred by a smile. "No, thank heaven," she repeated—"it's not you! Of course it wasn't to have been."

"Ah but it *was*," he gently insisted. And he stared before him now as he had been staring for so many weeks. "I was to have known myself."

"You couldn't!" she returned consolingly. And then reverting, and as if to account further for what she had herself done, "But it wasn't only *that*, that you hadn't been at home," she went on. "I waited till the hour at which we had found Mrs. Muldoon that day of my going with you; and she arrived, as I've told you, while, failing to bring any one to the door, I lingered in my despair on the steps. After a little, if she hadn't come, by such a mercy, I should have found means to hunt her up. But it wasn't," said Alice Staverton, as if once more with her fine intention—"it wasn't only that."

His eyes, as he lay, turned back to her. "What more then?"

She met it, the wonder she had stirred. "In the cold dim dawn, you say? Well, in the cold dim dawn of this morning I too saw you."

"Saw *me*—?"

"Saw *him*," said Alice Staverton. "It must have been at the same moment."

He lay an instant taking it in—as if he wished to be quite reasonable. "At the same moment?"

"Yes—in my dream again, the same one I've named to you. He came back to me. Then I knew it for a sign. He had come to you."

At this Brydon raised himself; he had to see her better. She helped him when she understood his movement, and he sat up, steadying himself beside her there on the window-bench and with his right hand grasping her left. "*He* didn't come to me."

"You came to yourself," she beautifully smiled.

"Ah I've come to myself now—thanks to you, dearest. But this brute, with his awful face—this brute's a black stranger. He's none of *me*, even as I *might* have been," Brydon sturdily declared.

But she kept the clearness that was like the breath of infallibility. "Isn't the whole point that you'd have been different?"

He almost scowled for it. "As different as *that*—?"

Her look again was more beautiful to him than the things of this world. "Haven't you exactly wanted to know *how* different? So this morning," she said, "you appeared to me."

"Like *him*?"

"A black stranger!"

"Then how did you know it was I?"

"Because, as I told you weeks ago, my mind, my imagination, had worked so over what you might, what you mightn't have been—to show you, you see, how I've thought of you. In the midst of that you came to me—that my wonder might be answered. So I knew," she went on; "and believed that, since the question held you too so fast, as you told me that day, you too would see for yourself. And when this morning I again saw I knew it would be because you had—and also then, from the first moment, because you somehow wanted me. *He* seemed to tell me of that. So why," she strangely smiled, "shouldn't I like him?"

It brought Spencer Brydon to his feet. "You 'like' that horror—?"

"I *could* have liked him. And to me," she said, "he was no horror. I had accepted him."

"'Accepted'—?" Brydon oddly sounded.

"Before, for the interest of his difference—yes. And as *I* didn't disown him, as *I* knew him—which you at last, confronted with him in his difference, so cruelly didn't, my dear—well, he must have been, you see, less dreadful to me. And it may have pleased him that I pitied him."

She was beside him on her feet, but still holding his hand—still with her arm supporting him. But though it all brought for him thus a dim light, "You 'pitied' him?" he grudgingly, resentfully asked.

"He has been unhappy; he has been ravaged," she said.

"And haven't I been unhappy? Am not I—you've only to look at me!—ravaged?"

"Ah I don't say I like him *better*," she granted after a thought. "But he's grim, he's worn—and things have happened to him. He doesn't make shift, for sight, with your charming monocle."

"No"—it struck Brydon: "I couldn't have sported mine 'downtown.' They'd have guyed[1] me there."

"His great convex pince-nez—I saw it, I recognised the kind— is for his poor ruined sight. And his poor right hand—!"

"Ah!" Brydon winced—whether for his proved identity or for his lost fingers. Then, "He has a million a year," he lucidly added. "But he hasn't you."

"And he isn't—no, he isn't—*you*!" she murmured as he drew her to his breast.

---

1 Made fun of.

The story had held us, round the fire, sufficiently breathless, but except the obvious remark that it was gruesome, as on Christmas Eve in an old house a strange tale should essentially be, I remember no comment uttered till somebody happened to note it as the only case he had met in which such a visitation had fallen on a child. The case, I may mention, was that of an apparition in just such an old house as had gathered us for the occasion—an appearance, of a dreadful kind, to a little boy sleeping in the room with his mother and waking her up in the terror of it; waking her not to dissipate his dread and soothe him to sleep again, but to encounter also herself, before she had succeeded in doing so, the same sight that had shocked him. It was this observation that drew from Douglas—not immediately, but later in the evening—a reply that had the interesting consequence to which I call attention. Some one else told a story not particularly effective, which I saw he was not following. This I took for a sign that he had himself something to produce and that we should only have to wait. We waited in fact till two nights later; but that same evening, before we scattered, he brought out what was in his mind.

"I quite agree—in regard to Griffin's ghost,[1] or whatever it was—that its appearing first to the little boy, at so tender an age, adds a particular touch. But it's not the first occurrence of its charming kind that I know to have been concerned with a child. If the child gives the effect another turn of the screw, what do you say to *two* children—?"

"We say of course," somebody exclaimed, "that two children give two turns! Also that we want to hear about them."

I can see Douglas there before the fire, to which he had got up to present his back, looking down at this converser with his hands in his pockets. "Nobody but me, till now, has ever heard. It's quite too horrible." This was naturally declared by several voices to give the thing the utmost price, and our friend, with quiet art, prepared his triumph by turning his eyes over the rest of us and going on: "It's beyond everything. Nothing at all that I know touches it."

"For sheer terror?" I remember asking.

He seemed to say it wasn't so simple as that; to be really at a loss how to qualify it. He passed his hand over his eyes, made a little wincing grimace. "For dreadful—dreadfulness!"

"Oh how delicious!" cried one of the women.

---

1 This is the only occasion when James uses the word "ghost" in this tale.

He took no notice of her; he looked at me, but as if, instead of me, he saw what he spoke of. "For general uncanny ugliness and horror and pain."

"Well then," I said, "just sit right down and begin."

He turned round to the fire, gave a kick to a log, watched it an instant. Then as he faced us again: "I can't begin. I shall have to send to town." There was a unanimous groan at this, and much reproach; after which, in his preoccupied way, he explained. "The story's written. It's in a locked drawer—it has not been out for years. I could write to my man and enclose the key; he could send down the packet as he finds it." It was to me in particular that he appeared to propound this—appeared almost to appeal for aid not to hesitate. He had broken a thickness of ice, the formation of many a winter; had had his reasons for a long silence. The others resented postponement, but it was just his scruples that charmed me. I adjured[1] him to write by the first post and to agree with us for an early hearing; then I asked him if the experience in question had been his own. To this his answer was prompt. "Oh thank God, no!"

"And is the record yours? You took the thing down?"

"Nothing but the impression. I took that *here*"—he tapped his heart. "I've never lost it."

"Then your manuscript—?"

"Is in old faded ink and in the most beautiful hand." He hung fire again.[2] "A woman's. She has been dead these twenty years. She sent me the pages in question before she died." They were all listening now, and of course there was somebody to be arch, or at any rate to draw the inference. But if he put the inference by without a smile it was also without irritation. "She was a most charming person, but she was ten years older than I. She was my sister's governess," he quietly said. "She was the most agreeable woman I've ever known in her position; she'd have been worthy of any whatever. It was long ago, and this episode was long before. I was at Trinity,[3] and I found her at home on my coming down the second summer. I was much there that year—it was a beautiful one; and we had, in her off-hours, some strolls and talks in the garden—talks in which she struck me as awfully clever and nice. Oh yes; don't grin: I liked

---

1 Begged.
2 Hesitated.
3 Trinity College, part of Cambridge University. Trinity was associated with the study of the supernatural since students there had formed a society to study ghosts. Several of those students were later associated with the Society for Psychical Research. See above, Introduction, pp. 28-29.

her extremely and am glad to this day to think she liked me too. If she hadn't she wouldn't have told me. She had never told any one. It wasn't simply that she said so, but that I knew she hadn't. I was sure; I could see. You'll easily judge why when you hear."

"Because the thing had been such a scare?"

He continued to fix me. "You'll easily judge," he repeated: "*you* will."

I fixed him too. "I see. She was in love."

He laughed for the first time. "You *are* acute. Yes, she was in love. That is she *had* been. That came out—she couldn't tell her story without its coming out. I saw it, and she saw I saw it; but neither of us spoke of it. I remember the time and the place—the corner of the lawn, the shade of the great beeches and the long hot summer afternoon. It wasn't a scene for a shudder; but oh—!" He quitted the fire and dropped back into his chair.

"You'll receive the packet Thursday morning?" I said.

"Probably not till the second post."

"Well then; after dinner—"

"You'll all meet me here?" He looked us round again. "Isn't anybody going?" It was almost the tone of hope.

"Everybody will stay!"

"*I* will—and *I* will!" cried the ladies whose departure had been fixed. Mrs. Griffin, however, expressed the need for a little more light. "Who was it she was in love with?"

"The story will tell," I took upon myself to reply.

"Oh I can't wait for the story!"

"The story *won't* tell," said Douglas; "not in any literal vulgar way."

"More's the pity then. That's the only way I ever understand."

"Won't *you* tell, Douglas?" somebody else enquired.

He sprang to his feet again. "Yes—to-morrow. Now I must go to bed. Good-night." And, quickly catching up a candlestick, he left us slightly bewildered. From our end of the great brown hall we heard his step on the stair; whereupon Mrs. Griffin spoke. "Well, if I don't know who she was in love with I know who *he* was."

"She was ten years older," said her husband.

"*Raison de plus*[1]—at that age! But it's rather nice, his long reticence."

---

1 All the more reason (French).

"Forty years!" Griffin put in.

"With this outbreak at last."

"The outbreak," I returned, "will make a tremendous occasion of Thursday night"; and every one so agreed with me that in the light of it we lost all attention for everything else. The last story, however incomplete and like the mere opening of a serial, had been told; we handshook and "candlestuck," as somebody said, and went to bed.

I knew the next day that a letter containing the key had, by the first post, gone off to his London apartments; but in spite of—or perhaps just on account of—the eventual diffusion of this knowledge we quite let him alone till after dinner, till such an hour of the evening in fact as might best accord with the kind of emotion on which our hopes were fixed. Then he became as communicative as we could desire, and indeed gave us his best reason for being so. We had it from him again before the fire in the hall, as we had had our mild wonders of the previous night. It appeared that the narrative he had promised to read us really required for a proper intelligence a few words of prologue. Let me say here distinctly, to have done with it, that this narrative, from an exact transcript of my own made much later, is what I shall presently give. Poor Douglas, before his death—when it was in sight—committed to me the manuscript that reached him on the third of these days and that, on the same spot, with immense effect, he began to read to our hushed little circle on the night of the fourth. The departing ladies who had said they would stay didn't, of course, thank heaven, stay: they departed, in consequence of arrangements made, in a rage of curiosity, as they professed, produced by the touches with which he had already worked us up. But that only made his little final auditory more compact and select, kept it, round the hearth, subject to a common thrill.

The first of these touches conveyed that the written statement took up the tale at a point after it had, in a manner, begun. The fact to be in possession of was therefore that his old friend, the youngest of several daughters of a poor country parson, had at the age of twenty, on taking service for the first time in the schoolroom, come up to London, in trepidation, to answer in person an advertisement that had already placed her in brief correspondence with the advertiser. This person proved, on her presenting herself for judgement at a house in

Harley Street[1] that impressed her as vast and imposing—this prospective patron proved a gentleman, a bachelor in the prime of life, such a figure as had never risen, save in a dream or an old novel, before a fluttered anxious girl out of a Hampshire vicarage.[2] One could easily fix his type; it never, happily, dies out. He was handsome and bold and pleasant, off-hand and gay and kind. He struck her, inevitably, as gallant and splendid, but what took her most of all and gave her the courage she afterwards showed was that he put the whole thing to her as a favour, an obligation he should gratefully incur. She figured him as rich, but as fearfully extravagant—saw him all in a glow of high fashion, of good looks, of expensive habits, of charming ways with women. He had for his town residence a big house filled with the spoils of travel and the trophies of the chase; but it was to his country home, an old family place in Essex, that he wished her immediately to proceed.

He had been left, by the death of his parents in India, guardian to a small nephew and a small niece, children of a younger, a military brother whom he had lost two years before. These children were, by the strangest of chances for a man in his position—a lone man without the right sort of experience or a grain of patience—very heavy on his hands. It had all been a great worry and, on his own part doubtless, a series of blunders, but he immensely pitied the poor chicks and had done all he could; had in particular sent them down to his other house, the proper place for them being of course the country, and kept them there from the first with the best people he could find to look after them, parting even with his own servants to wait on them and going down himself, whenever he might, to see how they were doing. The awkward thing was that they had practically no other relations and that his own affairs took up all his time. He had put them in possession of Bly, which was healthy and secure, and had placed at the head of their little establish-

---

1 A street in London, known for luxurious houses in the eighteenth and early nineteenth centuries; around the mid-nineteenth century, doctors living on the street began seeing patients and working with colleagues in their homes, thereby making the street a famous center for medicine. At the time of the story's events, the street was still known primarily for its wealthy residents.

2 Hampshire is a county southwest of London; a vicarage is the house provided to the vicar of the local Anglican church.

ment—but belowstairs[1] only—an excellent woman, Mrs. Grose, whom he was sure his visitor would like and who had formerly been maid to his mother. She was now housekeeper and was also acting for the time as superintendent to the little girl, of whom, without children of her own, she was by good luck extremely fond. There were plenty of people to help, but of course the young lady who should go down as governess would be in supreme authority. She would also have, in holidays, to look after the small boy, who had been for a term at school—young as he was to be sent, but what else could be done?—and who, as the holidays were about to begin, would be back from one day to the other. There had been for the two children at first a young lady whom they had had the misfortune to lose. She had done for them quite beautifully—she was a most respectable person—till her death, the great awkwardness of which had, precisely, left no alternative but the school for little Miles. Mrs. Grose, since then, in the way of manners and things, had done as she could for Flora; and there were further, a cook, a housemaid, a dairy-woman, an old pony, an old groom and an old gardener, all likewise thoroughly respectable.

So far had Douglas presented his picture when some one put a question. "And what did the former governess die of? Of so much respectability?"

Our friend's answer was prompt. "That will come out. I don't anticipate."

"Pardon me—I thought that was just what you *are* doing."

"In her successor's place," I suggested, "I should have wished to learn if the office brought with it—"

"Necessary danger to life?" Douglas completed my thought. "She did wish to learn, and she did learn. You shall hear to-morrow what she learnt. Meanwhile of course the prospect struck her as slightly grim. She was young, untried, nervous: it was a vision of serious duties and little company, of really great loneliness. She hesitated—took a couple of days to consult and consider. But the salary offered much exceeded her modest measure, and on a second interview she faced the music, she

---

1 Since much of the domestic housekeeping took place in a basement, "belowstairs" refers to the area in a large house in which the servants worked. The narrator thus distinguishes Mrs. Grose's social rank from that of a governess, whose status was higher than that of a servant.

engaged." And Douglas, with this, made a pause that, for the benefit of the company, moved me to throw in—

"The moral of which was of course the seduction exercised by the splendid young man. She succumbed to it."

He got up and, as he had done the night before, went to the fire, gave a stir to a log with his foot, then stood a moment with his back to us. "She saw him only twice."

"Yes, but that's just the beauty of her passion."

A little to my surprise, on this, Douglas turned round to me. "It *was* the beauty of it. There were others," he went on, "who hadn't succumbed. He told her frankly all his difficulty—that for several applicants the conditions had been prohibitive. They were somehow simply afraid. It sounded dull—it sounded strange; and all the more so because of his main condition."

"Which was—?"

"That she should never trouble him—but never, never: neither appeal nor complain nor write about anything; only meet all questions herself, receive all moneys from his solicitor, take the whole thing over and let him alone. She promised to do this, and she mentioned to me that when, for a moment, disburdened, delighted, he held her hand, thanking her for the sacrifice, she already felt rewarded."

"But was that all her reward?" one of the ladies asked.

"She never saw him again."

"Oh!" said the lady; which, as our friend immediately again left us, was the only other word of importance contributed to the subject till, the next night, by the corner of the hearth, in the best chair, he opened the faded red cover of a thin old-fashioned gilt-edged album. The whole thing took indeed more nights than one, but on the first occasion the same lady put another question. "What's your title?"

"I haven't one."

"Oh *I* have!" I said. But Douglas, without heeding me, had begun to read with a fine clearness that was like a rendering to the ear of the beauty of his author's hand.[1]

I

I remember the whole beginning as a succession of flights and drops, a little see-saw of the right throbs and the wrong. After rising, in town, to meet his appeal I had at all events a couple of

---

1   End of the first installment in *Collier's Weekly* (1898).

very bad days—found all my doubts bristle again, felt indeed sure I had made a mistake. In this state of mind I spent the long hours of bumping swinging coach that carried me to the stopping-place at which I was to be met by a vehicle from the house. This convenience, I was told, had been ordered, and I found, toward the close of the June afternoon, a commodious fly[1] in waiting for me. Driving at that hour, on a lovely day, through a country the summer sweetness of which served as a friendly welcome, my fortitude revived and, as we turned into the avenue, took a flight that was probably but a proof of the point to which it had sunk. I suppose I had expected, or had dreaded, something so dreary that what greeted me was a good surprise. I remember as a thoroughly pleasant impression the broad clear front, its open windows and fresh curtains and the pair of maids looking out; I remember the lawn and the bright flowers and the crunch of my wheels on the gravel and the clustered tree-tops over which the rooks circled and cawed in the golden sky. The scene had a greatness that made it a different affair from my own scant home, and there immediately appeared at the door, with a little girl in her hand, a civil person who dropped me as decent a curtsey as if I had been the mistress or a distinguished visitor. I had received in Harley Street a narrower notion of the place, and that, as I recalled it, made me think the proprietor still more of a gentleman, suggested that what I was to enjoy might be matter beyond his promise.

I had no drop again till the next day, for I was carried triumphantly through the following hours by my introduction to the younger of my pupils. The little girl who accompanied Mrs. Grose affected me on the spot as a creature too charming not to make it a great fortune to have to do with her. She was the most beautiful child I had ever seen, and I afterwards wondered why my employer hadn't made more of a point to me of this. I slept little that night—I was too much excited; and this astonished me too, I recollect, remained with me, adding to my sense of the liberality with which I was treated. The large impressive room, one of the best in the house, the great state bed, as I almost felt it, the figured full draperies, the long glasses[2] in which, for the first time, I could see myself from head to foot, all struck me—like the wonderful appeal of my small charge—as so many things thrown in. It was thrown in as well, from the first moment, that I should

---

1 Horse-drawn carriage.
2 Mirrors.

get on with Mrs. Grose in a relation over which, on my way, in the coach, I fear I had rather brooded. The one appearance indeed that in this early outlook might have made me shrink again was that of her being so inordinately glad to see me. I felt within half an hour that she was so glad—stout simple plain clean wholesome woman—as to be positively on her guard against showing it too much. I wondered even then a little why she should wish *not* to show it, and that, with reflection, with suspicion, might of course have made me uneasy.

But it was a comfort that there could be no uneasiness in a connexion with anything so beatific as the radiant image of my little girl, the vision of whose angelic beauty had probably more than anything else to do with the restlessness that, before morning, made me several times rise and wander about my room to take in the whole picture and prospect; to watch from my open window the faint summer dawn, to look at such stretches of the rest of the house as I could catch, and to listen, while in the fading dusk the first birds began to twitter, for the possible recurrence of a sound or two, less natural and not without but within, that I had fancied I heard. There had been a moment when I believed I recognised, faint and far, the cry of a child; there had been another when I found myself just consciously starting as at the passage, before my door, of a light footstep. But these fancies were not marked enough not to be thrown off, and it is only in the light, or the gloom, I should rather say, of other and subsequent matters that they now come back to me. To watch, teach, "form" little Flora would too evidently be the making of a happy and useful life. It had been agreed between us downstairs that after this first occasion I should have her as a matter of course at night, her small white bed being already arranged, to that end, in my room. What I had undertaken was the whole care of her, and she had remained just this last time with Mrs. Grose only as an effect of our consideration for my inevitable strangeness and her natural timidity. In spite of this timidity—which the child herself, in the oddest way in the world, had been perfectly frank and brave about, allowing it, without a sign of uncomfortable consciousness, with the deep sweet serenity indeed of one of Raphael's[1] holy infants, to be discussed, to be imputed to her and to determine us—I felt quite sure she would presently like me. It was part of what I already liked Mrs. Grose herself for, the pleasure I could see her feel in my admiration and wonder as I sat at

---

1 Italian artist (1483–1520).

supper with four tall candles and with my pupil, in a high chair, and a bib, brightly facing me between them over bread and milk. There were naturally things that in Flora's presence could pass between us only as prodigious and gratified looks, obscure and roundabout allusions.

"And the little boy—does he look like her? Is he too so very remarkable?"

One wouldn't, it was already conveyed between us, too grossly flatter a child. "Oh Miss, *most* remarkable. If you think well of this one!"—and she stood there with a plate in her hand, beaming at our companion, who looked from one of us to the other with placid heavenly eyes that contained nothing to check us.

"Yes; if I do—?"

"You *will* be carried away by the little gentleman!"

"Well, that, I think, is what I came for—to be carried away. I'm afraid, however," I remember feeling the impulse to add, "I'm rather easily carried away. I was carried away in London!"

I can still see Mrs. Grose's broad face as she took this in. "In Harley Street?"

"In Harley Street."

"Well, Miss, you're not the first—and you won't be the last."

"Oh I've no pretensions," I could laugh, "to being the only one. My other pupil, at any rate, as I understand, comes back to-morrow?"

"Not to-morrow—Friday, Miss. He arrives, as you did, by the coach, under care of the guard, and is to be met by the same carriage."

I forthwith wanted to know if the proper as well as the pleasant and friendly thing wouldn't therefore be that on the arrival of the public conveyance I should await him with his little sister; a proposition to which Mrs. Grose assented so heartily that I somehow took her manner as a kind of comforting pledge—never falsified, thank heaven!—that we should on every question be quite at one. Oh she was glad I was there!

What I felt the next day was, I suppose, nothing that could be fairly called a reaction from the cheer of my arrival; it was probably at the most only a slight oppression produced by a fuller measure of the scale, as I walked round them, gazed up at them, took them in, of my new circumstances. They had, as it were, an extent and mass for which I had not been prepared and in the presence of which I found myself, freshly, a little scared not less than a little proud. Regular lessons, in this agitation, certainly suffered some wrong; I reflected that my first duty was, by the gentlest arts I could contrive, to win the child into the sense of knowing me. I spent the day with her out of doors; I arranged with her, to her great satisfaction, that it should be she, she only, who might show me the place. She showed it step by step and room by room and secret by secret, with droll delightful childish talk about it and with the result, in half an hour, of our becoming tremendous friends. Young as she was I was struck, throughout our little tour, with her confidence and courage, with the way, in empty chambers and dull corridors, on crooked staircases that made me pause and even on the summit of an old machicolated square tower[1] that made me dizzy, her morning music, her disposition to tell me so many more things than she asked, rang out and led me on. I have not seen Bly since the day I left it, and I dare say that to my present older and more informed eyes it would show a very reduced importance. But as my little conductress, with her hair of gold and her frock of blue, danced before me round corners and pattered down passages, I had the view of a castle of romance inhabited by a rosy sprite, such a place as would somehow, for diversion of the young idea, take all colour out of story-books and fairy-tales. Wasn't it just a story-book over which I had fallen a-doze and a-dream? No; it was a big ugly antique but convenient house, embodying a few features of a building still older, half-displaced and half-utilised, in which I had the fancy of our being almost as lost as a handful of passengers in a great drifting ship. Well, I was strangely at the helm!

II

This came home to me when, two days later, I drove over with Flora to meet, as Mrs. Grose said, the little gentleman; and all the more for an incident that, presenting itself the second evening, had deeply disconcerted me. The first day had been, on the whole, as I have expressed, reassuring; but I was to see it wind up to a change of note. The postbag that evening—it came late—contained a letter for me which, however, in the hand of my employer, I found to be composed but of a few words enclosing another, addressed to himself, with a seal still unbroken. "This, I recognise, is from the head-master, and the head-master's an awful bore. Read him, please; deal with him; but mind you don't report. Not a word. I'm off!" I broke the seal with a great effort—

---

1 I.e., a gallery overhanging the tower, with openings for the projection of artillery onto enemy attackers.

so great a one that I was a long time coming to it; took the unopened missive at last up to my room and only attacked it just before going to bed. I had better have let it wait till morning, for it gave me a second sleepless night. With no counsel to take, the next day, I was full of distress; and it finally got so the better of me that I determined to open myself at least to Mrs. Grose.

"What does it mean? The child's dismissed his school."[1]

She gave me a look that I remarked at the moment; then, visibly, with a quick blankness, seemed to try to take it back. "But aren't they all—?"

"Sent home—yes. But only for the holidays. Miles may never go back at all."

Consciously, under my attention, she reddened. "They won't take him?"

"They absolutely decline."

At this she raised her eyes, which she had turned from me; I saw them fill with good tears. "What has he done?"

I cast about; then I judged best simply to hand her my document—which, however, had the effect of making her, without taking it, simply put her hands behind her. She shook her head sadly. "Such things are not for me, Miss."

My counsellor couldn't read! I winced at my mistake, which I attenuated as I could, and opened the letter again to repeat it to her; then, faltering in the act and folding it up once more, I put it back in my pocket. "Is he really *bad*?"

The tears were still in her eyes. "Do the gentlemen say so?"

"They go into no particulars. They simply express their regret that it should be impossible to keep him. That can have but one meaning." Mrs. Grose listened with dumb emotion; she forbore to ask me what this meaning might be; so that, presently, to put the thing with some coherence and with the mere aid of her presence to my own mind, I went on: "That he's an injury to the others."

At this, with one of the quick turns of simple folk, she suddenly flamed up. "Master Miles!—*him* an injury?"

There was such a flood of good faith in it that, though I had not yet seen the child, my very fears made me jump to the absurdity of the idea. I found myself, to meet my friend the better, offering it, on the spot, sarcastically. "To his poor little innocent mates!"

"It's too dreadful," cried Mrs. Grose, "to say such cruel things! Why he's scarce ten years old."

---

1 Been expelled from his boarding school.

"Yes, yes; it would be incredible."

She was evidently grateful for such a profession. "See him, Miss, first. *Then* believe it!" I felt forthwith a new impatience to see him; it was the beginning of a curiosity that, for all the next hours, was to deepen almost to pain. Mrs. Grose was aware, I could judge, of what she had produced in me, and she followed it up with assurance. "You might as well believe it of the little lady. Bless her," she added the next moment—"*look* at her!"

I turned and saw that Flora, whom, ten minutes before, I had established in the schoolroom with a sheet of white paper, a pencil and a copy of nice "round O's," now presented herself to view at the open door. She expressed in her little way an extraordinary detachment from disagreeable duties, looking at me, however, with a great childish light that seemed to offer it as a mere result of the affection she had conceived for my person, which had rendered necessary that she should follow me. I needed nothing more than this to feel the full force of Mrs. Grose's comparison, and, catching my pupil in my arms, covered her with kisses in which there was a sob of atonement.

None the less, the rest of the day, I watched for further occasion to approach my colleague, especially as, toward evening, I began to fancy she rather sought to avoid me. I overtook her, I remember, on the staircase; we went down together and at the bottom I detained her, holding her there with a hand on her arm. "I take what you said to me at noon as a declaration that *you've* never known him to be bad."

She threw back her head; she had clearly by this time, and very honestly, adopted an attitude. "Oh never known him—I don't pretend *that*!"

I was upset again. "Then you *have* known him—?"

"Yes indeed, Miss, thank God!"

On reflexion I accepted this. "You mean that a boy who never is—?"

"Is no boy for *me*!"

I held her tighter. "You like them with the spirit to be naughty?" Then, keeping pace with her answer, "So do I!" I eagerly brought out. "But not to the degree to contaminate—"

"To contaminate?"—my big word left her at a loss.

I explained it. "To corrupt."

She stared, taking my meaning in; but it produced in her an odd laugh. "Are you afraid he'll corrupt *you*?" She put the question with such a fine bold humour that with a laugh, a little silly doubtless, to match her own, I gave way for the time to the apprehension of ridicule.

But the next day, as the hour for my drive approached, I cropped up in another place. "What was the lady who was here before?"

"The last governess? She was also young and pretty—almost as young and almost as pretty, Miss, even as you."

"Ah then I hope her youth and her beauty helped her!" I recollect throwing off. "He seems to like us young and pretty!"

"Oh he *did*," Mrs. Grose assented: "it was the way he liked every one!" She had no sooner spoken indeed than she caught herself up. "I mean that's *his* way—the master's."

I was struck. "But of whom did you speak first?"

She looked blank, but she coloured. "Why of *him*."

"Of the master?"

"Of who else?"

There was so obviously no one else that the next moment I had lost my impression of her having accidentally said more than she meant; and I merely asked what I wanted to know. "Did *she* see anything in the boy—?"

"That wasn't right? She never told me."

I had a scruple, but I overcame it. "Was she careful—particular?"

Mrs. Grose appeared to try to be conscientious. "About some things—yes."

"But not about all?"

Again she considered. "Well, Miss—she's gone. I won't tell tales."

"I quite understand your feeling," I hastened to reply; but I thought it after an instant not opposed to this concession to pursue: "Did she die here?"

"No—she went off."

I don't know what there was in this brevity of Mrs. Grose's that struck me as ambiguous. "Went off to die?" Mrs. Grose looked straight out of the window, but I felt that, hypothetically, I had a right to know what young persons engaged for Bly were expected to do. "She was taken ill, you mean, and went home?"

"She was not taken ill, so far as appeared, in this house. She left it, at the end of the year, to go home, as she said, for a short holiday, to which the time she had put in had certainly given her a right. We had then a young woman—a nursemaid who had stayed on and who was a good girl and clever; and *she* took the children altogether for the interval. But our young lady never came back, and at the very moment I was expecting her I heard from the master that she was dead."

I turned this over. "But of what?"

"He never told me! But please, Miss," said Mrs. Grose, "I must get to my work."[1]

III

Her thus turning her back on me was fortunately not, for my just preoccupations, a snub that could check the growth of our mutual esteem. We met, after I had brought home little Miles, more intimately than ever on the ground of my stupefaction, my general emotion: so monstrous was I then ready to pronounce it that such a child as had now been revealed to me should be under an interdict.[2] I was a little late on the scene of his arrival, and I felt, as he stood wistfully looking out for me before the door of the inn at which the coach had put him down, that I had seen him on the instant, without and within, in the great glow of freshness, the same positive fragrance of purity, in which I had from the first moment seen his little sister. He was incredibly beautiful, and Mrs. Grose had put her finger on it: everything but a sort of passion of tenderness for him was swept away by his presence. What I then and there took him to my heart for was something divine that I have never found to the same degree in any child— his indescribable little air of knowing nothing in the world but love. It would have been impossible to carry a bad name with a greater sweetness of innocence, and by the time I had got back to Bly with him I remained merely bewildered—so far, that is, as I was not outraged—by the sense of the horrible letter locked up in one of the drawers in my room. As soon as I could compass a private word with Mrs. Grose I declared to her that it was grotesque.

She promptly understood me. "You mean the cruel charge—?"

"It doesn't live an instant. My dear woman, *look* at him!"

She smiled at my pretension to have discovered his charm. "I assure you, Miss, I do nothing else! What will you say then?" she immediately added.

"In answer to the letter?" I had made up my mind. "Nothing at all."

---

1 End of second installment.
2 Prohibition; in this case, Miles's expulsion from his school.

"And to his uncle?"

I was incisive. "Nothing at all."

"And to the boy himself?"

I was wonderful. "Nothing at all."

She gave with her apron a great wipe to her mouth. "Then I'll stand by you. We'll see it out."

"We'll see it out!" I ardently echoed, giving her my hand to make it a vow.

She held me there a moment, then whisked up her apron again with her detached hand. "Would you mind, Miss, if I used the freedom—"

"To kiss me? No!" I took the good creature in my arms and after we had embraced like sisters felt still more fortified and indignant.

This at all events was for the time: a time so full that as I recall the way it went it reminds me of all the art I now need to make it a little distinct. What I look back at with amazement is the situation I accepted. I had undertaken, with my companion, to see it out, and I was under a charm apparently that could smooth away the extent and the far and difficult connexions of such an effort. I was lifted aloft on a great wave of infatuation and pity. I found it simple, in my ignorance, my confusion and perhaps my conceit, to assume that I could deal with a boy whose education for the world was all on the point of beginning. I am unable even to remember at this day what proposal I framed for the end of his holidays and the resumption of his studies. Lessons with me indeed, that charming summer, we all had a theory that he was to have; but I now feel that for weeks the lessons must have been rather my own. I learnt something—at first certainly—that had not been one of the teachings of my small smothered life; learnt to be amused, and even amusing, and not to think for the morrow. It was the first time, in a manner, that I had known space and air and freedom, all the music of summer and all the mystery of nature. And then there was consideration—and consideration was sweet. Oh it was a trap—not designed but deep—to my imagination, to my delicacy, perhaps to my vanity; to whatever in me was most excitable. The best way to picture it all is to say that I was off my guard. They gave me so little trouble—they were of a gentleness so extraordinary. I used to speculate—but even this with a dim disconnectedness—as to how the rough future (for all futures are rough!) would handle them and might bruise them. They had the bloom of health and happiness; and yet, as if I had been in charge of a pair of little grandees, of princes of the blood, for whom everything, to be right, would have to be fenced about and ordered and arranged, the only form that in my fancy the after-years could take for them was that of a romantic, a really royal extension of the garden and the park. It may be of course above all that what suddenly broke into this gives the previous time a charm of stillness—that hush in which something gathers or crouches. The change was actually like the spring of a beast.

In the first weeks the days were long; they often, at their finest, gave me what I used to call my own hour, the hour when, for my pupils, tea-time and bed-time having come and gone, I had before my final retirement a small interval alone. Much as I liked my companions this hour was the thing in the day I liked most; and I liked it best of all when, as the light faded—or rather, I should say, the day lingered and the last calls of the last birds sounded, in a flushed sky, from the old trees—I could take a turn into the grounds and enjoy, almost with a sense of property that amused and flattered me, the beauty and dignity of the place. It was a pleasure at these moments to feel myself tranquil and justified; doubtless perhaps also to reflect that by my discretion, my quiet good sense and general high propriety, I was giving pleasure—if he ever thought of it!—to the person to whose pressure I had yielded. What I was doing was what he had earnestly hoped and directly asked of me, and that I *could*, after all, do it proved even a greater joy than I had expected. I dare say I fancied myself in short a remarkable young woman and took comfort in the faith that this would more publicly appear. Well, I needed to be remarkable to offer a front to the remarkable things that presently gave their first sign.

It was plump, one afternoon, in the middle of my very hour: the children were tucked away and I had come out for my stroll. One of the thoughts that, as I don't in the least shrink now from noting, used to be with me in these wanderings was that it would be as charming as a charming story suddenly to meet some one. Some one would appear there at the turn of a path and would stand before me and smile and approve. I didn't ask more than that—I only asked that he should *know*; and the only way to be sure he knew would be to see it, and the kind light of it, in his handsome face. That was exactly present to me—by which I mean the face was—when, on the first of these occasions, at the end of a long June day, I stopped short on emerging from one of the plantations and coming into view of the house. What arrested me on the spot—and with a shock much greater than any vision had allowed for—was the sense that my imagination had, in a flash, turned real. He did stand there!—but high up, beyond the lawn and at the very top of the tower to which, on that first morning, little Flora had conducted me. This tower was one of a pair—square incongruous crenellated[1] structures—that were distinguished, for some reason, though I could see little difference, as the new and the old. They flanked opposite ends of the house and were probably architectural absurdities, redeemed in a measure indeed by not being wholly disengaged nor of a height too pretentious, dating, in their gingerbread antiquity, from a romantic revival that was already a respectable past. I admired them, had fancies about them, for we could all profit in a degree, especially when they loomed through the dusk, by the grandeur of their actual battlements; yet it was not at such an elevation that the figure I had so often invoked seemed most in place.

It produced in me, this figure, in the clear twilight, I remember, two distinct gasps of emotion, which were, sharply, the shock of my first and that of my second surprise. My second was a violent perception of the mistake of my first: the man who met my eyes was not the person I had precipitately supposed. There came to me thus a bewilderment of vision of which, after these years, there is no living view that I can hope to give. An unknown man in a lonely place is a permitted object of fear to a young woman privately bred; and the figure that faced me was—a few more seconds assured me—as little anyone else I knew as it was the image that had been in my mind. I had not seen it in Harley Street—I had not seen it anywhere. The place moreover, in the strangest way in the world, had on the instant and by the very fact of its appearance become a solitude. To me at least, making my statement here with a deliberation with which I have never made it, the whole feeling of the moment returns. It was as if, while I took in what I did take in, all the rest of the scene had been stricken with death. I can hear again, as I write, the intense hush in which the sounds of evening dropped. The rooks stopped cawing in the golden sky and the friendly hour lost for the unspeakable minute all its voice. But there was no other change in nature, unless indeed it were a change that I saw with a stranger sharpness. The gold was still in the sky, the clearness in the air, and the man who looked at me over the battlements was as definite as a picture in a frame. That's how I thought, with extraordinary quickness, of each person that he might have been and that he wasn't. We were confronted across

---

1   A crenellated tower had at its top several rectangular cut-out spaces that allowed a castle's defenders to see and attack an invading enemy.

our distance quite long enough for me to ask myself with intensity who then he was and to feel, as an effect of my inability to say, a wonder that in a few seconds more became intense.

The great question, or one of these, is afterwards, I know, with regard to certain matters, the question of how long they have lasted. Well, this matter of mine, think what you will of it, lasted while I caught at a dozen possibilities, none of which made a difference for the better, that I could see, in there having been in the house—and for how long, above all?—a person of whom I was in ignorance. It lasted while I just bridled a little with the sense of how my office seemed to require that there should be no such ignorance and no such person. It lasted while this visitant, at all events—and there was a touch of the strange freedom, as I remember, in the sign of familiarity of his wearing no hat—seemed to fix me, from his position, with just the question, just the scrutiny through the fading light, that his own presence provoked. We were too far apart to call to each other, but there was a moment at which, at shorter range, some challenge between us, breaking the hush, would have been the right result of our straight mutual stare. He was in one of the angles, the one away from the house, very erect, as it struck me, and with both hands on the ledge. So I saw him as I see the letters I form on this page; then, exactly, after a minute, as if to add to the spectacle, he slowly changed his place—passed, looking at me hard all the while, to the opposite corner of the platform. Yes, it was intense to me that during this transit he never took his eyes from me, and I can see at this moment the way his hand, as he went, moved from one of the crenellations to the next. He stopped at the other corner, but less long, and even as he turned away still markedly fixed me. He turned away; that was all I knew.[1]

IV

It was not that I didn't wait, on this occasion, for more, since I was as deeply rooted as shaken. Was there a "secret" at Bly—a mystery of Udolpho or an insane, an unmentionable relative kept in unsuspected confinement?[2] I can't say how long I turned it over, or how long, in a confusion of curiosity and dread, I

---

1 End of third installment.
2 Ann Radcliffe (1764–1823) wrote her influential and popular Gothic novel *The Mysteries of Udolpho* in 1794; the young, courageous female protagonist suffers imprisonment in a remote castle and must confront

remained where I had had my collision; I only recall that when I re-entered the house darkness had quite closed in. Agitation, in the interval, certainly had held me and driven me, for I must, in circling about the place, have walked three miles; but I was to be later on so much more overwhelmed that this mere dawn of alarm was a comparatively human chill. The most singular part of it in fact—singular as the rest had been—was the part I became, in the hall, aware of in meeting Mrs. Grose. This picture comes back to me in the general train—the impression, as I received it on my return, of the wide white panelled space, bright in the lamplight and with its portraits and red carpet, and of the good surprised look of my friend, which immediately told me she had missed me. It came to me straightway, under her contact, that, with plain heartiness, mere relieved anxiety at my appearance, she knew nothing whatever that could bear upon the incident I had there ready for her. I had not suspected in advance that her comfortable face would pull me up, and I somehow measured the importance of what I had seen by my thus finding myself hesitate to mention it. Scarce anything in the whole history seems to me so odd as this fact that my real beginning of fear was one, as I may say, with the instinct of sparing my companion. On the spot, accordingly, in the pleasant hall and with her eyes on me, I, for a reason that I couldn't then have phrased, achieved an inward rev-olution—offered a vague pretext for my lateness and, with the plea of the beauty of the night and of the heavy dew and wet feet, went as soon as possible to my room.

Here it was another affair; here, for many days after, it was a queer affair enough. There were hours, from day to day—or at least there were moments, snatched even from clear duties—when I had to shut myself up to think. It wasn't so much yet that I was more nervous than I could bear to be as that I was remark-ably afraid of becoming so; for the truth I had now to turn over was simply and clearly the truth that I could arrive at no account whatever of the visitor with whom I had been so inexplicably and yet, as it seemed to me, so intimately concerned. It took me little time to see that I might easily sound, without forms of enquiry and without exciting remark, any domestic complication. The shock I had suffered must have sharpened all my senses; I felt

---

many apparently supernatural events. The "insane, unmentionable rela-tive" refers to *Jane Eyre* (1847) by Charlotte Brontë (1816–55), in which a madwoman is kept hidden in an attic, unbeknownst to the young governess, Jane Eyre.

sure, at the end of three days and as the result of mere closer attention, that I had not been practised upon by the servants nor made the object of any "game." Of whatever it was that I knew nothing was known around me. There was but one sane inference: someone had taken a liberty rather monstrous. That was what, repeatedly, I dipped into my room and locked the door to say to myself. We had been, collectively, subject to an intrusion; some unscrupulous traveller, curious in old houses, had made his way in unobserved, enjoyed the prospect from the best point of view and then stolen out as he came. If he had given me such a bold hard stare, that was but a part of his indiscretion. The good thing, after all, was that we should surely see no more of him.

This was not so good a thing, I admit, as not to leave me to judge that what, essentially, made nothing else much signify was simply my charming work. My charming work was just my life with Miles and Flora, and through nothing could I so like it as through feeling that to throw myself into it was to throw myself out of my trouble. The attraction of my small charges was a constant joy, leading me to wonder afresh at the vanity of my original fears, the distaste I had begun by entertaining for the probable grey prose of my office. There was to be no grey prose, it appeared, and no long grind; so how could work not be charming that presented itself as daily beauty? It was all the romance of the nursery and the poetry of the schoolroom. I don't mean by this of course that we studied only fiction and verse; I mean I can express no otherwise the sort of interest my companions inspired. How can I describe that except by saying that instead of growing deadly used to them—and it's a marvel for a governess: I call the sisterhood to witness!—I made constant fresh discoveries. There was one direction, assuredly, in which these discoveries stopped: deep obscurity continued to cover the region of the boy's conduct at school. It had been promptly given me, I have noted, to face that mystery without a pang. Perhaps even it would be nearer the truth to say that—without a word—he himself had cleared it up. He had made the whole charge absurd. My conclusion bloomed there with the real rose-flush of his innocence: he was only too fine and fair for the little horrid unclean school-world, and he had paid a price for it. I reflected acutely that the sense of such individual differences, such superiorities of quality, always, on the part of the majority—which could include even stupid sordid head-masters—turn infallibly to the vindictive.

Both the children had a gentleness—it was their only fault, and it never made Miles a muff[1]—that kept them (how shall I express it?) almost impersonal and certainly quite unpunishable. They were like those cherubs of the anecdote[2] who had—morally at any rate—nothing to whack! I remember feeling with Miles in especial as if he had had, as it were, nothing to call even an infinitesimal history. We expect of a small child scant enough "antecedents," but there was in this beautiful little boy something extraordinarily sensitive, yet extraordinarily happy, that, more than in any creature of his age I have seen, struck me as beginning anew each day. He had never for a second suffered. I took this as a direct disproof of his having really been chastised. If he had been wicked he would have "caught" it, and I should have caught it by the rebound—I should have found the trace, should have felt the wound and the dishonour. I could reconstitute nothing at all, and he was therefore an angel. He never spoke of his school, never mentioned a comrade or a master; and I, for my part, was quite too much disgusted to allude to them. Of course I was under the spell, and the wonderful part is that, even at the time, I perfectly knew I was. But I gave myself up to it; it was an antidote to any pain, and I had more pains than one. I was in receipt in these days of disturbing letters from home, where things were not going well. But with this joy of my children what things in the world mattered? That was the question I used to put to my scrappy retirements. I was dazzled by their loveliness.

There was a Sunday—to get on—when it rained with such force and for so many hours that there could be no procession to church; in consequence of which, as the day declined, I had arranged with Mrs. Grose that, should the evening show improvement, we would attend together the late service. The rain happily stopped, and I prepared for our walk, which, through the

---

1 A person who makes mistakes because of incompetence or awkwardness.

2 Possibly referring to a story recounted by writer Charles Lamb (1775–1834), who quotes a comment by his lifelong friend Samuel Taylor Coleridge (1772–1834) about the death of their former schoolmaster, James Boyer: "Poor J.B.!—may all his faults be forgiven; and may he be wafted to bliss by little cherub boys, all head and wings, with no *bottoms* to reproach his sublunary infirmities." R. Brimley Johnson, ed. *Christ's Hospital: Recollections of Lamb, Coleridge, and Leigh Hunt* (London: George Allen, 1896) 59.

park and by the good road to the village, would be a matter of twenty minutes. Coming downstairs to meet my colleague in the hall, I remembered a pair of gloves that had required three stitches and that had received them—with a publicity perhaps not edifying—while I sat with the children at their tea, served on Sundays, by exception, in that cold clean temple of mahogany and brass, the "grown-up" dining-room. The gloves had been dropped there, and I turned in to recover them. The day was grey enough, but the afternoon light still lingered, and it enabled me, on crossing the threshold, not only to recognise, on a chair near the wide window, then closed, the articles I wanted, but to become aware of a person on the other side of the window and looking straight in. One step into the room had sufficed; my vision was instantaneous; it was all there. The person looking straight in was the person who had already appeared to me. He appeared thus again with I won't say greater distinctness, for that was impossible, but with a nearness that represented a forward stride in our intercourse and made me, as I met him, catch my breath and turn cold. He was the same—he was the same, and seen, this time, as he had been seen before, from the waist up, the window, though the dining-room was on the ground floor, not going down to the terrace on which he stood. His face was close to the glass, yet the effect of this better view was, strangely, just to show me how intense the former had been. He remained but a few seconds—long enough to convince me he also saw and recognised; but it was as if I had been looking at him for years and had known him always. Something, however, happened this time that had not happened before; his stare into my face, through the glass and across the room, was as deep and hard as then, but it quitted me for a moment during which I could still watch it, see it fix successively several other things. On the spot there came to me the added shock of a certitude that it was not for me he had come there. He had come for someone else.

The flash of this knowledge—for it was knowledge in the midst of dread—produced in me the most extraordinary effect, starting, as I stood there, a sudden vibration of duty and courage. I say courage because I was beyond all doubt already far gone. I bounded straight out of the door again, reached that of the house, got in an instant upon the drive and, passing along the terrace as fast as I could rush, turned a corner and came full in sight. But it was in sight of nothing now—my visitor had vanished. I stopped, almost dropped, with the real relief of this; but I took in the whole scene—I gave him time to reappear. I call it time, but how long was it? I can't speak to the purpose to-day of the duration of these things. That kind of measure must have left me: they couldn't have lasted as they actually appeared to me to last. The terrace and the whole place, the lawn and the garden beyond it, all I could see of the park, were empty with a great emptiness. There were shrubberies and big trees, but I remember the clear assurance I felt that none of them concealed him. He was there or was not there: not there if I didn't see him. I got hold of this; then, instinctively, instead of returning as I had come, went to the window. It was confusedly present to me that I ought to place myself where he had stood. I did so; I applied my face to the pane and looked, as he had looked, into the room. As if, at this moment, to show me exactly what his range had been, Mrs. Grose, as I had done for himself just before, came in from the hall. With this I had the full image of a repetition of what had already occurred. She saw me as I had seen my own visitant; she pulled up short as I had done; I gave her something of the shock that I had received. She turned white, and this made me ask myself if I had blanched as much. She stared, in short, and retreated on just *my* lines, and I knew she had then passed out and come round to me and that I should presently meet her. I remained where I was, and while I waited I thought of more things than one. But there's only one I take space to mention. I wondered why *she* should be scared.

V

Oh she let me know as soon as, round the corner of the house, she loomed again into view. "What in the name of goodness is the matter—?" She was now flushed and out of breath.

I said nothing till she came quite near. "With me?" I must have made a wonderful face. "Do I show it?"

"You're as white as a sheet. You look awful."

I considered; I could meet on this, without scruple, any degree of innocence. My need to respect the bloom of Mrs. Grose's had dropped, without a rustle, from my shoulders, and if I wavered for the instant it was not with what I kept back. I put out my hand to her and she took it; I held her hard a little, liking to feel her close to me. There was a kind of support in the shy heave of her surprise. "You came for me for church, of course, but I can't go."

"Has anything happened?"

"Yes. You must know now. Did I look very queer?"

"Through this window? Dreadful!"

"Well," I said, "I've been frightened." Mrs. Grose's eyes expressed plainly that *she* had no wish to be, yet also that she knew too well her place not to be ready to share with me any marked inconvenience. Oh it was quite settled that she *must* share! "Just what you saw from the dining-room a minute ago was the effect of that. What *I* saw—just before—was much worse."

Her hand tightened. "What was it?"

"An extraordinary man. Looking in."

"What extraordinary man?"

"I haven't the least idea."

Mrs. Grose gazed round us in vain. "Then where is he gone?"

"I know still less."

"Have you seen him before?"

"Yes—once. On the old tower."

She could only look at me harder. "Do you mean he's a stranger?"

"Oh very much!"

"Yet you didn't tell me?"

"No—for reasons. But now that you've guessed—"

Mrs. Grose's round eyes encountered this charge. "Ah I haven't guessed!" she said very simply. "How can I if *you* don't imagine?"

"I don't in the very least."

"You've seen him nowhere but on the tower?"

"And on this spot just now."

Mrs. Grose looked round again. "What was he doing on the tower?"

"Only standing there and looking down at me."

She thought a minute. "Was he a gentleman?"

I found I had no need to think. "No." She gazed in deeper wonder. "No."

"Then nobody about the place? Nobody from the village?"

"Nobody—nobody. I didn't tell you, but I made sure."

She breathed a vague relief: this was, oddly, so much to the good. It only went indeed a little way. "But if he isn't a gentle-man—"

"What *is* he? He's a horror."

"A horror?"

"He's—God help me if I know *what* he is!"

Mrs. Grose looked round once more; she fixed her eyes on the duskier distance and then, pulling herself together, turned to me with full inconsequence. "It's time we should be at church."

"Oh I'm not fit for church!"

"Won't it do you good?"

"It won't do *them*—!" I nodded at the house.

"The children?"

"I can't leave them now."

"You're afraid—?"

I spoke boldly. "I'm afraid of *him*."

Mrs. Grose's large face showed me, at this, for the first time, the far-away faint glimmer of a consciousness more acute: I somehow made out in it the delayed dawn of an idea I myself had not given her and that was as yet quite obscure to me. It comes back to me that I thought instantly of this as something I could get from her; and I felt it to be connected with the desire she presently showed to know more. "When was it—on the tower?"

"About the middle of the month. At this same hour."

"Almost at dark," said Mrs. Grose.

"Oh no, not nearly. I saw him as I see you."

"Then how did he get in?"

"And how did he get out?" I laughed. "I had no opportunity to ask him! This evening, you see," I pursued, "he has not been able to get in."

"He only peeps?"

"I hope it will be confined to that!" She had now let go my hand; she turned away a little. I waited an instant; then I brought out: "Go to church. Goodbye. I must watch."

Slowly she faced me again. "Do you fear for them?"

We met in another long look. "Don't *you*?" Instead of answering she came nearer to the window and, for a minute, applied her face to the glass. "You see how he could see," I meanwhile went on.

She didn't move. "How long was he here?"

"Till I came out. I came to meet him."

Mrs. Grose at last turned round, and there was still more in her face. "*I* couldn't have come out."

"Neither could I!" I laughed again. "But I did come. I've my duty."

"So have I mine," she replied; after which she added: "What's he like?"

"I've been dying to tell you. But he's like nobody."

"Nobody?" she echoed.

"He has no hat." Then seeing in her face that she already, in this, with a deeper dismay, found a touch of picture, I quickly added stroke to stroke. "He has red hair, very red, close-curling, and a pale face, long in shape, with straight good features and little rather queer whiskers that are as red as his hair. His eyebrows are somehow darker; they look particularly arched and as if they might move a good deal. His eyes are sharp, strange—awfully; but I only know clearly that they're rather small and very fixed. His mouth's wide, and his lips are thin, and except for his little whiskers he's quite clean-shaven. He gives me a sort of sense of looking like an actor."

"An actor!" It was impossible to resemble one less, at least, than Mrs. Grose at that moment.

"I've never seen one, but so I suppose them. He's tall, active, erect," I continued, "but never—no, never!—a gentleman."

My companion's face had blanched as I went on; her round eyes started and her mild mouth gaped. "A gentleman?" she gasped, confounded, stupefied: "a gentleman *he*?"

"You know him then?"

She visibly tried to hold herself. "But he *is* handsome?"

I saw the way to help her. "Remarkably!"

"And dressed—?"

"In somebody's clothes. They're smart, but they're not his own."

She broke into a breathless affirmative groan: "They're the master's!"

I caught it up. "You *do* know him?"

She faltered but a second. "Quint!" she cried.

"Quint?"

"Peter Quint—his own man, his valet, when he was here!"

"When the master was?"

Gaping still, but meeting me, she pieced it all together. "He never wore his hat, but he did wear—well, there were waistcoats missed! They were both here—last year. Then the master went, and Quint was alone."

I followed, but halting a little. "Alone?"

"Alone with *us*." Then as from a deeper depth, "In charge," she added.

"And what became of him?"

She hung fire so long that I was still more mystified. "He went too," she brought out at last.

"Went where?"

Her expression, at this, became extraordinary. "God knows where! He died."

"Died?" I almost shrieked.

She seemed fairly to square herself, plant herself more firmly to express the wonder of it. "Yes. Mr. Quint's dead."[1]

VI

It took of course more than that particular passage to place us together in presence of what we had now to live with as we could, my dreadful liability to impressions of the order so vividly exemplified, and my companion's knowledge henceforth—a knowledge half consternation and half compassion—of that liability. There had been this evening, after the revelation that left me for an hour so prostrate—there had been for either of us no attendance on any service but a little service of tears and vows, of prayers and promises, a climax to the series of mutual challenges and pledges that had straightway ensued on our retreating together to the schoolroom and shutting ourselves up there to have everything out. The result of our having everything out was simply to reduce our situation to the last rigor of its elements. She herself had seen nothing, not the shadow of a shadow, and nobody in the house but the governess was in the governess's plight; yet she accepted without directly impugning my sanity the truth as I gave it to her, and ended by showing me on this ground an awestricken tenderness, a deference to my more than questionable privilege, of which the very breath has remained with me as that of the sweetest of human charities.

What was settled between us accordingly that night was that we thought we might bear things together; and I was not even sure that in spite of her exemption it was she who had the best of the burden. I knew at this hour, I think, as well as I knew later, what I was capable of meeting to shelter my pupils; but it took me some time to be wholly sure of what my honest comrade was prepared for to keep terms with so stiff an agreement. I was queer company enough—quite as queer as the company I received; but as I trace over what we went through I see how much common ground we must have found in the one idea that, by good fortune, *could* steady us. It was the idea, the second movement, that led me straight out, as I may say, of the inner chamber of my dread. I could take the air in the court, at least, and there Mrs. Grose could join me. Perfectly can I recall now the particular way strength came to me before we separated for the night. We had gone over and over every feature of what I had seen.

---

1 End of fourth installment.

"He was looking for someone else, you say—some one who was not you?"

"He was looking for little Miles." A portentous clearness now possessed me. "*That's* whom he was looking for."

"But how do you know?"

"I know, I know, I know!" My exaltation grew. "And *you* know, my dear!"

She didn't deny this, but I required, I felt, not even so much telling as that. She took it up again in a moment. "What if *he* should see him?"

"Little Miles? That's what he wants!"

She looked immensely scared again. "The child?"

"Heaven forbid! The man. He wants to appear to *them*." That he might was an awful conception, and yet somehow I could keep it at bay; which moreover, as we lingered there, was what I succeeded in practically proving. I had an absolute certainty that I should see again what I had already seen, but something within me said that by offering myself bravely as the sole subject of such experience, by accepting, by inviting, by surmounting it all, I should serve as an expiatory victim and guard the tranquility of the rest of the household. The children in especial I should thus fence about and absolutely save. I recall one of the last things I said that night to Mrs. Grose.

"It does strike me that my pupils have never mentioned—!"

She looked at me hard as I musingly pulled up. "His having been here and the time they were with him?"

"The time they were with him, and his name, his presence, his history, in any way. They've never alluded to it."

"Oh the little lady doesn't remember. She never heard or knew."

"The circumstances of his death?" I thought with some intensity. "Perhaps not. But Miles would remember—Miles would know."

"Ah don't try him!" broke from Mrs. Grose.

I returned her the look she had given me. "Don't be afraid." I continued to think. "It *is* rather odd."

"That he has never spoken of him?"

"Never by the least reference. And you tell me they were 'great friends.'"

"Oh, it wasn't *him*!" Mrs. Grose with emphasis declared. "It was Quint's own fancy. To play with him, I mean—to spoil him." She paused a moment; then she added: "Quint was much too free."

This gave me, straight from my vision of his face—*such* a face!—a sudden sickness of disgust. "Too free with *my* boy?"

"Too free with every one!"

I forbore for the moment to analyze this description further than by the reflexion that a part of it applied to several of the members of the household, of the half-dozen maids and men who were still of our small colony. But there was everything, for our apprehension, in the lucky fact that no discomfortable legend, no perturbation of scullions, had ever, within any one's memory, attached to the kind old place. It had neither bad name nor ill fame, and Mrs. Grose, most apparently, only desired to cling to me and to quake in silence. I even put her, the very last thing of all, to the test. It was when, at midnight, she had her hand on the schoolroom door to take leave. "I *have* it from you then—for it's of great importance—that he was definitely and admittedly bad?"

"Oh, not admittedly. *I* knew it—but the master didn't."

"And you never told him?"

"Well, he didn't like tale-bearing—he hated complaints. He was terribly short with anything of that kind, and if people were all right to *him*—"

"He wouldn't be bothered with more?" This squared well enough with my impressions of him: he was not a trouble-loving gentleman, nor so very particular perhaps about some of the company he himself kept. All the same, I pressed my informant. "I promise you *I* would have told!"

She felt my discrimination. "I dare say I was wrong. But really I was afraid."

"Afraid of what?"

"Of things that man could do. Quint was so clever—he was so deep."

I took this in still more than I probably showed. "You weren't afraid of anything else? Not of his effect—?"

"His effect?" she repeated with a face of anguish and waiting while I faltered.

"On innocent little precious lives. They were in your charge."

"No, they weren't in mine!" she roundly and distressfully returned. "The master believed in him and placed him here because he was supposed not to be quite in health and the country air so good for him. So he had everything to say. Yes"—she let me have it—"even about *them*."

"Them—that creature?" I had to smother a kind of howl. "And you could bear it?"

"No. I couldn't—and I can't now!" And the poor woman burst into tears.

A rigid control, from the next day, was, as I have said, to follow them; yet how often and how passionately, for a week, we came back together to the subject! Much as we had discussed it that Sunday night, I was, in the immediate later hours in especial—for it may be imagined whether I slept—still haunted with the shadow of something she had not told me. I myself had kept back nothing, but there was a word Mrs. Grose had kept back. I was sure moreover by morning that this was not from a failure of frankness, but because on every side there were fears. It seems to me indeed, in raking it all over, that by the time the morrow's sun was high I had restlessly read into the facts before us almost all the meaning they were to receive from subsequent and more cruel occurrences. What they gave me above all was just the sinister figure of the living man—the dead one would keep awhile!—and of the months he had continuously passed at Bly, which, added up, made a formidable stretch. The limit of this evil time had arrived only when, on the dawn of a winter's morning, Peter Quint was found, by a labourer going to early work, stone dead on the road from the village: a catastrophe explained—superficially at least—by a visible wound to his head; such a wound as might have been produced (and as, on the final evidence, *had* been) by a fatal slip, in the dark and after leaving the public-house, on the steepish icy slope, a wrong path altogether, at the bottom of which he lay. The icy slope, the turn mistaken at night and in liquor, accounted for much—practically, in the end and after the inquest and boundless chatter, for everything; but there had been matters in his life, strange passages and perils, secret disorders, vices more than suspected, that would have accounted for a good deal more.

I scarce know how to put my story into words that shall be a credible picture of my state of mind; but I was in these days literally able to find a joy in the extraordinary flight of heroism the occasion demanded of me. I now saw that I had been asked for a service admirable and difficult; and there would be a greatness in letting it be seen—oh in the right quarter!—that I could succeed where many another girl might have failed. It was an immense help to me—I confess I rather applaud myself as I look back!—that I saw my response so strongly and so simply. I was there to protect and defend the little creatures in the world the most bereaved and the most loveable, the appeal of whose helplessness had suddenly become only too explicit, a deep constant ache of one's own engaged affection. We were cut off, really, together; we were united in our danger. They had nothing but me, and I—well, I had *them*. It was in short a magnificent chance. This chance presented itself to me in an image richly material. I was a screen—I was to stand before them. The more I saw the less they would. I began to watch them in a stifled suspense, a disguised tension, that might well, had it continued too long, have turned to something like madness. What saved me, as I now see, was that it turned to another matter altogether. It didn't last as suspense—it was superseded by horrible proofs. Proofs, I say, yes—from the moment I really took hold.

This moment dated from an afternoon hour that I happened to spend in the grounds with the younger of my pupils alone. We had left Miles indoors, on the red cushion of a deep window-seat; he had wished to finish a book, and I had been glad to encourage a purpose so laudable in a young man whose only defect was a certain ingenuity of restlessness. His sister, on the contrary, had been alert to come out, and I strolled with her half an hour, seeking the shade, for the sun was still high and the day exceptionally warm. I was aware afresh with her, as we went, of how, like her brother, she contrived—it was the charming thing in both children—to let me alone without appearing to drop me and to accompany me without appearing to oppress. They were never importunate and yet never listless. My attention to them all really went to seeing them amuse themselves immensely without me: this was a spectacle they seemed actively to prepare and that employed me as an active admirer. I walked in a world of their invention—they had no occasion whatever to draw upon mine; so that my time was taken only with being for them some remarkable person or thing that the game of the moment required and that was merely, thanks to my superior, my exalted stamp, a happy and highly distinguished sinecure. I forget what I was on the present occasion; I only remember that I was something very important and very quiet and that Flora was playing very hard. We were on the edge of the lake, and, as we had lately begun geography, the lake was the Sea of Azof.[1]

Suddenly, amid these elements, I became aware that on the other side of the Sea of Azof we had an interested spectator. The way this knowledge gathered in me was the strangest thing in the world—the strangest, that is, except the very much stranger in

---

1 Small sea bordered by Ukraine to the north, Russia to the east, and the Crimean peninsula to the west.

which it quickly merged itself. I had sat down with a piece of work—for I was something or other that could sit—on the old stone bench which overlooked the pond; and in this position I began to take in with certitude and yet without direct vision the presence, a good way off, of a third person. The old trees, the thick shrubbery, made a great and pleasant shade, but it was all suffused with the brightness of the hot still hour. There was no ambiguity in anything; none whatever at least in the conviction I from one moment to another found myself forming as to what I should see straight before me and across the lake as a consequence of raising my eyes. They were attached at this juncture to the stitching in which I was engaged, and I can feel once more the spasm of my effort not to move them till I should so have steadied myself as to be able to make up my mind what to do. There was an alien object in view—a figure whose right of presence I instantly and passionately questioned. I recollect counting over perfectly the possibilities, reminding myself that nothing was more natural for instance then the appearance of one of the men about the place, or even of a messenger, a postman or a tradesman's boy, from the village. That reminder had as little effect on my practical certitude as I was conscious—still even without looking—of its having upon the character and attitude of our visitor. Nothing was more natural than that these things should be the other things that they absolutely were not.

Of the positive identity of the apparition I would assure myself as soon as the small clock of my courage should have ticked out the right second; meanwhile, with an effort that was already sharp enough, I transferred my eyes straight to little Flora, who, at the moment, was about ten yards away. My heart had stood still for an instant with the wonder and terror of the question whether she too would see; and I held my breath while I waited for what a cry from her, what some sudden innocent sign either of interest or of alarm, would tell me. I waited, but nothing came; then in the first place—and there is something more dire in this, I feel, than in anything I have to relate—I was determined by a sense that within a minute all spontaneous sounds from her had dropped; and in the second by the circumstance that also within the minute she had, in her play, turned her back to the water. This was her attitude when I at last looked at her—looked with the confirmed conviction that we were still, together, under direct personal notice. She had picked up a small flat piece of wood which happened to have in it a little hole that had evidently suggested to her the idea of sticking in another fragment that might figure as a mast and make the thing a boat. This second morsel, as I watched her, she was very markedly and intently attempting to tighten in its place. My apprehension of what she was doing sustained me so that after some seconds I felt I was ready for more. Then I again shifted my eyes—I faced what I had to face.

VII

I got hold of Mrs. Grose as soon after this as I could; and I can give no intelligible account of how I fought out the interval. Yet I still hear myself cry as I fairly threw myself into her arms: "They *know*—it's too monstrous: they know, they know!"

"And what on earth—?" I felt her incredulity as she held me.

"Why all that *we* know—and heaven knows what more besides!" Then as she released me I made it out to her, made it out perhaps only now with full coherency even to myself. "Two hours ago, in the garden"—I could scarce articulate—"Flora *saw*!"

Mrs. Grose took it as she might have taken a blow in the stomach. "She has told you?" she panted.

"Not a word—that's the horror. She kept it to herself! The child of eight,[1] *that* child!" Unutterable still for me was the stupefaction of it.

Mrs. Grose of course could only gape the wider. "Then how do you know?"

"I was there—I saw with my eyes: saw she was perfectly aware."

"Do you mean aware of *him*?"

"No—of *her*." I was conscious as I spoke that I looked prodigious things, for I got the slow reflexion of them in my companion's face. "Another person—this time; but a figure of quite as unmistakeable horror and evil: a woman in black, pale and dreadful—with such an air also, and such a face!—on the other side of the lake. I was there with the child—quiet for the hour; and in the midst of it she came."

"Came how—from where?"

"From where they come from! She just appeared and stood there—but not so near."

"And without coming nearer?"

"Oh for the effect and the feeling she might have been as close as you!"

---

1 In the *Collier's Weekly* version, Flora's age here is given as six, not eight; James raised her age in all subsequent editions.

My friend, with an odd impulse, fell back a step. "Was she someone you've never seen?"

"Never. But someone the child has. Someone *you* have." Then to show how I had thought it all out: "My predecessor—the one who died."

"Miss Jessel?"

"Miss Jessel. You don't believe me?" I pressed.

She turned right and left in her distress. "How can you be sure?"

This drew from me, in the state of my nerves, a flash of impatience. "Then ask Flora—*she's* sure!" But I had no sooner spoken than I caught myself up. "No, for God's sake *don't*!" She'll say she isn't—she'll lie!"

Mrs. Grose was not too bewildered instinctively to protest. "Ah how *can* you?"

"Because I'm clear. Flora doesn't want me to know."

"It's only then to spare you."

"No, no—there are depths, depths! The more I go over it the more I see in it, and the more I see in it the more I fear. I don't know what I *don't* see—what I *don't* fear!"

Mrs. Grose tried to keep up with me. "You mean you're afraid of seeing her again?"

"Oh no; that's nothing—now!" Then I explained. "It's of *not* seeing her."

But my companion only looked wan. "I don't understand."

"Why, it's that the child may keep it up—and that the child assuredly *will*—without my knowing it."

At the image of this possibility Mrs. Grose for a moment collapsed, yet presently to pull herself together again as from the positive force of the sense of what, should we yield an inch, there would really be to give way to. "Dear, dear—we must keep our heads! And after all, if she doesn't mind it—!" She even tried a grim joke. "Perhaps she likes it!"

"Like *such* things—a scrap of an infant!"

"Isn't it just a proof of her blest innocence?" my friend bravely inquired.

She brought me, for the instant, almost round. "Oh we must clutch at *that*—we must cling to it! If it isn't a proof of what you say, it's a proof of—God knows what! For the woman's a horror of horrors."

Mrs. Grose, at this, fixed her eyes a minute on the ground; then at last raising them, "Tell me how you know," she said.

"Then you admit it's what she was?" I cried.

"Tell me how you know," my friend simply repeated.

"Know? By seeing her! By the way she looked."

"At you, do you mean—so wickedly?"

"Dear me, no—I could have borne that. She gave me never a glance. She only fixed the child."

Mrs. Grose tried to see it. "Fixed her?"

"Ah with such awful eyes!"

She stared at mine as if they might really have resembled them. "Do you mean of dislike?"

"God help us, no. Of something much worse."

"Worse than dislike?"—this left her indeed at a loss.

"With a determination—indescribable. With a kind of fury of intention."

I made her turn pale. "Intention?"

"To get hold of her." Mrs. Grose—her eyes just lingering on mine—gave a shudder and walked to the window; and while she stood there looking out I completed my statement. "*That's* what Flora knows."

After a little she turned round. "The person was in black, you say?"

"In mourning—rather poor, almost shabby. But—yes—with extraordinary beauty." I now recognised to what I had at last, stroke by stroke, brought the victim of my confidence, for she quite visibly weighed this. "Oh, handsome—very, very," I insisted; "wonderfully handsome. But infamous."

She slowly came back to me. "Miss Jessel—*was* infamous." She once more took my hand in both her own, holding it as tight as if to fortify me against the increase of alarm I might draw from this disclosure. "They were both infamous," she finally said.

So for a little we faced it once more together; and I found absolutely a degree of help in seeing it now so straight. "I appreciate," I said, "the great decency of your not having hitherto spoken; but the time has certainly come to give me the whole thing." She appeared to assent to this, but still only in silence; seeing which I went on: "I must have it now. Of what did she die? Come, there was something between them."

"There was everything."

"In spite of the difference—?"

"Oh of their rank, their condition"—she brought it woefully out. "*She* was a lady."

I turned it over; I again saw. "Yes—she was a lady."

"And he so dreadfully below," said Mrs. Grose.

I felt that I doubtless needn't press too hard, in such company, on the place of a servant in the scale; but there was nothing to prevent an acceptance of my companion's own measure of my predecessor's abasement. There was a way to deal with that, and I dealt; the more readily for my full vision—on the evidence—of our employer's late clever good-looking "own" man; impudent, assured, spoiled, depraved. "The fellow was a hound."

Mrs. Grose considered as if it were perhaps a little a case for a sense of shades. "I've never seen one like him. He did what he wished."

"With *her*?"

"With them all."

It was as if now in my friend's own eyes Miss Jessel had again appeared. I seemed at any rate for an instant to trace their evocation of her as distinctly as I had seen her by the pond; and I brought out with decision: "It must have been also what *she* wished!"

Mrs. Grose's face signified that it had been indeed, but she said at the same time: "Poor woman—she paid for it!"

"Then you do know what she died of?" I asked.

"No—I know nothing. I wanted not to know; I was glad enough I didn't; and I thanked heaven she was well out of this!"

"Yet you had then your idea—"

"Of her real reason for leaving? Oh yes—as to that. She couldn't have stayed. Fancy it here—for a governess! And afterwards I imagined—and I still imagine. And what I imagine is dreadful."

"Not so dreadful as what *I* do," I replied; on which I must have shown her—as I was indeed but too conscious—a front of miserable defeat. It brought out again all her compassion for me, and at the renewed touch of her kindness my power to resist broke down. I burst, as I had the other time made her burst, into tears; she took me to her motherly breast, where my lamentation overflowed. "I don't do it!" I sobbed in despair; "I don't save or shield them! It's far worse than I dreamed—they're lost!"[1]

VIII

What I had said to Mrs. Grose was true enough: there were in the matter I had put before her depths and possibilities that I lacked resolution to sound; so that when we met once more in the wonder of it we were of a common mind about the duty of resistance to extravagant fancies. We were to keep our heads if we

---

1   End of fifth installment.

should keep nothing else—difficult indeed as that might be in the face of all that, in our prodigious experience, seemed least to be questioned. Late that night, while the house slept, we had another talk in my room; when she went all the way with me as to its being beyond doubt that I had seen exactly what I had seen. I found that to keep her thoroughly in the grip of this I had only to ask her how, if I had "made it up," I came to be able to give, of each of the persons appearing to me, a picture disclosing, to the last detail, their special marks—a portrait on the exhibition of which she had instantly recognised and named them. She wished, of course—small blame to her!—to sink the whole subject; and I was quick to assure her that my own interest in it had now violently taken the form of a search for the way to escape from it. I closed with her cordially on the article of the likelihood that with recurrence—for recurrence we took for granted—I should get used to my danger; distinctly professing that my personal exposure had suddenly become the least of my discomforts. It was my new suspicion that was intolerable; and yet even to this complication the later hours of the day had brought a little ease.

On leaving her, after my first outbreak, I had of course returned to my pupils, associating the right remedy for my dismay with that sense of their charm which I had already recognised as a resource I could positively cultivate and which had never failed me yet. I had simply, in other words, plunged afresh into Flora's special society and there become aware—it was almost a luxury!—that she could put her little conscious hand straight upon the spot that ached. She had looked at me in sweet speculation and then had accused me to my face of having "cried." I had supposed the ugly signs of it brushed away; but I could literally—for the time at all events—rejoice, under this fathomless charity, that they had not entirely disappeared. To gaze into the depths of blue of the child's eyes and pronounce their loveliness a trick of premature cunning was to be guilty of a cynicism in preference to which I naturally preferred to abjure my judgement and, so far as might be, my agitation. I couldn't abjure for merely wanting to, but I could repeat to Mrs. Grose—as I did there, over and over, in the small hours—that with our small friends' voices in the air, their pressure on one's heart and their fragrant faces against one's cheek, everything fell to the ground but their incapacity and their beauty. It was a pity that, somehow, to settle this once for all, I had equally to re-enumerate the signs of subtlety that, in the afternoon, by the lake, had made a miracle of my show of self-possession. It was a pity to be obliged to re-investigate the certitude of the moment itself and repeat how it had come to me as a revelation that the inconceivable communion I then surprised must have been for both parties a matter of habit. It was a pity that I should have had to quaver out again the reasons for my not having, in my delusion, so much as questioned that the little girl saw our visitant even as I actually saw Mrs. Grose herself, and that she wanted, by just so much as she did thus see, to make me suppose she didn't, and at the same time, without showing anything, arrive at a guess as to whether I myself did! It was a pity I needed to recapitulate the portentous little activities by which she sought to divert my attention—the perceptible increase of movement, the greater intensity of play, the singing, the gabbling of nonsense and the invitation to romp.

Yet if I had not indulged, to prove there was nothing in it, in this review, I should have missed the two or three dim elements of comfort that still remained to me. I shouldn't for instance have been able to asseverate to my friend that I was certain—which was so much to the good—that *I* at least had not betrayed myself. I shouldn't have been prompted, by stress of need, by desperation of mind—I scarce know what to call it—to invoke such further aid to intelligence as might spring from pushing my colleague fairly to the wall. She had told me, bit by bit, under pressure, a great deal; but a small shifty spot on the wrong side of it all still sometimes brushed my brow like the wing of a bat; and I remember how on this occasion—for the sleeping house and the concentration alike of our danger and our watch seemed to help—I felt the importance of giving the last jerk to the curtain. "I don't believe anything so horrible," I recollect saying; "no, let us put it definitely, my dear, that I don't. But if I did, you know, there's a thing I should require now, just without sparing you the least bit more—oh not a scrap, come!—to get out of you. What was it you had in mind when, in our distress, before Miles came back, over the letter from his school, you said, under my insistence, that you didn't pretend for him he hadn't literally *ever* been 'bad'? He has *not*, truly, 'ever,' in these weeks that I myself have lived with him and so closely watched him; he has been an imperturbable little prodigy of delightful loveable goodness. Therefore you might perfectly have made the claim for him if you had not, as it happened, seen an exception to take. What was your exception, and to what passage in your personal observation of him did you refer?"

It was a straight question enough, but levity was not our note, and in any case I had before the grey dawn admonished us to separate got my answer. What my friend had had in mind proved immensely to the purpose. It was neither more nor less than the particular fact that for a period of several months Quint and the boy had been perpetually together. It was indeed the very appropriate item of evidence of her having ventured to criticize the propriety, to hint at the incongruity, of so close an alliance, and even to go so far on the subject as a frank overture to Miss Jessel would take her. Miss Jessel had, with a very high manner about it, requested her to mind her business, and the good woman had on this directly approached little Miles. What she had said to him, since I pressed, was that *she* liked to see young gentlemen not forget their station.

I pressed again, of course, the closer for that. "You reminded him that Quint was only a base menial?"

"As you might say! And it was his answer, for one thing, that was bad."

"And for another thing?" I waited. "He repeated your words to Quint?"

"No, not that. It's just what he *wouldn't!*" she could still impress upon me. "I was sure, at any rate," she added, "that he didn't. But he denied certain occasions."

"What occasions?"

"When they had been about together quite as if Quint were his tutor—and a very grand one—and Miss Jessel only for the little lady. When he had gone off with the fellow, I mean, and spent hours with him."

"He then prevaricated about it—he said he hadn't?" Her assent was clear enough to cause me to add in a moment: "I see. He lied."

"Oh!" Mrs. Grose mumbled. This was a suggestion that it didn't matter; which indeed she backed up by a further remark. "You see, after all, Miss Jessel didn't mind. She didn't forbid him."

I considered. "Did he put that to you as a justification?"

At this she dropped again. "No, he never spoke of it."

"Never mentioned her in connexion with Quint?"

She saw, visibly flushing, where I was coming out. "Well, he didn't show anything. He denied," she repeated; "he denied."

Lord, how I pressed her now! "So that you could see he knew what was between the two wretches?"

"I don't know—I don't know!" the poor woman wailed.

"You do know, you dear thing," I replied; "only you haven't my dreadful boldness of mind, and you keep back, out of timidity and modesty and delicacy, even the impression that in the past, when you had, without my aid, to flounder about in silence, most of all made you miserable. But I shall get it out of you yet! There was something in the boy that suggested to you," I continued, "his covering and concealing their relation."

"Oh he couldn't prevent—"

"Your learning the truth? I dare say! But, heavens," I fell, with vehemence, a-thinking, "what it shows that they must, to that extent, have succeeded in making of him!"

"Ah nothing that's not nice *now*!" Mrs. Grose lugubriously pleaded.

"I don't wonder you looked queer," I persisted, "when I mentioned to you the letter from his school!"

"I doubt if I looked as queer as you!" she retorted with homely force. "And if he was so bad then as that comes to, how is he such an angel now?"

"Yes indeed—and if he was a fiend at school! How, how, how? Well," I said in my torment, "you must put it to me again, though I shall not be able to tell you for some days. Only put it to me again!" I cried in a way that made my friend stare. "There are directions in which I mustn't for the present let myself go." Meanwhile I returned to her first example—the one to which she had just previously referred—of the boy's happy capacity for an occasional slip. "If Quint—on your remonstrance at the time you speak of—was a base menial, one of the things Miles said to you, I find myself guessing, was that you were another." Again her admission was so adequate that I continued: "And you forgave him that?"

"Wouldn't *you*?"

"Oh yes!" And we exchanged there, in the stillness, a sound of the oddest amusement. Then I went on: "At all events, while he was with the man—"

"Miss Flora was with the woman. It suited them all!"

It suited me too, I felt, only too well; by which I mean that it suited exactly the particularly deadly view I was in the very act of forbidding myself to entertain. But I so far succeeded in checking the expression of this view that I will throw, just here, no further light on it than may be offered by the mention of my final observation to Mrs. Grose. "His having lied and been impudent are, I confess, less engaging specimens than I had hoped to have from you of the outbreak in him of the little natural man. Still," I mused, "they must do, for they make me feel more than ever that I must watch."

It made me blush, the next minute, to see in my friend's face how much more unreservedly she had forgiven him than her anecdote struck me as pointing out to my own tenderness any way to do. This was marked when, at the schoolroom door, she quitted me. "Surely you don't accuse *him*—"

"Of carrying on an intercourse that he conceals from me? Ah remember that, until further evidence, I now accuse nobody." Then before shutting her out to go by another passage to her own place, "I must just wait," I wound up.

IX

I waited and waited, and the days took as they elapsed something from my consternation. A very few of them, in fact, passing, in constant sight of my pupils, without a fresh incident, sufficed to give to grievous fancies and even to odious memories a kind of brush of the sponge. I have spoken of the surrender to their extraordinary childish grace as a thing I could actively promote in myself, and it may be imagined if I neglected now to apply at this source for whatever balm it would yield. Stranger than I can express, certainly, was the effort to struggle against my new lights. It would doubtless have been a greater tension still, however, had it not been so frequently successful. I used to wonder how my little charges could help guessing that I thought strange things about them; and the circumstance that these things only made them more interesting was not by itself a direct aid to keeping them in the dark. I trembled lest they should see that they *were* so immensely more interesting. Putting things at the worst, at all events, as in meditation I so often did, any clouding of their innocence could only be—blameless and foredoomed as they were—a reason the more for taking risks. There were moments when I knew myself to catch them up by an irresistible impulse and press them to my heart. As soon as I had done so I used to wonder—"What will they think of that? Doesn't it betray too much?" It would have been easy to get into a sad wild tangle about how much I might betray; but the real account, I feel, of the hours of peace I could still enjoy was that the immediate charm of my companions was a beguilement still effective even under the shadow of the possibility that it was studied. For if it occurred to me that I might occasionally excite suspicion by the little outbreaks of my sharper passion for them, so too I remember asking if I mightn't see a queerness in the traceable increase of their own demonstrations.

They were at this period extravagantly and preternaturally fond of me; which, after all, I could reflect, was no more than a graceful response in children perpetually bowed down over and hugged. The homage of which they were so lavish succeeded in truth for my nerves quite as well as if I never appeared to myself, as I may say, literally to catch them at a purpose in it. They had never, I think, wanted to do so many things for their poor protectress; I mean—though they got their lessons better and better, which was naturally what would please her most—in the way of diverting, entertaining, surprising her; reading her passages, telling her stories, acting her charades, pouncing out at her, in disguises, as animals and historical characters, and above all astonishing her by the "pieces" they had secretly got by heart and could interminably recite. I should never get to the bottom— were I to let myself go even now—of the prodigious private commentary, all under still more private correction, with which I in these days overscored their full hours. They had shown me from the first a facility for everything, a general faculty which, taking a fresh start, achieved remarkable flights. They got their little tasks as if they loved them; they indulged, from the mere exuberance of the gift, in the most unimposed little miracles of memory. They not only popped out at me as tigers and as Romans, but as Shakespeareans, astronomers, and navigators. This was so singularly the case that it had presumably much to do with the fact as to which, at the present day, I am at a loss for a different explanation: I allude to my unnatural composure on the subject of another school for Miles. What I remember is that I was content for the time not to open the question, and that contentment must have sprung from the sense of his perpetually striking show of cleverness. He was too clever for a bad governess, for a parson's daughter, to spoil; and the strangest if not the brightest thread in the pensive embroidery I just spoke of was the impression I might have got, if I had dared to work it out, that he was under some influence operating in his small intellectual life as a tremendous incitement.

If it was easy to reflect, however, that such a boy could postpone school, it was at least as marked that for such a boy to have been "kicked out" by a schoolmaster was a mystification without end. Let me add that in their company now—and I was careful almost never to be out of it—I could follow no scent very far. We lived in a cloud of music and affection and success and private theatricals. The musical sense in each of the children was of the quickest, but the elder in especial had a marvellous knack of catching and repeating. The schoolroom piano broke into all gruesome fancies; and when that failed there were confabulations in corners, with a sequel of one of them going out in the highest spirits in order to "come in" as something new. I had had brothers myself, and it was no revelation to me that little girls could be slavish idolaters of little boys. What surpassed everything was that there was a little boy in the world who could have for the inferior age, sex and intelligence so fine a consideration. They were extraordinarily at one, and to say that they never either quarrelled or complained is to make the note of praise coarse for their quality of sweetness. Sometimes perhaps indeed (when I dropped into coarseness) I perhaps came across traces of little understandings between them by which one of them should keep me occupied while the other slipped away. There is a naïf side, I suppose, in all diplomacy; but if my pupils practised upon me, it was surely with the minimum of grossness. It was all in the other quarter that, after a lull, the grossness broke out.

I find that I really hang back; but I must take my horrid plunge. In going on with the record of what was hideous at Bly I not only challenge the most liberal faith—for which I little care; but (and this is another matter) I renew what I myself suffered, I again push my dreadful way through it to the end. There came suddenly an hour after which, as I look back, the business seems to me to have been all pure suffering; but I have at least reached the heart of it, and the straightest road out is doubtless to advance. One evening—with nothing to lead up or prepare it—I felt the cold touch of the impression that had breathed on me the night of my arrival and which, much lighter then as I have mentioned, I should probably have made little of in memory had my subsequent sojourn been less agitated. I had not gone to bed; I sat reading by a couple of candles. There was a roomful of old books at Bly—last-century fiction some of it, which, to the extent of a distinctly deprecated renown, but never to so much as that of a stray specimen, had reached the sequestered home and appealed to the unavowed curiosity of my youth. I remember that the book I had in my hand was Fielding's "Amelia";[1] also that I was wholly awake. I recall further both a general conviction that it was horribly late and a particular objection to looking at my watch. I figure finally that the white curtain draping, in the fashion of those days, the head of Flora's little bed, shrouded, as I had assured myself long before, the perfection of childish rest. I recollect in short that though I was deeply interested in my

---

1 A novel (1751) by Henry Fielding (1707–54) about a kind young wife who forgives her husband for his many failings.

author I found myself, at the turn of a page and with his spell all scattered, looking straight up from him and hard at the door of my room. There was a moment during which I listened, reminded of the faint sense I had had, the first night, of there being something undefinably astir in the house, and noted the soft breath of the open casement just move the half-drawn blind. Then, with all the marks of a deliberation that must have seemed magnificent had there been anyone to admire it, I laid down my book, rose to my feet, and, taking a candle, went straight out of the room and, from the passage, on which my light made little impression, noiselessly closed and locked the door.

I can say now neither what determined nor what guided me, but I went straight along the lobby, holding my candle high, till I came within sight of the tall window that presided over the great turn of the staircase. At this point I precipitately found myself aware of three things. They were practically simultaneous, yet they had flashes of succession. My candle, under a bold flourish, went out, and I perceived, by the uncovered window, that the yielding dusk of earliest morning rendered it unnecessary. Without it, the next instant, I knew that there was a figure on the stair. I speak of sequences, but I required no lapse of seconds to stiffen myself for a third encounter with Quint. The apparition had reached the landing half-way up and was therefore on the spot nearest the window, where, at sight of me, it stopped short and fixed me exactly as it had fixed me from the tower and from the garden. He knew me as well as I knew him; and so, in the cold faint twilight, with a glimmer in the high glass and another on the polish of the oak stair below, we faced each other in our common intensity. He was absolutely, on this occasion, a living detestable dangerous presence. But that was not the wonder of wonders; I reserve this distinction for quite another circumstance: the circumstance that dread had unmistakably quitted me and that there was nothing in me unable to meet and measure him.

I had plenty of anguish after that extraordinary moment, but I had, thank God, no terror. And he knew I hadn't—I found myself at the end of an instant magnificently aware of this. I felt, in a fierce rigour of confidence, that if I stood my ground a minute I should cease—for the time at least—to have him to reckon with; and during the minute, accordingly, the thing was as human and hideous as a real interview: hideous just because it *was* human, as human as to have met alone, in the small hours, in a sleeping house, some enemy, some adventurer, some criminal. It was the dead silence of our long gaze at such close quarters that gave the whole horror, huge as it was, its only note of the unnatural. If I had met a murderer in such a place and at such an hour we still at least would have spoken. Something would have passed, in life, between us; if nothing had passed one of us would have moved. The moment was so prolonged that it would have taken but little more to make me doubt if even *I* were in life. I can't express what followed it save by saying that the silence itself—which was indeed in a manner an attestation of my strength—became the element into which I saw the figure disappear; in which I definitely saw it turn, as I might have seen the low wretch to which it had once belonged turn on receipt of an order, and pass, with my eyes on the villainous back that no hunch could have more disfigured, straight down the staircase and into the darkness in which the next bend was lost.[1]

X

I remained a while at the top of the stair, but with the effect presently of understanding that when my visitor had gone, he had gone; then I returned to my room. The foremost thing I saw there by the light of the candle I had left burning was that Flora's little bed was empty; and on this I caught my breath with all the terror that, five minutes before, I had been able to resist. I dashed at the place in which I had left her lying and over which—for the small silk counterpane and the sheets were disarranged—the white curtains had been deceivingly pulled forward; then my step, to my unutterable relief, produced an answering sound: I noticed an agitation of the window-blind, and the child, ducking down, emerged rosily from the other side of it. She stood there in so much of her candour and so little of her night-gown, with her pink bare feet and the golden glow of her curls. She looked intensely grave, and I had never had such a sense of losing an advantage acquired (the thrill of which had just been so prodigious) as on my consciousness that she addressed me with a reproach—"You naughty: where *have* you been?" Instead of challenging her own irregularity I found myself arraigned and explaining. She herself explained, for that matter, with the loveliest, eagerest simplicity. She had known suddenly, as she lay there, that I was out of the room, and had jumped up to see what had become of me. I had dropped, with the joy of her reappearance, back into my chair—feeling then, and then only, a little faint; and

---

1 End of sixth installment.

she had pattered straight over to me, thrown herself upon my knee, given herself to be held with the flame of the candle full in the wonderful little face that was still flushed with sleep. I remember closing my eyes an instant, yieldingly, consciously, as before the excess of something beautiful that shone out of the blue of her own. "You were looking for me out of the window?" I said. "You thought I might be walking in the grounds?"

"Well, you know, I thought someone was"—she never blanched as she smiled out that at me.

Oh how I looked at her now! "And did you see anyone?"

"Ah *no*!" she returned almost (with the full privilege of childish inconsequence) resentfully, though with a long sweetness in her little drawl of the negative.

At that moment, in the state of my nerves, I absolutely believed she lied; and if I once more closed my eyes it was before the dazzle of the three or four possible ways in which I might take this up. One of these for a moment tempted me with such singular force that, to resist it, I must have gripped my little girl with a spasm that, wonderfully, she submitted to without a cry or a sign of fright. Why not break out at her on the spot and have it all over?—give it to her straight in her lovely little lighted face? "You see, you see, you *know* that you do and that you already quite suspect I believe it; therefore why not frankly confess it to me, so that we may at least live with it together and learn perhaps, in the strangeness of our fate, where we are and what it means?" This solicitation dropped, alas, as it came: if I could immediately have succumbed to it I might have spared myself—well, you'll see what. Instead of succumbing I sprang again to my feet, looked at her bed and took a helpless middle way. "Why did you pull the curtain over the place to make me think you were still there?"

Flora luminously considered; after which, with her little divine smile: "Because I don't like to frighten you!"

"But if I had, by your idea, gone out—?"

She absolutely declined to be puzzled; she turned her eyes to the flame of the candle as if the question were as irrelevant, or at any rate as impersonal, as Mrs. Marcet[1] or nine-times-nine. "Oh but you know," she quite adequately answered, "that you might come back, you dear, and that you *have*!" And after a little, when she had got into bed, I had, for a long time, by almost sitting on her for the retention of her hand, to show how I recognised the pertinence of my return.

---

1 Jane Marcet (1769–1858), an author of children's science textbooks.

You may imagine the general complexion, from that moment, of my nights. I repeatedly sat up till I didn't know when; I selected moments when my room-mate unmistakeably slept, and, stealing out, took noiseless turns in the passage. I even pushed as far as to where I had last met Quint. But I never met him there again, and I may as well say at once that I on no other occasion saw him in the house. I just missed, on the staircase, nevertheless, a different adventure. Looking down it from the top I once recognised the presence of a woman seated on one of the lower steps with her back presented to me, her body half-bowed and her head, in an attitude of woe, in her hands. I had been there but an instant, however, when she vanished without looking round at me. I knew, for all that, exactly what dreadful face she had to show; and I wondered whether, if instead of being above I had been below, I should have had the same nerve for going up that I had lately shown Quint. Well, there continued to be plenty of call for nerve. On the eleventh night after my latest encounter with that gentleman—they were all numbered now—I had an alarm that perilously skirted it and that indeed, from the particular quality of its unexpectedness, proved quite my sharpest shock. It was precisely the first night during this series that, weary with vigils, I had conceived I might again without laxity lay myself down at my old hour. I slept immediately and, as I afterwards knew, till about one o'clock; but when I woke it was to sit straight up, as completely roused as if a hand had shaken me. I had left a light burning, but it was now out, and I felt an instant certainty that Flora had extinguished it. This brought me to my feet and straight, in the darkness, to her bed, which I found she had left. A glance at the window enlightened me further, and the striking of a match completed the picture.

The child had again got up—this time blowing out the taper, and had again, for some purpose of observation or response, squeezed in behind the blind and was peering out into the night. That she now saw—as she had not, I had satisfied myself, the previous time—was proved to me by the fact that she was disturbed neither by my re-illumination nor by the haste I made to get into slippers and into a wrap. Hidden, protected, absorbed, she evidently rested on the sill—the casement opened forward—and gave herself up. There was a great still moon to help her, and this fact had counted in my quick decision. She was face to face with the apparition we had met at the lake, and could now communicate with it as she had not then been able to do. What I, on my side, had to care for was, without disturbing her, to reach, from the corridor, some other window turned to the same quarter. I got to the door without her hearing me; I got out of it, closed it and listened, from the other side, for some sound from her. While I stood in the passage I had my eyes on her brother's door, which was but ten steps off and which, indescribably, produced in me a renewal of the strange impulse that I lately spoke of as my temptation. What if I should go straight in and march to *his* window?—what if, by risking to his boyish bewilderment a revelation of my motive, I should throw across the rest of the mystery the long halter of my boldness?

This thought held me sufficiently to make me cross to his threshold and pause again. I preternaturally listened; I figured to myself what might portentously be; I wondered if his bed were also empty and he also secretly at watch. It was a deep soundless minute, at the end of which my impulse failed. He was quiet; he might be innocent; the risk was hideous; I turned away. There was a figure in the grounds—a figure prowling for a sight, the visitor with whom Flora was engaged; but it wasn't the visitor most concerned with my boy. I hesitated afresh, but on other grounds and only a few seconds; then I had made my choice. There were empty rooms enough at Bly, and it was only a question of choosing the right one. The right one suddenly presented itself to me as the lower one—though high above the gardens—in the solid corner of the house that I have spoken of as the old tower. This was a large square chamber, arranged with some state as a bedroom, the extravagant size of which made it so inconvenient that it had not for years, though kept by Mrs. Grose in exemplary order, been occupied. I had often admired it and I knew my way about in it; I had only, after just faltering at the first chill gloom of its disuse, to pass across it and unbolt in all quietness one of the shutters. Achieving this transit I uncovered the glass without a sound and, applying my face to the pane, was able, the darkness without being much less than within, to see that I commanded the right direction. Then I saw something more. The moon made the night extraordinarily penetrable and showed me on the lawn a person, diminished by distance, who stood there motionless and as if fascinated, looking up to where I had appeared—looking, that is, not so much straight at me as at something that was apparently above me. There was clearly another person above me—there was a person on the tower; but the presence on the lawn was not in the least what I had conceived and had confidently hurried to meet. The presence on the lawn—I felt sick as I made it out—was poor little Miles himself.

XI

It was not till late next day that I spoke to Mrs. Grose; the rigour with which I kept my pupils in sight making it often difficult to meet her privately: the more as we each felt the importance of not provoking—on the part of the servants quite as much as on that of the children—any suspicion of a secret flurry or of a discussion of mysteries. I drew a great security in this particular from her mere smooth aspect. There was nothing in her fresh face to pass on to others the least of my horrible confidences. She believed me, I was sure, absolutely: if she hadn't I don't know what would have become of me, for I couldn't have borne the strain alone. But she was a magnificent monument to the blessing of a want of imagination, and if she could see in our little charges nothing but their beauty and amiability, their happiness and cleverness, she had no direct communication with the sources of my trouble. If they had been at all visibly blighted or battered she would doubtless have grown, on tracing it back, haggard enough to match them; as matters stood, however, I could feel her, when she surveyed them with her large white arms folded and the habit of serenity in all her look, thank the Lord's mercy that if they were ruined the pieces would still serve. Flights of fancy gave place, in her mind, to a steady fireside glow, and I had already begun to perceive how, with the development of the conviction that—as time went on without a public accident—our young things could, after all, look out for themselves, she addressed her greatest solicitude to the sad case presented by their deputy-guardian. That, for myself, was a sound simplification: I could engage that, to the world, my face should tell no tales, but it would have been, in the conditions, an immense added worry to find myself anxious about hers.

At the hour I now speak of she had joined me, under pressure, on the terrace, where, with the lapse of the season, the afternoon sun was now agreeable; and we sat there together while before us and at a distance, yet within call if we wished, the children strolled to and fro in one of their most manageable moods. They moved slowly, in unison, below us, over the lawn, the boy, as they went, reading aloud from a story-book and passing his arm round his sister to keep her quite in touch. Mrs. Grose watched them with positive placidity; then I caught the suppressed intellectual creak with which she conscientiously turned to take from me a view of the back of the tapestry. I had made her a receptacle of lurid things, but there was an odd recognition of my superiority—my accomplishments and my function—in her patience under my pain. She offered her mind to my disclosures as, had I wished to mix a witch's broth and proposed it with assurance, she would have held out a large clean saucepan. This had become thoroughly her attitude by the time that, in my recital of the events of the night, I reached the point of what Miles had said to me when, after seeing him, at such a monstrous hour, almost on the very spot where he happened now to be, I had gone down to bring him in; choosing then, at the window, with a concentrated need of not alarming the house, rather that method than any noisier process. I had left her meanwhile in little doubt of my small hope of representing with success even to her actual sympathy my sense of the real splendour of the little inspiration with which, after I had got him into the house, the boy met my final articulate challenge. As soon as I appeared in the moonlight on the terrace he had come to me as straight as possible; on which I had taken his hand without a word and led him, through the dark spaces, up the staircase where Quint had so hungrily hovered for him, along the lobby where I had listened and trembled, and so to his forsaken room.

Not a sound, on the way, had passed between us, and I had wondered—oh *how* I had wondered!—if he were groping about in his dreadful little mind for something plausible and not too grotesque. It would tax his invention, certainly, and I felt, this time, over his real embarrassment, a curious thrill of triumph. It was a sharp trap for any game hitherto successful. He could play no longer at perfect propriety, nor could he pretend to it; so how the deuce would he get out of the scrape? There beat in me indeed, with the passionate throb of this question, an equal dumb appeal as to how the deuce *I* should. I was confronted at last, as never yet, with all the risk attached even now to sounding my own horrid note. I remember in fact that as we pushed into his little chamber, where the bed had not been slept in at all and the window, uncovered to the moonlight, made the place so clear that there was no need of striking a match—I remember how I suddenly dropped, sank upon the edge of the bed from the force of the idea that he must know how he really, as they say, "had" me. He could do what he liked, with all his cleverness to help him, so long as I should continue to defer to the old tradition of the criminality of those caretakers of the young who minister to superstitions and fears. He "had" me indeed, and in a cleft stick; for who would ever absolve me, who would consent that I should go unhung, if, by the faintest tremor of an overture, I were the first to introduce into our perfect intercourse an element so dire? No, no: it was useless to attempt to convey to Mrs. Grose, just as it is scarcely less so to attempt to suggest here, how, during our short stiff brush there in the dark, he fairly shook me with admiration. I was of course thoroughly kind and merciful; never, never yet had I placed on his small shoulders hands of such tenderness as those with which, while I rested against the bed, I held him there well under fire. I had no alternative but, in form at least, to put it to him.

"You must tell me now—and all the truth. What did you go out for? What were you doing there?"

I can still see his wonderful smile, the whites of his beautiful eyes and the uncovering of his clear teeth, shine to me in the dusk. "If I tell you why, will you understand?" My heart, at this, leaped into my mouth. *Would* he tell me why? I found no sound on my lips to press it, and I was aware of answering only with a vague repeated grimacing nod. He was gentleness itself, and while I wagged my head at him he stood there more than ever a little fairy prince. It was his brightness indeed that gave me a respite. Would it be so great if he were really going to tell me? "Well," he said at last, "just exactly in order that you should do this."

"Do what?"

"Think me—for a change—*bad*!" I shall never forget the sweetness and gaiety with which he brought out the word, nor how, on top of it, he bent forward and kissed me. It was practically the end of everything. I met his kiss and I had to make, while I folded him for a minute in my arms, the most stupendous effort not to cry. He had given exactly the account of himself that permitted least my going behind it, and it was only with the effect of confirming my acceptance of it that, as I presently glanced about the room, I could say—

"Then you didn't undress at all?"

He fairly glittered in the gloom. "Not at all. I sat up and read."

"And when did you go down?"

"At midnight. When I'm bad I *am* bad!"

"I see, I see—it's charming. But how could you be sure I would know it?"

"Oh I arranged that with Flora." His answers rang out with a readiness! "She was to get up and look out."

"Which is what she did do." It was I who fell into the trap!

"So she disturbed you, and, to see what she was looking at, you also looked—you saw."

"While you," I concurred, "caught your death in the night air!"

He literally bloomed so from this exploit that he could afford radiantly to assent. "How otherwise should I have been bad enough?" he asked. Then, after another embrace, the incident and our interview closed on my recognition of all the reserves of goodness that, for his joke, he had been able to draw upon.

XII

The particular impression I had received proved in the morning light, I repeat, not quite successfully presentable to Mrs. Grose, though I re-enforced it with the mention of still another remark that he had made before we separated. "It all lies in half a dozen words," I said to her, "words that really settle the matter. 'Think, you know, what I *might* do!' He threw that off to show me how good he is. He knows down to the ground what he 'might' do. That's what he gave them a taste of at school."

"Lord, you do change!" cried my friend.

"I don't change—I simply make it out. The four, depend upon it, perpetually meet. If on either of these last nights you had been with either child you'd clearly have understood. The more I've watched and waited the more I've felt that if there were nothing else to make it sure it would be made so by the systematic silence of each. *Never*, by a slip of the tongue, have they so much as alluded to either of their old friends, any more than Miles has alluded to his expulsion. Oh yes, we may sit here and look at them, and they may show off to us there to their fill; but even while they pretend to be lost in their fairy-tale they're steeped in their vision of the dead restored to them. He's not reading to her," I declared; "they're talking of *them*—they're talking horrors! I go on, I know, as if I were crazy; and it's a wonder I'm not. What I've seen would have made *you* so; but it has only made me more lucid, made me get hold of still other things."

My lucidity must have seemed awful, but the charming creatures who were victims of it, passing and repassing in their interlocked sweetness, gave my colleague something to hold on by; and I felt how tight she held as, without stirring in the breath of my passion, she covered them still with her eyes. "Of what other things have you got hold?"

"Why of the very things that have delighted, fascinated and yet, at bottom, as I now so strangely see, mystified and troubled me. Their more than earthly beauty, their absolutely unnatural goodness. It's a game," I went on; "it's a policy and a fraud!"

"On the part of little darlings—?"

"As yet mere lovely babies? Yes, mad as that seems!" The very act of bringing it out really helped me to trace it—follow it all up and piece it all together. "They haven't been good—they've only been absent. It has been easy to live with them because they're simply leading a life of their own. They're not mine—they're not ours. They're his and they're hers!"

"Quint's and that woman's?"

"Quint's and that woman's. They want to get to them."

Oh how, at this, poor Mrs. Grose appeared to study them! "But for what?"

"For the love of all the evil that, in those dreadful days, the pair put into them. And to ply them with that evil still, to keep up the work of demons, is what brings the others back."

"Laws!" said my friend under her breath. The exclamation was homely, but it revealed a real acceptance of my further proof of what, in the bad time—for there had been a worse even than this!—must have occurred. There could have been no such justification for me as the plain assent of her experience to whatever depth of depravity I found credible in our brace of scoundrels. It was in obvious submission of memory that she brought out after a moment: "They *were* rascals! But what can they now do?" she pursued.

"Do?" I echoed so loud that Miles and Flora, as they passed at their distance, paused an instant in their walk and looked at us. "Don't they do enough?" I demanded in a lower tone, while the children, having smiled and nodded and kissed hands to us, resumed their exhibition. We were held by it a minute; then I answered: "They can destroy them!" At this my companion did turn, but the appeal she launched was a silent one, the effect of which was to make me more explicit. "They don't know as yet quite how—but they're trying hard. They're seen only across, as it were, and beyond—in strange places and on high places, the top of towers, the roof of houses, the outside of windows, the further edge of pools; but there's a deep design, on either side, to shorten the distance and overcome the obstacle: so the success of the tempters is only a question of time. They've only to keep to their suggestions of danger."

"For the children to come?"

"And perish in the attempt!" Mrs. Grose slowly got up, and I scrupulously added: "Unless, of course, we can prevent!"

Standing there before me while I kept my seat she visibly

turned things over. "Their uncle must do the preventing. He must take them away."

"And who's to make him?"

She had been scanning the distance, but she now dropped on me a foolish face. "You, Miss."

"By writing to him that his house is poisoned and his little nephew and niece mad?"

"But if they *are*, Miss?"

"And if I am myself, you mean? That's charming news to be sent him by a person enjoying his confidence and whose prime undertaking was to give him no worry."

Mrs. Grose considered, following the children again. "Yes, he do hate worry. That was the great reason—"

"Why those fiends took him in so long? No doubt, though his indifference must have been awful. As I'm not a fiend, at any rate, I shouldn't take him in."

My companion, after an instant and for all answer, sat down again and grasped my arm. "Make him at any rate come to you."

I stared. "To *me*?" I had a sudden fear of what she might do. "'Him?'"

"He ought to *be* here—he ought to help."

I quickly rose and I think I must have shown her a queerer face than ever yet. "You see me asking him for a visit?" No, with her eyes on my face she evidently couldn't. Instead of it even—as a woman reads another—she could see what I myself saw: his derision, his amusement, his contempt for the breakdown of my resignation at being left alone and for the fine machinery I had set in motion to attract his attention to my slighted charms. She didn't know—no one knew—how proud I had been to serve him and to stick to our terms; yet she nonetheless took the measure, I think, of the warning I now gave her. "If you should so lose your head as to appeal to him for me—"

She was really frightened. "Yes, Miss?"

"I would leave, on the spot, both him and you."[1]

---

1 The *Collier's Weekly* installment continues with the following exchange at this point, so that the seventh installment ended after this passage:

"Then what's your remedy?" she asked as I watched the children.

I continued, without answering, to watch them. "I would leave *them*," and went on.

"But what *is* your remedy?" she persisted.

It seemed, after all, to have come to me then and there. "To speak to them." And I joined them.

XIII

It was all very well to join them, but speaking to them proved quite as much as ever an effort beyond my strength—offered, in close quarters, difficulties as insurmountable as before. This situation continued a month, and with new aggravations and particular notes, the note above all, sharper and sharper, of the small ironic consciousness on the part of my pupils. It was not, I am as sure to-day as I was sure then, my mere infernal imagination: it was absolutely traceable that they were aware of my predicament and that this strange relation made, in a manner, for a long time, the air in which we moved. I don't mean that they had their tongues in their cheeks or did anything vulgar, for that was not one of their dangers: I do mean, on the other hand, that the element of the unnamed and untouched became, between us, greater than any other, and that so much avoidance couldn't have been made successful without a great deal of tacit arrangement. It was as if, at moments, we were perpetually coming into sight of subjects before which we must stop short, turning suddenly out of alleys that we perceived to be blind, closing with a little bang that made us look at each other—for, like all bangs, it was something louder than we had intended—the doors we had indiscreetly opened. All roads lead to Rome, and there were times when it might have struck us that almost every branch of study or subject of conversation skirted forbidden ground. Forbidden ground was the question of the return of the dead in general and of whatever, in especial, might survive, for memory, of the friends little children had lost. There were days when I could have sworn that one of them had, with a small invisible nudge, said to the other: "She thinks she'll do it this time—but she *won't!*" To "do it" would have been to indulge for instance—and for once in a way—in some direct reference to the lady who had prepared them for my discipline. They had a delightful endless appetite for passages in my own history to which I had again and again treated them; they were in possession of everything that had ever happened to me, had had, with every circumstance, the story of my smallest adventures and of those of my brothers and sisters and of the cat and the dog at home, as well as many particulars of the whimsical bent of my father, of the furniture and arrangement of our house, and of the conversation of the old women of our village. There were things enough, taking one with another, to chatter about, if one went very fast and knew by instinct when to go round. They pulled with an art of their own the strings of my invention and my memory; and nothing else perhaps, when I thought of such occasions afterwards, gave me so the suspicion of being watched from under cover. It was in any case over *my* life, *my* past and *my* friends alone that we could take anything like our ease; a state of affairs that led them sometimes without the least pertinence to break out into sociable reminders. I was invited—with no visible connexion—to repeat afresh Goody Gosling's celebrated *mot*[1] or to confirm the details already supplied as to the cleverness of the vicarage pony.

It was partly at such junctures as these and partly at quite different ones that, with the turn my matters had now taken, my predicament, as I have called it, grew most sensible. The fact that the days passed for me without another encounter ought, it would have appeared, to have done something toward soothing my nerves. Since the light brush, that second night on the upper landing, of the presence of a woman at the foot of the stair, I had seen nothing, whether in or out of the house, that one had better not have seen. There was many a corner round which I expected to come upon Quint, and many a situation that, in a merely sinister way, would have favoured the appearance of Miss Jessel. The summer had turned, the summer had gone; the autumn had dropped upon Bly and had blown out half our lights. The place, with its grey sky and withered garlands, its bared spaces and scattered dead leaves, was like a theatre after the performance—all strewn with crumpled playbills. There were exactly states of the air, conditions of sound and of stillness, unspeakable impressions of the *kind* of ministering moment, that brought back to me, long enough to catch it, the feeling of the medium in which, that June evening out of doors, I had had my first sight of Quint, and in which too, at those other instants, I had, after seeing him through the window, looked for him in vain in the circle of shrubbery. I recognised the signs, the portents—I recognised the moment, the spot. But they remained unaccompanied and empty, and I continued unmolested; if unmolested one could call a young woman whose sensibility had, in the most extraordinary fashion, not declined but deepened. I had said in my talk with Mrs. Grose on that horrid scene of Flora's by the lake—and had perplexed her by so saying—that it would from that moment distress me much more to lose my power than to keep it. I had then expressed what

---

1   Word (French). Goody (short for "Goodwife," a courtesy title for women of the lower classes) Gosling is probably one of her native village's old women.

was vividly in my mind: the truth that, whether the children really saw or not—since, that is, it was not yet definitely proved—I greatly preferred, as a safeguard, the fulness of my own exposure. I was ready to know the very worst that was to be known. What I had then had an ugly glimpse of was that my eyes might be sealed just while theirs were most opened. Well, my eyes *were* sealed, it appeared, at present—a consummation for which it seemed blasphemous not to thank God. There was, alas, a difficulty about that: I would have thanked him with all my soul had I not had in a proportionate measure this conviction of the secret of my pupils.

How can I retrace to-day the strange steps of my obsession? There were times of our being together when I would have been ready to swear that, literally, in my presence, but with my direct sense of it closed, they had visitors who were known and were welcome. Then it was that, had I not been deterred by the very chance that such an injury might prove greater than the injury to be averted, my exultation would have broken out. "They're here, they're here, you little wretches," I would have cried, "and you can't deny it now!" The little wretches denied it with all the added volume of their sociability and their tenderness, just in the crystal depths of which—like the flash of a fish in a stream—the mockery of their advantage peeped up. The shock had in truth sunk into me still deeper than I knew on the night when, looking out either for Quint or Miss Jessel under the stars, I had seen there the boy over whose rest I watched and who had immediately brought in with him—had straightway there turned on me—the lovely upward look with which, from the battlements above us, the hideous apparition of Quint had played. If it was a question of a scare my discovery on this occasion had scared me more than any other, and it was essentially in the scared state that I drew my actual conclusions. They harassed me so that sometimes, at odd moments, I shut myself up audibly to rehearse—it was at once a fantastic relief and a renewed despair—the manner in which I might come to the point. I approached it from one side and the other while, in my room, I flung myself about, but I always broke down in the monstrous utterance of names. As they died away on my lips I said to myself that I should indeed help them to represent something infamous if by pronouncing them I should violate as rare a little case of instinctive delicacy as any schoolroom probably had ever known. When I said to myself: "*They* have the manners to be silent, and you, trusted as you are, the baseness to speak!" I felt myself crimson and covered my face with my hands. After these secret scenes I chattered more than ever, going on volubly enough till one of our prodigious palpable hushes occurred—I can call them nothing else—the strange dizzy lift or swim (I try for terms!) into a stillness, a pause of all life, that had nothing to do with the more or less noise that we at the moment might be engaged in making and that I could hear through any intensified mirth or quickened recitation or louder strum of the piano. Then it was that the others, the outsiders, were there. Though they were not angels they "passed," as the French say, causing me, while they stayed, to tremble with the fear of their addressing to their younger victims some yet more infernal message or more vivid image than they had thought good enough for myself.

What it was least possible to get rid of was the cruel idea that, whatever I had seen, Miles and Flora saw *more*—things terrible and unguessable and that sprang from dreadful passages of intercourse in the past. Such things naturally left on the surface, for the time, a chill that we vociferously denied we felt; and we had all three, with repetition, got into such splendid training that we went, each time, to mark the close of the incident, almost automatically through the very same movements. It was striking of the children at all events to kiss me inveterately with a wild irrelevance and never to fail—one or the other—of the precious question that had helped us through many a peril. "When do you think he *will* come? Don't you think we *ought* to write?"—there was nothing like that enquiry, we found by experience, for carrying off an awkwardness. "He" of course was their uncle in Harley Street; and we lived in much profusion of theory that he might at any moment arrive to mingle in our circle. It was impossible to have given less encouragement than he had administered to such a doctrine, but if we had not had the doctrine to fall back upon we should have deprived each other of some of our finest exhibitions. He never wrote to them—that may have been selfish, but it was a part of the flattery of his trust of myself; for the way in which a man pays his highest tribute to a woman is apt to be but by the more festal celebration of one of the sacred laws of his comfort. So I held that I carried out the spirit of the pledge given not to appeal to him when I let our young friends understand that their own letters were but charming literary exercises. They were too beautiful to be posted; I kept them myself; I have them all to this hour. This was a rule indeed which only added to the satiric effect of my being plied with the supposition that he might at any moment be among us. It was exactly as if our young friends knew how almost more awkward than anything else that might be for me. There appears to me moreover as I look back no note in all this more extraordinary than the mere fact that, in spite of my tension and of their triumph, I never lost patience with them. Adorable they must in truth have been, I now feel, that I didn't in these days hate them! Would exasperation, however, if relief had longer been postponed, finally have betrayed me? It little matters, for relief arrived. I call it relief though it was only the relief that a snap brings to a strain or the burst of a thunderstorm to a day of suffocation. It was at least change, and it came with a rush.

XIV

Walking to church a certain Sunday morning, I had little Miles at my side and his sister, in advance of us and at Mrs. Grose's, well in sight. It was a crisp clear day, the first of its order for some time; the night had brought a touch of frost and the autumn air, bright and sharp, made the church-bells almost gay. It was an odd accident of thought that I should have happened at such a moment to be particularly and very gratefully struck with the obedience of my little charges. Why did they never resent my inexorable, my perpetual society? Something or other had brought nearer home to me that I had all but pinned the boy to my shawl, and that in the way our companions were marshalled before me I might have appeared to provide against some danger of rebellion. I was like a gaoler[1] with an eye to possible surprises and escapes. But all this belonged—I mean their magnificent little surrender—just to the special array of the facts that were most abysmal. Turned out for Sunday by his uncle's tailor, who had had a free hand and a notion of pretty waistcoats and of his grand little air, Miles's whole title to independence, the rights of his sex and situation, were so stamped upon him that if he had suddenly struck for freedom I should have had nothing to say. I was by the strangest of chances wondering how I should meet him when the revolution unmistakably occurred. I call it a revolution because I now see how, with the word he spoke, the curtain rose on the last act of my dreadful drama and the catastrophe was precipitated. "Look here, my dear, you know," he charmingly said, "when in the world, please, am I going back to school?"

Transcribed here the speech sounds harmless enough, particularly as uttered in the sweet, high, casual pipe with which, at all

---

1 Jailer (British spelling).

interlocutors, but above all at his eternal governess, he threw off intonations as if he were tossing roses. There was something in them that always made one "catch," and I caught at any rate now so effectually that I stopped as short as if one of the trees of the park had fallen across the road. There was something new, on the spot, between us, and he was perfectly aware I recognised it, though to enable me to do so he had no need to look a whit less candid and charming than usual. I could feel in him how he already, from my at first finding nothing to reply, perceived the advantage he had gained. I was so slow to find anything that he had plenty of time, after a minute, to continue with his suggestive but inconclusive smile: "You know, my dear, that for a fellow to be with a lady *always*—!" His "my dear" was constantly on his lips for me, and nothing could have expressed more the exact shade of the sentiment with which I desired to inspire my pupils than its fond familiarity. It was so respectfully easy.

But oh how I felt that at present I must pick my own phrases! I remember that, to gain time, I tried to laugh, and I seemed to see in the beautiful face with which he watched me how ugly and queer I looked. "And always with the same lady?" I returned.

He neither blanched nor winked. The whole thing was virtually out between us. "Ah of course she's a jolly 'perfect' lady; but after all I'm a fellow, don't you see? who's—well, getting on."

I lingered there with him an instant ever so kindly. "Yes, you're getting on." Oh but I felt helpless!

I have kept to this day the heartbreaking little idea of how he seemed to know that and to play with it. "And you can't say I've not been awfully good, can you?"

I laid my hand on his shoulder, for though I felt how much better it would have been to walk on I was not yet quite able. "No, I can't say that, Miles."

"Except just that one night, you know—!"

"That one night?" I couldn't look as straight as he.

"Why when I went down—went out of the house."

"Oh yes. But I forget what you did it for."

"You forget?"—he spoke with the sweet extravagance of childish reproach. "Why it was just to show you I could!"

"Oh yes—you could."

"And I can again."

I felt I might perhaps after all succeed in keeping my wits about me. "Certainly. But you won't."

"No, not *that* again. It was nothing."

"It was nothing," I said. "But we must go on."

He resumed our walk with me, passing his hand into my arm. "Then when *am* I going back?"

I wore, in turning it over, my most responsible air. "Were you very happy at school?"

He just considered. "Oh I'm happy enough anywhere!"

"Well then," I quavered, "if you're just as happy here—!"

"Ah but that isn't everything! Of course *you* know a lot—"

"But you hint that you know almost as much?" I risked as he paused.

"Not half I want to!" Miles honestly professed. "But it isn't so much that."

"What is it then?"

"Well—I want to see more life."

"I see; I see." We had arrived within sight of the church and of various persons, including several of the household of Bly, on their way to it and clustered about the door to see us go in. I quickened our step; I wanted to get there before the question between us opened up much further; I reflected hungrily that he would have for more than an hour to be silent; and I thought with envy of the comparative dusk of the pew and of the almost spiritual help of the hassock on which I might bend my knees. I seemed literally to be running a race with some confusion to which he was about to reduce me, but I felt he had got in first when, before we had entered the churchyard, he threw out—

"I want my own sort!"

It literally made me bound forward. "There aren't many of your own sort, Miles!" I laughed. "Unless perhaps dear little Flora!"

"You really compare me to a baby girl?"

This found me singularly weak. "Don't you then *love* our sweet Flora?"

"If I didn't—and you too; if I didn't—!" he repeated as if retreating for a jump, yet leaving his thought so unfinished that, after we had come into the gate, another stop, which he imposed on me by the pressure of his arm, had become inevitable. Mrs. Grose and Flora had passed into the church, the other worshippers had followed and we were, for the minute, alone among the old thick graves. We had paused, on the path from the gate, by a low oblong table-like tomb.

"Yes, if you didn't—?"

He looked, while I waited, about at the graves. "Well, you know what!" But he didn't move, and he presently produced something that made me drop straight down on the stone slab as if suddenly to rest. "Does my uncle think what *you* think?"

I markedly rested. "How do you know what I think?"

"Ah well, of course I don't; for it strikes me you never tell me. But I mean does *he* know?"

"Know what, Miles?"

"Why the way I'm going on."

I recognised quickly enough that I could make, to this enquiry, no answer that wouldn't involve something of a sacrifice of my employer. Yet it struck me that we were all, at Bly, sufficiently sacrificed to make that venial. "I don't think your uncle much cares."

Miles, on this, stood looking at me. "Then don't you think he can be made to?"

"In what way?"

"Why by his coming down."

"But who'll get him to come down?"

"*I* will!" the boy said with extraordinary brightness and emphasis. He gave me another look charged with that expression and then marched off alone into church.

XV

The business was practically settled from the moment I never followed him. It was a pitiful surrender to agitation, but my being aware of this had somehow no power to restore me. I only sat there on my tomb and read into what our young friend had said to me the fulness of its meaning; by the time I had grasped the whole of which I had also embraced, for absence, the pretext that I was ashamed to offer my pupils and the rest of the congregation such an example of delay. What I said to myself above all was that Miles had got something out of me and that the gage of it for him would be just this awkward collapse. He had got out of me that there was something I was much afraid of, and that he should probably be able to make use of my fear to gain, for his own purpose, more freedom. My fear was of having to deal with the intolerable question of the grounds of his dismissal from school, since that was really but the question of the horrors gathered behind. That his uncle should arrive to treat with me of these things was a solution that, strictly speaking, I ought now to have desired to bring on; but I could so little face the ugliness and the pain of it that I simply procrastinated and lived from hand to mouth. The boy, to my deep discomposure, was immensely in the right, was in a position to say to me: "Either you clear up with my guardian the mystery of this interruption of my studies, or you cease to expect me to lead with you a life that's so unnatural for a boy." What was so unnatural for the particular boy I was concerned with was this sudden revelation of a consciousness and a plan.

That was what really overcame me, what prevented my going in. I walked round the church, hesitating, hovering; I reflected that I had already, with him, hurt myself beyond repair. Therefore I could patch up nothing and it was too extreme an effort to squeeze beside him into the pew: he would be so much more sure than ever to pass his arm into mine and make me sit there for an hour in close mute contact with his commentary on our talk. For the first minute since his arrival I wanted to get away from him. As I paused beneath the high east window and listened to the sounds of worship I was taken with an impulse that might master me, I felt, and completely, should I give it the least encouragement. I might easily put an end to my ordeal by getting away altogether. Here was my chance; there was no one to stop me; I could give the whole thing up—turn my back and bolt. It was only a question of hurrying again, for a few preparations, to the house which the attendance at church of so many of the servants would practically have left unoccupied. No one, in short, could blame me if I should just drive desperately off. What was it to get away if I should get away only till dinner? That would be in a couple of hours, at the end of which—I had the acute prevision—my little pupils would play at innocent wonder about my non-appearance in their train.

"What *did* you do, you naughty bad thing? Why in the world, to worry us so—and take our thoughts off too, don't you know?— did you desert us at the very door?" I couldn't meet such questions nor, as they asked them, their false little lovely eyes; yet it was all so exactly what I should have to meet that, as the prospect grew sharp to me, I at last let myself go.

I got, so far as the immediate moment was concerned, away; I came straight out of the churchyard and, thinking hard, retraced my steps through the park. It seemed to me that by the time I reached the house I had made up my mind to cynical flight. The Sunday stillness both of the approaches and of the interior, in which I met no one, fairly stirred me with a sense of opportunity. Were I to get off quickly this way I should get off without a scene, without a word. My quickness would have to be remarkable, however, and the question of a conveyance was the great one to settle. Tormented, in the hall, with difficulties and obstacles, I remember sinking down at the foot of the staircase—suddenly collapsing there on the lowest step and then, with a revulsion, recalling that it was exactly where, more than a month before, in the darkness of night and just so bowed with evil things, I had seen the spectre of the most horrible of women. At this I was able to straighten myself; I went the rest of the way up; I made, in my turmoil, for the schoolroom, where there were objects belonging to me that I should have to take. But I opened the door to find again, in a flash, my eyes unsealed. In the presence of what I saw I reeled straight back upon resistance.

Seated at my own table in the clear noonday light I saw a person whom, without my previous experience, I should have taken at the first blush for some housemaid who might have stayed at home to look after the place and who, availing herself of rare relief from observation and of the schoolroom table and my pens, ink and paper, had applied herself to the considerable effort of a letter to her sweetheart. There was an effort in the way that, while her arms rested on the table, her hands, with evident weariness, supported her head; but at the moment I took this in I had already become aware that, in spite of my entrance, her attitude strangely persisted. Then it was—with the very act of its announcing itself—that her identity flared up in a change of posture. She rose, not as if she had heard me, but with an indescribable grand melancholy of indifference and detachment, and, within a dozen feet of me, stood there as my vile predecessor. Dishonoured and tragic, she was all before me; but even as I fixed and, for memory, secured it, the awful image passed away. Dark as midnight in her black dress, her haggard beauty and her unutterable woe, she had looked at me long enough to appear to say that her right to sit at my table was as good as mine to sit at hers. While these instants lasted indeed I had the extraordinary chill of feeling that it was I who was the intruder. It was as a wild protest against it that, actually addressing her—"You terrible miserable woman!"—I heard myself break into a sound that, by the open door, rang through the long passage and the empty house. She looked at me as if she heard me, but I had recovered myself and cleared the air. There was nothing in the room the next minute but the sunshine and the sense that I must stay.[1]

XVI

I had so perfectly expected the return of the others to be marked by a demonstration that I was freshly upset at having to find them

---

1 End of eighth installment.

merely dumb and discreet about my desertion. Instead of gaily denouncing and caressing me they made no allusion to my having failed them, and I was left, for the time, on perceiving that she too said nothing, to study Mrs. Grose's odd face. I did this to such purpose that I made sure they had in some way bribed her to silence; a silence that, however, I would engage to break down on the first private opportunity. This opportunity came before tea: I secured five minutes with her in the housekeeper's room, where, in the twilight, amid a smell of lately-baked bread, but with the place all swept and garnished, I found her sitting in pained placidity before the fire. So I see her still, so I see her best: facing the flame from her straight chair in the dusky shining room, a large clean picture of the "put away"—of drawers closed and locked and rest without a remedy.

"Oh yes, they asked me to say nothing; and to please them— so long as they were there—of course I promised. But what had happened to you?"

"I only went with you for the walk," I said. "I had then to come back to meet a friend."

She showed her surprise. "A friend—*you*?"

"Oh yes, I've a couple!" I laughed. "But did the children give you a reason?"

"For not alluding to your leaving us? Yes; they said you'd like it better. *Do* you like it better?"

My face had made her rueful. "No, I like it worse!" But after an instant I added: "Did they say why I should like it better?"

"No; Master Miles only said 'We must do nothing but what she likes!'"

"I wish indeed he would! And what did Flora say?"

"Miss Flora was too sweet. She said, 'Oh of course, of course!'—and I said the same."

I thought a moment. "You were too sweet too—I can hear you all. But nonetheless, between Miles and me, it's now all out."

"All out?" My companion stared. "But what, Miss?"

"Everything. It doesn't matter. I've made up my mind. I came home, my dear," I went on, "for a talk with Miss Jessel."

I had by this time formed the habit of having Mrs. Grose literally well in hand in advance of my sounding that note; so that even now, as she bravely blinked under the signal of my word, I could keep her comparatively firm. "A talk! Do you mean she spoke?"

"It came to that. I found her, on my return, in the schoolroom."

"And what did she say?" I can hear the good woman still, and the candour of her stupefaction.

"That she suffers the torments—!"

It was this, of a truth, that made her, as she filled out my picture, gape. "Do you mean," she faltered "—of the lost?"

"Of the lost. Of the damned. And that's why, to share them—" I faltered myself with the horror of it.

But my companion, with less imagination, kept me up. "To share them—?"

"She wants Flora." Mrs. Grose might, as I gave it to her, fairly have fallen away from me had I not been prepared. I still held her there, to show I was. "As I've told you, however, it doesn't matter."

"Because you've made up your mind? But to what?"

"To everything."

"And what do you call 'everything'?"

"Why to sending for their uncle."

"Oh Miss, in pity do," my friend broke out.

"Ah, but I will, I *will*! I see it's the only way. What's 'out,' as I told you, with Miles is that if he thinks I'm afraid to—and has ideas of what he gains by that—he shall see he's mistaken. Yes, yes; his uncle shall have it here from me on the spot (and before the boy himself if necessary) that if I'm to be reproached with having done nothing again about more school—"

"Yes, Miss—" my companion pressed me.

"Well, there's that awful reason."

There were now clearly so many of these for my poor colleague that she was excusable for being vague. "But—a—which?"

"Why the letter from his old place."

"You'll show it to the master?"

"I ought to have done so on the instant."

"Oh no!" said Mrs. Grose with decision.

"I'll put it before him," I went on inexorably, "that I can't undertake to work the question on behalf of a child who has been expelled—"

"For we've never in the least known what!" Mrs. Grose declared.

"For wickedness. For what else—when he's so clever and beautiful and perfect? Is he stupid? Is he untidy? Is he infirm? Is he ill-natured? He's exquisite—so it can be only *that*; and that would open up the whole thing. After all," I said, "it's their uncle's fault. If he left here such people—!"

"He didn't really in the least know them. The fault's mine." She had turned quite pale.

"Well, you shan't suffer," I answered.

"The children shan't!" she emphatically returned.

I was silent a while; we looked at each other. "Then what am I to tell him?"

"You needn't tell him anything. *I'll* tell him."

I measured this. "Do you mean you'll write—?" Remembering she couldn't, I caught myself up. "How do you communicate?"

"I tell the bailiff. *He* writes."

"And should you like him to write our story?"

My question had a sarcastic force that I had not fully intended, and it made her after a moment inconsequently break down. The tears were again in her eyes. "Ah, Miss, *you* write!"

"Well—to-night," I at last answered; and on this we separated.

XVII

I went so far, in the evening, as to make a beginning. The weather had changed back, a great wind was abroad, and beneath the lamp, in my room, with Flora at peace beside me, I sat for a long time before a blank sheet of paper and listened to the lash of the rain and the batter of the gusts. Finally I went out, taking a candle; I crossed the passage and listened a minute at Miles's door. What, under my endless obsession, I had been impelled to listen for was some betrayal of his not being at rest, and I presently caught one, but not in the form I had expected. His voice tinkled out. "I say, you there—come in." It was gaiety in the gloom!

I went in with my light and found him in bed, very wide awake but very much at his ease. "Well, what are *you* up to?" he asked with a grace of sociability in which it occurred to me that Mrs. Grose, had she been present, might have looked in vain for proof that anything was "out."

I stood over him with my candle. "How did you know I was there?"

"Why of course I heard you. Did you fancy you made no noise? You're like a troop of cavalry!" he beautifully laughed.

"Then you weren't asleep?"

"Not much! I lie awake and think."

I had put my candle, designedly, a short way off, and then, as he held out his friendly old hand to me, had sat down on the edge of his bed. "What is it," I asked, "that you think of?"

"What in the world, my dear, but *you*?"

"Ah the pride I take in your appreciation doesn't insist on that! I had so far rather you slept."

"Well, I think also, you know, of this queer business of ours."

I marked the coolness of his firm little hand. "Of what queer business, Miles?"

"Why the way you bring me up. And all the rest!"

I fairly held my breath a minute, and even from my glimmering taper there was light enough to show how he smiled up at me from his pillow. "What do you mean by all the rest?"

"Oh you know, you know!"

I could say nothing for a minute, though I felt as I held his hand and our eyes continued to meet that my silence had all the air of admitting his charge and that nothing in the whole world of reality was perhaps at that moment so fabulous[1] as our actual relation. "Certainly you shall go back to school," I said, "if it be that that troubles you. But not to the old place—we must find another, a better. How could I know it did trouble you, this question, when you never told me so, never spoke of it at all?" His clear listening face, framed in its smooth whiteness, made him for the minute as appealing as some wistful patient in a children's hospital; and I would have given, as the resemblance came to me, all I possessed on earth really to be the nurse or the sister of charity who might have helped to cure him. Well, even as it was I perhaps might help! "Do you know you've never said a word to me about your school—I mean the old one; never mentioned it in any way?"

He seemed to wonder; he smiled with the same loveliness. But he clearly gained time; he waited, he called for guidance. "Haven't I?" It wasn't for *me* to help him—it was for the thing I had met!

Something in his tone and the expression of his face, as I got this from him, set my heart aching with such a pang as it had never yet known; so unutterably touching was it to see his little brain puzzled and his little resources taxed to play, under the spell laid on him, a part of innocence and consistency. "No, never—from the hour you came back. You've never mentioned to me one of your masters, one of your comrades, nor the least little thing that ever happened to you at school. Never, little Miles—no never—have you given me an inkling of anything that *may* have happened there. Therefore you can fancy how much I'm in the dark. Until you came out, that way, this morning, you had since the first hour I saw you scarce even made a reference to anything in your previous life. You seemed so perfectly to accept the present." It was extraordinary how my absolute conviction of his

---

1 Fable-like.

secret precocity—or whatever I might call the poison of an influence that I dared but half-phrase—made him, in spite of the faint breath of his inward trouble, appear as accessible as an older person, forced me to treat him as an intellectual equal. "I thought you wanted to go on as you are."

It struck me that at this he just faintly coloured. He gave, at any rate, like a convalescent slightly fatigued, a languid shake of his head. "I don't—I don't. I want to get away."

"You're tired of Bly?"

"Oh no, I like Bly."

"Well then—?"

"Oh *you* know what a boy wants!"

I felt I didn't know so well as Miles, and I took temporary refuge. "You want to go to your uncle?"

Again, at this, with his sweet ironic face, he made a movement on the pillow. "Ah you can't get off with that!"

I was silent a little, and it was I now, I think, who changed colour. "My dear, I don't want to get off!"

"You can't even if you do. You can't, you can't!"—he lay beautifully staring. "My uncle must come down and you must completely settle things."

"If we do," I returned with some spirit, "you may be sure it will be to take you quite away."

"Well, don't you understand that that's exactly what I'm working for? You'll have to *tell* him—about the way you've let it all drop: you'll have to tell him a tremendous lot!"

The exultation with which he uttered this helped me somehow for the instant to meet him rather more. "And how much will *you*, Miles, have to tell him? There are things he'll ask you!"

He turned it over. "Very likely. But what things?"

"The things you've never told me. To make up his mind what to do with you. He can't send you back—"

"I don't want to go back!" he broke in. "I want a new field."

He said it with admirable serenity, with positive unimpeachable gaiety; and doubtless it was that very note that most evoked for me the poignancy, the unnatural childish tragedy, of his probable reappearance at the end of three months with all this bravado and still more dishonour. It overwhelmed me now that I should never be able to bear that, and it made me let myself go. I threw myself upon him and in the tenderness of my pity I embraced him. "Dear little Miles, dear little Miles—!"

My face was close to his, and he let me kiss him, simply taking it with indulgent good humour. "Well, old lady?"

"Is there nothing—nothing at all that you want to tell me?"

He turned off a little, facing round toward the wall and holding up his hand to look at as one had seen sick children look. "I've told you—I told you this morning."

Oh I was sorry for him! "That you just want me not to worry you?"

He looked round at me now as if in recognition of my understanding him; then ever so gently, "To let me alone," he replied.

There was even a singular little dignity in it, something that made me release him, yet, when I had slowly risen, linger beside him. God knows *I* never wished to harass him, but I felt that merely, at this, to turn my back on him was to abandon or, to put it more truly, lose him. "I've just begun a letter to your uncle," I said.

"Well then, finish it!"

I waited a minute. "What happened before?"

He gazed up at me again. "Before what?"

"Before you came back. And before you went away."

For some time he was silent, but he continued to meet my eyes. "What happened?"

It made me, the sound of the words, in which it seemed to me I caught for the very first time a small faint quaver of consenting consciousness—it made me drop to my knees beside the bed and seize once more the chance of possessing him. "Dear little Miles, dear little Miles, if you *knew* how I want to help you! It's only that, it's nothing but that, and I'd rather die than give you a pain or do you a wrong—I'd rather die than hurt a hair of you. Dear little Miles"—oh I brought it out now even if I *should* go too far—"I just want you to help me to save you!" But I knew in a moment after this that I had gone too far. The answer to my appeal was instantaneous, but it came in the form of an extraordinary blast and chill, a gust of frozen air and a shake of the room as great as if, in the wild wind, the casement had crashed in. The boy gave a loud high shriek which, lost in the rest of the shock of sound, might have seemed, indistinctly, though I was so close to him, a note either of jubilation or of terror. I jumped to my feet again and was conscious of darkness. So for a moment we remained, while I stared about me and saw the drawn curtains unstirred and the window tight. "Why, the candle's out!" I then cried.

"It was I who blew it, dear!" said Miles.

XVIII

The next day, after lessons, Mrs. Grose found a moment to say to me quietly: "Have you written, Miss?"

"Yes—I've written." But I didn't add—for the hour—that my letter, sealed and directed, was still in my pocket. There would be time enough to send it before the messenger should go to the village. Meanwhile there had been on the part of my pupils no more brilliant, more exemplary morning. It was exactly as if they had both had at heart to gloss over any recent little friction. They performed the dizziest feats of arithmetic, soaring quite out of *my* feeble range, and perpetrated, in higher spirits than ever, geographical and historical jokes. It was conspicuous of course in Miles in particular that he appeared to wish to show how easily he could let me down. This child, to my memory, really lives in a setting of beauty and misery that no words can translate; there was a distinction all his own in every impulse he revealed; never was a small natural creature, to the uninformed eye all frankness and freedom, a more ingenious, a more extraordinary little gentleman. I had perpetually to guard against the wonder of contemplation into which my initiated view betrayed me; to check the irrelevant gaze and discouraged sigh in which I constantly both attacked and renounced the enigma of what such a little gentleman could have done that deserved a penalty. Say that, by the dark prodigy I knew, the imagination of all evil *had* been opened up to him: all the justice within me ached for the proof that it could ever have flowered into an act.

He had never at any rate been such a little gentleman as when, after our early dinner on this dreadful day, he came round to me and asked if I shouldn't like him for half an hour to play to me. David playing to Saul[1] could never have shown a finer sense of the occasion. It was literally a charming exhibition of tact, of magnanimity, and quite tantamount to his saying outright: "The true knights we love to read about never push an advantage too far. I know what you mean now: you mean that—to be let alone yourself and not followed up—you'll cease to worry and spy upon me, won't keep me so close to you, will let me go and come. Well, I 'come,' you see—but I don't go! There'll be plenty of time for that. I do really delight in your society and I only want to show you that I contended for a principle." It may be imagined

---

1 In 1 Samuel 16:14ff, the young musician David plays the harp to soothe the Israelite leader Saul, who has been possessed of an evil spirit.

whether I resisted this appeal or failed to accompany him again, hand in hand, to the schoolroom. He sat down at the old piano and played as he had never played; and if there are those who think he had better have been kicking a football I can only say that I wholly agree with them. For at the end of a time that under his influence I had quite ceased to measure I started up with a strange sense of having literally slept at my post. It was after luncheon, and by the schoolroom fire, and yet I hadn't really in the least slept; I had only done something much worse—I had forgotten. Where all this time was Flora? When I put the question to Miles he played on a minute before answering, and then could only say: "Why, my dear, how do *I* know?"—breaking moreover into a happy laugh which immediately after, as if it were a vocal accompaniment, he prolonged into incoherent extravagant song.

I went straight to my room, but his sister was not there; then, before going downstairs, I looked into several others. As she was nowhere about she would surely be with Mrs. Grose, whom in the comfort of that theory I accordingly proceeded in quest of. I found her where I had found her the evening before, but she met my quick challenge with blank scared ignorance. She had only supposed that, after the repast, I had carried off both the children; as to which she was quite in her right, for it was the very first time I had allowed the little girl out of my sight without some special provision. Of course now indeed she might be with the maids, so that the immediate thing was to look for her without an air of alarm. This we promptly arranged between us; but when, ten minutes later and in pursuance of our arrangement, we met in the hall, it was only to report on either side that after guarded enquiries we had altogether failed to trace her. For a minute there, apart from observation, we exchanged mute alarms, and I could feel with what high interest my friend returned me all those I had from the first given her.

"She'll be above," she presently said—"in one of the rooms you haven't searched."

"No; she's at a distance." I had made up my mind. "She has gone out."

Mrs. Grose stared. "Without a hat?"

I naturally also looked volumes. "Isn't that woman always without one?"

"She's with *her*?"

"She's with *her*!" I declared. "We must find them."

My hand was on my friend's arm, but she failed for the moment, confronted with such an account of the matter, to respond to my pressure. She communed, on the contrary, where she stood, with her uneasiness. "And where's Master Miles?"

"Oh, *he's* with Quint. They'll be in the schoolroom."

"Lord, Miss!" My view, I was myself aware—and therefore I suppose my tone—had never yet reached so calm an assurance.

"The trick's played," I went on; "they've successfully worked their plan. He found the most divine little way to keep me quiet while she went off."

"'Divine?'" Mrs. Grose bewilderedly echoed.

"Infernal then!" I almost cheerfully rejoined. "He has provided for himself as well. But come!"

She had helplessly gloomed at the upper regions. "You leave him—?"

"So long with Quint? Yes—I don't mind that now."

She always ended at these moments by getting possession of my hand, and in this manner she could at present still stay me. But after gasping an instant at my sudden resignation, "Because of your letter?" she eagerly brought out.

I quickly, by way of answer, felt for my letter, drew it forth, held it up, and then, freeing myself, went and laid it on the great hall-table. "Luke will take it," I said as I came back. I reached the house-door and opened it; I was already on the steps.

My companion still demurred: the storm of the night and the early morning had dropped, but the afternoon was damp and grey. I came down to the drive while she stood in the doorway. "You go with nothing on?"

"What do I care when the child has nothing? I can't wait to dress," I cried, "and if you must do so I leave you. Try meanwhile yourself upstairs."

"With *them*?" Oh on this the poor woman promptly joined me![1]

XIX

We went straight to the lake, as it was called at Bly, and I dare say rightly called, though it may have been a sheet of water less remarkable than my untravelled eyes supposed it. My acquaintance with sheets of water was small, and the pool of Bly, at all events on the few occasions of my consenting, under the protection of my pupils, to affront its surface in the old flat-bottomed boat moored there for our use, had impressed me both with its

---

1 End of ninth installment.

extent and its agitation. The usual place of embarkation was half a mile from the house, but I had an intimate conviction that, wherever Flora might be, she was not near home. She had not given me the slip for any small adventure, and, since the day of the very great one that I had shared with her by the pond, I had been aware, in our walks, of the quarter to which she most inclined. This was why I had now given to Mrs. Grose's steps so marked a direction—a direction making her, when she perceived it, oppose a resistance that showed me she was freshly mystified. "You're going to the water, Miss?—you think she's *in*—?"

"She may be, though the depth is, I believe, nowhere very great. But what I judge most likely is that she's on the spot from which, the other day, we saw together what I told you."

"When she pretended not to see—?"

"With that astounding self-possession! I've always been sure she wanted to go back alone. And now her brother has managed it for her."

Mrs. Grose still stood where she had stopped. "You suppose they really *talk* of them?"

I could meet this with an assurance! "They say things that, if we heard them, would simply appal us."

"And if she *is* there—?"

"Yes?"

"Then Miss Jessel is?"

"Beyond a doubt. You shall see."

"Oh thank you!" my friend cried, planted so firm that, taking it in, I went straight on without her. By the time I reached the pool, however, she was close behind me, and I knew that, whatever, to her apprehension, might befall me, the exposure of sticking to me struck her as her least danger. She exhaled a moan of relief as we at last came in sight of the greater part of the water without a sight of the child. There was no trace of Flora on that nearer side of the bank where my observation of her had been most startling, and none on the opposite edge, where, save for a margin of some twenty yards, a thick copse came down to the pond. This expanse, oblong in shape, was so narrow compared to its length that, with its ends out of view, it might have been taken for a scant river. We looked at the empty stretch, and then I felt the suggestion in my friend's eyes. I knew what she meant and I replied with a negative headshake.

"No, no; wait! She has taken the boat."

My companion stared at the vacant mooring place and then again across the lake. "Then where is it?"

"Our not seeing it is the strongest of proofs. She has used it to go over, and then has managed to hide it."

"All alone—that child?"

"She's not alone, and at such times she's not a child: she's an old, old woman." I scanned all the visible shore while Mrs. Grose took again, into the queer element I offered her, one of her plunges of submission; then I pointed out that the boat might perfectly be in a small refuge formed by one of the recesses of the pool, an indentation masked, for the hither side, by a projection of the bank and by a clump of trees growing close to the water.

"But if the boat's there, where on earth's *she*?" my colleague anxiously asked.

"That's exactly what we must learn." And I started to walk further.

"By going all the way round?"

"Certainly, far as it is. It will take us but ten minutes, yet it's far enough to have made the child prefer not to walk. She went straight over."

"Laws!" cried my friend again; the chain of my logic was ever too strong for her. It dragged her at my heels even now, and when we had got halfway round—a devious tiresome process, on ground much broken and by a path choked with overgrowth—I paused to give her breath. I sustained her with a grateful arm, assuring her that she might hugely help me; and this started us afresh, so that in the course of but few minutes more we reached a point from which we found the boat to be where I had supposed it. It had been intentionally left as much as possible out of sight and was tied to one of the stakes of a fence that came, just there, down to the brink and that had been an assistance to disembarking. I recognised, as I looked at the pair of short thick oars, quite safely drawn up, the prodigious character of the feat for a little girl; but I had by this time lived too long among wonders and had panted to too many livelier measures. There was a gate in the fence, through which we passed, and that brought us after a trifling interval more into the open. Then "There she is!" we both exclaimed at once.

Flora, a short way off, stood before us on the grass and smiled as if her performance had now become complete. The next thing she did, however, was to stoop straight down and pluck—quite as if it were all she was there for—a big ugly spray of withered fern. I at once felt sure she had just come out of the copse. She waited for us, not herself taking a step, and I was conscious of the rare solemnity with which we presently approached her. She smiled and smiled, and we met; but it was all done in a silence by this time flagrantly ominous. Mrs. Grose was the first to break the spell: she threw herself on her knees and, drawing the child to her breast, clasped in a long embrace the little tender yielding body. While this dumb convulsion lasted I could only watch it—which I did the more intently when I saw Flora's face peep at me over our companion's shoulder. It was serious now—the flicker had left it; but it strengthened the pang with which I at that moment envied Mrs. Grose the simplicity of *her* relation. Still, all this while, nothing more passed between us save that Flora had let her foolish fern again drop to the ground. What she and I had virtually said to each other was that pretexts were useless now. When Mrs. Grose finally got up she kept the child's hand, so that the two were still before me; and the singular reticence of our communion was even more marked in the frank look she addressed me. "I'll be hanged," it said, "if *I'll* speak!"

It was Flora who, gazing all over me in candid wonder, was the first. She was struck with our bare-headed aspect. "Why where are your things?"

"Where yours are, my dear!" I promptly returned.

She had already got back her gaiety and appeared to take this as an answer quite sufficient. "And where's Miles?" she went on.

There was something in the small valour of it that quite finished me: these three words from her were in a flash like the glitter of a drawn blade the jostle of the cup that my hand for weeks and weeks had held high and full to the brim and that now, even before speaking, I felt overflow in a deluge. "I'll tell you if you'll tell *me*—" I heard myself say, then heard the tremor in which it broke.

"Well, what?"

Mrs. Grose's suspense blazed at me, but it was too late now, and I brought the thing out handsomely. "Where, my pet, is Miss Jessel?"

XX

Just as in the churchyard with Miles, the whole thing was upon us. Much as I had made of the fact that this name had never once, between us, been sounded, the quick smitten glare with which the child's face now received it fairly likened my breach of the silence to the smash of a pane of glass. It added to the interposing cry, as if to stay the blow, that Mrs. Grose at the same instant uttered over my violence—the shriek of a creature scared, or rather wounded, which, in turn, within a few seconds, was completed by a gasp of my own. I seized my colleague's arm. "She's there, she's there!"

Miss Jessel stood before us on the opposite bank exactly as she had stood the other time, and I remember, strangely, as the first feeling now produced in me, my thrill of joy at having brought on a proof. She was there, so I was justified; she was there, so I was neither cruel nor mad. She was there for poor scared Mrs. Grose, but she was there most for Flora; and no moment of my monstrous time was perhaps so extraordinary as that in which I consciously threw out to her—with the sense that, pale and ravenous demon as she was, she would catch and understand it—an inarticulate message of gratitude. She rose erect on the spot my friend and I had lately quitted, and there wasn't in all the long reach of her desire an inch of her evil that fell short. This first vividness of vision and emotion were things of a few seconds, during which Mrs. Grose's dazed blink across to where I pointed struck me as showing that she too at last saw, just as it carried my own eyes precipitately to the child. The revelation then of the manner in which Flora was affected startled me in truth far more than it would have done to find her also merely agitated, for direct dismay was of course not what I had expected. Prepared and on her guard as our pursuit had actually made her, she would repress every betrayal; and I was therefore at once shaken by my first glimpse of the particular one for which I had not allowed. To see her, without a convulsion of her small pink face, not even feign to glance in the direction of the prodigy I announced, but only, instead of that, turn at *me* an expression of hard still gravity, an expression absolutely new and unprecedented and that appeared to read and accuse and judge me—this was a stroke that somehow converted the little girl herself into a figure portentous. I gaped at her coolness even though my certitude of her thoroughly seeing was never greater than at that instant, and then, in the immediate need to defend myself, I called her passionately to witness. "She's there, you little unhappy thing—there, there, *there*, and you know it as well as you know me!" I had said shortly before to Mrs. Grose that she was not at these times a child, but an old, old woman, and my description of her couldn't have been more strikingly confirmed than in the way in which, for all notice of this, she simply showed me, without an expressional concession or admission, a countenance of deeper and deeper, of indeed suddenly quite fixed reprobation. I was by this time—if I can put the whole thing at all together—more appalled at what I may properly call her manner than at anything else, though it was quite simultaneously that I became aware of having Mrs. Grose also, and very formidably, to reckon with. My elder companion, the next moment, at any rate, blotted out everything but her own flushed face and her loud shocked protest, a burst of high disapproval. "What a dreadful turn, to be sure, Miss! Where on earth do you see anything?"

I could only grasp her more quickly yet, for even while she spoke the hideous plain presence stood undimmed and undaunted. It had already lasted a minute, and it lasted while I continued, seizing my colleague, quite thrusting her at it and presenting her to it, to insist with my pointing hand. "You don't see her exactly as *we* see?—you mean to say you don't now—*now*? She's as big as a blazing fire! Only look, dearest woman, *look*—!" She looked, just as I did, and gave me, with her deep groan of negation, repulsion, compassion—the mixture with her pity of her relief at her exemption—a sense, touching to me even then, that she would have backed me up if she had been able. I might well have needed that, for with this hard blow of the proof that her eyes were hopelessly sealed I felt my own situation horribly crumble, I felt—I *saw*—my livid predecessor press, from her position, on my defeat, and I took the measure, more than all, of what I should have from this instant to deal with in the astounding little attitude of Flora. Into this attitude Mrs. Grose immediately and violently entered, breaking, even while there pierced through my sense of ruin a prodigious private triumph, into breathless reassurance.

"She isn't there, little lady, and nobody's there—and you never see nothing, my sweet! How can poor Miss Jessel—when poor Miss Jessel's dead and buried? *We* know, don't we, love?"—and she appealed, blundering in, to the child. "It's all a mere mistake and a worry and a joke—and we'll go home as fast as we can!"

Our companion, on this, had responded with a strange quick primness of propriety, and they were again, with Mrs. Grose on her feet, united, as it were, in shocked opposition to me. Flora continued to fix me with her small mask of disaffection, and even at that minute I prayed God to forgive me for seeming to see that, as she stood there holding tight to our friend's dress, her incomparable childish beauty had suddenly failed, had quite vanished. I've said it already—she was literally, she was hideously hard; she had turned common and almost ugly. "I don't know what you mean. I see nobody. I see nothing. I never *have*. I think you're cruel. I don't like you!" Then, after this deliverance, which might have been that of a vulgarly pert little girl in the street, she hugged Mrs. Grose more closely and buried in her skirts the dreadful little face. In this position she launched an almost furious wail. "Take me away, take me away—oh take me away from *her*!"

"From *me*?" I panted.

"From you—from you!" she cried.

Even Mrs. Grose looked across at me dismayed; while I had nothing to do but communicate again with the figure that, on the opposite bank, without a movement, as rigidly still as if catching, beyond the interval, our voices, was as vividly there for my disaster as it was not there for my service. The wretched child had spoken exactly as if she had got from some outside source each of her stabbing little words, and I could therefore, in the full despair of all I had to accept, but sadly shake my head at her. "If I had ever doubted all my doubt would at present have gone. I've been living with the miserable truth, and now it has only too much closed round me. Of course I've lost you: I've interfered, and you've seen, under *her* dictation"—with which I faced, over the pool again, our infernal witness—"the easy and perfect way to meet it. I've done my best, but I've lost you. Goodbye." For Mrs. Grose I had an imperative, an almost frantic "Go, go!" before which, in infinite distress, but mutely possessed of the little girl and clearly convinced, in spite of her blindness, that something awful had occurred and some collapse engulfed us, she retreated, by the way we had come, as fast as she could move.

Of what first happened when I was left alone I had no subsequent memory. I only knew that at the end of, I suppose, a quarter of an hour, an odorous dampness and roughness, chilling and piercing my trouble, had made me understand that I must have thrown myself, on my face, to the ground and given way to a wildness of grief. I must have lain there long and cried and wailed, for when I raised my head the day was almost done. I got up and looked a moment, through the twilight, at the grey pool and its blank haunted edge, and then I took, back to the house, my dreary and difficult course. When I reached the gate in the fence the boat, to my surprise, was gone, so that I had a fresh reflexion to make on Flora's extraordinary command of the situation. She passed that night, by the most tacit and, I should add, were not the word so grotesque a false note, the happiest of arrangements, with Mrs. Grose. I saw neither of them on my return, but on the other hand I saw, as by an ambiguous compensation, a great deal of Miles. I saw—I can use no other phrase—so much of him that it fairly measured more than it had ever measured. No evening I had passed at Bly was to have had the portentous quality of this one; in spite of which—and in spite also of the deeper depths of consternation that had opened beneath my feet—there was literally, in the ebbing actual, an extraordinarily sweet sadness. On reaching the house I had never so much as looked for the boy; I had simply gone straight to my room to change what I was wearing and to take in, at a glance, much material testimony to Flora's rupture. Her little belongings had all been removed. When later, by the schoolroom fire, I was served with tea by the usual maid, I indulged, on the article of my other pupil, in no enquiry whatever. He had his freedom now—he might have it to the end! Well, he did have it; and it consisted—in part at least—of his coming in at about eight o'clock and sitting down with me in silence. On the removal of the tea-things I had blown out the candles and drawn my chair closer: I was conscious of a mortal coldness and felt as if I should never again be warm. So when he appeared I was sitting in the glow with my thoughts. He paused a moment by the door as if to look at me; then—as if to share them—came to the other side of the hearth and sank into a chair. We sat there in absolute stillness; yet he wanted, I felt, to be with me.[1]

XXI

Before a new day, in my room, had fully broken, my eyes opened to Mrs. Grose, who had come to my bedside with worse news. Flora was so markedly feverish that an illness was perhaps at hand; she had passed a night of extreme unrest, a night agitated above all by fears that had for their subject not in the least her former but wholly her present governess. It was not against the possible re-entrance of Miss Jessel on the scene that she protested—it was conspicuously and passionately against mine. I was at once on my feet, and with an immense deal to ask; the more that my friend had discernibly now girded her loins to meet me afresh. This I felt as soon as I had put to her the question of her sense of the child's sincerity as against my own. "She persists in denying to you that she saw, or has ever seen, anything?"

My visitor's trouble truly was great. "Ah Miss, it isn't a matter on which I can push her! Yet it isn't either, I must say, as if I much needed to. It has made her, every inch of her, quite old."

---

1 End of tenth installment.

"Oh I see her perfectly from here. She resents, for all the world like some high little personage, the imputation on her truthfulness and, as it were, her respectability. 'Miss Jessel indeed—*she!*' Ah, she's 'respectable,' the chit! The impression she gave me there yesterday was, I assure you, the very strangest of all; it was quite beyond any of the others. I *did* put my foot in it! She'll never speak to me again."

Hideous and obscure as it all was, it held Mrs. Grose briefly silent; then she granted my point with a frankness which, I made sure, had more behind it. "I think indeed, Miss, she never will. She do have a grand manner about it!"

"And that manner"—I summed it up—"is practically what's the matter with her now!"

Oh that manner, I could see in my visitor's face, and not a little else besides! "She asks me every three minutes if I think you're coming in."

"I see—I see." I, too, on my side, had so much more than worked it out. "Has she said to you since yesterday—except to repudiate her familiarity with anything so dreadful—a single other word about Miss Jessel?"

"Not one, Miss. And of course, you know," my friend added, "I took it from her by the lake that just then and there at least there *was* nobody."

"Rather! And naturally you take it from her still."

"I don't contradict her. What else can I do?"

"Nothing in the world! You've the cleverest little person to deal with. They've made them—their two friends, I mean—still cleverer even than nature did; for it was wondrous material to play on! Flora has now her grievance, and she'll work it to the end."

"Yes, Miss; but to *what* end?"

"Why that of dealing with me to her uncle. She'll make me out to him the lowest creature—!"

I winced at the fair show of the scene in Mrs. Grose's face; she looked for a minute as if she sharply saw them together. "And him who thinks so well of you!"

"He has an odd way—it comes over me now," I laughed, "—of proving it! But that doesn't matter. What Flora wants of course is to get rid of me."

My companion bravely concurred. "Never again to so much as look at you."

"So that what you've come to me now for," I asked, "is to speed me on my way?" Before she had time to reply, however, I had her in check. "I've a better idea—the result of my reflexions.

My going *would* seem the right thing, and on Sunday I was terribly near it. Yet that won't do. It's *you* who must go. You must take Flora."

My visitor, at this, did speculate. "But where in the world—?"

"Away from here. Away from *them*. Away, even most of all, now, from me. Straight to her uncle."

"Only to tell on you—?"

"No, not 'only'! To leave me, in addition, with my remedy."

She was still vague. "And what *is* your remedy?"

"Your loyalty, to begin with. And then Miles's."

She looked at me hard. "Do you think he—?"

"Won't, if he has the chance, turn on me? Yes, I venture still to think it. At all events I want to try. Get off with his sister as soon as possible and leave me with him alone." I was amazed, myself, at the spirit I had still in reserve, and therefore perhaps a trifle the more disconcerted at the way in which, in spite of this fine example of it, she hesitated. "There's one thing, of course," I went on: "they mustn't, before she goes, see each other for three seconds." Then it came over me that, in spite of Flora's presumable sequestration from the instant of her return from the pool, it might already be too late. "Do you mean," I anxiously asked, "that they *have* met?"

At this she quite flushed. "Ah, Miss, I'm not such a fool as that! If I've been obliged to leave her three or four times, it has been each time with one of the maids, and at present, though she's alone, she's locked in safe. And yet—and yet!" There were too many things.

"And yet what?"

"Well, are you so sure of the little gentleman?"

"I'm not sure of anything but *you*. But I have, since last evening, a new hope. I think he wants to give me an opening. I do believe that—poor little exquisite wretch!—he wants to speak. Last evening, in the firelight and the silence, he sat with me for two hours as if it were just coming."

Mrs. Grose looked hard through the window at the grey gathering day. "And did it come?"

"No, though I waited and waited I confess it didn't and it was without a breach of the silence, or so much as a faint allusion to his sister's condition and absence, that we at last kissed for goodnight. All the same," I continued, "I can't, if her uncle sees her, consent to his seeing her brother without my having given the boy—and most of all because things have got so bad—a little more time."

My friend appeared on this ground more reluctant than I could quite understand. "What do you mean by more time?"

"Well, a day or two—really to bring it out. He'll then be on *my* side—of which you see the importance. If nothing comes I shall only fail, and you at the worst have helped me by doing on your arrival in town whatever you may have found possible." So I put it before her, but she continued for a little so lost in other reasons that I came again to her aid. "Unless indeed," I wound up, "you really want *not* to go."

I could see it, in her face, at last clear itself; she put out her hand to me as a pledge. "I'll go—I'll go. I'll go this morning."

I wanted to be very just. "If you *should* wish still to wait I'd engage she shouldn't see me."

"No, no: it's the place itself. She must leave it." She held me a moment with heavy eyes, then brought out the rest. "Your idea's the right one. I myself, Miss—"

"Well?"

"I can't stay."

The look she gave me with it made me jump at possibilities. "You mean that, since yesterday you *have* seen—?"

She shook her head with dignity. "I've *heard*—!"

"Heard?"

"From that child—horrors! There!" she sighed with tragic relief. "On my honour, Miss, she says things—!" But at this evocation she broke down; she dropped with a sudden cry upon my sofa and, as I had seen her do before, gave way to all the anguish of it.

It was quite in another manner that I for my part let myself go. "Oh thank God!"

She sprang up again at this, drying her eyes with a groan. "'Thank God'?"

"It so justifies me!"

"It does that, Miss!"

I couldn't have desired more emphasis, but I just waited. "She's so horrible?"

I saw my colleague scarce knew how to put it. "Really shocking."

"And about me?"

"About you, Miss—since you must have it. It's beyond everything, for a young lady; and I can't think wherever she must have picked up—"

"The appalling language she applies to me? I can then!" I broke in with a laugh that was doubtless significant enough.

It only in truth left my friend still more grave. "Well, perhaps I ought to also—since I've heard some of it before! Yet I can't bear it," the poor woman went on while with the same movement she glanced, on my dressing-table, at the face of my watch. "But I must go back."

I kept her, however. "Ah if you can't bear it—!"

"How can I stop[1] with her, you mean? Why just *for* that: to get her away. Far from this," she pursued, "far from *them*—"

"She may be different? she may be free?" I seized her almost with joy. "Then in spite of yesterday you *believe*—"

"In such doings?" Her simple description of them required, in the light of her expression, to be carried no further, and she gave me the whole thing as she had never done."I believe."

Yes, it was a joy, and we were still shoulder to shoulder: if I might continue sure of that I should care but little what else happened. My support in the presence of disaster would be the same as it had been in my early need of confidence, and if my friend would answer for my honesty I would answer for all the rest. On the point of taking leave of her, none the less, I was to some extent embarrassed. "There's one thing of course—it occurs to me—to remember. My letter giving the alarm will have reached town before you."

I now felt still more how she had been beating about the bush and how weary at last it had made her. "Your letter won't have got there. Your letter never went."

"What then became of it?"

"Goodness knows! Master Miles—"

"Do you mean *he* took it?" I gasped.

She hung fire, but she overcame her reluctance. "I mean that I saw yesterday, when I came back with Miss Flora, that it wasn't where you had put it. Later in the evening I had the chance to question Luke, and he declared that he had neither noticed nor touched it." We could only exchange, on this, one of our deeper mutual soundings, and it was Mrs. Grose who first brought up the plumb with an almost elate "You see!"

---

1 Stay.

"Yes, I see that if Miles took it instead he probably will have read it and destroyed it."

"And don't you see anything else?"

I faced her a moment with a sad smile. "It strikes me that by this time your eyes are open even wider than mine."

They proved to be so indeed, but she could still almost blush to show it. "I make out now what he must have done at school." And she gave, in her simple sharpness, an almost droll disillusioned nod. "He stole!"

I turned it over—I tried to be more judicial. "Well—perhaps."

She looked as if she found me unexpectedly calm. "He stole *letters!*"

She couldn't know my reasons for a calmness after all pretty shallow; so I showed them off as I might. "I hope then it was to more purpose than in this case! The note, at all events, that I put on the table yesterday," I pursued, "will have given him so scant an advantage—for it contained only the bare demand for an interview—that he's already much ashamed of having gone so far for so little, and that what he had on his mind last evening was precisely the need of confession." I seemed to myself for the instant to have mastered it, to see it all. "Leave us, leave us"—I was already, at the door, hurrying her off. "I'll get it out of him. He'll meet me. He'll confess. If he confesses he's saved. And if he's saved—"

"Then *you* are?" The dear woman kissed me on this, and I took her farewell. "I'll save you without him!" she cried as she went.

XXII

Yet it was when she had got off—and I missed her on the spot—that the great pinch really came. If I had counted on what it would give me to find myself alone with Miles I quickly recognized that it would give me at least a measure. No hour of my stay in fact was so assailed with apprehensions as that of my coming down to learn that the carriage containing Mrs. Grose and my younger pupil had already rolled out of the gates. Now I *was*, I said to myself, face to face with the elements, and for much of the rest of the day, while I fought my weakness, I could consider that I had been supremely rash. It was a tighter place still than I had yet turned round in; all the more that, for the first time, I could see in the aspect of others a confused reflexion of the crisis. What had happened naturally caused them all to stare; there was too little of the explained, throw out whatever we might, in the suddenness of my colleague's act. The maids and the men looked blank; the effect of which on my nerves was an aggravation until I saw the necessity of making it a positive aid. It was in short by just clutching the helm that I avoided total wreck; and I dare say that, to bear up at all, I became that morning very grand and very dry. I welcomed the consciousness that I was charged with much to do, and I caused it to be known as well that, left thus to myself, I was quite remarkably firm. I wandered with that manner, for the next hour or two, all over the place and looked, I have no doubt, as if I were ready for any onset. So, for the benefit of whom it might concern, I paraded with a sick heart.

The person it appeared least to concern proved to be, till dinner, little Miles himself. My perambulations had given me meanwhile no glimpse of him, but they had tended to make more public the change taking place in our relation as a consequence of his having at the piano, the day before, kept me, in Flora's interest, so beguiled and befooled. The stamp of publicity had of course been fully given by her confinement and departure, and the change itself was now ushered in by our non-observance of the regular custom of the schoolroom. He had already disappeared when, on my way down, I pushed open his door, and I learned below that he had breakfasted—in the presence of a couple of the maids—with Mrs. Grose and his sister. He had then gone out, as he said, for a stroll; than which nothing, I reflected, could better have expressed his frank view of the abrupt transformation of my office. What he would now permit this office to consist of was yet to be settled: there was at the least a queer relief—I mean for myself in especial—in the renouncement of one pretension. If so much had sprung to the surface I scarce put it too strongly in saying that what had perhaps sprung highest was the absurdity of our prolonging the fiction that I had anything more to teach him. It sufficiently stuck out that, by tacit little tricks in which even more than myself he carried out the care for my dignity, I had had to appeal to him to let me off straining to meet him on the ground of his true capacity. He had at any rate his freedom now; I was never to touch it again; as I had amply shown, moreover, when, on his joining me in the schoolroom the previous night, I uttered, in reference to the interval just concluded, neither challenge nor hint. I had too much, from this moment, my other ideas. Yet when he at last arrived the difficulty of applying them, the accumulations of my problem, were brought straight home to me by the beautiful little presence on which what had occurred had as yet, for the eye, dropped neither stain nor shadow.

To mark, for the house, the high state I cultivated I decreed that my meals with the boy should be served, as we called it, downstairs; so that I had been awaiting him in the ponderous pomp of the room outside the window of which I had had from Mrs. Grose, that first scared Sunday, my flash of something it would scarce have done to call light. Here at present I felt afresh—for I had felt it again and again—how my equilibrium depended on the success of my rigid will, the will to shut my eyes as tight as possible to the truth that what I had to deal with was, revoltingly, against nature. I could only get on at all by taking "nature" into my confidence and my account, by treating my monstrous ordeal as a push in a direction unusual, of course, and unpleasant, but demanding after all, for a fair front, only another turn of the screw of ordinary human virtue. No attempt, none the less, could well require more tact than just this attempt to supply, one's self, *all* the nature. How could I put even a little of that article into a suppression of reference to what had occurred? How on the other hand could I make a reference without a new plunge into the hideous obscure? Well, a sort of answer, after a time, had come to me, and it was so far confirmed as that I was met, incontestably, by the quickened vision of what was rare in my little companion. It was indeed as if he had found even now—as he had so often found at lessons—still some other delicate way to ease me off. Wasn't there light in the fact which, as we shared our solitude, broke out with a specious glitter it had never yet quite worn?—the fact that (opportunity aiding, precious opportunity which had now come) it would be preposterous, with a child so endowed, to forgo the help one might wrest from absolute intelligence? What had his intelligence been given him for but to save him? Mightn't one, to reach his mind, risk the stretch of a stiff arm across his character? It was as if, when we were face to face in the dining-room, he had literally shown me the way. The roast mutton was on the table and I had dispensed with attendance. Miles, before he sat down, stood a moment with his hands in his pockets and looked at the joint, on which he seemed on the point of passing some humorous judgement. But what he presently produced was: "I say, my dear, is she really very awfully ill?"

"Little Flora? Not so bad but that she'll presently be better. London will set her up. Bly had ceased to agree with her. Come here and take your mutton."

He alertly obeyed me, carried the plate carefully to his seat and, when he was established, went on. "Did Bly disagree with her so terribly all at once?"

"Not so suddenly as you might think. One had seen it coming on."

"Then why didn't you get her off before?"

"Before what?"

"Before she became too ill to travel."

I found myself prompt. "She's *not* too ill to travel: she only might have become so if she had stayed. This was just the moment to seize. The journey will dissipate the influence"—oh I was grand!—"and carry it off."

"I see, I see"—Miles, for that matter, was grand too. He settled to his repast with the charming little "table manner" that, from the day of his arrival, had relieved me of all grossness of admonition. Whatever he had been expelled from school for, it wasn't for ugly feeding. He was irreproachable, as always, to-day; but was unmistakably more conscious. He was discernibly trying to take for granted more things than he found, without assistance, quite easy; and he dropped into peaceful silence while he felt his situation. Our meal was of the briefest—mine a vain pretence, and I had the things immediately removed. While this was done Miles stood again with his hands in his little pockets and his back to me—stood and looked out of the wide window through which, that other day, I had seen what pulled me up. We continued silent while the maid was with us—as silent, it whimsically occurred to me, as some young couple who, on their wedding-journey, at the inn, feel shy in the presence of the waiter. He turned round only when the waiter had left us. "Well—so we're alone!"[1]

XXIII

"Oh more or less." I imagine my smile was pale. "Not absolutely. We shouldn't like that!" I went on.

"No—I suppose we shouldn't. Of course we've the others."

"We've the others—we've indeed the others," I concurred.

"Yet even though we have them," he returned, still with his hands in his pockets and planted there in front of me, "they don't much count, do they?"

1   End of eleventh installment.

I made the best of it, but I felt wan. "It depends on what you call 'much'!"

"Yes"—with all accommodation—"everything depends!" On this, however, he faced to the window again and presently reached it with his vague restless cogitating step. He remained there a while with his forehead against the glass, in contemplation of the stupid shrubs I knew and the dull things of November. I had always my hypocrisy of "work,"[1] behind which I now gained the sofa. Steadying myself with it there as I had repeatedly done at those moments of torment that I have described as the moments of my knowing the children to be given to something from which I was barred, I sufficiently obeyed my habit of being prepared for the worst. But an extraordinary impression dropped on me as I extracted a meaning from the boy's embarrassed back—none other than the impression that I was not barred now. This inference grew in a few minutes to sharp intensity and seemed bound up with the direct perception that it was positively *he* who was. The frames and squares of the great window were a kind of image, for him, of a kind of failure. I felt that I saw him, in any case, shut in or shut out. He was admirable but not comfortable: I took it in with a throb of hope. Wasn't he looking through the haunted pane for something he couldn't see?—and wasn't it the first time in the whole business that he had known such a lapse? The first, the very first: I found it a splendid portent. It made him anxious, though he watched himself; he had been anxious all day and, even while in his usual sweet little manner he sat at table, had needed all his small strange genius to give it a gloss. When he at last turned round to meet me it was almost as if this genius had succumbed. "Well, I think I'm glad Bly agrees with *me*!"

"You'd certainly seem to have seen, these twenty-four hours, a good deal more of it than for some time before. I hope," I went on bravely, "that you've been enjoying yourself."

"Oh yes, I've been ever so far; all round about—miles and miles away. I've never been so free."

He had really a manner of his own, and I could only try to keep up with him. "Well, do you like it?"

He stood there smiling; then at last he put into two words—"Do *you*?"—more discrimination than I had ever heard two words contain. Before I had time to deal with that, however, he continued as if with the sense that this was an impertinence to be soft-

---

1 Knitting.

ened. "Nothing could be more charming than the way you take it, for of course if we're alone together now it's you that are alone most. But I hope," he threw in, "you don't particularly mind!"

"Having to do with you?" I asked. "My dear child, how can I help minding? Though I've renounced all claim to your company—you're so beyond me—I at least greatly enjoy it. What else should I stay on for?"

He looked at me more directly, and the expression of his face, graver now, struck me as the most beautiful I had ever found in it. "You stay on just for *that*?"

"Certainly. I stay on as your friend and from the tremendous interest I take in you till something can be done for you that may be more worth your while. That needn't surprise you." My voice trembled so that I felt it impossible to suppress the shake. "Don't you remember how I told you, when I came and sat on your bed the night of the storm, that there was nothing in the world I wouldn't do for you?"

"Yes, yes!" He, on his side, more and more visibly nervous, had a tone to master; but he was so much more successful than I that, laughing out through his gravity, he could pretend we were pleasantly jesting. "Only that, I think, was to get me to do something for *you*!"

"It was partly to get you to do something," I conceded. "But, you know, you didn't do it."

"Oh yes," he said with the brightest superficial eagerness, "you wanted me to tell you something."

"That's it. Out, straight out. What you have on your mind, you know."

"Ah then is *that* what you've stayed over for?"

He spoke with a gaiety through which I could still catch the finest little quiver of resentful passion; but I can't begin to express the effect upon me of an implication of surrender even so faint. It was as if what I had yearned for had come at last only to astonish me. "Well, yes—I may as well make a clean breast of it. It was precisely for that."

He waited so long that I supposed it for the purpose of repudiating the assumption on which my action had been founded; but what he finally said was: "Do you mean now—here?"

"There couldn't be a better place or time." He looked round him uneasily, and I had the rare—oh the queer!—impression of the very first symptom I had seen in him of the approach of immediate fear. It was as if he were suddenly afraid of me—which struck me indeed as perhaps the best thing to make him. Yet in the very pang of the effort I felt it vain to try sternness, and I heard myself the next instant so gentle as to be almost grotesque. "You want so to go out again?"

"Awfully!" He smiled at me heroically, and the touching little bravery of it was enhanced by his actually flushing with pain. He had picked up his hat, which he had brought in, and stood twirling it in a way that gave me, even as I was just nearly reaching port, a perverse horror of what I was doing. To do it in *any* way was an act of violence, for what did it consist of but the obtrusion of the idea of grossness and guilt on a small helpless creature who had been for me a revelation of the possibilities of beautiful intercourse? Wasn't it base to create for a being so exquisite a mere alien awkwardness? I suppose I now read into our situation a clearness it couldn't have had at the time, for I seem to see our poor eyes already lighted with some spark of a prevision of the anguish that was to come. So we circled about with terrors and scruples, fighters not daring to close. But it was for each other we feared! That kept us a little longer suspended and unbruised. "I'll tell you everything," Miles said—"I mean I'll tell you anything you like. You'll stay on with me, and we shall both be all right, and I *will* tell you—I *will*. But not now."

"Why not now?"

My insistence turned him from me and kept him once more at his window in a silence during which, between us, you might have heard a pin drop. Then he was before me again with the air of a person for whom, outside, someone who had frankly to be reckoned with was waiting. "I have to see Luke."

I had not yet reduced him to quite so vulgar a lie, and I felt proportionately ashamed. But, horrible as it was, his lies made up my truth. I achieved thoughtfully a few loops of my knitting. "Well then go to Luke, and I'll wait for what you promise. Only in return for that satisfy, before you leave me, one very much smaller request."

He looked as if he felt he had succeeded enough to be able still a little to bargain. "Very much smaller—?"

"Yes, a mere fraction of the whole. Tell me"—oh my work preoccupied me, and I was off-hand!—"if, yesterday afternoon, from the table in the hall, you took, you know, my letter."

XXIV

My grasp of how he received this suffered for a minute from something that I can describe only as a fierce split of my attention—a stroke that at first, as I sprang straight up, reduced me to the mere blind movement of getting hold of him, drawing him close, and, while I just fell for support against the nearest piece of furniture, instinctively keeping him with his back to the window. The appearance was full upon us that I had already had to deal with here: Peter Quint had come into view like a sentinel before a prison. The next thing I saw was that, from outside, he had reached the window, and then I knew that, close to the glass and glaring in through it, he offered once more to the room his white face of damnation. It represents but grossly what took place within me at the sight to say that on the second my decision was made; yet I believe that no woman so overwhelmed ever in so short a time recovered her command of the *act*. It came to me in the very horror of the immediate presence that the act would be, seeing and facing what I saw and faced, to keep the boy himself unaware. The inspiration—I can call it by no other name—was that I felt how voluntarily, how transcendently, I *might*. It was like fighting with a demon for a human soul, and when I had fairly so appraised it I saw how the human soul—held out, in the tremor of my hands, at arms' length—had a perfect dew of sweat on a lovely childish forehead. The face that was close to mine was as white as the face against the glass, and out of it presently came a sound, not low nor weak, but as if from much further away, that I drank like a waft of fragrance.

"Yes—I took it."

At this, with a moan of joy, I enfolded, I drew him close; and while I held him to my breast, where I could feel in the sudden fever of his little body the tremendous pulse of his little heart, I kept my eyes on the thing at the window and saw it move and shift its posture. I have likened it to a sentinel, but its slow wheel, for a moment, was rather the prowl of a baffled beast. My present quickened courage, however, was such that, not too much to let it through, I had to shade, as it were, my flame. Meanwhile the glare of the face was again at the window, the scoundrel fixed as if to watch and wait. It was the very confidence that I might now defy him, as well as the positive certitude, by this time, of the child's unconsciousness,[1] that made me go on. "What did you take it for?"

"To see what you said about me."

"You opened the letter?"

"I opened it."

---

1 Unawareness.

My eyes were now, as I held him off a little again, on Miles's own face, in which the collapse of mockery showed me how complete was the ravage of uneasiness. What was prodigious was that at last, by my success, his sense was sealed and his communication stopped: he knew that he was in presence, but knew not of what, and knew still less that I also was and that I did know. And what did this strain of trouble matter when my eyes went back to the window only to see that the air was clear again and—by my personal triumph—the influence quenched? There was nothing there. I felt that the cause was mine and that I should surely get *all*. "And you found nothing!"—I let my elation out.

He gave the most mournful, thoughtful little headshake. "Nothing."

"Nothing, nothing!" I almost shouted in my joy.

"Nothing, nothing," he sadly repeated.

I kissed his forehead; it was drenched. "So what have you done with it?"

"I've burnt it."

"Burnt it?" It was now or never. "Is that what you did at school?"

Oh what this brought up! "At school?"

"Did you take letters?—or other things?"

"Other things?" He appeared now to be thinking of something far off and that reached him only through the pressure of his anxiety. Yet it did reach him. "Did I *steal*?"

I felt myself redden to the roots of my hair as well as wonder if it were more strange to put to a gentleman such a question or to see him take it with allowances that gave the very distance of his fall in the world. "Was it for that you mightn't go back?"

The only thing he felt was rather a dreary little surprise. "Did you know I mightn't go back?"

"I know everything."

He gave me at this the longest and strangest look. "Everything?"

"Everything. Therefore *did* you—?" But I couldn't say it again.

Miles could, very simply. "No. I didn't steal."

My face must have shown him I believed him utterly; yet my hands—but it was for pure tenderness—shook him as if to ask him why, if it was all for nothing, he had condemned me to months of torment. "What then did you do?"

He looked in vague pain all round the top of the room and drew his breath, two or three times over, as if with difficulty. He might have been standing at the bottom of the sea and raising his eyes to some faint green twilight. "Well—I said things."

"Only that?"

"They thought it was enough!"

"To turn you out for?"

Never, truly, had a person "turned out" shown so little to explain it as this little person! He appeared to weigh my question, but in a manner quite detached and almost helpless. "Well, I suppose I oughtn't."

"But to whom did you say them?"

He evidently tried to remember, but it dropped—he had lost it. "I don't know!"

He almost smiled at me in the desolation of his surrender, which was indeed practically, by this time, so complete that I ought to have left it there. But I was infatuated—I was blind with victory, though even then the very effect that was to have brought him so much nearer was already that of added separation. "Was it to every one?" I asked.

"No; it was only to—" But he gave a sick little headshake. "I don't remember their names."

"Were they then so many?"

"No—only a few. Those I liked."

Those he liked? I seemed to float not into clearness, but into a darker obscure, and within a minute there had come to me out of my very pity the appalling alarm of his being perhaps innocent. It was for the instant confounding and bottomless, for if he *were* innocent, what then on earth was I? Paralysed, while it lasted, by the mere brush of the question, I let him go a little, so that, with a deep-drawn sigh, he turned away from me again; which, as he faced toward the clear window, I suffered, feeling that I had nothing now there to keep him from. "And did they repeat what you said?" I went on after a moment.

He was soon at some distance from me, still breathing hard and again with the air, though now without anger for it, of being confined against his will. Once more, as he had done before, he looked up at the dim day as if, of what had hitherto sustained him, nothing was left but an unspeakable anxiety. "Oh yes," he nevertheless replied—"they must have repeated them. To those *they* liked," he added.

There was somehow less of it than I had expected; but I turned it over. "And these things came round—?"

"To the masters? Oh, yes!" he answered very simply. "But I didn't know they'd tell."

"The masters? They didn't—they've never told. That's why I ask you."

He turned to me again his little beautiful fevered face. "Yes, it was too bad."

"Too bad?"

"What I suppose I sometimes said. To write home."

I can't name the exquisite pathos of the contradiction given to such a speech by such a speaker; I only know that the next instant I heard myself throw off with homely force: "Stuff and nonsense!" But the next after that I must have sounded stern enough. "What *were* these things?"

My sternness was all for his judge, his executioner; yet it made him avert himself again, and that movement made *me*, with a single bound and an irrepressible cry, spring straight upon him. For there again, against the glass, as if to blight his confession and stay his answer, was the hideous author of our woe—the white face of damnation. I felt a sick swim at the drop of my victory and all the return of my battle, so that the wildness of my veritable leap only served as a great betrayal. I saw him, from the midst of my act, meet it with a divination, and on the perception that even now he only guessed, and that the window was still to his own eyes free, I let the impulse flame up to convert the climax of his dismay into the very proof of his liberation. "No more, no more, no more!" I shrieked to my visitant as I tried to press him against me.

"Is she *here*?" Miles panted as he caught with his sealed eyes the direction of my words. Then as his strange "she" staggered me and, with a gasp, I echoed it, "Miss Jessel, Miss Jessel!" he with sudden fury gave me back.

I seized, stupefied, his supposition—some sequel to what we had done to Flora, but this made me only want to show him that it was better still than that. "It's not Miss Jessel! But it's at the window—straight before us. It's *there*—the coward horror, there for the last time!"

At this, after a second in which his head made the movement of a baffled dog's on a scent and then gave a frantic little shake for air and light, he was at me in a white rage, bewildered, glaring vainly over the place and missing wholly, though it now, to my sense, filled the room like the taste of poison, the wide overwhelming presence. "It's *he*?"

I was so determined to have all my proof that I flashed into ice to challenge him. "Whom do you mean by 'he'?"

"Peter Quint—you devil!" His face gave again, round the room, its convulsed supplication. "*Where*?"

They are in my ears still, his supreme surrender of the name and his tribute to my devotion. "What does he matter now, my own?—what will he *ever* matter? *I* have you," I launched at the beast, "but he has lost you forever!" Then for the demonstration of my work, "There, *there*!" I said to Miles.

But he had already jerked straight round, stared, glared again, and seen but the quiet day. With the stroke of the loss I was so proud of he uttered the cry of a creature hurled over an abyss, and the grasp with which I recovered him might have been that of catching him in his fall. I caught him, yes, I held him—it may be imagined with what a passion; but at the end of a minute I began to feel what it truly was that I held. We were alone with the quiet day, and his little heart, dispossessed, had stopped.[1]

---

1 End of final installment.

Appendix A: The Ghostly Tales: Inspiration and Reception

1. From Henry James, *A Small Boy and Others* (New York: Charles Scribner's Sons, 1913) 346–49

[In the first volume of his autobiography, *A Small Boy and Others* (1913), James shaped his earliest experiences into a model of the development of the artist as a young boy. In the passage below, he expounds on the meaning that the Galerie d'Apollon[1] of the Louvre took on for him when his brother William and he visited it as boys in their early teens, and then details a nightmare from a later date that was inspired by his trips to the museum. This section is often cited both for its explication of James's interest in art and as one source for "The Jolly Corner."]

... [I]n those beginnings I felt myself most happily cross that bridge over to Style constituted by the wondrous Galerie d'Apollon, drawn out for me as a long but assured initiation and seeming to form with its supreme coved ceiling and inordinately shining parquet a prodigious tube or tunnel through which I inhaled little by little, that is again and again, a general sense of *glory*. The glory meant ever so many things at once, not only beauty and art and supreme design, but history and fame and power, the world in fine raised to the richest and noblest expression. The world there was at the same time, by an odd extension or intensification, the local present fact, to my small imagination, of the Second Empire,[2] which was (for my notified consciousness) new and queer and perhaps even wrong, but on the spot so amply radiant and elegant that it took to itself, took under its protection with a splendor of insolence, the state and ancientry of the whole scene, profiting this, to one's dim historic vision, confusedly though it might be, by the unparalleled luxury and variety of its heritage. But who shall count the sources at which an intense young fancy (when a young fancy *is* intense) capriciously, absurdly drinks?—so that the effect is, in twenty connections, that of a love-philtre or fear-philtre which fixes for the sense their supreme symbol of the fair or the strange. The Galerie d'Apollon became for years what I can only term a splendid scene of things, even of the quite irrelevant or, as might be, almost unworthy; and I recall to this hour, with the last vividness, what a precious part it

---

1 Long gallery in the Louvre Museum, Paris.
2 The French regime of Napoléon III of France, who ruled as emperor, 1852–70.

played for me, and exactly by that continuity of honour, on my awaking, in a summer dawn many years later, to the fortunate, the instantaneous recovery and capture of the most appalling yet most admirable nightmare of my life. The climax of this extraordinary experience—which stands alone for me as a dream-adventure founded in the deepest, quickest, clearest act of cogitation and comparison, act indeed of lifesaving energy, as well as in unutterable fear—was the sudden pursuit, through an open door, along a huge high saloon, of a just dimlydescried figure that retreated in terror before my rush and dash (a glare of inspired reaction from irresistible but shameful dread,) out of the room I had a moment before been desperately, and all the more abjectly, defending by the push of my shoulder against hard pressure on lock and bar from the other side. The lucidity, not to say the sublimity, of the crisis had consisted of the great thought that I, in my appalled state, was probably still more appalling than the awful agent, creature or presence, whatever he was, whom I had guessed, in the suddenest wild start from sleep, the sleep within my sleep, to be making for my place of rest. The triumph of my impulse, perceived in a flash as I acted on it by myself at a bound, forcing the door outward, was the grand thing, but the great point of the whole was the wonder of my final recognition. Routed, dismayed, the tables turned upon him by my so surpassing him for straight aggression and dire intention, my visitant was already but a diminished spot in the long perspective, the tremendous, glorious hall, as I say, over the far-gleaming floor of which, cleared for the occasion of its great line of priceless vitrines[1] down the middle, he sped for *his* life, while a great storm of thunder and lightning played through the deep embrasures of high windows at the right. The lightning that revealed the retreat revealed also the wondrous place and, by the same amazing play, my young imaginative life in it of long before, the sense of which, deep within me, had kept it whole, preserved it to this thrilling use; for what in the world were the deep embrasures and the so polished floor but those of the Galerie d'Apollon of my childhood? The "scene of something" I had vaguely then felt it? Well I might, since it was to be the scene of that immense hallucination.

2. From Henry James Sr., *Society the Redeemed Form of Man: And the Earnest of God's Omnipotence in Human Nature* (Boston: Houghton, Osgood, 1879) 160–61

[While living in Windsor, England, in 1844 with his young family, Henry James Sr. experienced an event that shaped the rest of his life. He wrote about it not long before his death.]

---

1 Glass cabinets.

One day ... having eaten a comfortable dinner, I remained sitting at the table after the family had dispersed, idly gazing at the embers in the grate, thinking of nothing, and feeling only the exhilaration incident to a good digestion, when suddenly—in a lightning-flash as it were—"fear came upon me, and trembling, which made all my bones to shake." To all appearance it was a perfectly insane and abject terror, without ostensible cause, and only to be accounted for, to my perplexed imagination, by some damnèd shape squatting invisible to me within the precincts of the room, and raying out from his fetid personality influences fatal to life. The thing had not lasted ten seconds before I felt myself a wreck, that is, reduced from a state of firm, vigorous, joyful manhood to one of almost helpless infancy. The only self-control I was capable of exerting was to keep my seat. I felt the greatest desire to run incontinently to the foot of the stairs and shout for help to my wife,—to run to the roadside even, and appeal to the public to protect me; but by an immense effort I controlled these frenzied impulses, and determined not to budge from my chair till I had recovered my lost self-possession. This purpose I held to for a good long hour, as I reckoned time, beat upon meanwhile by an ever-growing tempest of doubt, anxiety, and despair, with absolutely no relief from any truth I had ever encountered save a most pale and distant glimmer of the divine existence....

3. From William James, *The Varieties of Religious Experience* (New York: Random House, 1929) 157–58

[William James gave a series of lectures on science and religion at the University of Edinburgh in 1901 and 1902. These lectures in edited form comprise his best-selling, highly influential book, *The Varieties of Religious Experience*. In this book, James writes of a Frenchman who experienced a sort of vastation very similar to that described by James's father, Henry Sr. In fact, James used the character of a Frenchman as a mask; he was speaking of his own encounter with a supernatural force.]

Whilst in this state of philosophic pessimism and general depression of spirits about my prospects, I went one evening into a dressing-room in the twilight to procure some article that was there; when suddenly there fell upon me without any warning, just as if it came out of the darkness, a horrible fear of my own existence. Simultaneously there arose in my mind the image of an epileptic patient whom I had seen in the asylum, a black-haired youth with greenish skin, entirely idiotic, who used to sit all day on one of the benches, or rather shelves against the wall, with his knees drawn up against his chin, and the coarse gray undershirt, which was his only garment, drawn over them inclosing his entire figure. He sat there like a sort of sculptured Egyptian cat or Peruvian mummy, moving nothing but his black eyes and looking absolutely non-human. This image and my fear entered into a species of combination with each other *That shape am I,* I felt, potentially. Nothing that I possess can defend me against that fate, if the hour for it should strike for me as it struck for him. There was such a horror of him, and such a perception of my own merely momentary discrepancy from him, that it was as if something hitherto solid within my breast gave way entirely, and I became a mass of quivering fear. After this the universe was changed for me altogether. I awoke morning after morning with a horrible dread at the pit of my stomach, and with a sense of the insecurity of life that I never knew before, and that I have never felt since. It was like a revelation; and although the immediate feelings passed away, the experience has made me sympathetic with the morbid feelings of others ever since. It gradually faded, but for months I was unable to go out into the dark alone.

In general I dreaded to be left alone. I remember wondering how other people could live, how I myself had ever lived, so unconscious of that pit of insecurity beneath the surface of life. My mother in particular, a very cheerful person, seemed to me a perfect paradox in her unconsciousness of danger, which you may well believe I was very careful not to disturb by revelations of my own state of mind. I have always thought that this experience of melancholia of mine had a religious bearing.

4. From Henry James, Letter to Mary Walsh James, 26 March 1870, in *Henry James: A Life in Letters*, ed. Philip Horne (New York: Viking, 1999) 37, 38

[Henry James's cousin and friend, Mary (Minny) Temple enjoyed a lively intelligence, wit, and curiosity about life that appealed to her reserved but admiring cousin. Many of James's biographers and critics believe that she served as an important inspiration for a number of his female characters in various short stories and novels. The following is from a letter the 26-year-old Henry wrote to his mother from England on 26 March 1870, responding to his parents' letter with the news of Minny's death.]

Time for you at home, will have begun to melt away the hardness of the thought of her being in future a simple memory of the mind—a mere pulsation of the heart: to me as yet it seems perfectly inadmissible....

But how much—how long—we have got to live without her! It's no more than a just penalty to pay, though, for the privilege of having been young with her. It will count in old age, when we live, more than now, in reflection, to have had such a figure in our youth.

5. From Henry James, *Notes of a Son and Brother* (New York: Charles Scribner's Sons, 1914) 515

[James ends his second autobiographical volume, *Notes of a Son and Brother* (1914), with a poignant meditation on how Minny's tragic death at age 24 changed him. As he had predicted so many years before, the figure that she had been for him lingered throughout his life.]

... [D]eath, at the last, was dreadful to her; she would have given any-thing to live—and the image of this, which was long to remain with me, appeared so of the essence of tragedy that I was in the far-off after-time to seek to lay the ghost by wrapping it, a particular occasion aiding, in the beauty and dignity of art. The figure that was to hover as the ghost has at any rate been of an extreme pertinence, I feel, to my doubtless too loose and confused general picture, vitiated perhaps by the effort to comprehend more than it contains. Much as this cher-ished companion's presence among us had represented for William and myself ... her death made a mark that must stand here for a too waiting conclusion. We felt it together as the end of our youth.

6. From Henry James, *The American Scene* (1907), in *Col-lected Travel Writings: Great Britain and America* (New York: The Library of America, 1993) 543–44

[As a young man of 32, James settled in Europe—first in Paris, then in London—for what turned out to be a permanent move. He returned to the United States for relatively brief visits (when his parents died) in 1881 and 1882 and did not make another trip back until over 20 years had passed, in 1904. During that time, the country had changed immeasurably—and New York City, the place of James's birth, shocked him with its transformations. In *The American Scene*, a set of essays published in 1907, James writes of his impressions of his native land. In the following excerpt, James describes a visit during his 1904–05 trip to his family's home on Ashburton Street in Cambridge, Massachusetts, where he lived as a young man in the mid-1860s.]

[T]he pair of ancient houses I was in quest of kept their tryst; a pleas-ant individual pair, mated with nothing else in the street, yet looking at that hour as if their old still faces had lengthened, their shuttered, lidded eyes had closed, their brick complexions had paled, above the good granite basements, to a fainter red—all as with the cold consciousness of a possible doom.

... The two years [in one of these two houses] had been those of a young man's, a very young man's earliest fond confidence in a "literary career," and the effort of actual attention was to recover on the spot some echo of ghostly footsteps—the sound as of taps on the window-pane heard in the dim dawn. The place itself was meanwhile, at all events, a conscious memento, with old secrets to keep and old stories to witness for, a saturation of life as closed together and preserved in it as the scent lingering in a folded pocket-handkerchief. But when, a month later, I returned again ... I found but a gaping void, the brutal effacement, at a stroke, of every related object, of the whole precious past. Both the houses had been levelled and the space to the corner cleared; hammer and pickaxe had evidently begun to swing on the very morrow of my previous visit—which had moreover been precisely the imminent doom announced, without my understanding it, in the poor scared faces. I had been present, by the oddest hazard, at the very last moments of the victim in whom I was most interested; the act of obliteration had been breathlessly swift, and if I had seen how fast history could be made I had doubtless never so felt that it could be unmade still faster. It was as if the bottom had fallen out of one's own biography, and one plunged backward into space without meeting anything.

7. From Henry James, Letter to Frederick A. Duneka, 28 August 1906, in *Henry James: A Life in Letters*, ed. Philip Horne (New York: Viking, 1999) 437

[In August 1906 James wrote to his agent, James Brand Pinker, that he had had an "excellent little idea through not having slept a wink last night *all* for thinking of it": he had envisioned the story that would become "The Jolly Corner." In the following excerpt of a letter James wrote to Frederick A. Duneka, an editor at *Harper's Monthly*, he describes the story (then titled "The Second House").]

Dear Mr. Duneka,

I am sending you with this a short story, "The Second House;" over which, in respect to brevity, I have had a big and desperate struggle—with the final effect of my being worsted. The thing is very much longer than you like, as I know; and yet, after taking earnest counsel with myself—to say nothing of desperate pains with *it*—I am still sending it, on the chance that, after all, you will feel it to have been worth your seeing—as a miraculous masterpiece in the line of the fantastic-gruesome, the supernatural-thrilling, or anything else of that sort it may best be called. I think the real reason I send it you, with all its length on its head, or rather at its tail, is that it is the best thing of this sort I've ever done; and that, as I wholly undertook it for your use, with my too fond and false estimate of the compass I could keep it down to—well, I just desperately pack it off. It is as short, by every sacrificed inch, as its magnificent subject permits! ...

8. From Henry James's Notebooks (1904–05), in *The Complete Notebooks of Henry James*, ed. Leon Edel and Lyall H. Powers (New York: Oxford UP, 1987) 237, 240

[While touring America during his 1904–05 visit, James was nearly overwhelmed by his impressions of his much-changed native land as well as by memories evoked by his visits to homes and haunts of his youth. In his journal, he captured those impressions and memories, and how he would transmute them into the "gold" of his art.]

Everything sinks in: nothing is lost; everything abides and fertilizes and renews its golden promise, making me think with closed eyes of deep and grateful longing when, in the full summer days of LH [i.e., Lamb House, his home in England], my long dusty adventure over, I shall be able to [plunge] my hand, my arm, *in*, deep and far, and up to the shoulder—into the heavy bag of remembrance—of suggestion—of imagination—of art—and fish out every little figure and felicity, every little fact and fancy that can be to my purpose. These things are all packed away, now, thicker than I can penetrate, deeper than I can fathom, and there let them rest for the present, in their sacred cool darkness, till I shall let in upon them the mild still light of dear old LH—in which they will begin to gleam and glitter and take form like the gold and jewels of a mine....

... Isn't the highest deepest note of the whole thing the never-to-be-lost memory of that evening hour at Mount Auburn—at the Cambridge Cemetery when I took my way alone—after much waiting for the favouring hour—to that unspeakable group of graves.[1] It was late, in November; the trees all bare, the dusk to fall early, the air all still (at Cambridge, in general *so* still), with the western sky more and more turning to that terrible, deadly, pure polar pink that shows behind American winter woods. But I can't go over this—I can only, oh, so gently, so tenderly, brush it and breathe upon it—breathe upon it and

---

1 James was visiting the graves of his parents, his sister Alice, and an infant nephew (a son of William James).

brush it. It was the moment; it was the hour, it was the blessed flood of emotion that broke out at the touch of one's sudden *vision* and carried me away. I seemed then to know why I had done this; I seemed then to know why I had *come*—and to feel how not to have come would have been miserably, horribly to miss it. It made everything right—it made everything priceless. The moon was there, early, white and young, and seemed reflected in the white face of the great empty Stadium, forming one of the boundaries of Soldiers' Field,[1] that looked over at me, stared over at me, through the clear twilight, from across the Charles. Everything was there, everything *came*; the recognition, stillness, the strangeness, the pity and the sanctity and the terror, the breath-catching passion and the divine relief of tears. William's inspired transcript, on the exquisite little Florentine urn of Alice's ashes, William's divine gift to us, and to *her*, of the Dantean lines—

Dopo lungo exilio e martiro
Viene a questa pace—[2]

took me so at the throat by its penetrating *rightness*, that it was as if one sank down on one's knees in a kind of anguish of gratitude before something for which one had waited with a long, deep *ache*. But why do I write of all the unutterable and the all abysmal? Why does my pen not drop from my hand on approaching the infinite pity and tragedy of all the past? It does, poor helpless pen, with what it meets of the ineffable, what it meets of the cold Medusa-face[3] of life, of all the life *lived*, on every side. *Basta, basta!*[4]

---

1 A stretch of land near Harvard University, named to honor a small group of New Englanders who died in the Civil War (1861–65).

2 Edel and Powers note that James misquotes Dante's lines; James's lines can be translated, "After long exile and martyrdom [she/he/it] comes to this peace," whereas the actual quotation is "... ed essa da martiro / e da essilio venne a questa pace" ("and [she/it] from martyrdom and from exile came to this peace." Sharon Cameron has noted that James removes the feminine pronoun "essa" (in Dante, referring to the feminine noun for "soul"), thereby allowing the lines to apply to himself as well to his sister. See Cameron, *Thinking in Henry James* (Chicago: U of Chicago P, 1989) 14–16.

3 Medusa was a Gorgon—a monster in Greek mythology whose face was so horrific that whoever looked upon her would be turned to stone.

4 Enough, enough! (Italian).

9. Contemporary Reviews of "The Altar of the Dead"

[James published "The Altar of the Dead" in a collection of short stories, called *Terminations*, in 1895.]

a. *Harper's New Monthly Magazine*, 92 (May 1896): 12

[In this review, the critic said little else about *Terminations* except to make a rather strong claim for "The Altar of the Dead."]

[The tale's] quality of distinction is not surpassed by any previous effort of this author, nor perhaps by any short story in the English language ...

b. William Dean Howells, *Harper's Weekly* (27 July 1896): 701

Everywhere the admirable book is marked by a wise and sensitive reticence, which sometimes shades into the defect of its virtue, perhaps; but I am not sure of this. It is all in the minor key, but it is full of a distinction which is hard to preserve in the effects of pathos, whether it is the pathos that weeps or the pathos that laughs. The first is so easily maudlin, the last is so easily sardonic, but neither is imaginable of Mr. James, whose appeals to the sympathy of his reader are never such as to involve a loss of self-respect with the most responsive. One quits his company pensive with the sense of life which has been lived, and will be lived again and again.

10. Contemporary Reviews of *The Turn of the Screw*

[This novella was one of two stories in a collection called *The Two Magics*. Virtually all James's contemporaries read *The Turn of the Screw* as a tale involving some form of the supernatural; the famous critical debate—the so-called apparitionist versus non-apparitionist argument—would not really begin until the 1920s.]

a. Oscar Wilde, Letter to Robert Boss ([?]12 January 1899), in *The Letters of Oscar Wilde*, ed. Rupert Hart-Davis (New York: Harcourt Brace, 1962) 776

I think it is a most wonderful, lurid, poisonous little tale, like an Elizabethan tragedy. I am greatly impressed by it. James is developing, but he will never arrive at passion, I fear.

b. From *Literature*, 52 (15 October 1898): 351

It is not our fault if we fail to understand Mr. James's new book. He leaves everything unexplained.... [The story] is full of apparition, generally in broad daylight, but it is not a ghost story. Its subject, we hope, will not become a common motive with novelists, for it is nothing less than the demoniac possession of two young and otherwise delightful children.... So far as there is a story, the trials of the new governess (she has no name) form the story.

c. From "Mr. James's New Stories," *Athenaeum* 3704 (22 October 1898): 564–65

[After giving a negative review to one of James's tales also published in 1898, *In the Cage*, the writer of the following excerpt compares *The Turn of the Screw* to that story.]

... [*The Turn of the Screw*] is one of the most engrossing and terrifying ghost stories we have ever read. It is a real creation, and the idea of it is quite novel. Briefly, it is about the influence which two evil ghosts have on the lives of two young children, and about the efforts made by their governess to overcome the sinister attacks. Here the author makes triumphant use of his subtlety; instead of obscuring, he only adds to the horror of his conception by occasionally withholding the actual facts and just indicating them without unnecessarily ample details. A touch where a coarser hand would write a full-page description, a hint at unknown terrors where another would talk of bloody hands or dreadful crimes, and the impression is heightened in a way which would have made even Hawthorne envious on his own ground. And here, too, the style—braced up, as it were, to the task of not missing a detail of the author's effects—loses its flabbiness and indistinctness, and only gains in stimulating power where a curious turn of phrase is substituted for a more hackneyed expression.

d. From "Henry James as a Ghost Raiser," *Life* 32 (10 November 1898): 368

Henry James has frequently given his readers shivers by the coldness with which he treats intense emotions. But it is a new thing for him to create a semblance of terror by a genuine story of "uncanny ugliness and horror and pain.".... He calls the story *The Turn of the Screw*, and he does not hesitate to give it the extra twist that makes the reader writhe under it. And when you sift the terror to its essential facts, there does not seem to be anything in it to make a fuss about. That two supremely beautiful children should be under the evil spell of the ghosts of a dead governess and a wicked valet is not, on the face of it, a very awe-inspiring situation. Indeed, the ludicrousness of it, in these enlightened days, is always in danger of breaking through the hedge which the author has ingeniously constructed around it.

But right there is the place for the literary artist to show what he can do—and Henry James does it in a way to raise goose-flesh! He creates the atmosphere of the tale with those slow, deliberate phrases which seem fitted only to differentiate the odors of rare flowers. Seldom does he make a direct assertion, but qualifies and negatives and doubles negatives, and then throws in a handful of adverbs, until the image floats away upon a verbal smoke. But while the image lasts, it is, artistically, a thing of beauty. When he seems to be vague he is by elimination creating an effect of terror, of unimaginable horrors.

While his art is present in every sentence, the artist is absolutely obliterated. His personality counts for nothing in the effect. He is like a perfect lens which focuses light, but is itself absolutely colorless.

e. From *Illustrated London News* 113 (3 December 1898): 834

... [Henry James] has rarely written anything so subtle, so delicate in workmanship, so intense in feeling, so entirely artistic. And what a subject has he chosen to spend all this art and emotion upon! There are readers, we believe, who have faced the horrible in several literatures, and who will come to the conclusion that Mr. James has capped it all. The subject will outrage many minds far from prudish, with its sickening suggestion of evil nestling in the fairest of all fair places, the souls of little children. To us it appears gratuitously painful. But the land of art is wide and free, and we cannot say it excludes studies of morbidity and of demoniac possession. As such must we describe this story to ourselves, if we are to tolerate it at all.... There is something really great in the story, and assuredly the skill is superb. But surely we are not merely sentimentalists in our protest against children being made the pawns in this horrible contest.

Appendix B: The Study of the Supernatural in Nineteenth-Century England and America

1. From William James, "Certain Phenomena of Trance" (1890), in *The Works of William James: Essays in Psychical Research*, Frederick Burkhardt, General Editor, Fredson Bowers, Textual Editor (Cambridge, MA: Harvard University Press, 1986) 80–81

[In 1882, a group of well-respected scholars founded the Society for Psychical Research in London. Both William and Henry James were friends with several of the original founders and members; William helped found the American Society in 1885 and served as president of the British Society in 1894–95.[1] The excerpt below is a report that William wrote about a medium, Mrs. Leonora Piper ("Mrs. P."), whose work he had been observing. Because William could not be in London to give the report, Henry read it for him on 31 October 1890. William wrote to Henry a few days before, "I think your reading my Piper letter ... is the most comical thing I ever heard of."[2]]

... I remember playing the *esprit fort*[3] on that occasion before my feminine relatives, and seeking to explain by simple considerations the marvellous character of the facts which they brought back. This did not, however, prevent me from going myself a few days later, in

---

1 Peter G. Beidler has identified motifs in *The Turn of the Screw* that appear regularly in ghost stories collected by various researchers of supernatural phenomena and published before James wrote his own tale. Given his brother William's involvement with the Society for Psychical Research and his own friendship with several SPR members, James would almost certainly have been familiar with at least some of these stories. Beidler identifies 14 motifs from *The Turn of the Screw* that also occur in over 2,000 stories that he examined: ghosts appearing to two children; noises in the night; the face at the window; the upper part of the figure; the fixed stare; precise description of ghosts; identifying the ghost; the sad face; the felt presence of ghosts; ponds, stable and stairs; a feeling of cold; cold winds; extinguished lights; selective seeing of ghosts (Peter G. Beidler, *Ghosts, Demons and Henry James: "The Turn of the Screw" at the Turn of the Century* [Columbia: U of Missouri P, 1989] 77.

2 *The Works of William James: Essays in Psychical Research* (Cambridge, MA: Harvard UP, 1986) 465.

3 Free thinker (French).

company with my wife, to get a direct personal impression. The names of none of us up to this meeting had been announced to Mrs. P, and Mrs. J. and I were, of course, careful to make no reference to our relatives who had preceded. The medium, however, when entranced, repeated most of the names of "spirits" whom she had announced on the two former occasions and added others. The names came with difficulty, and were only gradually made perfect. My wife's father's name of Gibbens was announced first as Niblin, then as Giblin. A child Herman (whom we had lost the previous year) had his name spelt out as Herrin. I think that in no case were both Christian and surnames given on this visit. But the *facts predicated* of the persons named made it in many instances impossible not to recognize the particular individuals who were talked about....

My impression after this first visit was, that Mrs. P. was either possessed of supernormal powers, or knew the members of my wife's family by sight and had by some lucky coincidence become acquainted with such a multitude of their domestic circumstances as to produce the startling impression which she did. My later knowledge of her sittings and personal acquaintance with her has led me absolutely to reject the latter explanation, and to believe that she has supernatural powers.

2. From *The Times* (28 December 1898): 10

[The London *Times*'s reviewer of *The Turn of the Screw* criticized the tale because it deviated from the information about ghosts provided by the Society for Psychical Research.]

A ghost story ought to be short, persuasive, and in harmony, nowadays, with the provisional conclusions of psychical science.... Now, Mr. Henry James's tale, *The Turn of the Screw*, in his newest volume, *The Two Magics*, is not short (169 pages), is not persuasive (we could read it unmoved at midnight in a haunted house), it is not in conformity with the results of science, and the ghosts are too punctual and frequent. Out of the vast collections of phantasms brought together by the S.P.R., almost no sign of purpose on the ghost's side is offered, and when he may be suspected of a purpose he scarcely ever manages to make its nature intelligible. He somnambulizes,[1] so to speak, in a restless, incoherent dream. On the other hand Mr. James's two phantasms have their purpose sun-clear before them and are most pertinacious. Their idea is to corrupt two very nice children, brother and sister. The

---

1 Sleepwalks.

male ghost is that of Peter Quint, a bad menial; the lady ghost is that of his mistress, recently governess to the children. These are pretty ideas for a fable! The narrative is supposed to be written, many years ago, by another governess, who had developed Mr. James's style, down to an occasional Americanism.... The narrative concludes with the death of the poor little boy and the removal of his sister from home. But are ghosts purely local? One is recorded to have followed a family from Brompton to Bayswater,[1] and the banshee of an Irish house has turned up in Barbados and India. If the defunct governess was not purely local there would be no use in removing the little girl. In short, a ghost story does not seem to be within Mr. James's artistic resources. If Mr. James's friend, mentioned at the opening to the story, knows only one case of a child seeing a phantasm, he must be inexpert in these matters.

3. From Catherine S. Crowe, *The Night-Side of Nature or Ghosts and Ghost-Seers* (New York: Redfield, 1848) 300–01

[Catherine S. Crowe published *The Night-Side of Nature* in 1848, a collection of supposedly real-life ghost stories that went through several editions throughout the nineteenth century. Several of the stories foreshadow various events in Henry James's own ghostly tales. In the following excerpt, the wife of a family who has taken an isolated country estate has an encounter reminiscent of those in *The Turn of the Screw*. Whether James had read this actual account does not matter; the popularity of Crowe's book suggests a standard for ghost stories that James's reading audience would have recognized.]

They had been some considerable time in the house without the occurrence of anything remarkable, when one evening, towards dusk, Mrs. C., on going into what was called the oak bed-room, saw a female figure near one of the windows. It was apparently a young woman with dark hair hanging over her shoulders, a silk petticoat, and a short white robe, and she appeared to be looking eagerly through the window, as if expecting somebody. Mrs. C. clapped her hand upon her eyes "as thinking she had seen something she ought not to have seen," and when she looked again the figure had disappeared.

Shortly after this, a young girl who filled the situation of under nursery-maid, came to her in great agitation, saying that she had had a terrible fright, from seeing a very ugly old woman looking in upon her as she passed the window in the lobby. The girl was trembling vio-

---

1 Areas of London.

lently, and almost crying, so that Mrs. C. entertained no doubts of the reality of her alarm. She, however, thought it advisable to laugh her out of her fear, and went with her to the window, which looked into a closed court, but there was no one there, neither had any of the other servants seen such a person.

4. From William T. Stead, *Real Ghost Stories* (1897) (New York: George Doran, 1921) 58–60

[In another very popular collection of "true" ghost stories, *Real Ghost Stories* (1897), the English journalist William T. Stead brought together stories of premonitions, doppelgängers, and ghostly apparitions. In the excerpts below, he tells of an exchange between a well-educated friend and himself about body doubles.]

... I found that there had been a ghost in the trim new little villa in which I was quartered! It didn't appear to me—at least, it has not done so as yet. But it appeared to some friends of mine whose statement is explicit enough. Here was a find indeed. I spent most of my boyhood within a mile of the famous haunted house or mill at Willington, but I had never slept before in a place which ghosts used as a trysting place. I asked my hostess about it. She replied, "Yes, it is quite true; but, although you may not believe it, I am the ghost." "You? How?" "Yes," she replied, quite seriously; "it is quite true what your friends have told you. They did see what you would correctly describe as an apparition. That is to say, they saw a more or less shadowy figure, which they at once identified, and which then gradually faded away. It was an apparition in the true sense of the word. It entered the room without using the door or window, it was visibly manifested before them, and then it vanished. All that is quite true. But it is also true that the ghost, as you call it, was my ghost." "Your ghost, but——" "I am not dead, you are going to say. Precisely. But surely you must be well aware of the fact that the ghosts of the living are much better authenticated than ghosts of the dead."...

... "But what is a Thought Body?" [I asked.] My hostess smiled: "It is difficult to explain truths on the plane of thought to those who are immersed body and soul in matter. I can only tell you that every person has, in addition to this natural body of flesh, bones, and blood, a Thought Body, the exact counterpart in every respect of this material frame. It is contained within the material body, as air is contained in the lungs and in the blood. It is of finer matter than the gross fabric of our outward body. It is capable of motion with the rapidity of thought. The laws of space and time do not exist for the mind...."

Appendix C: Excerpts from Henry James's Nonfiction Writing about the Supernatural

1. **From Henry James, "Is There Life After Death?" (1910), in** *Henry James on Culture: Collected Essays on Politics and the American Social Scene*, **ed. Pierre A. Walker (Lincoln, NE: U of Nebraska P, 1999) 120–21, 122–24**

[Around 1909, Elizabeth Garver Jordan, the editor of *Harper's Bazaar*, invited several prominent writers, including Henry James, to contribute essays on life after death. James's essay appeared in two installments in early 1910. Critic Richard Hocks regards this essay as equal to his late (and greatest) tales and finds evocations of Spencer Brydon's experiences in "The Jolly Corner."[1] The first part of the essay examines the arguments against life after death.]

... [W]e begin by pitying the remembered dead, even for the very danger of our indifference to them, and we end by pitying ourselves for the final demonstration, as it were, of their indifference to us. "They must be dead, indeed," we say; "they must be as dead as 'science' affirms, for this consecration of it on such a scale, and with these tremendous rites of nullification, to take place." We think of the particular cases of those who could have been backed, as we call it, not to fail, on occasion, of somehow reaching us. We recall the forces of passion, of reason, of personality, that lived in them, and what such forces had made them, to our sight, capable of; and then we say, conclusively, "Talk of triumphant identity if *they*, wanting to triumph, haven't done it!"

[In the second part of the essay, James reflects on the change that the question has taken on for him over his lifetime. As a young man, he says, he was not interested in the issue, but as he aged, that changed.]

...What had happened, in short, was that all the while I had been practically, though however dimly, trying to take the measure of my consciousness—on this appropriate and prescribed basis of its being so finite—I had learned, as I may say, to live in it more, and with the con-

---

1   Richard Hocks, *Henry James and Pragmatistic Thought* (Chapel Hill, NC: U of North Carolina P, 1974) 217, 221.

sequence of thereby not a little undermining the conclusion most unfavorable to it. I had doubtless taken thus to increased living in it by reaction against so grossly finite a world—for it at least *contained* the world, and could handle and criticize it, could play with it and deride it; it had *that* superiority: which meant, all the while, such successful living that the abode itself grew more and more interesting to me, and with this beautiful sign of its character that the more and the more one asked of it the more and the more it appeared to give....

... It is not that I have found in growing older any one marked or momentous line in the life of the mind or in the play and the freedom of the imagination to be stepped over; but that a process takes place which I can only describe as the accumulation of the very treasure itself of consciousness....

Living, or feeling one's exquisite curiosity about the universe fed and fed, rewarded and rewarded—though I of course don't say definitely answered and answered—becomes thus the highest good I can conceive of, a million times better than not living (however *that* comfort may at bad moments have solicited us); all of which illustrates what I mean by the consecrated "interest" of consciousness. It so peoples and animates and extends and transforms itself; it so gives me the chance to take, on behalf of my personality, these inordinate intellectual and irresponsible liberties with the idea of things.... As more or less of one [i.e., an artist] myself, for instance, I deal with being, I invoke and evoke, I figure and represent, I seize and fix, as many phases and aspects and conceptions of it as my infirm hand allows me strength for; and in so doing I find myself—I can't express it otherwise—in communication with *sources*; sources to which I owe the apprehension of far more and far other combinations than observation and experience, in their ordinary sense, have given me the pattern of.

2. Henry James's Review of *The Strange Case of Dr. Jekyll and Mr. Hyde* (1888), in *Henry James: Literary Criticism: Essays on Literature, American Writers, English Writers*, ed. Leon Edel (New York: Library of America, 1984) 1251–53

[In 1888, James published a review of several of Robert Louis Stevenson's works, including *The Strange Case of Dr. Jekyll and Mr. Hyde*. James was impressed with this fictional case study of one man's struggle with the evil that lurks within him. The story's foreboding atmosphere and the moral and ethical dichotomy that so tortures Dr. Jekyll foreshadow similar elements in *The Turn of the Screw* and "The Jolly Corner." In fact, James's review of *Jekyll* describes Stevenson's story with almost exactly the same phrase that he will later use to describe his own tale in his preface to *The Turn of the Screw*: *Jekyll* is "the most ingenious and irresponsible of fictions," while *The Turn* is a "perfectly independent and irresponsible little fiction."]

Is *Dr. Jekyll and Mr. Hyde* a work of high philosophic intention, or simply the most ingenious and irresponsible of fictions? It has the stamp of a really imaginative production, that we may take it in different ways, but I suppose it would generally be called the most serious of the author's tales. It deals with the relation of the baser parts of man to his nobler, of the capacity for evil that exists in the most generous natures; and it expresses these things in a fable which is a wonderfully happy invention. The subject is endlessly interesting, and rich in all sorts of provocation, and Mr. Stevenson is to be congratulated on having touched the core of it. I may do him injustice, but it is, however, here, not the profundity of the idea which strikes me so much as the art of the presentation—the extremely successful form. There is a genuine feeling for the perpetual moral question, a fresh sense of the difficulty of being good and the brutishness of being bad; but what there is above all is a singular ability in holding the interest. I confess that that, to my sense, is the most edifying thing in the short, rapid, concentrated story, which is really a masterpiece of concision. There is something almost impertinent in the way, as I have noticed, in which Mr. Stevenson achieves his best effects without the aid of the ladies, and *Doctor Jekyll* is a capital example of his heartless independence. It is usually supposed that a truly poignant impression cannot be made without them, but in the drama of Mr. Hyde's fatal ascendency they remain altogether in the wing. It is very obvious—I do not say it cynically—that they must have played an important part in his development. The gruesome tone of the tale is, no doubt, deepened by their absence; it is like the late afternoon light of a foggy winter Sunday, when even inanimate objects have a kind of wicked look. I remember few situations in the pages of mystifying fiction more to the purpose than the episode of Mr. Utterson's going to Dr. Jekyll's to confer with the butler when the doctor is locked up in his laboratory, and the old servant, whose sagacity has hitherto encountered successfully the problems of the sideboard and the pantry, confesses that this time he is utterly baffled. The way the two men, at the door of the laboratory, discuss the identity of the mysterious personage inside, who has revealed himself in two or three inhuman glimpses to Poole, has those touches of which irresistible shudders are made. The butler's theory is that his master has been murdered, and that the murderer is in the room, personating him with a sort of clumsy diabolism. "Well, when that masked thing like a monkey jumped from among the chemicals and whipped into the cabinet, it went down my spine like ice." That is the effect upon the reader of most of the story. I say of most rather than all, because the ice rather melts in the sequel, and I have some difficulty in accepting the business of the powders, which seems to me too explicit and explanatory. The powders constitute the machinery of the transformation, and it will probably have struck many readers that this uncanny process would be more conceivable (so far as one may speak of the conceivable in such a case), if the author had not made it so definite.

3. From Henry James's Prefaces to the Tales (1906–08)

[From 1906 through 1908, James wrote prefaces for a new collection of his works, which he called the New York Edition. Those prefaces constitute an important part of James's nonfiction work and helped establish him as one of the most significant novelists who also wrote substantially *about* the novel and short story as a major art form.]

a. From the Preface to *The Turn of the Screw*, in *The Aspern Papers; The Turn of the Screw; The Liar; The Two Faces*, vol. 12, *The Novels and Tales of Henry James*, The New York Edition (New York: Charles Scribner's Sons, 1937): xiv–xxii

[T]his perfectly independent and irresponsible little fiction rejoices, beyond any rival on a like ground, in a conscious provision of prompt retort to the sharpest question that may be addressed to it. For it has the small strength—if I shouldn't say rather the unattackable ease—of a perfect homogeneity, of being, to the very last grain of its virtue, all of a kind; the very kind, as happens, least apt to be baited by earnest criticism, the only sort of criticism of which account need be taken. To have handled again this so full-blown flower of high fancy is to be led back by it to easy and happy recognitions. Let the first of these be that of the starting-point itself—the sense, all charming again, of the circle, one winter afternoon, round the hall-fire of a grave old country-house where (for all the world as if to resolve itself promptly and obligingly into convertible, into "literary" stuff) the talk turned, on I forget what homely pretext, to apparitions and night-fears, to the marked and sad drop in the general supply, and still more in the general quality, of such commodities. The good, the really effective and heart-shaking ghost-stories (roughly so to term them) appeared all to have been told, and neither new crop nor new type in any quarter awaited us. The new type indeed, the mere modern "psychical" case, washed clean of all queerness as by exposure to a flowing laboratory tap, and equipped with credentials vouching for this—the new type clearly promised little, for the more it was respectably certified the less it seemed of a nature to rouse the dear old sacred terror. Thus it was, I remember, that amid our lament for a beautiful lost form, our distinguished host expressed the wish that he might but have recovered for us one of the scantest of fragments of this form at its best. He had never forgotten the impression made on him as a young man by the withheld glimpse, as it were, of a dreadful matter that had been reported years before, and with as few particulars, to a lady with whom he had youthfully talked. The story would have been thrilling could she but have found herself in better possession of it, dealing as it did with a couple of small children in an out-of-the-way place, to whom the spirits of certain "bad" servants, dead in the employ of the house, were believed to have appeared with the design of "getting hold" of them. This was all, but there had been more, which my friend's old converser had lost the thread of: she could only assure him of the wonder of the allegations as she had anciently heard them made. He himself could give us but this shadow of a shadow—my own appreciation of which, I need scarcely say, was exactly wrapped up in that thinness. On the surface there wasn't much, but another grain, none the less, would have spoiled the precious pinch addressed to its end as neatly as some modicum extracted from an old silver snuff-box and held between finger and thumb. I was to remember the haunted children and the prowling servile spirits as a "value," of the disquieting sort, in all conscience sufficient; so that when, after an interval, I was asked for something seasonable by the promoters of a periodical dealing in the time-honoured Christmas-tide toy, I bethought myself at once of the vividest little note for sinister romance that I had ever jotted down.

Such was the private source of *The Turn of the Screw*; and I wondered, I confess, why so fine a germ, gleaming there in the wayside dust of life, had never been deftly picked up. The thing had for me the immense merit of allowing the imagination absolute freedom of hand, of inviting it to act on a perfectly clear field, with no "outside" control involved, no pattern of the usual or the true or the terrible "pleasant" (save always of course the high pleasantry of one's very form) to consort with. This makes in fact the charm of my second reference, that I find here a perfect example of an exercise of the imagination unassisted, unassociated—playing the game, making the score, in the phrase of our sporting day, off its own bat. To what degree the game was worth playing I needn't attempt to say: the exercise I have noted strikes me now, I confess, as the interesting thing, the imaginative faculty acting with the *whole* of the case on its hands. The exhibition involved is in other words a fairy-tale pure and simple—save indeed as to its springing not from an artless and measureless, but from a conscious and cultivated credulity. Yet the fairy-tale belongs mainly to either of two classes, the short and sharp and single, charged more or less with the compactness of anecdote (as to which let the familiars of our childhood, Cinderella and Blue-Beard and Hop o' my Thumb and Little Red Riding Hood and many of the gems of the Brothers Grimm directly testify), or else the long and loose, the copious, the various, the endless, where, dramatically speaking, roundness is quite sacrificed— sacrificed to fulness, sacrificed to exuberance, if one will: witness at hazard almost any one of the Arabian Nights.[1] The charm of all these things for the distracted modern mind is in the clear field of experience, as I call it, over which we are thus led to roam; an annexed but independent world in which nothing is right save as we rightly imagine it. We have to do *that*, and we do it happily for the short spurt and in the smaller piece, achieving so perhaps beauty and lucidity; we flounder, we lose breath, on the other hand—that is we fail, not of continuity, but of an agreeable unity, of the "roundness" in which beauty and lucidity largely reside—when we go in, as they say, for great lengths and breadths. And this, oddly enough, not because "keeping it up" isn't abundantly within the compass of the imagination appealed to in certain conditions, but because the finer interest depends just on *how* it is kept up.

Nothing is so easy as improvisation, the running on and on of invention; it is sadly compromised, however, from the moment its stream breaks bounds and gets into flood. Then the waters may spread indeed, gathering houses and herds and crops and cities into their arms and wrenching off, for our amusement, the whole face of the land–only violating by the same stroke our sense of the course and the channel, which is our sense of the uses of a stream and the virtue of a story. Improvisation, as in the Arabian Nights, may keep on terms with encountered objects by sweeping them in and floating them on its breast; but the great effect it so loses—that of keeping on terms with itself. This is ever, I intimate, the hard thing for the fairy-tale; but by just so much as it struck me as hard did it in *The Turn of the Screw* affect me as irresistibly prescribed. To improvise with extreme freedom and yet at the same time without the possibility of ravage, without the hint of a flood; to keep the stream, in a word, on something like ideal terms with itself: that was here my definite business. The thing was to aim at absolute singleness, clearness and roundness, and yet to depend on an imagination working freely, working (call it) with extravagance; by which law it wouldn't be thinkable except as free and wouldn't be amusing except as controlled. The merit of the tale, as it stands, is accordingly, I judge, that it has struggled successfully with its dangers. It is an excursion into chaos while remaining, like Blue-Beard and

---

1 Collection of folktales from the Middle East, which were commonly adapted for children's literature in the nineteenth century.

Cinderella, but an anecdote—though an anecdote amplified and highly emphasised and returning upon itself; as, for that matter, Cinderella and Blue-Beard return. I need scarcely add after this that it is a piece of ingenuity pure and simple, of cold artistic calculation, an *amusette*[1] to catch those not easily caught (the "fun" of the capture of the merely witless being ever but small), the jaded, the disillusioned, the fastidious. Otherwise expressed, the study is of a conceived "tone," the tone of suspected and felt trouble, of an inordinate and incalculable sort—the tone of tragic, yet of exquisite, mystification. To knead the subject of my young friend's, the supposititious narrator's, mystification thick, and yet strain the expression of it so clear and fine that beauty would result: no side of the matter so revives for me as that endeavour. Indeed if the artistic value of such an experiment be measured by the intellectual echoes it may again, long after, set in motion, the case would make in favour of this little firm fantasy—which I seem to see draw behind it to-day a train of associations. I ought doubtless to blush for thus confessing them so numerous that I can but pick among them for reference. I recall for instance a reproach made me by a reader capable evidently, for the time, of some attention, but not quite capable of enough, who complained that I hadn't sufficiently "characterised" my young woman engaged in her labyrinth; hadn't endowed her with signs and marks, features and humours, hadn't in a word invited her to deal with her own mystery as well as with that of Peter Quint, Miss Jessel and the hapless children. I remember well, whatever the absurdity of its now coming back to me, my reply to that criticism—under which one's artistic, one's ironic heart shook for the instant almost to breaking. "You indulge in that stricture at your ease, and I don't mind confiding to you that—strange as it may appear!— one has to choose ever so delicately among one's difficulties, attaching one's self to the greatest, bearing hard on those and intelligently neglecting the others. If one attempts to tackle them all one is certain to deal completely with none; whereas the effectual dealing with a few casts a blest golden haze under cover of which, like wanton mocking goddesses in clouds, the others find prudent to retire. It was 'déjà très joli,'[2] in *The Turn of the Screw*, please believe, the general proposition of our young woman's keeping crystalline her record of so many intense anomalies and obscurities—by which I don't of course mean her explanation of them, a different matter; and I saw no way, I feebly grant (fighting, at the best too, periodically, for every grudged inch of my space) to exhibit her in relations other than those; one of which,

---

1 Plaything (French).
2 Already very pretty (French).

precisely, would have been her relation to her own nature. We have surely as much of her own nature as we can swallow in watching it reflect her anxieties and inductions. It constitutes no little of a character indeed, in such conditions, for a young person, as she says, 'privately bred,' that she is able to make her particular credible statement of such strange matters. She has 'authority,' which is a good deal to have given her, and I couldn't have arrived at so much had I clumsily tried for more."

For which truth I claim part of the charm latent on occasion in the extracted reasons of beautiful things—putting for the beautiful always, in a work of art, the close, the curious, the deep. Let me place above all, however, under the protection of that presence the side by which this fiction appeals most to consideration: its choice of its way of meeting its gravest difficulty. There were difficulties not so grave: I had for instance simply to renounce all attempt to keep the kind and degree of impression I wished to produce on terms with the to-day so copious psychical record of cases of apparitions. Different signs and circumstances, in the reports, mark these cases; different things are done—though on the whole very little appears to be—by the persons appearing; the point is, however, that some things are never done at all: this negative quantity is large—certain reserves and proprieties and immobilities consistently impose themselves. Recorded and attested "ghosts" are in other words as little expressive, as little dramatic, above all as little continuous and conscious and responsive, as is consistent with their taking the trouble—and an immense trouble they find it, we gather—to appear at all. Wonderful and interesting therefore at a given moment, they are inconceivable figures in an *action*—and *The Turn of the Screw* was an action, desperately, or it was nothing. I had to decide in fine between having my apparitions correct and having my story "good"—that is producing my impression of the dreadful, my designed horror. Good ghosts, speaking by book, make poor subjects, and it was clear that from the first my hovering prowling blighting presences, my pair of abnormal agents, would have to depart altogether from the rules. They would be agents in fact; there would be laid on them the dire duty of causing the situation to reek with the air of Evil. Their desire and their ability to do so, visibly measuring meanwhile their effect, together with their observed and described success—this was exactly my central idea; so that, briefly, I cast my lot with pure romance, the appearances conforming to the true type being so little romantic.

This is to say, I recognise again, that Peter Quint and Miss Jessel are not "ghosts" at all, as we now know the ghost, but goblins, elves, imps, demons as loosely constructed as those of the old trials for witchcraft; if not, more pleasingly, fairies of the legendary order, wooing their victims forth to see them dance under the moon. Not indeed that I suggest their reducibility to any form of the pleasing pure and simple; they please at the best but through having helped me to express my subject all directly and intensely. Here it was—in the use made of them—that I felt a high degree of art really required; and here it is that, on reading the tale over, I find my precautions justified. The essence of the matter was the villainy of motive in the evoked predatory creatures; so that the result would be ignoble—by which I mean would be trivial—were this element of evil but feebly or inanely suggested. Thus arose on behalf of my idea the lively interest of a possible suggestion and process of *adumbration*; the question of how best to convey that sense of the depths of the sinister without which my fable would so woefully limp. Portentous evil—how was I to save that, as an intention on the part of my demon-spirits, from the drop, the comparative vulgarity, inevitably attending, throughout the whole range of possible brief illustration, the offered example, the imputed vice, the cited act, the limited deplorable presentable instance? To bring the bad dead back to life for a second round of badness is to warrant them as indeed prodigious, and to become hence as shy of specifications as of a waiting anti-climax. One had seen, in fiction, some grand form of wrong-doing, or better still of wrong-being, imputed, seen it promised and announced as by the hot breath of the Pit—and then, all lamentably, shrink to the compass of some particular brutality, some particular immorality, some particular infamy portrayed: with the result, alas, of the demonstration's falling sadly short. If *my* bad things, for *The Turn of the Screw*, I felt, should succumb to this danger, if they shouldn't seem sufficiently bad, there would be nothing for me but to hang my artistic head lower than I had ever known occasion to do.

The view of that discomfort and the fear of that dishonour, it accordingly must have been, that struck the proper light for my right, though by no means easy, short cut. What, in the last analysis, had I to give the sense of? Of their being, the haunting pair, capable, as the phrase is, of everything—that is of exerting, in respect to the children, the very worst action small victims so conditioned might be conceived as subject to. What would *be* then, on reflexion, this utmost conceivability?—a question to which the answer all admirably came. There is for such a case no eligible *absolute* of the wrong; it remains relative to fifty other elements, a matter of appreciation, speculation, imagination—these things moreover quite exactly in the light of the spectator's, the critic's, the reader's experience. Only make the reader's general vision of evil intense enough, I said to myself—and that already is a charming job—and his own experience, his own imagination, his own sympathy (with the children) and horror (of their false friends) will supply him quite sufficiently with all the particulars.

Make him *think* the evil, make him think it for himself, and you are released from weak specifications. This ingenuity I took pains—as indeed great pains were required—to apply; and with a success apparently beyond my liveliest hope. Droll enough at the same time, I must add, some of the evidence—even when most convincing—of this success. How can I feel my calculation to have failed, my wrought suggestion not to have worked, that is, on my being assailed, as has befallen me, with the charge of a monstrous emphasis, the charge of all indecently expatiating? There is not only from beginning to end of the matter not an inch of expatiation, but my values are positively all blanks save so far as an excited horror, a promoted pity, a created expertness—on which punctual effects of strong causes no writer can ever fail to plume himself—proceed to read into them more or less fantastic figures. Of high interest to the author meanwhile—and by the same stroke a theme for the moralist—the artless resentful reaction of the entertained person who has abounded in the sense of the situation. He visits his abundance, morally, on the artist—who has but clung to an ideal of faultlessness. Such indeed, for this latter, are some of the observations by which the prolonged strain of that clinging may be enlivened!

b. From the Preface to "The Altar of the Dead," "The Beast in the Jungle," and "The Jolly Corner," in Preface to "The Altar of the Dead," "The Beast in the Jungle," "The Birthplace," and Other Tales, vol. 17, *The Novels and Tales of Henry James*, The New York Edition (New York: Charles Scribner's Sons, 1937): v–xxix

The "Altar of the Dead" forms part of a volume bearing the title of *Terminations*, which appeared in 1895. Figuring last in that collection of short pieces, it here stands at the head of my list, not as prevailing over its companions by length, but as being ample enough and of an earlier date than several. I have to add that with this fact of its temporal order, and the fact that, as I remember, it had vainly been "hawked about," knocking, in the world of magazines, at half a dozen editorial doors impenetrably closed to it, I shall have exhausted my fund of allusion to the influences attending its birth. I consult memory further to no effect; so that if I should seem to have lost every trace of "how I came to think" of such a motive, didn't I, by a longer reach of reflexion, help myself back to the state of not having *had* to think of it? The idea embodied in this composition must in other words never have been so absent from my view as to call for an organised search. It was "there"—it had always, or from ever so far back, been there, not interfering with other conceits, yet at the same time not interfered with; and it naturally found expression at the first hour something more urgently undertaken happened not to stop the way. The way here, I recognise, would ever have been easy to stop, for the general patience, the inherent waiting faculty, of the principle of interest involved, was conscious of no strain, and above all of no loss, in amusedly biding its time. Other conceits might indeed come and go, born of light impressions and passing hours, for what sort of free intelligence would it be that, addressed to the human scene, should propose to itself, all vulgarly, never to be waylaid or arrested, never effectively inspired, by some imaged appeal of the lost Dead? The subject of my story is obviously, and quite as usual, the exhibition of a case; the case being that of an accepted, a cultivated habit (the cultivation is really the point) of regularly taking thought for them. Frankly, I can but gather, the desire, at last of the acutest, to give an example and represent an instance of some such practised communion, was a foredoomed consequence of life, year after year, amid the densest and most materialised aggregation of men upon earth, the society most wedded by all its conditions to the immediate and the finite. More exactly speaking, it was impossible for any critic or "creator" at all worth his wage not, as a matter of course, again and again to ask himself what may not become of individual sensibility, of the faculty and the fibre itself, when everything makes against the indulgence of it save as a conscious, and indeed highly emphasised, dead loss.

The impression went back for its full intensity, no doubt, neither to a definite moment nor to a particular shock; but the author of the tale before us was long to cherish the memory of a pair of illuminating incidents that, happily for him—by which I mean happily for the generalisation he here makes—placed themselves, at no great distance apart, so late in a sustained experience of London as to find him profitably prepared for them, and yet early enough to let confirmatory matter gather in abundance round. Not to this day, in fine, has he forgotten the hard, handsome, gentlemanly face, as it was expressionally affected in a particular conjunction, of a personage occasionally met in other years at one of the friendliest, the most liberal of "entertaining" houses and then lost to sight till after a long interval. The end of all mortal things had, during this period, and in the fulness of time, overtaken our delightful hosts and the scene of their long hospitality, a scene of constant welcome to my personage, as I have called him (a police-magistrate then seated, by reason of his office, well in the eye of London, but as conspicuous for his private urbanity as for his high magisterial and penal mask). He too has now passed away, but what could exactly better attest the power of prized survival in personal signs than my even yet felt chill as I saw the old penal glare rekindled in him by the form of my aid to his memory. "We used sometimes to meet, in the old days, at the dear So-and-So's, you may recall." "The

So-and-So's?" said the awful gentleman, who appeared to recognise the name, across the table, only to be shocked at the allusion. "Why, they're Dead, sir—dead these many years." "Indeed they are, sir, alas," I could but reply with spirit; "and it 's precisely why I like so to speak of them!—Il ne manquerait plus que cela,[1] that because they're dead I shouldn't!" is what I came within an ace of adding; or rather *might* have come hadn't I felt my indecency too utterly put in its place. I was left with it in fact on my hands—where however I was quite everlastingly, as you see, to cherish it. My anecdote is mild and its companion perhaps milder; but impressions come as they can and stay as they will.

A distinguished old friend, a very eminent lady and highly marked character, though technically, as it were, a private person, unencompassed by literary luggage or other monumental matter, had dropped from the rank at a great age and, as I was to note after a sufficient interval, to my surprise, with a singularly uncommemorated and unchronicled effect: given, I mean, her social and historical value. One blushed, as the days passed, for the want of manners in it—there being twenty reasons in the case why manners should have been remembered. A friend of the interesting woman, thereupon, seeing his opportunity, asked leave of an acquaintance of his own, the conductor of a "high class" periodical, to intervene on behalf of her memory in the pages under the latter's control. The amiable editor so far yielded to a first good impulse as to welcome the proposal; but the proposer was disconcerted to receive on the morrow a colder retractation. "I really don't see why I should publish an article about Mrs. X *because*—and because *only*, so far as I can make out—she's dead." Again I felt the inhibition, as the psychologists say, that I had felt in the other case; the vanity, *in the conditions*, of any yearning plea that this was the most beautiful of reasons. Clearly the conditions were against its being for an effective moment felt as such; and the article in question never appeared—nor, to the best of my knowledge, anything else of the sort: which fact was to take its place among other grim values. These pointed, as they all too largely accumulated, to the general black truth that London was a terrible place to die in; doubtless not so much moreover by conscious cruelty or perversity as under the awful doom of general dishumanisation. It takes space to feel, it takes time to know, and great organisms as well as small have to pause, more or less, to possess themselves and to be aware. Monstrous masses are, by this truth, so impervious to vibration that the sharpest forces of feeling, locally applied, no more penetrate than a pin or a paper-cutter penetrates an elephant's hide. Thus the very tradition of sensibility would

---

1 That would be the last straw! (French).

perish if left only to their care. It has here and there to be rescued, to be saved by independent, intelligent zeal; which type of effort however, to avail, has to fly in the face of the conditions.

These are easily, one is obliged to add, too many for it; nothing being more visible for instance than that the life of inordinately numerous companies is hostile to friendship and intimacy—unless indeed it be the impropriety of such names applied to the actual terms of intercourse. The sense of the state of the dead is but part of the sense of the state of the living; and, congruously with that, life is cheated to almost the same degree of the finest homage (precisely this our possible friendships and intimacies) that we fain would render it. We clutch indeed at some shadow of these things, we stay our yearning with snatches and stop-gaps; but our struggle yields to the other arrayed things that defeat the *cultivation*, in such an air, of the finer flowers—creatures of cultivation as the finer flowers essentially are. We perforce fall back, for the application of that process, on the coarser— which form together the rank and showy bloom of "success," of multiplied contact and multiplied motion; the bloom of a myriad many-coloured "relations"—amid which the precious plant that is rare at the best becomes rare indeed. "The Altar of the Dead" then commemorates a case of what I have called the individual independent effort to keep it none the less tended and watered, to cultivate it, as I say, with an exasperated piety. I am not however here reconstituting my more or less vivid fable, but simply glancing at the natural growth of its prime idea, that of an invoked, a restorative reaction against certain general brutalities. Brutal, more and more, to wondering eyes, the great fact that the poor dead, all about one, were nowhere so dead as there; where to be caught in any rueful glance at them was to be branded at once as "morbid." "Mourir, à Londres, c'est être bien mort!"[1]—I have not forgotten the ironic emphasis of a distinguished foreign friend, for some years officially resident in England, as we happened once to watch together a funeral-train, on its way to Kensal Green or wherever, bound merrily by. That truth, to any man of memories, was too repeatedly and intolerably driven home, and the situation of my depicted George Stransom is that of the poor gentleman who simply at last couldn't "stand" it.

To desire, amid these collocations, to place, so far as possible, like with like, was to invite "The Beast in the Jungle" to stand here next in order. As to the accidental determinant of which composition, once more—of comparatively recent date and destined, like its predecessor, first to see the light in a volume of miscellanies (*The Better Sort*, 1903)—I remount the stream of time, all enquiringly, but to come

---

1 To die in London is to be truly dead! (French).

back empty-handed. The subject of this elaborated fantasy—which, I must add, I hold a successful thing only as its motive may seem to the reader to stand out sharp—can't quite have belonged to the immemorial company of such solicitations; though in spite of this I meet it, in ten lines of an old note-book, but as a recorded conceit and an accomplished fact. Another poor sensitive gentleman, fit indeed to mate with Stransom of "The Altar"—my attested predilection for poor sensitive gentlemen almost embarrasses me as I march!—was to have been, after a strange fashion and from the threshold of his career, condemned to keep counting with the unreasoned prevision of some extraordinary fate; the conviction, lodged in his brain, part and parcel of his imagination from far back, that experience would be marked for him, and whether for good or for ill, by some rare distinction, some incalculable violence or unprecedented stroke. So I seemed to see him start in life—under the so mixed star of the extreme of apprehension and the extreme of confidence; all to the logical, the quite inevitable effect of the complication aforesaid: his having to wait and wait for the right recognition; none of the mere usual and normal human adventures, whether delights or disconcertments, appearing to conform to the great type of his fortune. So it is that he's depicted. No gathering appearance, no descried or interpreted promise or portent, affects his superstitious soul either as a damnation deep enough (if damnation be in question) for his appointed *quality* of consciousness, or as a translation into bliss sublime enough (on *that* hypothesis) to fill, in vulgar parlance, the bill. Therefore as each item of experience comes, with its possibilities, into view, he can but dismiss it under this sterilising habit of the failure to find it good enough and thence to appropriate it.

His one desire remains of course to meet his fate, or at least to divine it, to see it as intelligible, to learn it, in a word; but none of its harbingers, pretended or supposed, speak his ear in the true voice; they wait their moment at his door only to pass on unheeded, and the years ebb while he holds his breath and stays his hand and—from the dread not less of imputed pride than of imputed pusillanimity—stifles his distinguished secret. He perforce lets everything go—leaving all the while his general presumption disguised and his general abstention unexplained; since he's ridden by the idea of what things may lead to, since they mostly always lead to human communities, wider or intenser, of experience, and since, above all, in his uncertainty, he mustn't compromise others. Like the blinded seeker in the old-fashioned game he "burns," on occasion, as with the sense of the hidden thing near—only to deviate again however into the chill; the chill that indeed settles on him as the striking of his hour is deferred. His career thus resolves itself into a great negative adventure, my report of which presents, for its centre, the fine case that has caused him most tor-

mentedly to "burn," and then most unprofitably to stray. He is afraid
to recognise what he incidentally misses, since what his high belief
amounts to is not that he shall have felt and vibrated less than any one
else, but that he shall have felt and vibrated more; which no acknowledgement of the minor loss must conflict with. Such a course of existence naturally involves a climax—the final flash of the light under
which he reads his lifelong riddle and sees his conviction proved. He
has indeed been marked and indeed suffered his fortune—which is
precisely to have been the man in the world to whom nothing whatever was to happen. My picture leaves him overwhelmed—at last he
has understood; though in thus disengaging my treated theme for the
reader's benefit I seem to acknowledge that this more detached
witness may not successfully have done so. I certainly grant that any
felt merit in the thing must all depend on the clearness and charm
with which the subject just noted expresses itself.

... I dare say, to conclude, that whenever, in quest, as I have noted,
of the amusing, I have invoked the horrific, I have invoked it, in such
air as that of *The Turn of the Screw*, that of "The Jolly Corner," ... in
earnest aversion to waste and from the sense that in art economy is
always beauty. The apparitions of Peter Quint and Miss Jessel, in the
first of the tales just named, the elusive presence nightly "stalked"
through the New York house by the poor gentleman in the second, are
matters as to which in themselves, really, the critical challenge (essentially nothing ever but the spirit of fine attention) may take a hundred
forms—and a hundred felt or possibly proved infirmities is too great a
number. Our friends' respective minds about them, on the other hand,
are a different matter—challengeable, and repeatedly, if you like, but
never challengeable without some consequent further stiffening of the
whole texture. Which proposition involves, I think, a moral. The
moving accident, the rare conjunction, whatever it be, doesn't make
the story—in the sense that the story is our excitement, our amusement, our thrill and our suspense; the human emotion and the human
attestation, the clustering human conditions we expect presented, only
make it. The extraordinary is most extraordinary in that it happens to
you and me, and it's of value (of value for others) but so far as visibly
brought home to us. At any rate, odd though it may sound to pretend
that one feels on safer ground in tracing such an adventure as that of
the hero of "The Jolly Corner" than in pursuing a bright career among
pirates or detectives, I allow that composition to pass as the measure
or limit, on my own part, of any achievable comfort in the "adventure-
story"; and this not because I may "render"—well, what my poor gentleman attempted and suffered in the New York house—better than I
may render detectives or pirates or other splendid desperadoes,
though even here too there would be something to say; but because

the spirit engaged with the forces of violence interests me most when I can think of it as engaged most deeply, most finely and most "subtly" (precious term!). For then it is that, as with the longest and firmest prongs of consciousness, I grasp and hold the throbbing subject; *there* it is above all that I find the steady light of the picture....

[T]he strange and sinister embroidered on the very type of the normal and easy ... was to be again, after years, the idea entertained for "The Jolly Corner," about the composition of which there would be more to say than my space allows; almost more in fact than categorical clearness might see its way to. A very limited thing being on this occasion in question, I was moved to adopt as my motive an analysis of some one of the conceivably rarest and intensest grounds for an "unnatural" anxiety, a *malaise* so incongruous and discordant, in the given prosaic prosperous conditions, as almost to be compromising. Spencer Brydon's adventure however is one of those finished fantasies that, achieving success or not, speak best even to the critical sense for themselves ...

4. From Henry James's Notebooks (1879–1914), in *The Complete Notebooks of Henry James*, ed. Leon Edel and Lyall H. Powers (New York: Oxford UP, 1987)

[James kept extensive notes about ideas, or "germs," as he often called them, for his fiction. Interspersed with those ideas are his meditations on living a literary life, in which he would often invoke his "good angel" whom he sometimes addressed in French as "*mon bon.*" The notebooks give us a fascinating glimpse into the inner sanctum of the artist at work, but it is important to remember that the final text itself often differs from the plans, both in content and in treatment.]

Notebook Entry on *The Turn of the Screw*, 12 January 1895

Note here the ghost-story told me at Addington (evening of Thursday 10th), by the Archbishop of Canterbury: the mere vague, undetailed, faint sketch of it—being all he had been told (very badly and imperfectly), by a lady who had no art of relation, and no clearness: the story of the young children (indefinite number and age) left to the care of servants in an old country-house, through the death, presumably, of parents. The servants, wicked and depraved, corrupt and deprave the children; the children are bad, full of evil, to a sinister degree. The servants *die* (the story vague about the way of it) and their apparitions, figures, return to haunt the house *and* children, to whom they seem to beckon, whom they invite and solicit, from across dangerous places, the deep ditch of a sunk fence, etc.—so that the children may destroy themselves, lose themselves by responding, by getting into their power. So long as the children are kept from them, they are not lost: but they try and try and try, these evil presences, to get hold of them. It is a question of the children "coming over to where they are." It is all obscure and imperfect, the picture, the story, but there is a suggestion of strangely gruesome effect in it. The story to be told—tolerably obviously—by an outside spectator, observer [*Notebooks* 109].

Notebook Entry on "The Altar of the Dead," 29 September 1894

I seem to see a pretty idea for a short tale in a small fancy to which I should give the name of "The Altar of the Dead." The name, at least, is happy; if the story may be half as much so! I imagine a man whose noble and beautiful religion is the worship of the Dead. It is the only religion he has; and it is a refuge and a consolation to him. He cherishes for the silent, for the patient, the unreproaching dead, a tenderness in which all his private need of something, not of this world, to cherish, to be pious to, to make the object of a donation, finds a sacred, and almost a secret, expression. He is struck with the way they are forgotten, are unhallowed—unhonoured, neglected, shoved out of sight; allowed to become so much more dead, even, than the fate that has overtaken them has made them. He is struck with the rudeness, the coldness, that surrounds their memory—the want of place made for them in the life of the survivors. The essence of his religion is really to make and to keep such a place. This place I call—he calls—their altar; an altar that, in the obscurity of his spiritual spaces, seems to blaze with lights and flowers. *His* dead, at least, are there, and there is a great perpetual taper for each of them. The situation, the action, that makes the idea a subject, comes to me vaguely as something like this. Let me first say that I had first fancied the "altar" as a merely spiritual one—an altar in his mind, in his soul, more splendid to the spiritual eye than any shrine in any actual church. But I probably can't get an adequate action unless I enlarge this idea. Let me suppose for the moment, at any rate, that he has set up a spiritual altar—either in some Catholic church or in some apartment or chapel of his own house. The latter alternative is, I think, much the *least* practicable. The idea of the story, in its simplest expression, is that, loving and cherishing his altar, he feels that it doesn't become complete—that it won't be, can't be, till his *own* taper is lighted there. It's to that end, as a climax, that the little tale must work. I think I see it, and that it comes to me. He begins it with the death of his mother—or at any rate with the loss of some dear friend. The thing takes place in London, vaguely, fancifully, obscurely, without "realism" or dots upon the *i*'s. He wanders in his bereavement into a Catholic church. He sits there—in the darkness of a winter afternoon—before a lighted altar; and the comfort and the peace are sweet to him. It could all be much better abroad; but that is a detail, and tact, and art, the divine, circumvent everything. Abroad or in London, at any rate, he sees an old woman paying for a taper—for one of *her* poor dead; and that gives him the fancy, the hint. He finds one of the side-altars of the church obscure and neglected—and he makes an arrangement by which, on payment of a sum of money, *he* may establish certain perpetual candles there [*Notebooks* 98–99].

2 October 1894

I came back to town yesterday—and I see my little subject comparatively clear—I think. My hero's altar has long been a "spiritual" one—lighted in the gloom of his own soul. Then it *becomes* a material one, and the event is *determined* in a manner that the story relates. He wanders into a suburban (of course, Catholic) church on a winter afternoon. He is under the *coup*, the effect, of some *fresh* perception of the way the Dead are forgotten, dishonoured, in the manner I have hinted at [*Notebooks* 99].

24 October 1894

I broke off there—but I wrote the greater part of a very short tale on those lines: with the effect, unusual for me, of quite losing conceit of my subject, within sight of the close, and asking myself if it is worth going on with: or rather feeling that it isn't. I shall put it by—perhaps it will, the humour of it, come back to me. But the thing is a "conceit," after all, a little fancy which doesn't hold a great deal. Such things betray one—that I more and more (if possible) feel. *Plus je vais,*[1] the more intensely it comes home to me that solidity of subject, importance, emotional capacity of subject, is the only thing on which, henceforth, it is of the slightest use for me to expend myself. Everything else breaks down, collapses, turns thin, turns poor, turns wretched—betrays one miserably. Only the fine, the large, the human, the natural, the fundamental, the passionate things. It is true, of course, that in the case of a little thing like this "Altar of the Dead," a short thing, as to which its modest dimensions speak for it, it need not be of much moment, one way or the other, if one *does* go on with it. What one *has* seen in it is probably there, and pressing a little will bring it out. One's claim for it is, on the very face of the matter, slight [*Notebooks* 99–100].

---

1 The more I go along (French).

Notebook Entry on "The Jolly Corner," 5 February 1895

There comes back to me, à propos of it, and as vaguely and crookedly hooking itself on to it, somehow, that *concetto*[1] that I have jotted down in another notebook—that of the little tragedy of the man who has renounced his ambition, the dream of his youth, his genius, talent, vocation—with all the honour and glory it might have brought him: sold it, bartered it, exchanged it for something very different and inferior, but mercenary and worldly.... What I fanced in this last mentioned was that this Dead Self of the poor man's lives for him still in some indirect way, in the sympathy, the fidelity (the relation of some kind) of another.... [W]hat I wanted not to let slip altogether was simply some reminder of the beauty, the little tragedy, attached perhaps to the situation of the man of genius who, in some accursed hour of his youth, has bartered away the fondest vision of that youth and lives ever afterwards in the shadow of the bitterness of the regret. My other little note contained the fancy of his *recovering* a little of the lost joy, of the Dead Self, in his intercourse with some person, some woman, who knows what that self was, in whom it still lives a little. This intercourse is his real life.... [*Notebooks* 112–13].

27 August 1901

Meanwhile there is something else—a very tiny *fantaisie* probably—in small notion that comes to me of a man haunted by the fear more and more, throughout life, that *something will happen to him*: he doesn't quite know what. His life *seems* safe and ordered, his liabilities and exposures (as a *result* of the fear) a good deal curtailed and cut down, so that the years go by and the stroke doesn't fall. Yet "It *will* come, it will still come," he finds himself believing—and indeed saying to some one, some second-consciousness in the anecedote. "It will come before death; I shan't die without it." Finally I think it must be *he* who sees—not the 2d consciousness. Mustn't indeed the "2d consciousness" be some woman, and it be she who *helps* him to see? She has always loved him—yet, *that*, for the story, "pretty," and he, saving, protecting, exempting his life (always, really, with and *for* the fear), has never known it. He likes her, talks to her, confides in her, sees her often—*la côtoie*,[2] as to her hidden passion, but never guesses. She meanwhile, all the time, sees his life as it is. It is to her that he tells his fear—yes, she is the "2d consciousness." At first she *feels* herself, for

---

1 Conceit (Italian). James is using the term "conceit" as he did in his notes on the origins of "The Altar of the Dead" (noted above).

2 He stays close to her side.

him, his feeling of his fear, and is tender, reassuring, protective. Then she reads, as I say, his real case, and is, though unexpressedly, *lucid*. The years go by and *she sees the thing not happen*. At last one day they are somehow, some day, face to face over it, and then she speaks. "It *has*, the great thing you've always lived in dread of, had the foreboding of—it *has* happened to you." He wonders—when, how, what? "What is it?—why it is that *nothing* has happened!" Then, later on, I think, to keep up the prettiness, it must be that HE sees, that he understands. She has loved him always—and *that* might have happened. But it's too late—she's dead. That, I think, at least, he comes to later on, after an interval, after her death. She is dying, or ill, when she says it. He *then* DOESN'T understand, doesn't see—or so far, only, as to agree with her, ruefully, that that very well *may* be it: that nothing has happened. He goes back; she is gone: she is dead. *What* she has said to him has in a way, by its truth, created the need for her, made him want her, *positively* want her, more. But she is gone, he has lost her, and *then* he sees all she has meant. She has loved him. *(It must come for the* READER *thus, at this moment.)* With his base safety and shrinkage he never knew. *That* was what might have happened, and what *has* happened is that it didn't [*Notebooks* 199].

[On three separate occasions, James made a note about a motif that would become an element in "The Jolly Corner": a ghostly knocking. Towards the end of his life, he wrote extensively about a novel that he did not finish, *The Sense of the Past*. In that "statement," as he called his plans for the novel, he remembers using his ideas for this novel in "The Jolly Corner."]

22 January 1879

Imagine a door—either walled-up, or that has been long locked—at which there is an occasional knocking—a knocking which—as the other side of the door is inaccessible—can only be ghostly. The occupant of the house or room, containing the door, has long been familiar with the sound; and, regarding it as ghostly, has ceased to heed it particularly—as the ghostly presence remains on the other side of the door, and never reveals itself in other ways. But this person may be imagined to have some great and constant trouble; and it may be observed by another person, relating the story, that the knocking increases with each fresh manifestation of the trouble. He breaks open the door and the trouble ceases—as if the spirit had desired to be admitted, that it might interpose, redeem and protect [*Notebooks* 10].

16 May 1899

Note the idea of the knock at the door (*petite fantaisie*)[1] that comes to a young man (3 loud taps, etc.) *everywhere*—in all rooms and places he successively occupies—going from one to the other. *I* tell it—am with him: (*he* has told *me*); share a little (though joking him always) his wonder, worry, suspense. I've my idea of what it means. His fate, etc. "sometime there *will* be something there—some one." I am *with* him once when it happens, I am with him the 1st time—I mean the 1st time *I* know about it. (He doesn't notice—I do; then he explains: "Oh, I thought it was only—" He opens; there *is* some one—natural and ordinary. It is my *entrée en matière*.)[2] The denouement is all. What *does* come—at last? What *is* there? This to be ciphered out [*Notebooks* 183].

Notes for *The Sense of the Past*, 1914

The most intimate idea of *that* ["The Jolly Corner"] is that my hero's adventure there takes the form so to speak of his turning the tables, as I think I called it, on a "ghost" or whatever, a visiting or haunting apparition otherwise qualified to appal *him*; and thereby winning a sort of victory by the appearance, and the evidence, that this personage or presence was more overwhelmingly affected by him than he by it [*Notebooks* 507].

---

1   Little fantasy (French).
2   Introduction (French).

Appendix D: Other Writers and Artists on James

1. From Edith Wharton, *A Backward Glance* (New York: Appleton-Century, 1934) 193–94

[Henry James and Edith Wharton first met in 1887 but did not pursue a friendship until 1899, when Wharton sent James her first collection of stories. Their friendship grew over the years; each visited the other in England and the United States, and they traveled together in New England and in France. In the passage below from her autobiography, *A Backward Glance*, Wharton writes of James's ability to bring the dead to life through what she describes as his incantatory use of language.]

In one respect Henry James stood alone among the great talkers I have known, for while he was inexhaustible in repartee, and never had the least tendency to monopolize the talk, yet it was really in monologue that he was most himself. I remember in particular one summer evening, when we sat late on the terrace at the Mount,[1] with the lake shining palely through dark trees, and one of us suddenly said to him (in response to some chance allusion to his Albany relations): "And now tell us about the Emmets—tell us all about them."

The Emmet and Temple families composed, as we knew, the main element of his vast and labyrinthine cousinship—"the Emmetry," as he called it—and for a moment he stood there brooding in the darkness, murmuring over to himself: "Ah, my dear, the Emmets—ah, the Emmets!" Then he began, forgetting us, forgetting the place, forgetting everything but the vision of his lost youth that the question had evoked, the long train of ghosts flung with his enchanter's wand across the wide stage of the summer night. Ghostlike indeed at first, wavering and indistinct, they glimmered at us through a series of disconnected ejaculations, epithets, allusions, parenthetical rectifications and restatements, till not only our brains but the clear night itself seemed filled with a palpable fog; and then, suddenly, by some miracle of shifted lights and accumulated strokes, there they stood before us as they lived, drawn with a million filament-like lines, yet sharp as an

---

1   Wharton's home in the Berkshire mountains near Lenox, Massachusetts.

Ingres, dense as a Rembrandt;[1] or, to call upon his own art for an analogy, minute and massive as the people of Balzac.[2]

I often saw the trick repeated; saw figures obscure or famous summoned to the white square of his magic-lantern, flickering and wavering there, and slowly solidifying under the turn of his lens; but never perhaps anything so ample, so sustained, as that summoning to life of dead-and-gone Emmets and Temples, old lovelinesses, old follies, old failures, all long laid away and forgotten under old crumbling gravestones. I wonder if it may not have been that very night, the place and his re-awakened associations aiding, that they first came to him and constrained him to make them live for us again in the pages of "A Small Boy" and "A Son and Brother?"

2. From T.S. Eliot, "On Henry James" (1918), in *Henry James: Critical Assessments*, vol. 1 (Mountfield, East Sussex: Helm Information, 1991) 303–04

[Like Henry James, T.S. Eliot was an expatriate American who moved to England and eventually became a British citizen. In the following excerpt from an essay on James published not long after his death, Eliot makes a comment that has been often quoted and almost as often misinterpreted about James's mind being so fine that "no idea could violate it." As the context shows, Eliot intended to praise James.]

... Compared with James's, other novelists' characters seem to be only accidentally in the same book. Naturally, there is something terrible, as disconcerting as a quicksand, in this discovery, though it only becomes absolutely dominant in such stories as *The Turn of the Screw*. It is partly foretold in Hawthorne, but James carried it much further. And it makes the reader, as well as the *personae*, uneasily the victim of a merciless clairvoyance.

James's critical genius comes out most tellingly in his mastery over, his baffling escape from, Ideas; a mastery and an escape which are perhaps the last test of a superior intelligence. He had a mind so fine that no idea could violate it.... In England ideas run wild and pasture on the emotions; instead of thinking with our feelings (a very different thing) we corrupt our feelings with ideas; we produce the political, the emotional idea, evading sensation and thought.... James in his novels is like the best French critics in maintaining a point of view, a viewpoint untouched by the parasite idea. He is the most intelligent man of his generation.

---

1 Jean Auguste Dominique Ingrès, French painter (1780–1867) and Rembrandt von Rijn (1606–69), Dutch painter.

2 Honoré de Balzac, French novelist (1799–1850).

3. From Virginia Woolf, "Henry James's Ghost Stories" (1921), in *Granite and Rainbow: Essays by Virginia Woolf* (London: Hogarth Press, 1981) 71–72

[The young Virginia Stephen knew Henry James through her father, Leslie Stephen, the editor at the *Cornhill Magazine* who published James's early novella, *Daisy Miller*. Like James, Woolf wrote extensively about other writers and their works.]

Henry James's ghosts have nothing in common with the violent old ghosts—the blood-stained sea captains, the white horses, the headless ladies of dark lanes and windy commons. They have their origins within us. They are present whenever the significant overflows our powers of expressing it; whenever the ordinary appears ringed by the strange. The baffling things that are left over, the frightening ones that persist—these are the emotions that he takes, embodies, makes consoling and companionable.... What does it matter, then, if we do pick up the [sic] *Turn of the Screw* an hour or so before bedtime? After an exquisite entertainment we shall, if the other stories are to be trusted, end with this fine music in our ears, and sleep the sounder.

Perhaps it is the silence that first impresses us. Everything at Bly is so profoundly quiet. The twitter of birds at dawn, the far-away cries of children, faint footsteps in the distance stir it but leave it unbroken. It accumulates; it weighs us down; it makes us strangely apprehensive of noise. At last the house and garden die out beneath it. "I can hear again, as I write, the intense hush in which the sounds of evening dropped. The rooks stopped cawing in the golden sky, and the friendly hour lost for the unspeakable minute all its voice." It is unspeakable. We know that the man who stands on the tower staring down at the governess beneath is evil. Some unutterable obscenity has come to the surface.... It is Quint who hangs about us in the dark; who is there in that corner and again there in that. It is Quint who must be reasoned away, and for all our reasoning returns. Can it be that we are afraid? But it is not a man with red hair and a white face whom we fear. We are afraid of something, perhaps, in ourselves. In short, we turn on the light. If by its beams we examine the story in safety, note how masterly the telling is, how each sentence is stretched, each image filled, how the inner world gains from the robustness of the outer, how beauty and obscenity twined together worm their way to the depths—still we must own that something remains unaccounted for. We must admit that Henry James has conquered. That courtly, worldly, sentimental old gentleman can still make us afraid of the dark.

4. Charles Demuth's Illustrations for "The Beast in the Jungle"

[The American painter Charles Demuth (1883–1935), best known for his watercolors, illustrated three of James's stories: "The Beast in the Jungle," "The Real Thing," and *The Turn of the Screw*. Demuth did not intend for his watercolors to accompany a particular edition of James's texts; instead, his paintings served as visual renderings of his own interpretations of the literary texts.]

Charles Demuth: The Boat Ride from Sorrento (1919)

Charles Demuth: The Revelation Comes to May Bartram in Her Drawing Room (1919)

Charles Demuth: Marcher Receives His Revelation at May Bartram's Tomb (1919)

5. Max Beerbohm on James's Return to the United States (1904)

[Max Beerbohm (1872–1956) was an English author and artist, famous for his witty parodies and caricatures of his era's celebrities. Beerbohm knew James personally and admired him, both as a person and as an artist. This caricature depicts James upon his return to the United States in 1904.]

Max Beerbohm (1872–1956), English, *Mr. Henry James revisiting America*, c. 1906. Pen, ink, and watercolour, 41.7 X 33.7 cm (sheet). Purchased 1953, National Gallery of Victoria, Melbourne (3156-4)

In balloon to left of James: Mr. Henry James revisiting America *Extract from His Unspoken Thoughts*:

"So that, in fine, let, without further beating about the bush, me make to myself amazed acknowledgement that, but for the certificate of birth which I have—so quite indubitably—*on* me, I might, in regarding (and, as it somewhat were, overseeing) *à l'oeil de voyageur*, these dear good people, find hard to swallow, or even to take by subconscious injection, the great idea that I am—oh, ever so indigenously!—one of them" . . . .

In each character's balloon, moving clockwise from James's left:

"My! Ain't he cree-ative?"
"We wants yer mightly badly. Yas, we *doo!*"
"Guess 'e ken shoot char'cter at sight!"
"Hail, great white novelist! Tuniyaba—the Spinner of fine cobwebs!"
"Why, it's Masser Henry! Come to your old nurse's arms, honey!"
"What's—the matter with—*James?*"
"*He's*—all—right!"
"*Who's*—all-right?"
"*James!*"

Select Bibliography and Filmography

Editions of Henry James's Works

James, Henry. *The Novels and Tales of Henry James: The New York Edition*. New York: Scribner; London: Macmillan, 1907–09. 24 volumes. (Two volumes added in 1917.)

From the Library of America (New York):
Collected Travel Writings: The Continent. 1993.
Collected Travel Writings: Great Britain and America. 1993.
Complete Stories 1864–1874. 1999.
Complete Stories 1874–1884. 1999.
Complete Stories 1884–1891. 1999.
Complete Stories 1892–1898. 1996.
Complete Stories 1898–1910. 1996.
Literary Criticism: Volume One: Essays on Literature, American Writers & English Writers. 1984.
Literary Criticism: Volume Two: French Writers, Other European Writers, The Prefaces to the New York Edition. 1984.
Novels 1871–1880. 1983.
Novels 1881–1886. 1985.
Novels 1886–1890. 1989.
Novels 1896–1899. 2003.
Novels 1901–1902. 2006.

Biographical Studies

Edel, Leon and Lyall H. Powers, eds. *The Complete Notebooks of Henry James*. New York: Oxford UP, 1987.
Edel, Leon. *Henry James: The Untried Years 1843–1870* (1953); *Henry James: The Conquest of London 1870–1881* (1962); *Henry James: The Middle Years 1882–1895* (1962); *Henry James: The Treacherous Years 1895–1901* (1969); *Henry James: The Master 1901–1916* (1972). Philadelphia: Lippincott.
Horne, Philip. *Henry James: A Life in Letters*. New York: Viking, 1999.
Kaplan, Fred. *Henry James: The Imagination of Genius*. New York: William Morrow, 1992.
Lewis, R.W.B. *The Jameses: A Family Narrative*. New York: Farrar, 1991.

Critical Studies

Banta, Martha. *Henry James and the Occult: The Great Extension.* Bloomington: Indiana UP, 1972.

Bazargan, Susan. "Illustrating the Invisible: 'The Beast in the Jungle' as Edition de luxe." *The Henry James Review* 29:1 (Winter 2008): 54–64.

Beidler, Peter G. *Ghosts, Demons, and Henry James: "The Turn of the Screw" at the Turn of the Century.* Columbia: U of Missouri P, 1989.

Bell, Millicent. "*The Turn of the Screw.*" *Meaning in Henry James.* Cambridge: Harvard UP, 1991. 223–44.

Brown, Arthur A. "Death and the Reader: James's 'The Beast in the Jungle.'" *Postmodern Approaches to the Short Story.* Ed. Farhat Iftekharrudin, et al. Westport, CT: Praeger, 2003. 39–50.

Cameron, Sharon. *Thinking in Henry James.* Chicago: U of Chicago P, 1989.

Claggett, Shalyn. "Narcissism and the Conditions of Self-Knowledge in James's 'The Jolly Corner.'" *The Henry James Review* 26:2 (Spring 2005): 189–200.

Cornwell, Neil, and Maggie Malone, eds. *"The Turn of the Screw" and "What Maisie Knew": Contemporary Critical Essays.* New York: St. Martin's, 1998.

Davis, Colin. *Haunted Subjects: Deconstruction, Psychoanalysis and the Return of the Dead.* Basingstoke, Hampshire: Palgrave Macmillan, 2007.

Fahy, Christopher A. "Of Sacred Art and the Artist: Henry James's 'The Altar of the Dead.'" *Christianity and Literature* 51:2 (Winter 2002): 209–18.

Felman, Shoshana. *Literature and Psychoanalysis: The Question of Reading: Otherwise.* Baltimore: Johns Hopkins UP, 1982.

Freud, Sigmund. "The Uncanny." *The Uncanny.* Trans. David McClintock. Ed. Adam Phillips. New York: Penguin, 2003. 123–62.

Gilbert, Geoffrey. "The Origins of Modernism in the Haunted Properties of Literature." *The Victorian Supernatural.* Ed. Nicola Brown, et al. Cambridge: Cambridge UP, 2004. 239–57.

Griffin, Susan M. *Henry James Goes to the Movies.* Lexington: UP of Kentucky, 2002.

Haralson, Eric. "'His little heart, dispossessed': Ritual Sexorcism in *The Turn of the Screw.*" In *Questioning the Master: Gender and Sexuality in Henry James's Writings*, ed. Peggy McCormack. Newark, DE: U of Delaware P, 2002. 133–48.

Heller, Terry. *"The Turn of the Screw": Bewildered Vision*. Boston: Twayne, 1989.

Hocks, Richard. *Henry James: A Study of the Short Fiction*. Boston: Twayne, 1990.

Hoople, Robin P. *Distinguished Discord: Discontinuity and Pattern in the Critical Tradition of "The Turn of the Screw."* Lewisburg: Bucknell UP, 1997.

Lustig, T.J. *Henry James and the Ghostly*. Cambridge: Cambridge UP, 1994.

Rovit, Earl. "The Language and Imagery of 'The Jolly Corner.'" *"The Finer Thread, The Tighter Weave": Essays on the Short Fiction of Henry James*. Ed. Joseph Dewey and Brooke Horvath. West Lafayette, IN: Purdue UP, 2001.

Rowe, John Carlos. *The Theoretical Dimensions of Henry James*. Madison: U of Wisconsin P, 1984.

Savoy, Eric. "The Queer Subject of the 'Jolly Corner.'" *The Henry James Review* 20:1 (Winter 1999): 1–21.

Sedgwick, Eve Kosofsky. *Epistemology of the Closet*. Berkeley: U of California P, 1990.

Tintner, Adeline R. *Henry James's Legacy: The Afterlife of His Figure and Fiction*. Baton Rouge: Louisiana State UP, 1998.

Ward, Geoff. "'The Strength of Applied Irony': James's 'The Altar of the Dead.'" *Henry James: The Shorter Fiction, Reassessments*. Ed. N.H. Reeve. Basingstoke, Hampshire: Macmillan; New York: St. Martin's, 1997. 60–76.

Zacharias, Greg, ed. *A Companion to Henry James*. London: Blackwell, 2008.

Select Filmography

The Green Room (La Chambre verte). Screenplay by François Truffaut and Jean Gruault. Dir. François Truffaut. Perf. François Truffaut (Julien), Nathalie Baye (Cecilia), et al. Les Films du Carosse SA/Les Productions Artistes Associés / United Artists, color, 95 mins., 1978. Videocassette. MGM/UA Home Video, 1993. [Inspired by "The Altar of the Dead" as well as other short stories by Henry James, including "The Beast in the Jungle."]

The Jolly Corner. Teleplay by Arthur Barron. Dir. Arthur Barron. Perf. Fritz Weaver (Spencer Brydon), Salome Jens (Alice Staverton). *American Short Story*, color, 43 mins., 1975.

The Innocents. Screenplay by William Archibald, Truman Capote, and John Mortimer. Dir. Jack Clayton. Music George Auric. Perf. Deborah Kerr (Miss Giddens, the governess), Michael Redgrave (the uncle), Megs Jenkins (Mrs. Grose), Martin Stephens (Miles), Pamela Franklin (Flora), Peter Wyngarde (Peter Quint), Clytie Jessop (Miss Jessel). Twentieth Century Fox / Achilles, bw, 99 mins., 1962.

The Turn of the Screw. Teleplay by Nick Dear. Dir. Ben Bolt. Perf. Jodhi May (the governess), Pam Ferris (Mrs. Grose), Colin Firth (the uncle), Caroline Pegg (Miss Jessel), Jason Salkey (Peter Quint), Joe Sowerbutts (Miles), Grace Robinson (Flora). Martin Pope Productions / WGBH, color, 100 mins, 1999.

from the publisher

A name never says it all, but the word "broadview" expresses a good deal of the philosophy behind our company. We are open to a broad range of academic approaches and political viewpoints. We pay attention to the broad impact book publishing and book printing has in the wider world; we began using recycled stock more than a decade ago, and for some years now we have used 100% recycled paper for most titles. As a Canadian-based company we naturally publish a number of titles with a Canadian emphasis, but our publishing program overall is internationally oriented and broad-ranging. Our individual titles often appeal to a broad readership too; many are of interest as much to general readers as to academics and students.

Founded in 1985, Broadview remains a fully independent company owned by its shareholders—not an imprint or subsidiary of a larger multinational.

If you would like to find out more about Broadview and about the books we publish, please visit us at **www.broadviewpress.com**. And if you'd like to place an order through the site, we'd like to show our appreciation by extending a special discount to you: by entering the code below you will receive a 20% discount on purchases made through the Broadview website.

Discount code: **broadview20%**

Thank you for choosing Broadview.

Please note: this offer applies only to sales of bound books within the United States or Canada.